Born in Zurich, Paul Witcover is a writer and critic. He is the author of the novels *Waking Beauty*, *Tumbling After* and *Asylum* and, with Elizabeth Hand, created the cult comic book series, *Anima*. He has also served as the curator of the *New York Review of Science Fiction*.

Paul lives in New York City and is currently working on the sequel to *The Emperor of All Things*.

Acclaim for *The Emperor of All Things*:

'A hugely entertaining read ... comparisons to Neil Stephenson and Susanna Clarke are only very slightly premature. As with the finest timepiece, *The Emperor of All Things* is ultimately a rather beautiful thing'
INDEPENDENT ON SUNDAY

'An excitingly and brilliantly realised, poetically written tale of magic, subterfuge and intrigue. Not to mention clocks'
SFFWORLD.COM

'Witcover conjures an enlightenment-punk vision of England, before taking detours to the Alps, subterranean London and the utterly fantastic. ****'
SFX magazine

Also by Paul Witcover

WAKING BEAUTY
TUMBLING AFTER
DRACULA: ASYLUM
EVERLAND AND OTHER STORIES

THE
EMPEROR
OF ALL THINGS

Book 1 of
The Productions of Time

PAUL WITCOVER

BANTAM BOOKS

LONDON • TORONTO • SYDNEY • AUCKLAND • JOHANNESBURG

TRANSWORLD PUBLISHERS
61–63 Uxbridge Road, London W5 5SA
A Random House Group Company
www.transworldbooks.co.uk

THE EMPEROR OF ALL THINGS
A BANTAM BOOK: 9780857501592

First published in Great Britain
in 2013 by Bantam Press
an imprint of Transworld Publishers
Bantam edition published 2014

Addresses for Random House Group Ltd companies outside the UK
can be found at: www.randomhouse.co.uk
The Random House Group Ltd Reg. No. 954009

The Random House Group Limited supports the Forest Stewardship Council®
(FSC®), the leading international forest-certification organisation. Our books
carrying the FSC label are printed on FSC®-certified paper. FSC is the only
forest-certification scheme supported by the leading environmental organisations,
including Greenpeace. Our paper procurement policy can be found at
www.randomhouse.co.uk/environment

Typeset in 11/14pt Dante by Falcon Oast Graphic Art Ltd.
Printed and bound by CPI Group (UK) Ltd, Croydon, CR0 4YY.

2 4 6 8 10 9 7 5 3 1

For Cynthia Babak

and

Christopher Schelling

Eternity is in love with the productions of time.
– William Blake, *Proverbs of Hell*

*You shall swear to be true to our Sovereign Lord the King's Majesty,
his heirs and successors, and at all times obedient to the Master and
Wardens of this Fellowship and Society, and their successors after
them, in all honest and lawful things touching the affairs of this
Fellowship. You shall be ready at all manner of Summons, and bear
scot and lot in all manner of reasonable contributions of and to this
Fellowship, and the Fellowship of the Company of Clockmakers of
the City of London you shall to the best of your skill, power and
ability, uphold and maintain. You shall not know nor suspect any
manner of meetings, conspiracies, plots, devices against the King's
Majesty, his heirs or successors, or the Government of this
Fellowship, but you shall the same to the utmost of your power, let
and hinder and speedily disclose to the Master or one of the Wardens
of this Society. And this City of London and Fellowship of
Clockmakers you shall keep harmless, as much as in you lieth: also
you shall be ready at all times to be at the Quarter Days, and every
other assembly, matter or cause that you shall be warned or called
unto for the affairs of this Fellowship, unless you shall have lawful or
reasonable excuse in that behalf. And all other Ordinances of this
Fellowship or Society, ratified according to the laws of this Realm,
or otherwise lawful for this Fellowship or Society to make and
ordain, you shall, to the utmost of your power well and truly submit
yourself unto and keep. So help you God.*
– Oath of the Worshipful Company of Clockmakers

PART ONE

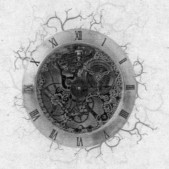

Prologue

CLOCKS. CLOCKS EVERYWHERE, ON THE WOODEN SHELVES AND tables, even upon the sawdust-covered floor of the attic room: clocks of all shapes and sizes limned in the light of a gibbous moon that did not so much pierce the skylight as sift through its sooty glass – tall clocks in finely carved and polished casings of exotic woods with brass pendulums winking back and forth; ornate mantel clocks of ormolu and mahogany, marble and tortoiseshell; clocks of gold and silver set into or alongside precious metal and porcelain renderings of human figures in varied states of dress and undress as well as representations of beasts real and fabulous: lions consorting with unicorns, eagles and gryphons roosting side by side; cuckoo clocks and carriage clocks and tambour clocks and skeleton clocks; even pocket watches with their chains and ribbons neatly coiled or dangling free and loose as slipped lanyards. The ticking of so many timepieces, no two synchronized, filled the space with a facsimile of whispered conversation, as if some ghostly parliament were meeting in the dead of night.

Scattered among the clocks were glass flasks and vials of assorted shapes and sizes, some containing clear or opaque liquids, others quite empty, along with mortars and pestles, iron tongs, funnels, crucibles, and other such instruments bespeaking the practice of alchemy. Set in a row along one wall were three brick furnaces, one in the shape of a tower and as tall as a man, the other two smaller and squat in shape, like ornamental toads.

A mouse was making its way across the surface of one table, nosing amid a clutter of clock parts and tools: pins, clicks, rivets, coiled springs, tweezers, clamps, winders, files, and like essentials of the horologist's trade. Every so often it rose off its tiny front paws to sniff the air, whiskers twitching, eyes aglitter like apple seeds in a bed of ash.

From a shelf overhead, a black cat followed its progress with glowing tourmaline eyes. The noise in the back of its throat, somewhere between a growl and a purr, was cloaked by the gossipy muttering of the clocks. The tip of its tail lashed from side to side like a metronome.

When the meanderings of the mouse brought it conveniently near, the cat moved with the grace of a gliding shadow, seeming as insubstantial . . . until it struck. In leaping to the table top, it did not disturb a single item yet knocked the rodent onto its side, pressing the half-stunned creature down with one paw and slashing with its teeth at the grey fur.

The cat tensed and flattened at a sound from overhead: a faint click followed by a drawn-out creaking, as if the old house were settling on its foundations. Hissing, the cat darted a glance upwards as a thin rope dropped through the now-open skylight to dangle above the floor a few feet away. The rope had not reached the end of its length before the cat bolted, with less stealth or silence than just moments before; small gears and other items scattered under its paws as it fled into the shadows. An empty vial slipped to the floor and shattered. The mouse was long gone. Drops of its blood glistened on the table, dark as oil.

A svelte figure slid down the rope and dropped soundlessly to the floor. The intruder was dressed in grey: soft grey boots, grey breeches, a grey shirt beneath a grey cloak. Strapped to its back was a small crossbow, and a blade as slender as a rapier yet no longer than a short sword hung in a grey scabbard from its belt, as did six leather pouches, also grey. A grey kerchief pulled across the nose hid the bottom half of the face; a grey hood cloaked the upper; in between, eyes as dark as the mouse's glittered as they probed the shadowy corners of the room. The intruder strode to one of the tables.

The timepieces on this particular table were clearly the work of master craftsmen. Many were made with precious metals; not a few were inset with jewels. A single one of these clocks, selected at random, would have made a rich prize for a thief. Yet the grey-clad figure reached without hesitation for a mantel clock that appeared as out of place as an ordinary goblet set alongside the Holy Grail.

At a whisper of displaced air, the intruder turned, clock in one hand, the rapier-like blade in the other.

The casing of a tall clock some twelve feet away swung open. Out stepped a gentleman of middling height wearing a powdered wig and an elegant sky-blue coat over a lace-adorned white shirt and embroidered waistcoat, yellow breeches with pale blue hose, and embroidered green silk slippers. His powdered face glowed corpse white in the moonlight; a conspicuous beauty mark adorned his left cheek, and his lips were as red as cherries half sunk in a bowl of cream. He had the look of extreme age masquerading as youth . . . or perhaps it was the other way around. But the most striking feature of his appearance was the cocked duelling pistol that he held in the most negligent manner imaginable, as though it was by the merest chance that this object happened to be pointing at the breast of the intruder. 'So good of you to drop in, Grimalkin,' he drawled.

The hooded figure executed a slight but meticulous bow. 'Lord Wichcote.'

'I had thought you retired – or dead.'

'Merely . . . elsewhere. Now, as you see, I have returned.'

'And come to pay me a visit. I'm honoured. But my guests generally call at the front door. Many of them are thieves, it is true, but few take the trouble to mask themselves. Are you a coward, sir?'

'Simply modest, my lord,' answered the one addressed as Grimalkin.

'Why, damn me if you are not a smooth-tongued rascal! But I will see who is beneath that mask.' He gestured with the pistol. 'Remove it, sir.'

'As your lordship can see, my hands are occupied at present.'

'Then I suggest you un-occupy them.'

'Gladly, but your pistol is making me somewhat nervous.'

'Afraid it might go off? You should be.'

'I am more concerned that, in my nervousness, I might drop the clock.'

The tremor that shook the hand holding the pistol was evident in the man's voice as well. 'If you damage that clock, sir, I will kill you.'

'Such is already your intent, is it not?'

'Even if it were, some deaths are less pleasant than others. Now, set the clock down, sir. Gently.'

'Since you will shoot me the instant I do so, that would be most foolish.'

'Perhaps I will shoot you in any case.'

'I think not. Even a steady hand is no guarantee of accuracy at this distance, in this poor light, and your hand is far from steady. Should you fire, you are as likely to strike the clock as to strike me. And if you do strike me, why, then I will drop the clock after all, and your precious timepiece will suffer the very damage you seek to avoid.'

'I would sooner see it destroyed than give it up to you and your masters.'

'I serve no masters,' Grimalkin stated.

This provoked a laugh. 'Come now, sir. It is common knowledge that you are, or at any rate used to be, an agent of those confounded meddlers, the Worshipful Company of Clockmakers.'

'Common knowledge often masks uncommon ignorance.'

'Hmph. How else would you know the value of that particular timepiece?'

'Why, half of London knows it, sir, the way you have been broadcasting your acquisition of it! Indeed, the wonder is that no one has got here before me.'

'It was to entice you to my workshop that I spoke so freely,' Lord Wichcote said. 'I had heard rumours of your return, and wished to see for myself.'

'That was obvious. Still, I am nothing if not curious. And so I accepted your lordship's invitation. I take it you are not normally in the habit of leaving the skylight unlocked, or your treasures unguarded.'

'Most assuredly not.'

Grimalkin bowed again, making a mocking flourish with the blade, then straightened and said: 'In that case, put up your pistol, sir. I do not think you have gone to so much trouble merely to kill me.'

Lord Wichcote cackled. 'I like you, sir, damned if I do not!' He kept the pistol pointed at the other's chest, however. 'Very well then: to business. It happens that I am an admirer of your peculiar talents. I have followed your career, if I may term it such, with avid interest, despite your efforts to cover your trail. Your pursuit of rare and unusual timepieces has led you from far Cathay to the New World and everywhere in between. The mysterious Grimalkin – the grey shadow whose identity is known to no man! Some say you are of noble, even royal blood. Others maintain you are naught but a brash commoner. Still others hold that you are no man at all, but a devil sworn to the service of Lucifer.'

Grimalkin shrugged. 'People say many things, my lord. One grows weary of idle talk.'

'Then I shall come straight to the point. I wish to employ you as my confidential agent, sir. Whatever the Worshipful Company is paying you, I shall double it. They need never know.'

'I have told you that I am not in the service of that guild.'

'Who then?' A look of repugnance, as if an offensive odour had wafted into the room, came over the powdered features. 'Surely not the Frogs?'

'I serve no master,' Grimalkin repeated. 'Not English, not French. None.'

Lord Wichcote smirked, revealing teeth as yellow as aged ivory. 'Every man serves a master, my dear Grimalkin. Whether king or commoner, all of us bend the knee to someone or something.'

'And who is your master, my lord?'

'Why, His Majesty, of course. And Almighty God.'

'So say you. Yet by the laws of His Majesty, only the

Worshipful Company of Clockmakers has the right to such a workshop as this.'

The man bristled. 'Do you take me for a shopkeeper, sir? A common artisan? I am a peer of the realm! Such petty restrictions do not apply to the likes of me. Nor do I claim exemption on the grounds of rank alone. I am a natural scientist. An investigator into the secret nature of the most elusive and mysterious of all substances in God's creation. I refer, of course, to time. That is our true master, is it not, Grimalkin? *Tempus Rerum Imperator,* as the Worshipful Company has it. Time, the emperor of all things.'

'Not of me.'

'You would be time's master?' Lord Wichcote laughed. 'You have the heart of a rebel, I find. Well, no matter. Worship who or what you will, or nothing at all, if it please you. I care only for my collection and my experiments. With your help, Grimalkin, that collection can be the finest in the world, and the fruit of my labours can be yours to share.'

'What fruit?'

'The very distillate of time, sir.'

'You seek immortality?'

Lord Wichcote twitched the barrel of the pistol in a dismissive fashion. 'That is the least of it. What men call time is the mind of God in its most subtle manifestation. Its purest essence, if you will. Imagine the potency of that divine essence, distilled into an elixir! To drink of it would be to become as God Himself.'

Now it was Grimalkin's turn to laugh. 'And you call *me* a rebel?'

'I had hoped that you, of all men, might understand.'

'Oh, I understand very well, my lord. Very well indeed.

How much of this fabulous elixir have you managed to distil thus far?'

Lord Wichcote frowned. 'Certain . . . difficulties in the refining process remain to be overcome, but—'

'In other words, none,' Grimalkin interrupted. 'I thought as much. Alas, I fear I must decline your offer.'

'Do not be hasty. You will not find a more generous patron. My fortune is vast, my influence at court vaster still. All I require to succeed are various timepieces that I regret to say are beyond my reach at present. My reach, but not yours.'

'Your confidence is flattering. But the only collection that interests me is my own. As for this elixir of yours, it smacks more of alchemy than natural science. I do not believe that you have the skill to make it, nor even that it can be made.'

'Is that your final answer?'

'I'm afraid so.'

Lord Wichcote sighed. 'A pity. But not entirely unexpected.' He pulled the trigger of the duelling pistol. There was a spark, a roar, a cloud of smoke that reeked of sulphur.

Grimalkin flinched as the clock, struck, was torn free of the hand that held it.

At the same instant, the front panels of three other tall clocks swung open. From each emerged a man with a drawn rapier. One to Grimalkin's right; another to the left; the third stood beside Lord Wichcote, who seemed vastly amused.

'The clock,' he said, 'was of course a facsimile only.'

'I am relieved to hear it,' said Grimalkin, flexing the fingers of a now-empty hand. 'Your lordship is a most excellent shot.'

'I spend an hour each day at target practice.' As he spoke, Lord Wichcote began the laborious process of reloading his pistol. 'I want him alive,' he added, addressing the three swordsmen without bothering to look up. 'And take care you do not damage any of my timepieces in the process.'

'Aye, m'lud,' chorused the new arrivals. Rapiers held en garde, they converged on the intruder with the wary grace of professionals; they were met by a grey blur. The music of swordplay filled the room, providing a lively accompaniment to the stolid ticking of so many clocks.

Preoccupied with the pistol, it was some seconds before Lord Wichcote, in response to a groan that seemed more a product of dismay than pain, glanced up to gauge the progress of the fight. There were now two men facing the masked intruder; the third was sprawled on the floor, a rose blooming on his chest. Frowning, Lord Wichcote returned to his work, a certain agitation visible in his movements. When next he glanced up, the intruder was facing but a single man. Lord Wichcote's efforts now took on an unmistakable urgency, accompanied by a marked deterioration in manual dexterity. Gunpowder spilled over his shirt, and the ball he was trying to insert into the pistol's muzzle seemed possessed of a perverse desire to go elsewhere. At last he rammed it home. But no sooner had he done so than he found the red-stained tip of a blade hovering near his throat.

'Perhaps you should devote more time in your practice sessions to the loading rather than the firing of your pistols,' Grimalkin suggested, somewhat breathlessly.

'No doubt you have a point,' Lord Wichcote conceded through gritted teeth.

'Indeed I do. And you will become more intimately acquainted with my point unless you drop your pistol.'

The pistol dropped.

Grimalkin kicked the weapon aside.

'You would not dare to shed even a single drop of my blood,' Lord Wichcote declared, though he did not sound convinced of it. The powder on his face was streaked with sweat. The skin underneath was neither so white nor so smooth.

'Would I not?' The tip of the blade indented his throat, where the skin was as yellowed – and as thin – as ancient parchment. A red bead appeared there.

The man gasped but said nothing more.

'Give me your parole, as a gentleman and a peer of the realm, that you will not cry out or otherwise attempt to impede me, and I will take my leave without doing you graver injury.' Grimalkin pulled the blade back a fraction of an inch.

'You have it,' Lord Wichcote said.

As Grimalkin retreated a step, still holding the blade ready, the other pressed a white handkerchief to his throat and said in a tone of deepest disapproval, 'What manner of fencing do you call that, sir? Three of my finest swordsmen dispatched in under two minutes! I have never seen a man wield a blade in such an outlandish fashion!'

'I have travelled widely, my lord, and learned much along the way – not all of it to do with clocks.' Grimalkin leaned forward to wipe the blade clean on the edge of his lordship's sky-blue coat, then returned it to its scabbard.

This affront Lord Wichcote bore with barely controlled fury. 'Do you know, Grimalkin, I don't believe you are a gentleman at all.'

'I have never claimed that distinction. And now, sir, I bid you adieu.' Grimalkin gave another precise bow and backed away, moving towards the rope that dangled from the open skylight. In passing a table bestrewn with timepieces in various stages of assembly and disassembly – the very table, as it happened, where cat and mouse had earlier disported them-selves – Grimalkin paused. A grey-gloved hand shot out.

Lord Wichcote gave a wordless cry.

'I'll take this for my trouble.' A clock very like the one that had been the target of the gentleman's pistol disappeared into the folds of Grimalkin's cloak – as, moving more swiftly still, like a liquid shadow, did the mouse that had escaped the cat. 'Did you really think you could hide it from me?'

The gentleman's only reply was to begin shouting for help at the top of his lungs.

'I don't know what England is coming to when the parole of a lord cannot be trusted by an honest thief,' Grimalkin muttered, reaching into a belt pouch. A small glass vial glittered in an upraised hand, then was flung to the floor. Thick clouds of smoke boiled up, filling the room.

By the time the air in the attic had cleared, the masked intruder stood on an empty rooftop half a mile away. Tendrils of fog and coal smoke eeled through the streets below, but a strong breeze, carrying the effluvial reek of the Thames, had swept the rooftops clear. Grimalkin fished out the timepiece and turned it this way and that in the silvery light of the moon. The exterior was unremarkable.

The whiskered nose of the mouse peeked out inquisitively from the collar of the grey hood.

'Well, Henrietta,' whispered the thief. 'Let us see what hatches out of—'

A muffled footfall. Grimalkin spun, blade already sliding from scabbard . . .

Too late. With a sharp crack, the hilt of a rapier slammed into the side of the grey hood. The thief crumpled without another word.

1

Honour

DANIEL QUARE, JOURNEYMAN OF THE WORSHIPFUL COMPANY OF Clockmakers and confidential agent of the Most Secret and Exalted Order of Regulators, stood in flickering candlelight and listened to the synchronized ticking of the dozens of timepieces that filled the room. The longer he listened, the more the sound suggested the marching of a vast insect army to his weary yet overstimulated brain. He could picture it clearly, row upon row of black ants, as many of them as the number of seconds ordained from the Creation until the Last Judgement. He felt as though he had been standing here for a substantial part of that time already. His injured leg, which had stiffened overnight, throbbed painfully.

Before him was an oaken desk of such prodigious dimensions that a scout from that ant army might have spent a considerable portion of its life journeying from one side to the other. An immensely fat man wearing a powdered wig and a dark blue greatcoat sat across the desk from him in a high-backed wooden chair of thronelike proportions. The windowless room was stifling, with a fire burning in a tiled fireplace set into one wall amid shelves filled with clocks and leather-bound books. It might have been the dead of winter and not midway through an unseasonably warm September. Quare was sweating profusely.

So was the man behind the desk. The play of light across his features made it appear as if invisible fingers were moulding the soft wax of his face. At one moment he seemed a well-preserved man of sixty, flush with vigour; in the next, he had aged a good twenty years; and which of these two impressions, if either, struck closest to the truth, Quare did not know. Moisture dripped from the man's round, red, flabby-jowled face, yet he made no move to wipe the sweat away or to divest himself of his powdered wig or greatcoat, as if oblivious to the heat, to everything save the disassembled clock spread out before him. He examined its innards closely, hunched over the desktop and squinting through a loupe as he wielded a variety of slender metal tools with the dexterity of a surgeon. Jewelled rings flashed on the plump sausages of his fingers. Occasionally, without glancing up, he reached out to shift the position of a large silver and crystal candelabrum, drawing it closer or pushing it away. His breathing was laboured, as if from strenuous physical activity, and was interspersed with low grunts of inscrutable import.

Quare had been ushered into the room by a servant who'd announced him in a mournful voice, bowed low, and departed. Not once in the interminable moments since had the man behind the desk looked up or acknowledged his presence in any way, though Quare had cleared his throat more than once. He did so again now.

The man raised his head with the slow deliberation of a tortoise. The loupe dropped from an eye as round and blue as a cephalopod's. It came to rest, suspended on a fine silver chain, upon the mountainous swell of the man's belly. He scrunched his eyes shut and then opened them wide, as if he were in some doubt as to the substantiality of the young man before him. 'Ah, Journeyman Quare,' he wheezed at last. 'Been expecting you.'

Quare gave a stiff bow. 'Grandmaster Wolfe.'

The grandmaster waved a massive hand like a king commanding a courtier. 'Sit you down, sir, sit you down. You must be weary after last night's exertions.'

That was an understatement. Quare had returned to the guild hall late, and had not repaired to his own lodgings, and to bed, until even later – only to be summoned back two hours ago, at just past eight in the morning. Still, that was more sleep than Grandmaster Wolfe had managed, by the look of him. Quare perched on the edge of an armchair so lavishly upholstered and thickly pillowed he feared it might swallow him if he relaxed into its embrace.

'Comfortable, are you?' inquired Grandmaster Wolfe with the same look of sceptical curiosity he had worn while examining the clock. He seemed to be considering the possibility that Quare was a timekeeping mechanism . . . and a flawed one at that, in need of repair.

'Yes, thank you, Sir Thaddeus.'

'Hmph.' The man took a ready-filled long-stemmed clay pipe from a stand on the desk. He touched a spill to the flame of one of the candles in the candelabrum and held it above the bowl, puffing fiercely. Grey smoke wreathed his flushed and perspiring face.

Quare waited. Sir Thaddeus Wolfe, who had led the Worshipful Company for more than thirty years, was notoriously difficult to please. The fact that Quare completed his mission successfully was no guarantee of praise from the man who masters and journeymen alike referred to – though never to his face – as the Old Wolf.

'You were dispatched to secure a certain timepiece,' Wolfe said now, speaking in a measured tone, like a barrister setting out the facts of a case. 'A timepiece illegally in the possession of a gentleman whose connections at Court precluded a more . . . direct approach. Thanks to your efforts, that clock, and its secrets, now belong to us. And yet, a greater prize was within your grasp. Do you take my meaning, sir?'

'I do.'

'Has it a name, this prize?'

Quare did not hesitate. 'Grimalkin.'

'Grimalkin,' the Old Wolf echoed with a growl that sent smoke billowing from between his lips. 'Our enemies have no more skilful agent than that cursed man. For all his absurd affectations – the grey clothing, the mask, the infernal devices, the ridiculous name itself – he has never failed his masters . . . until now. You, sir, a mere neophyte but recently admitted to the active ranks of our Most Secret and Exalted Order, achieved what your more experienced brethren have long dreamed of accomplishing. You tracked Grimalkin, took him by surprise, rendered him unconscious. And then . . . did you kill him?'

'No.'

'Did you, perhaps, question him?'

'I did not.'

'No, you did neither of these things. May I ask why you chose to spare the enemy of your guild, your king, and your country?'

Quare frowned. He had expected the question, and had prepared an answer, but he had hoped his success in procuring the timepiece would have earned him a measure of leniency. 'As you say, Grimalkin was unconscious. To kill him under the circumstances would have been cold-blooded murder. It would not have been honourable.'

Alarming quantities of smoke poured from between the grandmaster's lips and jetted from his nostrils. 'And was it also a consideration of honour that prevented you from peeking beneath the rascal's mask to discover his identity?'

'It did not seem the act of a gentleman,' Quare affirmed. His words sounded foolish even to his own ears.

'A gentleman, is it?' The smoke grew denser still. 'I was under the impression that I had dispatched a spy.'

'I hope I may still comport myself as befits a gentleman.'

A choking sound emerged from the old man, and he spat out upon the desk what Quare at first took to be a tooth but then realized was the tip of the pipe stem, bitten off. Grandmaster Wolfe flung the ruined pipe down to one side of the exposed clockworks, sending a scattering of coals across the desktop; burn marks on the wood indicated that this was not the first time he had done so. 'Dolt!' he thundered, red-faced. 'Imbecile! You will comport yourself in whatever manner best advances the interests of His Majesty and this guild!' Then, his voice tightly controlled, he continued: 'As to considerations of honour, Mr Quare, allow me to instruct you, as it appears Master Magnus has been lax in seeing to your education on this point. A regulator must be many things. A gentleman, yes, if circumstances warrant. But also a thief. An assassin. Or a cold-blooded murderer. In short, sir, a chameleon. A regulator does not have the luxury of weighing his actions against abstract notions of gentlemanly honour – notions which, in any case, do not apply to you, as neither your present rank of journeyman nor your condition as bastard entitles you to claim them. Is that clear?'

'Yes, Grandmaster,' said Quare. But inside he was seething; how long would his bastardy be held against him? Would nothing he achieved be sufficient to weigh against it? Oh, to discover the name of his true father, the cowardly blackguard! If he could but solve that riddle, he would pay the man a visit, no matter how high his rank, and demand acknowledgement . . . or satisfaction.

'And what of putting Grimalkin to the question while he was in your power?' the Old Wolf went on meanwhile. 'How, may I ask, did that offend your fine scruples?'

'It did not. I merely thought it was more important that I return with the timepiece, in case he had associates near by, ready to come to his aid. I did bind him, and made report of where I had left him as soon as I returned to the guild hall.'

'And by the time we dispatched a team to the rooftop, the villain was long gone.' The Old Wolf took a fresh pipe from the stand on his desk and lit it with the spill. 'You are talented, Mr Quare. When it comes to the horological arts, you are most promising. But I find myself questioning whether you have the temperament to be an effective regulator.'

'I—'

'How old are you, sir?' Grandmaster Wolfe interrupted through puffs of smoke.

'Twenty-one,' Quare admitted.

'That is young for a regulator.'

'Master Magnus did not think so when he recruited me for the Order.'

'I remember his report. I thought that he was being overhasty, bringing you along too quickly. Patience is not among Magnus's many virtues. Still, he argued your case persuasively, and in the end I gave approval for your induction. I feel now that I may have been mistaken.'

'Begging your pardon, Sir Thaddeus, but that is most unjust!' The words were out before Quare could consider the wisdom of saying them. 'I completed the mission successfully, despite the unforeseen complication of Grimalkin! I brought back the clock, and you must have noted the innovation to the verge escapement . . .'

'In this business, Mr Quare, a missed opportunity can be worse than outright failure,' answered the Old Wolf. 'As in a game of chess, when a player blunders and puts his queen in jeopardy, only a fool passes up the chance to sweep that lady from the board. As for the escapement, I am surprised to hear you mention it. That is not your affair. You were dispatched to gain possession of a timepiece, not to plumb its secrets. Your orders were explicit on that point, were they not?'

'I-I merely wished to make certain it had not been damaged,' Quare stammered.

'Do not compound the severity of your transgression by inventing feeble excuses. You know very well that the secrets of this particular clock were reserved for the masters of the guild alone.'

'A moment ago, you criticized me for not displaying initiative. Yet now it seems you would prefer me to follow my orders to the letter, without departing from them in any respect whatsoever!'

'That is a specious argument, sir.' The Old Wolf jabbed the end of his pipe towards Quare. 'Save such pettifoggery for the barristers, if you please. The difference is this: in the former case, you would have been acting in the interests of your king and your guild, while in the latter, you were merely satisfying your own curiosity and ambition. There is a time for initiative and a time for obedience, and you need to start distinguishing between the two if you ever hope to rise above the rank of journeyman, my lad. Do I make myself clear?'

'Abundantly,' said Quare.

The old man puffed at his pipe for a moment, then sighed.

'Well, what's done is done. You have seen what you have seen. I would hear your opinion.'

'I-I didn't examine the escapement in detail . . .'

'The truth, sir, I pray you.'

Quare cleared his throat. 'The innovation to the mechanism is clever but not significant. It is an elegant if somewhat impractical solution to a problem that others are close to solving. In truth, I was surprised; it didn't seem substantial enough to account for the urgency of my mission or the interest of Grimalkin. I can only assume I missed something.'

The Old Wolf gave a phlegmatic chuckle. 'You missed nothing. Your assessment is entirely correct. When Lord Wichcote began to boast of his recent acquisition, claiming that it represented an astonishing breakthrough in the horological arts, we had no choice but to act with dispatch, sending the only regulator available, despite your regrettable lack of experience. Who controls the measurement of time controls the world, Mr Quare. It is imperative that every major horological advance become the exclusive property of this guild . . . and, through us, of His Majesty. Luckily, Wichcote is as deficient in his knowledge of horology as in his exercise of discretion.' He waved the pipe over the disassembled clockworks like a priest dispensing a blessing of incense over a corpse. 'As you point out, the innovation to the escapement is clever but no more than that. Spying, like clock-making, is unfortunately an imprecise art.'

'Then it was for nothing.'

'Nothing?' Grandmaster Wolfe shook his head; a fine dust of powder sifted down from his wig to settle on the shoulders of his greatcoat. 'Every scrap of knowledge is valuable in itself. And consider that Grimalkin did not have an opportunity to examine the clock. The fact that it was stolen from him before he could do so will only support the rumour that it embodied some grand stroke of genius. Our enemies will now assume that we possess this knowledge, and we can use their assumption, mistaken though it may be, to our advantage.'

'So I was right after all not to kill him.'

'That we can turn your failure to good account does not excuse it. I would rather have Grimalkin dead than possess a thousand clever clocks. Yet it's possible his masters will dispatch him to retrieve the clock or to learn its secrets. In that case, we may have the opportunity to rectify your mistake.'

'Surely not even Grimalkin would dare to come here!'

'Perhaps not. But as long as we have the proper bait, we may lay a trap for him wherever we please. And this time, I dare say, that grey-suited rogue will not escape.'

'I hope I will be allowed the chance to redeem my honour.'

'There is that detestable word again,' said the Old Wolf with a sour grimace. 'No, Mr Quare, I think you've had enough of honour for now. Perhaps it is best that you put aside the cloak and dagger of the regulator and return for a time to a typical journeyman's life. There you may learn the value of obedience.'

Quare had thought himself prepared for the blow, yet it was a moment before he found his voice again. 'Am I expelled from the Order, then?'

'Suspended, rather. You need a bit of seasoning, I find. Some added experience under your belt before you can be trusted with the responsibilities of membership in the Most Secret and Exalted Order of Regulators.'

Quare stood, hands clenched at his sides. 'If you would give me another chance . . .'

Grandmaster Wolfe studied him through impassive blue eyes. 'I am giving you that chance, sir, provided you have the wit to take it.' He waved the pipe stem in the direction of the door. 'You are dismissed.'

Quare bowed more stiffly than before, turned, and stalked from the stifling room.

A servant waited outside. Guild hall servants dressed in identical livery, wore identical wigs, even had identical expressions painted on their identically powdered faces, making it difficult if not impossible to tell them apart, especially since they were all of middling heft and height, as if cast from the same mould. There was an ongoing conflict between the journeymen of the guild and its servants, a kind of low-grade class warfare that took place within well-defined boundaries and was fought with weapons of juvenile provocation, on the one hand, and, on the other, a sangfroid so impermeable as to verge on the inhuman. Indeed, Quare's friend and fellow journeyman Pickens maintained, not entirely facetiously, that the servants were not human beings at all but automatons, sophisticated mechanical devices crafted by the masters, golems of natural science.

'Master Magnus wishes to see you, sir,' the servant intoned. His powdered face, rouged lips, and pale blue livery put Quare in mind of a well-spoken carp.

Quare gestured for the servant to precede him, then limped in his wake. Candles set in wall sconces cast a murky, tremulous light, like moonlight sifting into a sunken ship. Quare always felt a peculiar shortness of breath here in the guild hall, as if the presence of so many clocks had concentrated time itself, causing a change of state analogous to the condensation of a gas into a liquid. He even thought he could smell it – time, that is: an odour composed of smoke and wax and human sweat, of ancient wood, and stone more ancient still, of lives forgotten but not entirely vanished, ghostly remnants of all those who had walked these halls.

Dark oil paintings of guild masters and grandmasters from the last three hundred and fifty years glowered down at him from the walls of the narrow hallway like Old Testament prophets. *Bastard*, he imagined them sneering. *Failure*. Now he must face the judgement of Master Magnus.

Magnus and the Old Wolf were rivals for power, each believing that he and he alone knew the best way to shepherd the Worshipful Company through these perilous times. Grandmaster Wolfe clung to the past, to the guild's traditional prerogatives, as a bulwark against the uncertainties of change, while Magnus championed a future in which innovation, rather than hoarded knowledge, would be the guarantor of the guild's wealth and influence. Each man had his followers, but Quare – although his personal sympathies were with Master Magnus – had done his best to steer a middle course between them, knowing that the key to advancement lay in keeping his options open. He had no father or family to look to for support and could depend only upon his own native wit. Yet despite his care, he had become caught between them, like Odysseus between Scylla and Charybdis. Now, if he were not careful, they would grind him down to nothing. Indeed, he reflected gloomily, had not the process already begun?

At last the servant pushed open a door and stepped aside. Quare walked past him into a small room whose wood panelling bore gilded bas-reliefs of grandfatherly, bearded Chronos with his hourglass and hungry scythe, winged cherubs carrying bows and arrows in their pudgy hands, and scantily clad nymphs cavorting amidst scenery symbolizing the changing of the seasons. There was a smell of beeswax, though the candles were unlit, the room illuminated by the morning sun streaming through two large windows. One of these looked out upon a busy street – whose cacophony of carriages and wagons, pedestrians, sedan chairs, and pedlars crying their wares was so intrinsic a part of London's aural landscape that Quare scarcely noticed it any more, though upon his arrival in the city just over five years ago he had imagined himself in a very Bedlam of noise – the other upon a time garden: a secluded outdoor space, reserved for the meditations of the masters, in which a variety of timepieces antique and modern, from simple gnomons to more fanciful sundials, along with water clocks, hourglasses, and other constructs, sprouted with the profligacy of weeds.

In the centre of the room, on a spindly-legged wooden table so delicate in appearance that it seemed in danger of collapsing under the weight of Quare's gaze, was a clock topped by the figure of fleet-footed Hermes captured in mid stride, caduceus upraised. A settee upholstered in red and white striped satin stood against one wall, beneath a large oval mirror set in a dark wooden frame carved into the semblance of a wreath of burgeoning grape vines. Against the wall opposite were two chairs done in the same style as the settee.

The room was otherwise empty; there was no door save the one through which he had entered. Quare did not think he had come here before, though it was difficult to be sure; the layout of the guild hall – the gloomy corridors, tight, twisty staircases, and mazelike clusters of rooms – seemed to change from one visit to the next. 'I thought you were bringing me to Master Magnus,' he said, turning to the servant.

'The master asks that you wait,' the servant answered. He bowed low and departed, pulling the door shut behind him.

When he had gone, no sign of the door was visible in the carved panelling. Likely there were other concealed doors in the room. And not only doors. Quare felt the prickly sensation of unseen eyes. In the guild hall, it was always safest to assume that someone was looking on or listening; the Old Wolf and Master Magnus, along with their factions and others harbouring ambitions or resentments, schemed incessantly with and against each other, jockeying for information and the power that came with it. Let them look, he thought; he would betray nothing. That was one lesson among many that bastardy had taught him, and he had learned it well.

Quare approached the mirror. His light brown coat and the cream-coloured waistcoat beneath it, as well as the white shirt under that, bore sweat stains from the inferno of the Old Wolf's private study. He could do nothing about that. But he could and did wipe the sweat from his stubbled face and neck – he had not had time to shave – with an almond-scented handkerchief, then gathered up some lank black locks that had slipped free from the ribbon with which he usually secured his long hair; he detested wigs and wore them as seldom as possible.

Turning from the mirror, Quare fished his pocket watch from his coat and checked it: seventeen minutes past ten. He was gratified to note that the table clock showed the identical time, to the minute. He'd crafted the watch himself, incorporating certain innovations he'd come across in his travels . . . innovations proscribed to the general public.

By royal decree, the Worshipful Company of Clockmakers was the sole arbiter of the techniques and tools that horologists throughout Britain, whether members of the guild or amateurs, were permitted to employ in the manufacture of timepieces. All journeymen of the Worshipful

Company had the duty of protecting its patents and interests. Any timepiece that utilized an already forbidden technology was destroyed, its maker reported to the local authorities, while those clocks evidencing new technologies and methods were confiscated and sent to London for study. The prosperity and safety of the nation depended upon superiority in business as well as in battle, and nothing was a surer guarantee of dominance in both realms than the ability to measure the passage of time more accurately than one's adversaries. Whether coordinating the shipment and delivery of merchandise over land and sea or troop movements upon a battlefield, the advantage belonged to the side with the best timepieces.

Quare considered himself as patriotic as the next fellow, but it was really his fascination with clocks – or, rather, with time itself – that had caused him to accept Master Magnus's invitation to join the Most Secret and Exalted Order of Regulators, an elite corps of journeymen trained as spies and dispatched on missions throughout the country and beyond.

But in this, too, he found himself at odds with Grandmaster Wolfe and his faction: men who regarded all horological innovation with profound mistrust, forever apprehensive that the measurement of time would slip out of their grasp and control, rendering the guild superfluous. Such had been the fate of other guilds, left behind by the rapid changes of the modern world. Thus they behaved as jealous priests, with-holding approval from all but the most innocuous improvements while keeping the truly important advances to themselves. As a consequence, the timepieces made by the journeymen and masters of the Worshipful Company, whether for the public or for private collectors, no longer embodied the latest technologies, as they once had; now, by design, they were always some years behind the true state of the art. Only the scientists of the Royal Society, and of course the army and navy, received the benefit of the guild's secret knowledge, and even there, or so Quare would have been willing to bet, certain things were kept back. The result of this (in his view) short-sighted policy was that practical innovation in the horological arts no longer came from within the guild, but from without: from self-taught amateurs – like Lord Wichcote, he was chagrined to admit – whose work was often strange and eccentric, wild. Quare loved the life of a journeyman because it brought him into contact with ideas and methods that had not yet come to the attention of the guild's censorious authorities. On occasion – by no means often, yet not infrequently, either – he had encountered time-pieces of such radical ingenuity, not to say genius, that he had trembled with excitement as he plumbed their workings and let the beauty of another man's ideas take fire in his mind. No matter that his sworn oath required him to destroy or confis-cate these timepieces and suppress the knowledge behind them; he took no pleasure in his inquisitorial powers but exercised them with cold-blooded efficiency because that was the price of admission to and advancement within the guild. He had accepted Master Magnus's invitation to join the Most Secret and Exalted Order for the same reason, figuring that, as a regulator, he would be able to dip into streams of knowledge more esoteric still, though he'd realized that his acceptance would make it more difficult to avoid becoming enmeshed in the byzantine coils of guild politics . . . as indeed had been the case.

His mission to the attic workshop of the very eccentric, very wealthy, and very well-connected collector and inventor Lord Wichcote had been his first solo assignment after more than a year of intensive training in spycraft, swordplay, and bare-knuckle boxing . . . among other subjects he had never thought to learn. Master Magnus had told him only that the viscount had acquired a most unusual and potentially valuable timepiece, one whose secrets could not be allowed to fall into the wrong hands, either within the country or abroad – not with war between the Great Powers in this Year of Our Lord 1758 approaching a climax on which the fate of England hinged.

Quare had set off at nightfall from the top of the guild hall and made his way swiftly but with care across the eerie moon-lit and fog-wrapped roofscape of London, his only witnesses skulking cats and startled birds, until he reached Wichcote House, an imposing edifice that towered immodestly above its neighbours. He had studied plans of the house and knew that access to the attic could be had through a skylight; to reach it, he would have to climb.

The brickwork afforded sufficient purchase for him to clamber up the wall with ease, moving with a silence that was already second nature. And this ingrained caution was rewarded: before his head topped the ledge, he heard the faint sound of a creaking hinge from above. He froze, clinging to the wall, whose bricks soon showed themselves to be far less suited for hanging on to than for climbing. He dug in with his fingers and toes, muscles aching and sweat drenching his clothes. When some moments had passed with no further sound, he ventured to peek above the parapet.

At this height, the fog was thinner than it had been when he'd started his climb, and the moonlight was bright enough to read by, quite diminishing the stars. As he'd suspected, the skylight had been opened. The roof was deserted; whoever had opened the skylight was now inside the workshop below.

His pulse quickened: the mission had just grown more complicated – and dangerous – than he'd been led to expect. But what of it? Whoever had entered the workshop would have to leave it at some point, no doubt through the skylight, and Quare would be waiting when he came out. The fact that someone else should be prowling about the roof of this particular house of all houses, on this particular night of all nights, was sufficient proof for Quare that the prowler, whoever it was, was here for the same purpose as he. Quare would allow the interloper to do all the work and then step in to claim the prize.

He hoisted himself onto the roof and took cover behind one of the house's many chimneys. From there he had a clear view of the skylight, though he could neither see nor hear what was taking place in the attic below. He drew his primed and loaded pistol, and waited.

It was not long before the sound of a pistol firing broke the silence, sending pigeons wheeling from their roosts and making Quare start and curse under his breath. Seconds later, the music of swordplay rose from the open skylight. Part of Quare's training as a regulator had involved learning to distinguish the salient details of a melee by sound alone, and he judged that there were at least four men engaged below. In a belated rush of understanding, he realized how close he had come to walking into a trap.

The sounds of fighting ceased. The always surprising quiet of a London night resettled over the rooftop. What was happening down there?

'Help! Help!'

Quare drew back behind the chimney at the shrill cries rising from the attic. When he peeked again, billowing clouds of grey smoke were pouring from the skylight. Then, from the midst of the fog, like a materializing phantom, stepped a figure cloaked all in grey.

Quare felt a thrill of fear: it could only be the notorious thief, assassin and spy, Grimalkin.

Nothing was known for certain about Grimalkin. His name, his face, his history: all was mysterious, the subject of endless gossip and conjecture among the apprentices, journeymen and masters of the Worshipful Company. Some said he was a rich and eccentric private collector, of the same irresponsible stamp as Lord Wichcote. Others held him to be a member – or former member – of the Worshipful Company. Still others maintained that he was a spy in the service of a foreign power: France or Austria, or even of an ally, like Prussia, for alliances were matters of expedience among the Great Powers, and allies no more to be trusted than enemies . . . indeed, sometimes rather less so.

Not even Master Magnus, with the resources of the Most Secret and Exalted Order of Regulators at his fingertips, and his connections to the vast intelligence-gathering network of Mr Pitt, had been able to dig up any useful information about Grimalkin. For years, the man had been hunted . . . without success. All the efforts of the Order had failed to kill, capture, or even, it appeared, inconvenience the rogue – which had only led to another surmise, the most outrageous of all: that Grimalkin was himself a regulator.

Grimalkin had not been seen in the city for some years, leading to the general belief – or rather hope – that he had been captured or killed elsewhere. But recently there had been rumours of his return – rumours that were apparently well founded.

The thief, without a glance in Quare's direction, set off across the roof at a loping run and disappeared over the ledge.

The outraged shouts from below convinced Quare that it was time for him to make his escape as well. Tucking away his pistol, he followed Grimalkin across the roof, pausing at the ledge to peer down – just in time to see a lithe grey figure sprint up and over the tiled roof of a neighbouring town-house. Grimalkin had left a rope behind, which Quare wasted no time in shimmying down.

The chase was on.

In his training, Quare had played the roles of fox and hound in gambols across the rooftops of London, but those affairs were mere amusements compared to the reality he experienced now. The need to remain unseen was paramount, and yet he also had to keep his quarry in sight while managing not to fall to his death – three imperatives that proved difficult to reconcile given the speed and daring with which Grimalkin navigated a terrain as treacherous – and starkly beautiful – as the crags and crevices of a desolate mountain range. Yet even as he laboured to keep up, Quare couldn't help admiring the man's graceful athleticism. There was something almost uncanny about the sureness of Grimalkin's balance and the swiftness of his reactions as he hurtled along narrow ledges of marble or slate tiles slick with damp soot and the slimy droppings of birds and leapt without hesitation across open spaces where the slightest misstep meant certain death. Equally amazing was the fact that he made no more sound than his feline namesake might have done.

Quare could not keep pace; with each rooftop he surmounted, scrambling up the tiles, heart hammering in his chest, Grimalkin was farther away, a shadow half lost amidst other shadows. Nor could Quare, for all his efforts, keep quiet; tiles came loose beneath his feet, skittering down the long slopes to crash upon the ground – yet not once did

Grimalkin glance back, as if ignorant or scornful of pursuit.

Just when Quare was about to give up the chase, Grimalkin halted. Quare flung himself flat, but his quarry appeared to take no notice. Instead, angled to make the most of the moonlight – which kept his back to Quare – he pulled an object from the folds of his cape. Quare's heart throbbed. The clock – for so the object must be, though he could not see more than the rough shape and size of it, as big as a big man's fist – was nearly in his grasp. All thought of Grimalkin's fabled fighting prowess was gone from his mind; a predatory instinct welled up from he knew not where. He slid back down the slope of the roof, then rose to a crouch and circled to the right, where, he had ascertained from his former perch, a path led to Grimalkin across a series of connected rooftops.

After what seemed an eternity, he crossed to the flat roof on which Grimalkin stood, intent on his prize. A warm breeze freighted with the stink of the Thames kept the fog at bay. Holding his breath, he slid his rapier from its sheath and crept forward a step, then another.

A tile shifted beneath his foot.

Grimalkin spun, sword in hand, with a speed beyond anything Quare had ever seen . . . but Quare was already lunging to close the distance and could not pull back. All his training in swordplay deserted him in that terrifying instant. He made no attempt to bring his point en garde but instead stepped close, inside Grimalkin's guard, and punched wildly, frantically. More by luck than skill, the hilt of the rapier slammed into the grey-hooded skull, and the man collapsed like a puppet with cut strings.

The clock dropped from Grimalkin's hand and fell towards the roof. Almost indolently, Quare plucked it from the air. Then reeled, stumbling, as if the weight of the clock had unbalanced him. But really it was just the weight of all that had happened this night: the unlooked-for appearance of Grimalkin; the long, harrowing chase by moonlight; the confusion of his clumsy attack – which had by some miracle ended with Grimalkin, a master swordsman, lying unconscious at his feet. Or was the villain shamming?

Quare took a step towards the man, then halted at another wave of dizziness. His hands were trembling; he felt an incongruous urge to laugh. Perhaps he would have – if a sudden burning sensation in the vicinity of his thigh had not directed his eyes downward to torn fabric and a spreading stain. His legs gave way, and he sprawled on the roof alongside Grimalkin – who, he was now certain, was truly unconscious.

Dropping his rapier – though his other hand maintained its hold on the clock – Quare examined his leg as best he could by the light of the moon. The wound did not seem deep: just a long and bloody gash along the outside of his thigh. It burned like hell, though. Recalling how quickly Grimalkin had turned to meet him, he felt almost sick with a visceral understanding of how lucky he had been: a fraction of an inch to one side, and the odd-looking weapon of his grey-cloaked adversary would have punched into his thigh; a fraction higher, and the same move that had ended the fight would instead have impaled him on Grimalkin's blade.

Wounded as he was, he would be even less of a match for the man now. He had to get away before Grimalkin regained consciousness. Or, no … Quare drew a deep breath and mastered his emotions. He knew his duty and would not shirk it, however unpleasant.

Quare shifted his legs beneath him – grimacing as the movement aggravated his wound – and pushed himself to his knees. Grimalkin had fallen onto his back and lay as if peacefully sleeping, one arm flung over his head, the other draped across his chest. All that Quare could see of the man's face between his grey hood and mask were his eyes, and even they were closed. He drew his dagger, then hesitated.

What was he doing? He was about to murder a man who was at his mercy. Surely what was wanted now was questioning, not killing. Here was an opportunity to learn not only Grimalkin's identity but that of his masters.

Setting down the clock, Quare used his dagger to cut lengths from the coiled rope he carried, then bound Grimalkin's wrists and ankles. All the while, Grimalkin lay motionless, though his light eyelashes fluttered and a faint moan escaped his lips, as if he were coming round.

Quare reached out to remove the grey mask covering the lower half of the man's face. It was not only curiosity that impelled him; should the rogue awaken and begin shouting for help, he could use the mask as a gag. But it was fastened tightly and would not come away, so he began to tug it down instead, past the nose, the lips . . .

Quare rocked back on his heels. Disbelieving, he yanked the hood away . . . and saw a luxuriant coil of blonde hair silvered in moonlight.

Grimalkin – renowned spy, deadly fighter, consummate thief – was a woman.

2

Master Mephistopheles

A SECTION OF PANELLING SCYTHED INWARDS, AND A LIVERIED servant glided into the room like a spectre. Quare, who had just lowered himself gingerly onto the settee – his leg was troubling him – sprang up with an oath upon catching sight of the man.

'For God's sake,' he cried in irritation, 'must you skulk about like some damned red Indian?' No sooner were the words out of his mouth than he regretted them; the real source of his anger was the Old Wolf, not this blameless – and to all appearances bloodless – factotum . . . but it was too late now; he would not apologize to a servant.

'Very good, sir,' the man intoned as if incapable of taking offence. He inclined his head towards the open door through which he had entered the room. 'Master Magnus will see you now.'

Quare strode past him into a closet bare of all amenities save a thin wooden railing that circled the enclosed space at waist height, two wall sconces with burning candles caged in glass, and a tasselled bell pull hanging in one corner, beside the door. He did not understand why the master would want to meet him in such close confines. Mystified, he turned to address the servant, who, meanwhile, had stepped in behind him and pulled the door shut. Before Quare could get a word out, the man, with no warning or explanation, tugged the bell pull.

The closet jerked and slid sideways, throwing Quare into the servant. Almost immediately, it changed direction like a swerving carriage, and he was flung away, his shoulder striking hard against the opposite wall. 'What in God's name . . . !'

'Your pardon, sir.'

'The room is moving!'

'Indeed, sir.'

Grasping the railing with both hands, Quare shot the imperturbable servant an exasperated glance but knew better than to press him further: the guild hall servants could make life miserable for journeymen if they chose – as, no doubt, he was being reminded after his impolitic outburst of a moment ago. Nor, to be honest, was he capable of speech. Indeed, it was all he could do to keep from screaming, for the closet now abandoned the horizontal for the vertical, dropping like a stone.

It was a common conceit among the journeymen of the Worshipful Company that the guild hall was itself a great clock, and that to step through its doors was not merely to enter into its workings but to become a part of them, in-corporated into a vast and intricate – if maddeningly obscure – design; Quare suddenly felt that this was no mere metaphor but the literal truth, and that he stood now inside the plung-ing weight of what must be the guild hall's remontoir. Though he was well acquainted with the functioning of this device, which provided motive force to the escapement of a timepiece, his mechanical knowledge was no comfort. On the contrary, as in a nightmare, the familiar was turned strange and inimical. His heart was racing, his reason overcome by a vertiginous terror that shamed him but could not be dispelled by any appeal to reason. The tight dimensions of the closet only made things worse, as if he had been locked, still alive, in a coffin that devils were dragging down to hell. Quare squeezed his eyes shut and glued his hands to the railing.

At last there came a loud clicking noise, followed by a drawn-out growl that made him wince and brace in expectation of a shattering impact. The closet began to shudder, but it also began to slow, and the more it slowed, the less it shuddered, until, mercifully, it came to rest. Quare let out a breath he hadn't been aware of holding and dared to open his eyes.

The door through which he had entered the closet was open again, and beyond it, like a vision of some dishevelled paradise, lay the private study of Master Magnus, though there was no sign of the master himself. Nor did Quare wait for one. He bolted from the room like a prisoner escaping his cell. Once outside, he turned to examine the torture chamber that had conveyed him here, but the servant was already pulling the door closed.

'Wait, damn you—'

Too late; the door snicked shut, fitting so snugly into the wall that there was no sign of its ever having been there at all; nor was there a knob or handle of any sort to pull it open again.

Quare laid his hand against the wall. He felt a steady vibration through his palm, an industrious humming that suggested a hive of bees. Intrigued, he placed his ear where his hand had been and heard the muted music of gears and pulleys – a pleasing harmony nothing at all like the cacophony of screeches and rattles that had attended his arrival. *Why, the impudent rogue*, Quare thought, straightening up. The servant had interfered somehow with the proper working of this device, whatever it was, in order to teach him a lesson. Such cavalier treatment went well beyond the pale; he would have to devise a suitable revenge.

But this was not the time. Sighing, he turned about. As ever, Master Magnus's study was in a state of disorder bordering on chaos. Books and papers covered every available surface, including the floor and the tiled fireplace across the room, in whose capacious interior bound volumes and loose papers were piled as if in readiness for an auto-da-fé. In fact, with candles as likely to be found balanced on stacks of manuscripts as stowed in sconces and candelabra, it was a wonder the master hadn't burned the entire guild hall to the ground by now. On one wall, behind the mound of debris that Quare knew from previous visits marked the master's desk, was a map of Europe reflecting the boundaries drawn in the second Treaty of Aix-la-Chapelle, which had ended the War of the Austrian Succession ten years before, in 1748 – boundaries the current conflict had rendered irrelevant. The map's surface bristled with pins that had variously coloured ribbons attached, giving the appearance of a half-unravelled tapestry; these indicated the locations of regulators dispatched across the Channel as well as other spies and agents in the master's wide-flung network of informants. The wall opposite was given over to bookshelves that stretched from floor to ceiling; so packed were the books in this space that Quare doubted a mouse could have wriggled between them. Master Magnus had charge of the guild library, and he treated its contents as his personal property. Though the other masters grumbled at this presumption, the Old Wolf tolerated it for reasons beyond Quare's understanding.

Quare, picking up a candle along the way, trod a careful path across the room to the shelves, still favouring his wounded leg, and let his eyes rove over the books assembled there. They were not organized by title, author, date of publication, or any other discernible bibliographical system; they weren't even all upright, with spines facing outward for ease of inspection, but jammed higgledy-piggledy wherever there was space, like fieldstones in a wall. It bothered Quare to see books treated like stones; there were treasures in the library of the Worshipful Company that could be found nowhere else in the world, ancient horological texts long forgotten or believed irretrievably lost, as well as more recent publications and private correspondence by some of the greatest minds of Europe, the Orient, and the New World. Master Magnus respected knowledge, indeed had an insatiable appetite for it, but he was less than scrupulous about books, like a connoisseur of wine who cared nothing for the bottles it came in. Why, there, wedged into a space that would not have easily admitted a volume half its size, was the *Horologium Oscillatorium* of Huyghens! Quare reached for it.

'I have always maintained, if one wishes to discover the true character of a man, it is but necessary to set him loose in a library and let him think himself unobserved.'

Quare turned towards the voice, a smile on his lips. 'Your pardon, Master Magnus. I did not see you.'

'Few do,' came the reply, 'unless I wish to be seen.'

Across the room, beside the desk, a vigorous-looking elderly man as slender and hooked as a sickle stood hunched over a pair of stout black walking sticks. The pronounced curvature of his spine forced him to look up at Quare, although if he could have stood unbowed he would have been Quare's equal in height. His dark breeches were finely tailored but could not disguise how twisted were the legs within, and from the cut of his blocky shoes it seemed more likely that they contained pig's trotters than human feet. He had a pronounced humpback, a nose that echoed his posture in miniature, and a wild if thinning mane of white hair that framed his craggy face as if the area around his head were subject to violent crosswinds. A pair of round, dark-tinged spectacles reflected the flames of the candles scattered about the room, giving Quare the disconcerting impression of being stared at by a creature with eyes of fire. Little wonder that fearful, malicious apprentices had bestowed the nickname Master Mephistopheles upon him. Twining in and out of the space between his legs and the two sticks were a number of cats that, like the man, seemed to have materialized out of thin air. The notion that this person could make himself inconspicuous or unseen would have been laughable were it not for the fact that Quare had ample evidence of its truth.

'The moving closet, master,' he burst out, navigating his way past piled books and manuscripts on which certain of the cats – there seemed to be more of the animals by the second – had taken up residence; some ignored him, others regarded him through slitted eyes with something like contempt, a few hissed at his passage. 'Is it your invention? How does it work?'

Master Theophilus Magnus bared white teeth in the feral grimace that served him for a smile. Those teeth were the only uncrooked thing about him. 'You like that, eh? Just a little something I threw together. Employs the same principle as the gravity escapement. Saves me the trouble of climbing stairs. I call it the "stair-master".'

'Ingenious,' said Quare.

Master Magnus tossed his head dismissively. 'A curiosity, nothing more. Of use only to cripples like me.'

'What is the name of the man who operated it?'

'Ha ha! Did the rascal give you a scare? Ruffled your dignity, did he? I'll speak to the fellow, never fear. Now, my boy, take a seat and tell me how things went with Sir Thaddeus. Don't worry – here of all places, in the very bowels of the guild hall, you may speak freely. This is my domain.'

Quare could not find a chair that wasn't covered with books or cats, or both, so remained standing. 'As well – that is to say as badly – as one could have hoped. I am suspended from the Most Secret and Exalted Order of Regulators.'

'Capital,' said Master Magnus, flashing his bright grimace again. 'The Old Wolf took the bait, eh?'

'I begged him to reconsider, but he refused.'

'Of course he did. Predictable as a pendulum. And the clock? Any suspicions there?'

'Not that I could see. He identified the improvement to the escapement and dismissed it out of hand, just as you said he would. But I confess, I don't understand the need for this obfuscation.'

'It is obedience that I require from you, Mr Quare, not understanding,' Master Magnus replied.

'But surely you don't suspect the Old Wolf of treason!'

'I suspect everyone, yourself included. That is the task appointed to me by Mr Pitt and His Majesty. Your task is to follow my orders without tedious questions and objections. And I must say, my boy, you did well with Sir Thaddeus. Very well indeed. Should your horological talents ever desert you, I advise you to take up the stage.' Raising one stick in a swordsman's flourish, he repeated: 'Now, sit, sir – take the weight off that leg of yours.'

As Quare sank dejectedly into the nearest chair, a calico cat leapt clear with a yowl. 'If I were on the stage, at least my efforts would be applauded.'

'Have I not applauded them? You must be satisfied with an audience of one, my boy. Such is a regulator's lot.'

'But thanks to you, I am no longer a regulator.'

'Pishposh. Regardless of what Sir Thaddeus and the rest of the Order may believe, you are a regulator until I say otherwise.'

'That is small consolation, sir, for the public humiliation. News travels fast within these walls – and beyond them. Soon all of London will think me disgraced.'

'Hardly all. All of London does not know of our Most Secret Order's existence. Even the masters of the Worshipful Company know little enough of our business, and the majority of journeymen still less. We are a subject of rumour and speculation, not knowledge. But perhaps you deserve a little disgrace, sir. You let a rare opportunity slip. That grey-clad popinjay has robbed us of too many prizes.'

'But—'

'You had Grimalkin at your mercy,' Master Magnus interrupted sternly. 'With only the moon as witness. Sir Thaddeus may be wrong about any number of things when it comes to the management of this guild, but he is right to be angry when a regulator fails in the clear requirements of his duty.'

'Master, as I told you when I placed the clock into your hands last night, I was concerned about my wound and feared the rogue's blade was poisoned. There was no time to question or dispatch him.'

'I know you, Mr Quare. I trained you. You are no milksop to flinch from what needs doing. So do not think to pull the wool over these eyes. There is more to your rooftop encounter with Grimalkin than you have divulged to me. I knew it at once, as soon as you began to spin your preposterous tale, but I decided to wait until this morning, after your interview with Sir Thaddeus, to prise the truth out of you. I knew it would be easier for you to play your part with the Old Wolf if you believed your story had taken me in. So I pretended to believe that poppycock about a poisoned blade, and I pretended to be relieved when my surgeon determined the wound was not poisoned after all. That you should attempt to deceive me was surprising, I confess – but I had other priorities than ferreting out the truth just then. Namely, the clock you had placed into my hands, the secrets of which could not be trusted to anyone else but me, not even Sir Thaddeus. That is why I rehearsed you in a tale more preposterous still, a tale of gross ineptitude conducted under the flag of honour, a tale apt to be so infuriating to a man of Sir Thaddeus's saturnine temperament that he would overlook any inconsistencies in the timepiece before him and focus instead on the inadequacies of the man who had recovered it.'

'I did as you asked, and look what it has cost me. Do I not deserve to know why?'

'Why? Because it suits my purposes to have the Old Wolf and his partisans believe you dismissed from the Order and out of my favour. But do not attempt to divert me, Mr Quare. You would do well to remember that I am not so credulous as Sir Thaddeus. No, not by a long shot. So do not try my patience with any more flimsy fictions, sir – or you will find me as temperate as the Lisbon earthquake. Now, if you please, the truth. What really happened between you and Grimalkin on that rooftop?'

Quare swallowed, his mouth gone dry. 'I fear you will not believe me.'

'I will believe the truth, when I hear it.'

'Will you hold it in confidence?'

'Why, damn your impudence!' Master Magnus slammed one of his sticks hard against the floor, putting a passel of cats to flight. 'I will not parley with you! If you would remain a regulator, then speak. But understand this – one way or another, I will learn the truth. I have other devices at my disposal, devices every bit as ingenious as the stair-master . . . though much less pleasant to ride upon, I assure you.'

At this, Quare realized that the servant had been following Master Magnus's orders in conveying him here so roughly. The master had foreseen this moment from the first and had planned accordingly; truly, he had a better chance of trouncing the great Philidor across a chessboard than of winning a battle of wits with Master Theophilus Magnus, who had built the Most Secret and Exalted Order of Regulators into a secret service said to rival that of Pitt himself. Yet the knowledge that he was almost certainly overmatched served only to stiffen his spine. 'I do not take kindly to threats,' he said, glowering.

'Think of it rather as a reminder,' Master Magnus answered.

'A reminder of what?'

'Of the oath you swore upon becoming a journeyman of this company. Why, one would think you were trying to protect Grimalkin!'

'It's not that. It's . . . Well, it's . . .'

'Out with it, sir!'

Quare sighed. There was no help for it. 'He . . . Grimalkin, that is . . . is a woman.'

For a moment, the only sound was the purring of the cats. Quare had always found a cat's purr soothing, but there was a peculiar quality about a roomful of purring cats that was, he decided, not very soothing at all. Master Magnus, meanwhile, studied him from behind those dark lenses filled with flickering flames. That wasn't too soothing, either. Despite his twisted legs, or rather because of them, the master possessed unusual upper-body strength – Quare had seen him lift, with minimal effort, gear assemblies for tower clocks that two men would have struggled to raise – and to watch him now, propped upon his sticks, ominously silent, was to see not a crippled man but a coiled spring. 'A woman,' he said at last. 'Grimalkin a woman, you say?'

'There can be no doubt of it.'

'Grimalkin, who has outfought the deadliest swordsmen in Europe and outthought their masters, not once but again and again, that Grimalkin, the spy supreme, the paragon of thieves, is a female.'

'It's hard to believe, I know. But it's true. I saw her with my own eyes. That's why I couldn't— You said the moon was the only witness, master. But God was watching, too. How could I slay a woman in cold blood?'

Master Magnus grunted as if he might be prepared to offer some practical suggestions. But instead he said, 'Tell me everything that happened from the moment you first saw Grimalkin. Leave nothing out, Mr Quare, no matter how insignificant it may seem.'

Quare related how he had seen Grimalkin emerge, wreathed in smoke, from the attic skylight of Lord Wichcote's house, then shadowed the grey-clad figure from rooftop to rooftop under the gibbous moon, crept close enough to deliver a knockout blow, more by luck than skill, and at the cost of a painful gash to his leg, and then lifted the grey mask only to find himself gazing at a face unmistakably female. Apart from the lifting of the mask, and what he had found beneath it, it was all as he had related to Master Magnus the previous night, while his leg was being tended to.

'Describe this woman,' Master Magnus instructed with sceptical interest.

'It was not a face I had seen before,' Quare replied. 'Youngish, I would say.'

'Attractive?'

'I was too taken aback to notice.'

'Were you? In my experience, regardless of the circumstances, the attractiveness of a young female is among the few things a young male may be depended upon to notice.'

Quare felt himself blushing. 'The light was poor, and one side of her face was bruised and bleeding,' he explained.

'Did you move her? Staunch the bleeding?'

'No, master.'

'You did not . . . touch her at all?'

Quare bristled. 'What do you mean?'

Master Magnus raised a bushy white eyebrow above the gold frames of his spectacles. 'You would not be the first to take advantage of such an opportunity. Alone with a helpless young woman – a woman, moreover, who by her wanton actions might be said to have forfeited the protections a civilized society accords the weaker sex.'

'Do you think I would spare a woman's life only to violate that which is more precious than life?'

'Fine sentiments, sir. They do you credit, I'm sure. Yet I cannot help but notice that you did not attempt to aid her. A strange sort of chivalry, that.'

'I . . .'

'No matter. Surely you questioned the woman once she had regained consciousness.'

Quare started as a cat – the same calico he had evicted

earlier – leapt into his lap. He stroked the animal, grateful for the distraction. 'Er, no. In truth, I *was* worried that her blade had been poisoned. You will grant, master, that poison is a woman's weapon.'

At this, Master Magnus gave a stiff nod, as though compelled against his will to acknowledge the point.

Encouraged, Quare went on. 'I thought it best to return the timepiece to you as quickly as possible – before the poison took effect or any accomplices came to Grimalkin's aid. I was loath to lose the prize so soon after having won it.'

Master Magnus chuckled. 'I do not mean to denigrate your bravery and resourcefulness, my boy. But even you must realize how unlikely – inconceivable, rather – it is that a regulator of your limited experience could take a seasoned agent like Grimalkin by surprise. No, sir, no. That alone proves – were the idea itself not absurd on its face – that the woman you overcame on the rooftop was not Grimalkin, but an imposter.'

'An imposter! But she stole the clock from Lord Wichcote – and, by the sound of it, crossed blades with more than one adversary to do so!'

'Pishposh. By your own testimony, you did not see what went on in that attic. For all you know, the woman was aided by an accomplished swordsman, who sacrificed his life – or at least his liberty – in order to facilitate her escape. That seems more likely, does it not, than a lone woman besting multiple swordsmen? No doubt the woman and her accomplice believed their chances of robbing Lord Wichcote would be improved if one of them dressed as the notorious Grimalkin. Such a stratagem would also enable the woman to conceal her gender beneath a mask – thus giving Lord Wichcote the mistaken impression that he was facing two men.'

'But I saw no evidence of an accomplice!'

'Absence of evidence is not evidence of absence.'

'If only you had seen the speed and skill with which she moved, master. She very nearly skewered me! How do you explain that?'

'You believed you were facing Grimalkin – and believing made it so. Preconceptions colour perceptions, my boy.'

'What of *your* preconceptions, then? Because you cannot entertain the possibility of a female Grimalkin, you spin hypotheses out of whole cloth!'

'No, sir, no,' the master repeated, giving the floor another thump with his stick. 'Why, it were as likely for me to dance a jig atop this desk as for Grimalkin to be a woman! Put the notion from your mind. That was not Grimalkin you fought. And a good thing, too, else you would not have survived, much less come back in triumph, bearing the prize.'

Quare was not in a mood to be mollified. 'If not Grimalkin, then who?'

'That is precisely the question, Mr Quare. And you may rest assured that it is a question I mean to get to the bottom of. Not just the woman's identity – and that of her accomplice, should he be proved to exist – but the identity of the person or persons who engaged them to steal that timepiece from Lord Wichcote. I do not believe they were common criminals. Far from it. They were in the service of England's enemies, of that I have no doubt.'

'Then perhaps they are allied with Grimalkin in some way.'

'That is indeed a troubling possibility.' Master Magnus adopted a severe expression. 'You were wrong to try and keep this from me, Mr Quare, as you were wrong not to question the woman posing as Grimalkin. But I will forgive these wrongs, just this once, because you did bring the clock to me, after all, and played your part to perfection with the Old Wolf. Yet I must say, I find your account, even in its amended form, an odd one – so odd, in fact, that I cannot help but wonder if you are holding something back even now.'

'I've told you everything, master – I swear it!'

'We shall see,' he answered, and his expression turned more ominous still. 'You were not my first choice for this assignment, Mr Quare. Had a more seasoned regulator been available, I would have sent him. But with the French, Russians, and Austrians moving against us on the Continent, as well as in Scotland and in Ireland, to say nothing of the Colonies, I've had to dispatch my best men far and wide, and you – to be blunt – were simply the best of what remained. I was, I confess, somewhat apprehensive as to your chances. Nor has your success in securing the timepiece against all odds laid those apprehensions to rest – on the contrary, in some respects what you have just told me has exacerbated them. If you are to continue as my special agent, I must have your solemn oath that you are prepared to harden your heart, put conscience aside, and act in the best interests of your country and your guild as circumstances require. Can you do that, Mr Quare? Because I assure you, if you cannot, I can find another man who will.'

'I am your man,' Quare said, anxious to assuage the master's doubts. It had not only been from a desire to draw closer to the mysteries of time that he had accepted Master Magnus's invitation to become a regulator; the master had promised to utilize his intelligence network on Quare's behalf, to uncover the identity of his father. He did not wish to jeopardize that promise now. 'You have my word.'

'Hmm ... Perhaps there is someone I can assign to help you,' Master Magnus said. 'Someone with more experience ...'

'I thought all the experienced agents were on assignment,' Quare said. 'Anyway, I prefer to work alone.'

'Your preferences do not concern me,' the master answered. 'There are regulators no longer on active duty but still competent enough to support you in the field.'

'To spy on me, you mean.'

This the master did not trouble to deny. 'Do we have an understanding, Mr Quare?'

'It appears I have no choice.'

'Quite.'

'Then, yes, I agree, of course. Who will you assign to me?'

'I must think on it.' And with that, the storm clouds lifted from the master's expression, and he looked younger, almost boyish – as if the flames dancing in his spectacles had burned away half a lifetime in an instant. The change did not make his appearance any more regular or pleasing to behold, yet it made Quare smile even so, for he had never yet witnessed this transformation in Master Magnus without being rewarded by some astonishing glimpse into the man's fertile mind: a hint of some heretofore veiled mystery of time, or a wondrous invention like the stair-master, which put horological principles to unexpected use.

'Now, my boy,' said Master Magnus, a mischievous lilt to his voice, his stature seeming to grow straighter as he spoke, 'would you care to have a look at the timepiece you have risked – and sacrificed – so much to procure?'

3

Three Questions

USING HIS WALKING STICKS, MASTER MAGNUS PULLED HIMSELF across the floor of the study. He stabbed one forward, then the other, dragging his legs along behind with sharp wrenchings of his hips, like a man toiling through drifts of snow. Once again Quare was struck by the strength of his arms and upper body. Mewling cats slipped in and out of his path, rubbing against the sticks and his twisted legs. He ignored them.

'Word of what I am about to show you can go no further,' he said. 'Is that understood?'

'Yes, of course,' said Quare, wondering what was about to be revealed to him. He would have risen to assist Master Magnus but knew from experience that any such attempt would meet with an angry rejection.

The master paused before Quare, his face shining with sweat. Now it was his own reflection Quare beheld in the dark spectacles; though he was seated, his eyes were nearly level with the master's, so pronounced was the curvature of his spine. 'Swear it,' growled Master Magnus. 'Swear it on your *honour*.'

There was more mischief than malice to the barb; still, Quare couldn't help flinching as it struck home. 'I swear it.'

'One day I will perfect a set of mechanical limbs,' the master said as he resumed his halting progress. 'Think of it, sir. Legs for the legless. Arms for the armless. Hands as clever and supple as your own. Better, even. Stronger. Then cripples such as I will be envied instead of scorned.'

His destination was the bookshelves. A cluttered space Quare could have crossed in five seconds was for Master Magnus a labour of as many minutes, though he did not once complain of it. But at last he stood before the solid mass of books and papers, his misshapen back to Quare. The phlegmatic rasp of his breathing was the loudest sound in the room, but it did not drown out the purring of the cats; it seemed almost to rise out of those lesser rumblings, riding above them like the foaming crest of a wave. Quare felt an answering vibration in himself, transmitted through the air, or through the calico cat still curled on his lap, as if all his nerves, pulled taut, had been plucked like the strings of a guitar. He got to his feet (displacing the cat, which leapt to the floor) and stepped – or, rather, felt himself drawn – towards the shelves. Was the timepiece hidden there?

'Bring a light,' said Master Magnus, who must have heard Quare move, for he had not turned to look at him, his attention fixed on the shelves before him. He reached up with one of his walking sticks to stab at the fat, leather-bound spine of a nameless volume. There came a clicking sound, and a section of shelving slid away from the rest, scattering cats as it pivoted through one hundred and eighty degrees to bring into view a worktable outfitted with all the familiar accoutrements of the clockmaker's trade . . . and some not so familiar.

Quare's heart was beating fast as he joined the master, who motioned for him to set down the candlestick he had fetched along. This Quare managed with difficulty, as the surface of the worktable was strewn with disassembled or partially assembled clocks and watches – a spilled cornucopia of gears and gauges, wheels and wires and other glittery objects he would have given much to examine at his leisure. Though he had spent a fair amount of time in Master Magnus's study of late, and had on occasion even assisted him in his researches, he had never before seen this hidden worktable, or so much as suspected its existence. How many other secrets were concealed here?

'Now, where did I put the cursed thing?' muttered the master. Having set one of his sticks against the worktable, he leaned upon the other as he rummaged one-handed, and with a roughness that made Quare wince, through the mechanical treasure trove atop the table. 'I could have sworn . . . ah!' His hand rose, still empty, and plunged into the pocket of his waistcoat, whence it emerged clutching an object about the size and shape of a quail's egg. This he held up between thumb and forefinger as if presenting a precious jewel for Quare's inspection.

It was, he saw at once, a pocket watch of the type known as a hunter, the case of which included a metal lid covering the dial. The watch was ovoid, as he had already noted, the case of polished but otherwise unembellished silver, including the cover.

'Well, sir?' demanded Master Magnus.

'But that is not the clock I brought you!'

'No, it is not . . . and yet it is. Here, take it.'

Quare accepted the watch. It was unusually thin, less than half the width of his index finger, and lighter than he had expected. He prised the cover apart with his thumbnail and swung it open, revealing a mi-concave crystal and an enamel dial with twelve black symbols – neither numbers nor astrological signs; at least, not any that he recognized – painted upon it. His horological studies had exposed him to the alphabetic and numerical systems of foreign lands: he could recognize Cyrillic, Chinese, and Arabic, among others, but these symbols were new to him, rendered in a style so fluid as to almost swim before his eyes, as if the marks were changing in subtle ways beyond his ability to register. He found it difficult to focus on them; they seemed to squirm not only against the backdrop of the dial but, as it were, against the backdrop of his mind. The sensation was uncomfortable enough that he let his gaze slide away, to the inside of the silver cover, which he noticed was engraved. He held it closer to the candle, angling it until he could make out the initials *JW* in fancy script, and a date: *1652*.

Quare frowned; given the thinness and lightness of the watch, he would have guessed it to be of more recent manufacture. The hour and minute hands were gilded and fancifully shaped to resemble the head and tail, respectively, of a dragon, and, as he determined after a quick check against his own pocket watch, were not positioned to anything near the correct time. He raised the watch to his ear, but heard no ticking; the mainspring had run down and was in need of winding. But the stem proved decorative only, and there was no opening for a key. Nor any indication that there ever had been. He shot Master Magnus a questioning look, but the master returned his gaze expressionlessly.

'Well?' he repeated.

'An intriguing watch,' Quare acknowledged. 'Am I to infer that you found it secreted inside the clock I brought you?'

'Like a pearl within an oyster.'

'Was there a master with the initials JW on the rolls of the Worshipful Company in 1652?'

'More than one,' said Master Magnus, manoeuvring himself towards a nearby armchair covered with loose papers and cat hair, into which he collapsed with a grunt of voluptuous satisfaction. 'Journeymen, too. But after studying the archives thoroughly, I have ruled out each of them as the maker.'

'Perhaps JW was a foreigner,' Quare mused. 'Or an amateur, like Lord Wichcote—' He paused, struck by a sudden notion: 'What is that gentleman's first name, by the way?'

'It is Josiah,' the master said, stroking a fat black and white cat that had wasted no time in leaping into his lap and settling itself there with an air of entitlement a pasha would have envied. 'But that is mere coincidence. Why, the man was not yet born in 1652! And his father, the late Lord Wichcote, was named Cecil . . . and had no better acquaintance with the insides of a timepiece than does this cat. No, it is the watch you should be interrogating, sir, not me. The answers you seek lie there, provided you can unlock them.'

Quare accepted the challenge with a nod, remembering how, at his first meeting with Master Magnus, years before, the master had similarly challenged him with a pocket watch. Now, turning back to the worktable, he fished a loupe from his waistcoat pocket and held it to his eye while examining the watch more closely in the candlelight – though, as before, his eyes slid past the figures painted onto the dial, as if their flowing shapes offered no purchase for his sight.

'These markings are most curious.'

'Indeed,' Master Magnus agreed. 'What do you make of them?'

'I assume they are numbers, though none that I recognize. Still, there are twelve of them, arranged in the traditional manner upon the face – what else could they be?'

Master Magnus shrugged in a most maddening manner.

Quare told himself that he would subject the numbers – if numbers they were – to a more rigorous inspection at some later time. They were, after all, the very least of the wonders and mysteries of what was unquestionably a masterpiece. The detail of the draconic hands was particularly well done, the filigree as fine as gilded frost, evidence of a keen eye and an exceptionally steady hand. Yet the secret of its winding eluded him, unless . . .

Could the watch be self-winding? Such a timepiece was theoretically possible, and many gifted clockmakers, Master Magnus included, had sought to solve the considerable practical difficulties involved in making one. Yet as far as Quare knew, no one had succeeded, or come close to succeeding. Certainly his own efforts in that line had met with abject failure. How likely was it that some solitary genius had done it more than a century ago? He needed to open the case.

Quare could feel Master Magnus's probing gaze. The master was studying him as intently as he was studying the watch . . . and with an identical purpose: to divine his secrets. He had said he trusted no one, suspected everyone, and just because Quare was no traitor did not mean he had no secrets he wished to hide.

Of course, Master Magnus had been correct in his suspicion that Quare had not been entirely forthcoming about his rooftop encounter with the woman – a woman whom, despite the master's scorn, he still believed to have been the real Grimalkin and not an imposter.

After all, she had told him so.

She had regained consciousness while he was still marvelling at her unmasking. Master Magnus had asked if he had found her attractive, but the truth was that neither at the time nor later had he thought in such conventional terms. The woman was not beautiful but uncanny, her pale blonde hair seemingly spun out of moonlight, her skin like ivory, an exotic cast to her angled features – features streaked now with soot and grime and blood from where he had struck her – that provoked his fascination rather than his admiration. He saw a blend of races there but could not identify the mixture. She might have fallen from the moon, a handmaiden of Selene.

She didn't make a sound. All at once the dark pools of her eyes opened, and she regarded him with frank but calm curiosity. Such self-possession threw Quare further off his mark. It was as if their positions had been reversed, and he was the one who had been surprised and rendered helpless, his secret exposed, his prize stolen, his honour – indeed, his very life – hanging by the thread of a stranger's mercy. He felt interrogated by her stare and drew back, as if, bound though she was, she still constituted a danger. 'I warn you,' he said. 'Do not cry out.'

She laughed softly . . . and, he thought, sadly; the sound sent a shiver down his spine. 'I congratulate you, sir.'

'What?' Her voice made him think of fresh country breezes and springtime rain showers, as if he were back in his native Dorchester and not squatting upon a foul London rooftop. Her accent, like her features, was hard to place.

'You have caught the great Grimalkin.' She seemed to mock herself, and him. 'Now, what will you do with her?'

Quare felt drunk, or under a spell. He swallowed and attempted to marshal his wits. 'You are my prisoner, madam. I will ask the questions.'

She laughed again, but this time there was no sadness in it; eagerness, rather. 'Ask, then. I am bound to answer.'

'Are you really Grimalkin? A woman?'

'Have I not said it? You are a spendthrift with your questions, man. That is one of your three gone already.'

'Three? What folly is this?'

She grinned. 'And there is question two, fled as quickly as a man's life. But I shall answer, as I must. You have captured me, sir, knocked me out and restrained me as I lay senseless. Yet it is not these ropes that bind me. By ancient compact must I answer truthfully three questions put to me by any man who holds me in his power.'

'You're mad,' he said.

'Ask your third question, and you shall see my madness,' she promised. And there was that in her voice and her dark eyes which made him shudder and draw back farther still.

'I know not what tricks you have up your sleeve, nor do I care.' Quare sheathed his dagger and drew his pistol, which he cocked and held at the ready. 'Do not think your sex will save you. Believe me, I will not hesitate to fire.'

This seemed to recall the woman to the reality of her circumstances. Or perhaps it was the reassuring feel of the pistol grip in his hand that made him see her in a more realistic light. In any case, she no longer seemed so eerie. The wild provocation of her manner, which had puffed her up like the bristling fur of a cat seeking to warn off a larger enemy, fell away, revealing a bedraggled creature more to be pitied than feared, a young woman – certainly no older than he, and perhaps younger – who lay entirely at his mercy. 'Don't,' she said, and shrank back against the filthy tiles of the roof. 'I beg you . . .'

'I won't, unless you force me to it,' he reassured her. 'Now, you will tell me who you are working for, and why you have stolen this timepiece from Lord Wichcote.'

She answered with another question. 'What is your name?'

'Give me yours, and perhaps I will tell you.'

'You know my name.'

'Grimalkin? That is but an alias. I mean your true name.'

She glared at him defiantly.

He shrugged. 'No matter. I am more interested in hearing the name of your masters.'

'I know *your* masters,' she replied. 'You are of the Worshipful Company. There is the stink of the regulator about you.'

'The existence of the Worshipful Company is no secret,' he said, 'but few indeed are those who know of the regulators, and common thieves are not of that number.'

'There is nothing common about me,' she declared, eyes flashing with a trace of their former fire.

In that, he was forced to agree, though he was not about to admit it to her. 'Come now,' he said instead. 'I watched you enter Lord Wichcote's attic through the skylight and leave the same way, bearing your prize. Those are the actions of a thief.'

'A thief steals the property of others. I take what belongs to me, wherever I chance to find it.'

'Chance?' He laughed. 'I suppose you will tell me next that you were simply out for a moonlight stroll across the rooftops of London and happened to fall through Lord Wichcote's open skylight!'

She glowered but said nothing in reply.

Keeping the pistol trained upon her, he lifted the clock from the rooftop with his free hand. 'So, you maintain that this clock is your property. That Lord Wichcote stole it from you, and you were but retrieving it.'

'Careful,' she cautioned, and it seemed to him that there was more than just concern for a rare and valuable timepiece in the tone of her voice.

'It seems an ordinary clock to me.'

'It is no more ordinary than I am.'

'Indeed? I am glad to hear it. I should hate to think I have engaged in this merry chase for nothing.'

'You are a fool.'

He felt the blood rush to his face. 'At least I am no traitor, madam. You would betray your country, and your king.'

'There is more to the world than England. If my allegiance lies elsewhere, that does not make me a traitor.'

'No matter. Whatever you are, my masters will ferret out your secrets. Just as they will the secrets of this timepiece.'

'I do not think so.' Suddenly the woman was free, her hands no longer bound behind her; they were pointing at him, and they were not empty, either, but held a brace of small pistols. He had seen only a grey blur. He cursed, realizing too late that she hadn't been cowering at all but somehow cutting herself free of the ropes he had lashed about her wrists. Or, no . . . not cutting herself free, but instead being freed by the sharp teeth of a small grey mouse that he now saw scamper up her sleeve and disappear into the folds of her cloak.

Though he could scarcely believe his eyes, he forced himself to show no surprise. 'Your little pet is resourceful,' he said.

'Henrietta is no pet but a friend and companion. And now' – she gave him a mocking smile – 'hand over the clock, and I will spare your life.'

He shook his head. 'Lay down your pistols, and I shall spare yours.'

'Why do you not fire?' she demanded. 'Are you a coward?'

Truthfully, he did not think he could beat her to the trigger. She was that fast. He would have to find another way. 'You have not fired, either,' he observed. 'It would appear we are at an impasse.'

For a moment, they faced off in silence. Then the woman groaned with frustration. 'Damn you, sir, for a dunce! Why will you not ask your third question?'

'I beg your pardon?'

'Your third question, man! Until you ask it, I am bound to do you no harm, unless you should first attempt to harm me. If you would but try to shoot, or if you would but ask – yet you do neither, as if you somehow know our ways!'

He blinked, taken aback by the return of the madwoman of moments before. Mad, yes, but could he not use that to his advantage? 'Perhaps I am not such a dunce after all, madam. And perhaps I know more of your ways than you think.'

She regarded him with something like horror. 'No. That is not possible.'

'And yet, as you say, I have not posed my third question.' Until she'd spoken of it, he'd had no idea that he hadn't asked her a third question; indeed, even now he could not have sworn to it with certainty. Yet she obviously believed it, and, with the capricious logic of the mad, attached a dire significance to the omission. Thus Quare resolved to continue as he had started – though he soon discovered that it was more difficult to avoid asking a question than he would have imagined, even knowing that his mission, and likely his life, hung in the balance. What ignorance had allowed him to accomplish with thoughtless ease took all his concentration to continue now that his mind was fixed upon it. 'Nor shall I pose it,' he added. 'No, nor attack you, either, though I will not hesitate to defend myself. I have the clock, after all, and I reckon that my masters and I may pose it as many questions as we like without fear of retribution.'

'You could not be more wrong.'

He couldn't help chuckling at such arrant lunacy.

71

'Why, you speak as if I held a weapon rather than a timepiece!'

'That is precisely what you hold. A weapon so dangerous, so deadly, that it cannot be allowed to fall into careless hands. That is why I was sent to retrieve it from that supercilious bumbler, Lord Wichcote. And why you must return it to me now. Believe me, it is for your own sake. For the sake of all mankind.'

A thousand questions clustered at his lips; he bit them back. 'Better that such a weapon – if weapon it be – fall into English hands than into the hands of the French and their allies. These are perilous times for England, madam. We fight for our survival against foes – as I have no doubt you know very well – who would show us not a scintilla of mercy. Against such enemies, the champions of an absolutism abhorrent to every freeborn Englishman and woman, we must grasp at every advantage, no matter how slight. It is our duty, to ourselves and our posterity.'

'You speak of your petty wars as if they matter.'

'They matter to me.'

'There are other wars, sir, greater wars than you know, the consequences of which you cannot begin to imagine.'

'Then I will leave such imaginings to you.'

'If only you would. Yet in your ignorance, you and your masters thrust yourselves into matters that are beyond you in every way. In doing so, you will bring ruin upon the very posterity whose safety you seek to ensure.'

'I am touched by your concern.'

Now it was the woman's turn to chuckle. 'If that were all, I would leave you to your fate, and gladly. But like curious children bearing lit candles into a cellar where gunpowder is stored, thinking to find toys and sweetmeats hidden amid the barrels, your greedy stupidity threatens more than your own lives. This clock will not yield up its secrets to such as you – no, nor to your masters, not even the greatest of them. Believe me, rather than answer your questions, it will punish you for asking them – and it will be a punishment that strikes the guilty and the innocent alike.'

'What sort—' He stopped himself in time. 'That is to say, even if this clock were stuffed with gunpowder and primed to explode like a grenado, it would scarcely pose a danger to any-one beyond its immediate vicinity.'

'Were I to explain, you would think me madder than you do already,' she answered. '"There are more things in heaven and earth than are dreamt of in your philosophy."'

'I am no Horatio, madam; nor, I think, are you Prince Hamlet – though I begin to wonder if you are but mad north-northwest. You speak in riddles and hint at powers beyond mortal ken, yet whether you truly believe these things or say them to play upon my fancy, as if I were some superstitious rustic or smooth-cheeked schoolboy, I cannot tell. But it matters not. I am a man of science. I place my faith in reason. Thus will we unlock the secrets of this clock. Thus will we make use of them in defence of our hard-won liberties. And now' – he struggled to his feet, keeping his pistol trained upon her and ignoring the sharp, stabbing pain in his thigh, as if his movements had started his wound to bleeding again – 'as much as I have enjoyed matching wits with you, the hour grows late. I—'

'But you are wounded!' she interrupted, her pale face turn-ing paler still. 'Blood has been spilled!'

'Indeed, we have spilled each other's blood this night.'

'Then it is already too late,' she said, and, to his astonish-ment, lowered her pistols. Even more astonishing, a tear rolled down her ivory cheek. Most astonishing of all, at the sight of that glistening track, silvered in moonlight, he felt an answering shiver pass across his heart, and an impulse to comfort her so strong that it took all his will to resist it. 'But perhaps not,' she said, wiping the tear away and looking up at him with pleading eyes. 'There may yet be time to undo what you have unwittingly set in motion, or at least to avert the worst of it. Give me the clock, I beg you. I will take my leave, and no one need be the wiser. You will never see me again, I swear it.'

And those words, too, flew straight to his heart, echoing in that chamber with a hollow pang. Why should the thought of never seeing her again seem like such a terrible thing? 'Madam, I cannot. My duty is clear.'

'Then you have doomed us all.' She put her pistols away – where they went, Quare didn't see; one second they were in her hands; the next, her hands were empty. She stood with graceful dignity, her eyes fixed on him all the while, full of reproach and disappointment. 'Would that I had slain you,' she said with quiet bitterness. 'Or that you had killed me. Better still if we had never been born. But I see now that there could be no escaping this moment for either of us. From the very beginning, we two were fated to mingle our blood upon this rooftop.'

As she spoke, her voice heavy with resignation, she pulled the hood back over her head and drew the scarf up to cover her mouth and nose. Yet it was not just a rearrangement of clothing; her voice, her posture, even the quality of her eyes underwent a transformation, until, at the end of it, the woman was gone so thoroughly as to never have existed, and in her place stood Grimalkin. It was a change so convincing, so complete, that Quare stepped back and brought his pistol – which, without noticing, he had lowered – back into line.

'You do not need to fear me,' said Grimalkin, sounding very

much as if she wished it were otherwise. 'Even were you to ask your third question, I could not harm you now. We are bound, you and I, by ties of blood and destiny.'

But Quare asked nothing. He could not find his voice, and even if he could have spoken, he would not have questioned her, wary of a trick. He watched, heart pounding.

'Besides,' Grimalkin added with a weary shrug, 'my time here is done. The sky grows pale with the approach of dawn, and I am called Otherwhere.'

That was news to Quare; as far as he could tell, sparing a quick glance upwards, the sky was as dark as ever, and the light of the moon had no rival. He did not think it could be any later than three in the morning; dawn was hours off.

The noise of a small concussion, a hollow popping sound, drew his attention. Clouds of thick grey smoke boiled up from the rooftop to cloak the figure of Grimalkin. He cursed himself for a fool. But he would not compound his foolishness by entering that cloud to grapple with her; nor could he bring himself to fire into it. Instead, keeping his pistol raised, he backed away. The cloud seemed to follow him with an intent all its own, as if it might reach out with smoky tendrils to snatch the clock from his grasp.

'We are not finished, you and I,' came her voice from out of the murk. 'We shall meet again, I promise you.'

He saw – or thought he saw – a serpentine form flex within the billowing, and at that he cursed again, in fear this time, and pulled the trigger. The pistol misfired, the hammer clicking without effect. But already the cloud was thinning, breaking into patchy wisps that drifted with the wind, indistinguishable from the general fog of the city. Another moment, and no trace remained. He stood alone on the rooftop. Grimalkin was gone.

Nor did Quare linger, afraid she would return, either alone or with allies who would not let an unasked question keep them from their objective. He set off at once for the guild hall, retracing his path across the roofs, cursing himself for having misloaded the pistol. He had been lucky many times over this night.

He moved slowly, thanks to his injured leg, which had resumed bleeding and soon stiffened into the bargain. All the while, he debated what to tell Master Magnus. It was crystal clear to him that he couldn't relate all that had occurred, not if he wished to continue as a regulator, or, for that matter, a journeyman in good standing. He knew there was no way he could make the master understand why he had not captured or killed Grimalkin; he did not really understand it himself. It wasn't because he had found himself facing a woman – or not only because of that . . . and there, too, was a thing better left unsaid; without proof, no one would credit such an outlandish claim. Grimalkin a woman? He scarcely believed it himself. As for her warnings about the clock . . . What were they but the ravings of a lunatic? Even if the workings of the timepiece belied its plain exterior, he did not see how this clock, or, indeed, any clock, could be a weapon, unless the woman had spoken metaphorically, referring to some martial use to which the secrets of its mechanism might be put, beating plough-share into sword, as it were, but even that possibility did not seem of sufficient gravity to warrant such desperate words.

No, he would say nothing of that, either. He would hand over the clock and leave the rest to Master Magnus. Yet he would have to mention Grimalkin; Lord Wichcote was the sort of man who would take a perverse pride in having been robbed by the notorious Grimalkin, and he would no more be able to resist boasting of his attic encounter than he had of possessing the clock that had occasioned it. The news would no doubt spread quickly, reaching the ears of Master Magnus in short order. So he must confess that much, at least. And, too, there was his wounded leg to explain. It occurred to him that the latter might serve as an excuse for his failure to kill or capture Grimalkin.

Thus it was that by the time he returned to the guild hall, Quare had concocted the story, a blend of truth, lies, and omissions, that he had related to Master Magnus while suffering the none-too-gentle ministrations of the man's surgeon. And thus it was that he had found himself caught in the strands of his own web – or, rather, swept up in the larger web of Master Magnus, who, after seeing his wound treated, had ensnared him in a further fabrication, this one directed at no less a target than Grandmaster Wolfe himself. As Quare took a carriage home in the early morning hours, a luxury provided by Master Magnus, he'd cursed the luck that had caused this night's mission to fall into his lap; the result of his success had not been the praise and advancement he deserved but an injured leg and recruitment into a power struggle between two giants who could crush him as thoughtlessly as he might crush a fly.

He had sought to make his own way in the Worshipful Company, beholden to no faction but to his talents only; no doubt he had been naïve. But that was finished now. Or would be, once he was called before the Old Wolf to give his report, a summons that Master Magnus had advised him to expect by the afternoon at the latest. Then he would relate the fabrication he had been rehearsed in and suffer the consequences of it – disgrace, suspension, perhaps outright expulsion – all in the service of a scheme whose purpose was as obscure to him as were the plans of the Almighty. Yet as he lay back on the cushions of the carriage seat, it was not the base machinations of guild politics that whirled feverishly through his brain but instead the features of the woman he had discovered behind Grimalkin's mask.

Those exotic features were still present in his mind, or at the back of his mind, seeming, as it were, to gaze down over his shoulder as he examined the hunter that Master Magnus had placed into his hands. The woman's dire warnings echoed in his memory. They seemed crazier than ever now that their object had been revealed to be a pocket watch barely thicker than his dagger's blade; yet though he could not credit her warnings, neither could he dismiss them, any more than he could dismiss the memory of the woman herself: her vernal voice, the quickness of her wit and of her movements, the sense that there had been, and perhaps still was, a connection between them, one that went deeper than words unsaid, questions unasked, and ancient compacts born of a moon-struck fancy: a bond brought into being by the shedding and, as she had put it, the mingling of blood, as though what had passed between them on that rooftop had been some kind of ceremony and not a shabby paroxysm of violence that had left her unconscious from a blow to the head and himself run through the leg and lucky to be alive. He wondered if he would ever see her again, and though he felt no certainty that he would survive a second encounter, he found that he desired it almost as much as he desired to possess the secret of the timepiece he had taken from her.

Now, after clearing a work space on the cluttered table, he set loupe and hunter down and pulled from an interior pocket of his waistcoat a well-worn leather-bound wallet tied shut with a length of dark ribbon. This he untied, placed on the table to one side, and flicked open with practised ease. Laid out within was a tidy assortment of files, callipers, pliers, tweezers, wires, springs, small glass vials containing various chemicals, a watchmaker's hammer, an equally diminutive screwdriver, and other items needful for the interrogation and repair of timepieces. He glanced at Master Magnus for permission.

The master inclined his head while continuing to stroke the cat in his lap. 'Have you enough light?'

Quare nodded; the single candle, while not ideal, would suffice for now. Turning back to the table, he screwed the loupe to his left eye and bent to his work. In one hand he held the watch; in the other, a long, scalpel-like tool he had adapted for horological use from a surgeon's kit. Many of his most useful tools were based on or even made from surgical implements; the clockmaker and the surgeon, he had found, had much in common. But before he could begin in earnest, a movement to one side startled him, and he stepped back as a small black cat leapt onto the table.

Behind him, Master Magnus laughed. 'Why, it would appear that Calpurnia wishes to observe your technique!'

The small cat sat regarding him through unblinking green-gold eyes, its tail curled primly about its front paws. It might almost have been a marble statuette, save for the vigorous purring that seemed to emanate from its entire body. 'That is a very large purr for such a small cat,' Quare remarked. 'But if she has any advice, I would welcome it.'

'Cats do not advise,' said Master Magnus. 'They command.'

At present, Calpurnia seemed inclined to do neither. Once, Quare would have found the animal's presence a distraction, but among the many things he had learned from Master Magnus was a tolerance, even a kind of grudging affection, for cats. The master had an absolute mania for the creatures; he could identify each of his vast menagerie by name, and seemed to prefer their company to that of human beings.

'They accept me for who I am,' he had once told Quare. 'They do not judge by appearances but see past the surface of things. Dogs have no choice but to love us; it is how they are made. Despite their many fine qualities, one cannot help but pity them. A cat, however, bestows its affections where it will. Thus the companionship of a cat is to be more highly valued, for cats are like mirrors in which we may see ourselves as we truly are, not as we appear to others, and still less as we would prefer ourselves to be.'

The cases of most pocket watches were easily removed, opening from the back, but in this, too, the watch at hand proved an exception to the rule: the case was all of a piece. The crystal came away without trouble, but once he had laid it upon the inside flap of his tool kit, Quare was baffled. There seemed no way inside. The edge of the dial met the side of the case precisely, and not even the fine, sharp edge of his scalpel could find purchase there. He did not probe too forcibly, however, for fear of scratching the dial.

He straightened with a sigh, replacing the loupe on the table, and rubbed his watering eye as Calpurnia gave a querulous miaow.

'Giving up so soon?' Master Magnus echoed rather smugly.

Quare couldn't help but glare. 'I suppose you opened it right away, without any trouble.'

'On the contrary, it took me the better part of an hour.'

'And you expect me to do it faster? You must have a higher opinion of my abilities than you've admitted so far, Master Magnus.'

'No higher than your own,' the master replied.

Quare opened his mouth to answer, then thought better of it; he couldn't decide if he'd just been complimented or insulted. He returned his attention to the watch. It was infuriating but at least would not talk back. Cupping it in one hand, he used the scalpel to push the fancifully shaped hands around the dial, once again experiencing that strange disinclination to focus upon the glyphs painted there; his gaze glided over each one as smoothly as did the hands themselves . . . which, as he now ascertained, moved with equal facility in a counterclockwise direction. But these idle exercises brought him no nearer to his goal. What was he missing? He ground his teeth in frustration. Again he thought of Grimalkin. He did not doubt for an instant that she would have already prised the watch open somehow. He felt clumsy and stupid, like a thief standing before a locked steel vault deep in the bowels of the Bank of England.

Then Quare smiled. Of course. The master himself had provided a clue. Watches and locks were not so different, after all. Not inside, where it counted. He gave a little laugh of admiration at the cleverness of it.

'Got it, have you?' asked Master Magnus.

'We'll see.' What if the number inscribed on the inside of the cover, 1652, was not just a date but a combination? It was both obvious and ingenious; yet there were many possible ways of representing that number, or sequence of numbers, using the hour and minute hands of the watch. For all he knew, some complicated formula was required. But he would eliminate the obvious choices before worrying about more arcane possibilities. Could it be as simple as moving one hand to sixteen and the other to fifty-two? The strange glyphs on the face of the watch had no meaning to him in themselves, but that did not mean they could not correspond to the numbers he knew; after all, there were twelve of them, just as with any ordinary timepiece. But on further reflection, that solution made no sense . . . for then the case would automatically open twice every twenty-four hours, whenever the minute and hour hands, in their quotidian revolutions, passed over the necessary points on the watch face: not at all the sort of feature typically valued by purchasers of pocket watches.

Indeed, this objection held for any sequence of numbers arrived at by rotating the hands in a clockwise direction. Thus, Quare reasoned, the numbers of the combination, or at least one of them, must be arrived at by means of a retrograde motion, by which the locking mechanism would be engaged or disengaged. He began to try various possibilities, moving the hands backwards and forwards around the dial until, after no more than five minutes, to the accompaniment of a sharp click, he felt the back of the watch detach from the case and drop into his palm.

'Bravo,' said Master Magnus. 'Well done!'

'You provided the clue,' Quare acknowledged, grinning, 'when you challenged me to unlock the secrets of the watch. Otherwise I could never have opened it so quickly, if at all.'

'You would have hit upon it sooner or later,' the master said. 'But that is only one mystery solved. You have work yet to do.'

Quare nodded and turned back to the table, feeling quite pleased with himself – an opinion not shared by the black cat, Calpurnia, who was grooming herself fastidiously, taking no notice of him whatsoever. A man could not get too full of himself, Quare reflected, in the company of a cat.

Placing the scalpel on the table beside the loupe, Quare shifted the watch to his free hand and set the detached back of the case on the flap of his tool kit alongside the crystal he'd placed there earlier. Only then did he turn the watch over to reveal the exposed movement.

His initial impression was of a three-quarter plate construction, with overlapping wheels and pinions neatly packed into the available space, all of a silver so pale that it seemed almost translucent. Yet no clockmaker with an ounce of experience or common sense would choose silver over brass and steel for the inner workings of a watch. But then, he thought, perhaps the metal was not silver after all. He was reaching for his loupe when a sudden hissing caused him to start. 'What the devil?'

Beside him, standing with spine arched, tail stiff, ears flat, and fur gone all spiky, a hissing and growling Calpurnia eyed the watch in Quare's hand as if it were a serpent poised to strike.

'God in heaven, what's got into the beast?' Quare demanded.

'Fascinating,' said Master Magnus. The black and white cat in his lap had fled at Calpurnia's outburst, and now Calpurnia herself did likewise, springing down from the table and rushing headlong away. Her fear had transmitted itself to the other cats, and, in the blink of an eye, the study became a roiling mass of fast-moving felines and their shadows, the two not always distinguishable in the candlelight. Yowls and hisses filled the air. Stacks of books and papers toppled, which further agitated the cats, who in turn knocked over more stacks in a chain reaction that continued for some time as Quare and Master Magnus looked on in astonishment.

'That didn't happen when I opened the case,' the master commented when things had quieted somewhat. He sounded almost regretful. 'But then,' he continued, 'no cat was as near to the watch as Calpurnia was just now. She smelled the strangeness of it, no doubt. Or saw something. They are per-spicacious creatures, cats.'

'They're only animals, master,' Quare said with a laugh. 'They start at moonbeams and chase shadows. They know nothing of watches.'

'What do any of us know?'

'Master?'

He shook his head. 'Go on, Quare. The test isn't over yet.'

'Is that what this is? A test?'

Now it was the master's turn to laugh. But he did not otherwise answer, merely gestured with one hand for Quare to get back to work.

Quare bent close over the watch. With the aid of the loupe, he saw that, as he'd begun to suspect before Calpurnia had gone mad, the wheels and pinions and plates of the movement were not made of silver. Indeed, they did not appear to be made of metal at all. The substance looked more like wood . . . which perhaps accounted for the lightness of the watch. Yet the grain was curious, like no wood he was familiar with, and not even birch had such a silvery shine. Nor, as far as he knew, was wood of any kind suitable for the stresses and strains, the wear and tear, of a watch movement: even less so than silver, in fact. But perhaps the wood had been treated with some chemical unknown to him to give it added strength and resilience. He set down the loupe and retrieved the scalpel. He scraped softly at one wheel, to no effect. Whatever it was, it was *hard*. He gave the wheel a cautious tap with the tip of the scalpel. 'Why, it's hollow!' he exclaimed in wonder, looking to Master Magnus, who, after his peculiar fashion, grinned – that is, grimaced – in reply. Quare tapped the escapement, the fusee. 'They're *all* hollow! Master, I don't believe this is a real watch at all.'

'Isn't it?'

'I confess I thought at first that it might be self-winding, but now I perceive that it lacks a winding mechanism of any kind. There is simply no source of power. Yet the wheels turn easily; the teeth of the gears fall smoothly into place; the escapement, the fusee – all else is as it should be. This is a model of a watch, a toy, not the thing itself. And even if it could be wound, what time would it keep, with its parts all of hollow wood?'

'What kind of wood is it, then, Quare, at once light, hard, and hollow?'

He shrugged. 'I'm no wood-carver.' An idea struck him: 'Why, he wasn't a clockmaker at all! The mysterious JW, I mean. No wonder he wasn't mentioned in the archives. He must have been a master wood-carver.'

'Perhaps,' said Master Magnus, lurching to his feet with an abrupt rocking motion. He swayed for an instant, then planted his walking sticks on the floor and hauled himself over to Quare, again seeming to wade through some invisible medium sensible to himself alone, as if the air around him were as thick as mud. 'But do you know, I don't believe it *is* carved of wood.'

'Indeed? What then?'

'Bone.'

'Bone?' Quare glanced at the watch in his hand and shook his head sceptically. 'What kind of bone is so hard, yet so light?'

'That I cannot say. But I have examined the movement under the microscope, compared the grain of the stuff with samples of wood and of bone, and though I did not find an exact match, it is unquestionably closer in nature to the latter than to the former.'

Quare shrugged. 'Even so, it is still no more than a curiosity, a toy.'

'Do you suppose I would attach so much importance to a mere curiosity? Would Lord Wichcote risk so much to possess it, or the thief you encountered upon the rooftop go to such trouble to steal it?'

'I don't understand . . .'

'I wonder if I might borrow that sharp little tool of yours.'

'Of course.' Quare reversed the scalpel and held it out.

Resting his weight on one stick and letting the other fall back against his hip, the master took the tool in a rock-steady hand. Before Quare could react, the hand darted out.

Quare yelped, more in surprise than pain, and watched a bead of blood appear on the tip of his finger. 'What—'

'Quickly,' Master Magnus interrupted. 'Hold it over the watch!'

Quare was too stunned to do anything but obey. Drop after drop of his blood dripped into the pale silver insides of the watch. It pooled there like the shadow of the sun creeping across the face of the moon in swift eclipse, a dark stain that must soon spill over.

But it did not spill over.

Instead, it seeped into the watch. The parts of the movement, the wheels and pinions and plates, the escapement, the fusee, all the pieces so cunningly carved out of . . . something . . . sucked in the blood. Drank it in like water absorbed by a sponge. And as they did, they changed colour, took on the redness of Quare's blood. Or perhaps it was that they turned translucent as glass, only seeming to take on the hue of what filled them.

But Quare was not interested in such distinctions. He stood transfixed with awe and creeping horror, mesmerized by the sight of the watch so engorged with blood that it seemed to glow like a hot coal in the palm of his hand. He would not have been surprised had it burned him. But the watch, already warmed to his body temperature, grew not a whit warmer.

Then he felt it faintly shudder. Felt a convulsion spark and bloom within the watch and pass through it into his flesh, his blood, like a call seeking answer.

He would have dropped it then, cast it from him like a loathsome, cursed thing, but Master Magnus took hold of his wrist in an unbreakable grip, preventing him.

Quare moaned, words as far beyond him as thought, as reason. For now, as if his heart had answered the call, the watch throbbed to life, pulsing in time to the rhythm in his chest, the wheels and pinions turning, the teeth meshing: the movement running, keeping time.

'*There* is your source of power,' Master Magnus said, his voice fierce, triumphant.

4

Pig and Rooster

QUARE DREW ON HIS PIPE AND TILTED HIS CHAIR BACK AGAINST THE wall, gazing through a fog of tobacco smoke at the other tavern patrons eating and drinking at tables and along the bar. Wheels of candles hanging on chains from the beams of the ceiling provided a wan illumination. According to the clock on the wall above the fireplace, it was approaching nine o'clock. Quare had no reason to doubt the time, though he had not checked it against his pocket watch as he was normally wont to do. Nor could he locate in himself the remotest desire to do so.

The Pig and Rooster was packed, the atmosphere boisterous. A man wearing an eye patch had taken out a fiddle and begun scratching a tune in the far corner, and an appreciative audience had gathered round, clapping and shouting encouragement as a little capuchin monkey done up as a Turk, a bright red turban strapped to its head, capered and turned somersaults on a table beside the fiddler. Elsewhere, men were playing at cards, chess and draughts, and at a nearby table a rowdy group of apprentices from assorted guilds, including his own, was engaged in a – so far – good-natured drinking game mediated by a pair of dice . . . or perhaps it was a dice game mediated by draughts of ale. Three barmaids – a brunette, Martha, and two blondes, Arabella and Clara, who looked enough alike to be sisters – hustled back and forth across the sawdust-covered floor with loaded trays, bantering with the men they served while expertly dodging groping and grasping hands . . . and just as expertly, it seemed, failing to dodge others. A fire crackled in the hearth, adding to the smoke and heat.

Quare sat at the back of the tavern, his only companions a mug of ale and a steak and kidney pie, both barely touched. Beside them on the stained and gouged table top a candle burned in a battered tin holder, the flame bending and sway-ing. He had come to the Pig and Rooster, a favourite haunt, to lose himself in the easy good-fellowship of the public house, yet instead he felt cut off from everything and everyone around him, as if the smoke from his pipe had wrapped him in a hazy cocoon.

The horror of all that had happened in Master Magnus's study lingered like a nightmare that refused to fade. It clung to him like a leech – a leech of the mind. Of the very soul. He could still feel the throbbing pulse of the hunter in his hand, strong and regular as the beat of a living heart. Against his palm, like the ticklish scrabbling of an insect, he had felt the hands of the watch moving. He would have dropped it, thrown it away, but Master Magnus had clamped his wrist in a grip of iron.

'Control yourself, sir! Master your fear, damn you, or you're of no use to me!'

He'd turned his head away with a groan.

'Look at it!' Master Magnus had hissed. 'And you call your-self a clockmaker? Look you, sir. *Look* you!'

Quare looked.

The fiery crimson glow of the pocket watch had faded to something like the cherry blush of colour on a young girl's cheek. The rotation of the wheels and pinions was slowing, and the vigour of the pulsations communicating themselves through the case to his hand was weakening, the interval between them growing wider. The watch was running down. Its ruddy colour waned, passing from apple red to strawberry to rose to a wan pink, like wine diluted in water, as the fuel of Quare's blood thinned, consumed by the uncanny engine in his hand. Another moment and the movement had returned to its original appearance of pale, unblemished silver, and the wheels once again were still.

The watch had stopped.

Only then did Master Magnus release him. Quare gasped, vaguely conscious that he'd been holding his breath. His thoughts were sluggish; he felt as if he'd taken a blow to the head. His fingers opened reflexively, and the watch slid to the table top; it landed face up, and Quare saw that the hands had moved from their former positions, pointing now at sigils whose significance he did not know any more than he had a moment ago but which nevertheless seemed invested with sinister import. He drew back as though afraid the watch might fling itself upon him.

'What in God's name is that thing?' he demanded. And then: 'How does it *work*?'

At which the master gave a satisfied chuckle. 'You'll do, Quare. You'll do.' He reached past Quare to retrieve watch, case, and crystal, tucking all three into his waistcoat pocket without pausing to reassemble them. When he turned, his eyes narrowed and he said, 'You might want to tend to that finger.'

'What? Oh.' Blood oozed from the cut. He had thought the

master had but pricked his finger; now it was clear the blade had sunk deeper. Digging a handkerchief from his pocket, he fashioned a makeshift bandage. The finger throbbed as though from a bee sting, reminding him of how the watch had pulsed in his palm. He shot Master Magnus a trenchant look and opened his mouth to demand an accounting, but before he could get a word out, a shadow passed before his eyes like the wing of a great black bird.

The next thing he knew, he was gazing up at the frowning face of Master Magnus, which seemed to be suspended some considerable distance above him, hanging down as if attached by invisible wires to the still-more-distant ceiling.

'Well,' demanded that face, 'are you going to lie there all day like a lazy dog? Get up, sir! Get up! We have much to discuss.' And one of the walking sticks struck against his shoulder.

Or, no, not a walking stick. A cat, butting its head against him. In fact, numerous cats were prowling about his person, rubbing against him, patting him with their paws, purring as if very pleased indeed to find him stretched out upon the floor. No doubt they were just being friendly, but even so there were rather a lot of them. He sat up with alacrity, and they scattered.

'I never figured you for a fainter,' Master Magnus said with a sniff. 'Does this happen often?'

Head swimming, Quare climbed to his feet. 'I've never fainted in my life,' he protested, steadying himself with one hand upon a stack of books that was almost more in need of steadying than he was. 'I don't know what—' He stopped short at the sight of the handkerchief swaddling his finger.

'God help me,' sighed the master, rolling his eyes. 'You're not going to faint again, are you?'

Quare glared at him. 'I appreciate your concern, Master. I'm quite well.'

'I should hope so. What possible use will you be if you go around fainting every five minutes like some overdelicate young miss suffering from the vapours?'

'I don't know what use I can be at all,' he answered. 'You've told me nothing, explained nothing, just shown me something possible by no natural science with which I am acquainted – a watch that runs on human blood. *My* blood, as it happens, drawn without a by-your-leave! And you wonder, after such shocks to the body and the mind, that a man might find himself a trifle unsteady on his feet?'

Master Magnus shrugged. '*I* did not faint when it happened to me. Oh, yes, my boy – how do you think I knew to prick your finger? I cut myself accidentally while examining the watch, and my blood was drawn into the movement just as yours was, and with the same intriguing if admittedly disquieting result. But why do you look at me so sceptically, sir? You have experienced for yourself the truth of what I am telling you.'

'I am merely surprised to find that blood and not oil circulates in your veins.'

'Hmph. Come, let us sit and talk.' As he spoke, the master swung himself about on his sticks and led Quare to a small round table flanked by a pair of chairs, all three pieces of furniture covered with various combinations of books and cats and their respective sheddings of loose pages and hair.

'Clear them away,' he directed, and Quare evicted all the cats save one, a fat old orange tom that lay draped in a peculiarly boneless fashion over two books whose much-clawed bindings had the look of despoiled antiquity. This surly beast hissed and swatted a hefty paw at him when he made to remove it, and he baulked at a further attempt, deciding that he had already been wounded enough for one day. Master Magnus, not so easily deterred, delivered a thump with his stick that sent the feline yowling in retreat.

'The books as well,' he said in a tone of impatience, gesturing with the stick as though threatening Quare with the same treatment.

'Where shall I put them?'

'Anywhere. It doesn't matter.'

Quare transferred the books and papers to the floor. There was no organizing principle to maintain; Greek and Arabian treatises on horology lay alongside volumes by Newton, Descartes, Leibniz and Spinoza, which in turn sat upon anonymous pamphlets setting forth systems of astrology, alchemy and numerology. Interspersed throughout were pages covered with diagrams and calculations and Latin scribblings in the master's own crabbed hand.

'You should have all this put in the proper order,' Quare admonished, not for the first time. He couldn't help thinking that the books and papers – the property of the Worshipful Company, after all – deserved a kinder master, or at any rate a more meticulous one.

'I like to keep them near to hand,' Master Magnus said, manoeuvring himself in front of a chair and then toppling back into it with a grunt. His misshapen legs flew up, resembling the flippers of a seal. 'This way, I know exactly where everything is.' He laid his walking sticks against the side of the chair.

'But what of the other masters?' Quare persisted. 'What if they should require a particular book? How will they ever find it?'

'They will ask me, and I will procure it for them. The

system is practical and convenient. Now, sit you down, sir.'

Quare began to brush cat hair from the upholstery of the remaining chair. But he soon gave it up as a lost cause and seated himself with a sigh. Master Magnus, he noted with some foreboding, was once again gazing at him with that unsettling grimace-cum-smile. Without a word, the master reached into his pocket. Quare flinched, fearing that he was about to draw forth the watch; despite his curiosity, he was not eager to renew his acquaintance with the timepiece just yet. But instead, Master Magnus produced a small tin whistle. Putting it to his lips, he blew three shrill blasts in quick succession.

A door opened, and a servant entered the room carrying a tray on which sat two glasses and a bottle of port. The man approached smoothly, something of a feat considering that he did not glance even once at the array of animate and inanimate obstacles bestrewing his path, but avoided them as if by instinct or some sense other than sight, his gaze fixed on a distant point. Quare studied him, trying to ascertain if this was the same servant who had fetched him in the stair-master, but there was no way of telling; perhaps if the servant had spoken he might have recognized the man's voice, but he lowered the tray to the table without a word and then, with a stiff bow, his powdered face so devoid of expression that it seemed to indicate a lack of consciousness itself, turned and left the room, shutting the door behind him.

The master filled the glasses. He lifted one and indicated that Quare should do likewise. Half wondering if he were still unconscious and dreaming, for he had that sense, peculiar to dreams, that the most fantastic events could take place at any moment, and indeed most probably would take place, and, moreover, if he but knew it, were very likely taking place already, Quare followed suit. Master Magnus made the toast: 'To His Majesty.'

'His Majesty,' echoed Quare, rising to his feet and drinking.

'No need to be so formal, Quare. It's just the two of us, after all.' The master refilled his own glass, then reached up with the bottle to refill Quare's. '*Tempus Imperator Rerum.*'

The motto of the Worshipful Company. Time, Emperor of All Things. A reminder that even His Majesty had a master greater still. As did all men.

Quare drank. The sweet wine went straight to his head, accentuating his sense of inhabiting a dream. He cleared his throat, set the glass down on the table as though to reassure himself of its solidity, and his own, and took his seat again. 'How did the servant know to bring the wine, Master?'

'Oh, I've got them trained,' said Master Magnus, holding up the whistle. 'They're under strict orders not to enter unless summoned with this. I've devised a kind of code, you see, to communicate simple commands by means of the number and duration of blasts on a whistle. It's quicker and more effective than calling them in here and explaining what I want. The Vikings used a similar method in bygone days. The longboats of a raiding party would speak to each other over great distances or through inclement weather by blowing upon their horns. My system adapts their barbarous custom for civilized use. I call it "Norse Code".'

'Impressive,' said Quare. 'But still, the servant must have been expecting the command. He appeared immediately with his tray.'

'Despite all that has transpired, you remain observant. Excellent.' The master gave a satisfied nod. 'Yes, Mr Quare, he was expecting the command. I thought it only right that we celebrate your success with a glass or two.'

'Then you knew I would succeed in opening the watch.'

'Your horological talents have never been questioned. At least, not by me.'

Quare sighed, reminded of his interview with Grandmaster Wolfe.

'Your suspension irks you,' Master Magnus said. 'You feel the insult keenly.'

'Wouldn't you?'

'Indeed, I would not! The Most Secret and Exalted Order of Regulators. Bah! How secret can they be when they are named thus?'

'But, Master, it was you who created the Order. You who named it. You recruit the regulators from among the journeymen of the Worshipful Company, oversee their training, dispatch them on their missions—'

'Then perhaps you will grant that I know what I am talking about,' Master Magnus interrupted. He reached for the port, then seemed to think better of it, making a dismissive motion as if shooing the bottle away. 'Oh, the Order serves its purpose. The regulators do good and necessary work in thwarting the efforts of our enemies and their agents. But they are men of reason. Men of science. And there are other forces at work in the world, as you have now experienced for yourself. Thus I require other agents. Agents who belong to no named order, however secretly styled.'

'I am surprised to hear you, of all people, disparage reason and science.'

'I do not disparage them. On the contrary, I embrace them as fervently as I can. I have struggled my whole life to see them triumph. Look at me, Mr Quare. What do you see in this twisted body of mine?'

Quare hesitated, uncertain how to answer.

'Come now, sir. Am I a spawn of evil? Does my misshapen outer aspect proclaim a soul bent equally out of true?'

'Of course not.'

'Yet many would say otherwise, even today, in this supposedly enlightened age. Do you know how many years it has been since I dared to leave the safety of the guild hall? It is my sanctuary and my prison all in one, for I cannot walk the streets of London without being followed by whispers of the devil. Adults mock me, children hurl insults and worse.'

'Ignorance and superstition. No thinking man believes such foolishness.'

'Perhaps not. Unfortunately, there are few men who can truly be said to think, even among the so-called educated classes. Why, even here in the Worshipful Company, I am looked upon as a monster. Apprentices fear me. Journeymen mock me, call me Master Mephistopheles. And my fellow masters, while content to reap the rewards of my genius, keep me hidden away, buried alive in the very bowels of the guild hall.'

The master paused, but before Quare could interject a word, he raised a forestalling hand; taking this for an invitation, a blue-grey cat jumped into his lap. He stroked it as he continued. 'Do not misunderstand me, Quare. I am grateful to the guild. It gave me shelter, a home. I do not believe I would be alive today if the guild hadn't taken me in, a friendless orphan, and trained me. But am I permitted to express my gratitude openly, like other men? Can I acknowledge my debt before the world and be seen by the world to pay it back tenfold, a hundredfold, a thousand, so that people might say, "Behold Theophilus Magnus, a credit to his guild and to his city!"? No. I must keep to the shadows like a skulking kobold. Allow lesser men to take credit for my work and receive the rewards and honours that rightfully belong to me. While it is true that I have the ear of Pitt, I do not believe that His Majesty even knows I exist!'

'But surely Grandmaster Wolfe—'

'Do not speak to me of that mendacious mediocrity! He has stolen everything from me. Everything! Do you think he would stand at the head of our guild if my back and legs were straight? Eh? Sir Thaddeus, indeed! Where is my title, I should like to know?' He gave a bitter laugh.

Quare had seen Master Magnus lose his temper, but never his self-control. Yet here he was, the legendary Master Mephistopheles, he of the iron will and clockwork heart, confessing a petty litany of secret hurts and thwarted ambitions such as might be found smouldering in the breast of any disgruntled apprentice set to scrubbing floors. It was a breach of decorum every bit as shocking as the baring of his hump would have been.

'But here is one thing he will not steal,' the master continued. He drew the still-disassembled watch from his pocket and brandished it triumphantly; the silvery movement winked between his fingers, looking more like metal than any kind of bone with which Quare was familiar. 'With this, I will pull the teeth from the Old Wolf and— God in heaven!'

A spitting and hissing ball of blue-grey fury had replaced the cat purring placidly in his lap. Master Magnus stared goggle-eyed at the animal, the watch raised level with his ear.

'Do you see, Quare?' demanded the master. All peevishness had vanished from his voice, replaced by boyish enthusiasm. 'As with Calpurnia a moment ago, her instincts tell her plainly what our vaunted intellects strain uselessly to comprehend! If only you could speak, Marissa!' He brought the watch closer to the cat, intent on her reaction. 'If only you c—'

He broke off with a curse as claws raked the back of his hand. Blood flew, and so did both cat and watch, the latter sailing high in the air behind the master, the former leaping after it as though it were a bird. Still cursing, Master Magnus groped for his walking sticks but succeeded only in pushing them out of reach, and, for good measure, knocking the bottle of port off the table. Quare, meanwhile, remained rooted in place, watching the timepiece as it tumbled through the air, the movement no longer silver but red: a baleful crimson eye.

'Get it, you fool!' cried the master.

The room was in an uproar. Earlier, Calpurnia's distress had infected the other cats. Now the rage of Marissa transmitted itself, and when the watch fell to the floor in the centre of the room, bouncing twice on the thick carpet, what seemed a single furry mass of teeth and claws fell upon it with a ferocity that curdled Quare's blood.

'Mr Quare!' the master half shrieked, having turned himself within the prison of his chair to gaze in horror at the frenzied swarm.

The anguished voice pierced the caterwauling, jolting Quare out of his daze. He did not relish the idea of wading into that angry mob, but neither, he discovered, could he allow such a marvellous timepiece to come to harm. He sprang from his chair.

A flicker of darkness. It was as though all the candles in the room had gone out at once, then rekindled. Or a great black wing had passed before his eyes. Had he fainted again? But no: he was still on his feet, the cats still . . .

He stopped short. His heart throbbed in his chest, as if he had run for miles across the rooftops of London and not merely taken a few quick steps across the floor of the study.

The cats . . .

In the stillness and silence of the room, the drawn-out howl that issued from the mouth of Master Magnus seemed all the more terrible. It was like the sound of a hinge creaking as a door was forced open that had been rusted shut for centuries.

Quare stepped wonderingly into the midst of them. They lay motionless in concentric circles radiating out from a point of pale silver that seemed to shine with a light of its own. The outermost rings were sparsely populated, giving Quare room to walk, if he placed his feet with care, but the inner rings were so packed with bodies that he knew he would have to clear a path if he wished to reach the centre. There must have been close to fifty, perhaps even more.

'Quare, are they . . . are they *all* . . .'

'It would seem so.' He felt giddy, as if he might break into laughter, although in fact he had never been so frightened in his life. Yet he couldn't turn away. Something held him, a sense of being implicated in what had taken place, not simply as a witness to it – or rather to its aftermath, for whatever had been unleashed here had done its work in darkness, in the blink of an eye – but as a participant, however unwilling or unaware. Perhaps it was that he had been spared. He and the master both. As if, because the watch had drunk their blood, they were connected to it now. Part of it somehow. And therefore complicitous in its actions – for despite how little he understood of what had happened, he had no doubt that the watch had lashed out in self-defence, like a living thing.

The words of Grimalkin came back to him: 'This clock will not yield up its secrets to such as you – no, nor to your masters, not even the greatest of them. Believe me, rather than answer your questions, it will punish you for asking them –

and it will be a punishment that strikes the guilty and the innocent alike.'

He shuddered, wondering if the effect was limited to this room or extended beyond it, into the rest of the guild hall, the city, the world. If Master Magnus should blow on his whistle now, who would answer the summons? Was there anyone left to answer?

From behind him came the sounds of ragged sobbing, and it seemed to Quare that the master was grieving a loss greater than his precious cats. But he didn't want to learn the truth of it. Didn't want to witness the master's mourning or even acknowledge it. Instead, he picked his way among the outliers, stooping here and there as he went, looking for some sign of what had killed them, as if that were the only question that mattered. But he could find no evidence of injury: bodies unmarked, unbloodied, limbs whole and positioned with the regal insouciance common to sleeping cats, so that he found it difficult to remember at times that they were not sleeping.

When Master Magnus next spoke, his voice was raw. 'And the watch?'

'I-it appears to be undamaged, Master. But I need to clear a path—'

'You shall not touch them!'

This was no voice he knew. Quare turned at the shrill and fearful cry, nearly crying out himself at the sight that greeted him. The master seemed to have aged ten years or more.

The horror that came over him then was so much greater than what he'd felt before as to deserve another name. He told himself that the watch was responsible, that it had killed the cats by aging them, and that Master Magnus – and, no doubt, himself as well – had been similarly aged. But then he realized that it was an illusion, a trick of candlelight and the naked play of emotions across the master's tearful face. He had not grown older; rather, a customary mask had fallen away, a mask of iron self-control that disguised his true age, made him seem not younger, exactly, but ageless. Now that mask was gone, and Quare beheld a face that Master Magnus himself might not have recognized had he chanced to see it in a mirror: the ravaged face of a man whose greatest solace has been ripped from him. But the understanding of what he was seeing came as no relief to Quare. Nor did the swift return of the mask.

'Forgive me, Mr Quare.' The master's voice was as it always had been ... only more so. It made Quare shudder to hear it.

'Of course, Master,' he somehow managed to bring himself to say.

'You are quite correct. It is the watch that matters. Clear your path and bring it to me.'

Quare hesitated. He had no desire to touch the cats, and even less, if possible, to touch the watch. 'Perhaps the servants . . . ?'

'No,' the master said in a tone that brooked no argument. 'There will be talk enough among the servants as it is. But the existence of the watch must remain our secret. At least for now, until we can understand better what has happened, and how. Move the cats aside. But do it gently, sir, I beg you. As gently as ever you can.'

'Care for some company?'

Startled out of his reverie, Quare looked up to see a woman standing beside the table and smiling down at him, her eyes hooded by a ruffled blue bonnet but rest of her face garishly painted, so that it was impossible to tell what her true features, or even her age, might be. 'Sorry, love,' he answered. 'Not in the mood tonight.'

Like many such establishments, the Pig and Rooster had its share of prostitutes who either worked outright for the business or kicked back a share of their earnings in exchange for the right to troll the premises.

Rather than accepting the rebuff, the woman seated herself.

'See here—' Quare began.

She interrupted: 'I believe you have mistaken me, sir.'

Quare knew that voice. Those dark eyes newly revealed in the light of the candle. 'Grimalkin,' he whispered.

With infuriating insouciance, she lifted his mug of ale, saluted him, and sipped from it. 'I promised we would meet again.'

'You are a fool to come here.' He made to rise, then stopped as the point of a sword pricked his belly. He felt the blood drain from his face. The minx had drawn on him under the table.

'Do not prove yourself a bigger fool. Sit down, Mr Quare.'

He settled back in the chair. 'How do you know my name?'

The sword point did not retreat an inch, even as she took another sip of ale. 'I have many resources at my disposal,' she said with a smile made grotesque by the red paint smeared over her lips. When she lowered the mug to the table, a grey mouse darted from her sleeve, ran across the table top to his plate, and nibbled at his steak and kidney pie.

'Look here!' he exclaimed, and would have shot to his feet had not the tip of the sword impressed upon him the wisdom of remaining seated. 'Can you not control that infernal rodent?'

'Come, Henrietta,' she called, and the mouse, after standing upon its hind legs to observe him, pink nose twitching, scampered back up her sleeve like a witch's familiar.

'Why do you carry that vermin upon your person?'

'You have seen yourself how useful she can be,' Grimalkin replied. 'Now, sir: to business.'

'I do not see what business you can possibly have with me, or I with you.'

'Can you not? Have you forgotten that we are linked, you and I? Blood calls to blood, Mr Quare.'

'Blood . . .' He could not suppress a shudder. 'Has this aught to do with that cursed timepiece?'

'Cursed, is it? You were singing a different tune last night.'

'I have since had the opportunity to examine its workings more . . . intimately.' His finger throbbed at the memory.

'Then you understand the danger.'

'I understand nothing whatsoever! How it works, or how such a thing could even exist. 'Tis unnatural, an affront to God and science alike.'

'That's as may be. Yet it does exist.'

'What do you know of it?' he asked. 'Who made it, and why?'

'None of that matters now,' she said. 'I have come to ask your help – to beg it, rather.'

'Beg, is it? At swordpoint? I believe the proper word is threaten.'

She winced at that, and, beneath the table, he felt the blade withdraw. 'Your pardon. We must trust each other, you and I.'

'You have given me no reason to trust you.'

'I have not killed you. Is that not reason enough?'

'You said yourself there were other reasons for that – reasons that have remained as cloaked in mystery as everything else about you. You wish my trust? Then speak plainly.'

'Very well. Bring me the watch, Mr Quare. I would steal it

back myself, but I dare not enter your guild hall. It is not safe for such as I.'

'What, for a thief, you mean?'

'If you like. Will you help me?'

'I did not give you the watch last night, madam, when I knew nothing of its true nature. Now, having experienced the horror of it for myself, I am even less inclined to do so. I know nothing of who you are, really, or of why you want the watch. I only know that it is too dangerous to fall into the wrong hands.'

'Where that watch is concerned, there are no right hands,' she said.

'Right or wrong, I should prefer it remain in English hands.'

She frowned; for an instant he thought to feel himself pierced by her blade. But then she sighed, and her shoulders slumped. 'I was a fool after all. To come here and expect your help. Why should you help me when you understand nothing of what is at stake?'

'Enlighten me, then. After all, we are bound, are we not? Blood to blood?'

Her eyes flashed. 'You would not joke if you understood what that meant. It is the watch that binds us, for it has drunk of our blood.'

'You speak as if it were alive.'

'It contains life and death, yet is beyond both.'

'More obfuscation. I begin to wonder—'

A shout interrupted him. 'Quare! Ho, Quare, old son!'

Quare turned his head and squinted through the drifting smoke towards the front of the Pig and Rooster, where four men had just entered. He recognized three of them as friends and fellow journeymen. The quartet made for him at once, calling loudly for ale.

Grimacing at the interruption, Quare turned back to Grimalkin. She was gone. He shot to his feet, searching for the blue bonnet, but there was no sign of it, or of her, amidst the patrons of the Pig and Rooster. Once again, it was as if she had vanished into thin air.

He was still standing, mouth agape, when the new arrivals reached him: Francis Farthingale, a handsome, dark-haired giant who claimed to be the illegitimate son of a European monarch – which monarch, he was never prepared to say, but his insistence upon this circumstance, plus the fact that he received a regular sum of money from a mysterious source, had earned him the nickname Prince Farthing; fat Henry Mansfield, whose round, smallpox-ravaged face always wore a baffled smile, as if the world were a perpetual wonderment to him; and Gerald Pickens, the youngest son of a master clock-maker in far-away Boston in the Colonies, who had a comfortable allowance from his father but no hope of inheriting the prosperous family shop, which would go to his elder brother. The fourth man, a slender, red-haired youth, Quare did not know.

'You look as though you have seen a ghost,' said Mansfield, clapping Quare on the back. He pulled out a chair and sat down, as did the others.

Quare sank back into his own chair. Not a ghost, he thought, yet was there not something ghostlike about Grimalkin? She was as uncanny in her way as the timepiece she sought. And as dangerous.

Mansfield reached for the steak and kidney pie. 'I say, Quaresie, are you going to finish this?'

Before Quare could reply, Farthingale interjected with a laugh: 'Speaking of ghosts, did you hear about Master Mephistopheles? It seems the old boy poisoned his pussycats!'

Quare bristled. 'You shouldn't be spreading lies, Farthingale.'

'It's true,' the dark-haired youth protested indignantly, looking to his fellows for support. 'I had it from one of the servants, who saw it with his own eyes. A whole roomful of dead cats! And the master right there in the midst of them, cool as you please, picking out corpses for dissection as if choosing melons at the market!'

Mansfield spoke around a mouthful of steak and kidney pie, his lips glistening with grease. 'His children, he liked to call 'em, remember? Some father, eh?' He licked his fingers as fastidiously as any cat cleaning itself.

'It's as close to paternity as he's ever likely to come,' laughed Farthingale. 'Even if he could pay a woman enough to lie with him, what's between his legs is probably just as shrivelled and useless as they are!'

'For God's sake, Farthingale,' said Mansfield. 'Some of us are trying to eat!'

'Even if it were true,' Quare said tight-lipped, ignoring the sniggers provoked by Mansfield's remark, 'it must have been an accident.' He wanted to say more, but the master had sworn him to silence. And even if he had not been so sworn, he knew that he could not unburden himself of what he had seen and experienced, not to this audience or any other. Men of reason would dismiss him as a lunatic, while the religious would see proof of witchery. Nor was he by any means certain that witchery had not been involved. Or lunacy, for that matter.

He doubted that he would ever forget those fraught, disjointed moments, the dark flash of the event itself, and, in some ways worse, the dreadful aftermath: how he'd cleared a path through the cats, gingerly lifting the limp, still-warm bodies and moving them aside, and then, more gingerly still, as if reaching for an infernal device primed to explode, picked up the watch ... or tried to, for the timepiece, which was glowing with an unnatural white light, like a scale of moon-stuff fallen to earth, had burned his fingers, though with cold rather than fire, forcing him to fetch a pair of iron tongs from the fireplace in order to ferry it back to the worktable.

There a shaken Master Magnus had confessed himself unable to go on. He'd instructed Quare to come back in the morning, when, the master promised, he would answer his questions as best he could and give him a new assignment: a confidential brief that would make up for the sting of his suspension from the Most Secret and Exalted Order.

Now, surrounded by his high-spirited fellows, Quare was sensible of a gulf between them – a gulf of knowledge and experience. Of terror. He looked at their lively, animated faces with a pang of loss, and of envy.

'Accident or not,' Mansfield said meanwhile, 'what's he doing with poison anyhow? Is the man a clockmaker or an apothecary, eh?' He helped himself to Quare's mug of ale.

Gerald Pickens spoke up for the first time. 'Why, he's both, Henry. And a bit of an alchemist into the bargain. After all, he is in charge of the Most Secret and Exalted Order. Oh, don't fret, Daniel,' he added, noting Quare's sharp, admonitory glance towards the fourth member of the quartet, the slight, red-headed stranger, who had been following the conversation with glittering blue eyes and a ready if rather brittle laugh, 'I'm not spilling any secrets. Aylesford here is a fellow journey-man, newly arrived from ... from ... what was the name of your village, Tom?'

Aylesford, who appeared to be still in his teens, his cheeks smooth as a maid's, blushed scarlet in what Quare took for shyness . . . until he spoke. 'Rannaknok,' he declared rather too loudly, in an assertive tone and a rough Scots accent, as if daring anyone to dispute him. ' 'Tis a town on the Meggerny River, in Perth.'

'Nobody ever said it wasn't,' said Farthingale, rolling his eyes.

'You wouldn't think it to look at him,' Pickens confided to Quare with a wink, 'but young Tom is quite the swordsman. He's been in London for but two days and has already fought four duels.'

'Five,' Aylesford corrected, then added ruefully: 'But Grandmaster Wolfe has forbidden me to fight any more. He says I may draw my sword only in self-defence.'

'That is the rule of the guild,' Quare pointed out. 'We are, after all, supposed to repair timepieces, not put holes in their owners.'

'I have come to London to be confirmed as a master clock-man,' Aylesford stated, eyeing Quare as if daring him to dispute the assertion. It was little wonder the fellow had found himself embroiled in five duels, thought Quare, if this was his customary manner of conversation. He was as brazen and dis-putatious as a bantam rooster. But Quare had no interest in quarrelling, not on this night of all nights, when he craved dis-traction above anything. True enough, Aylesford seemed too young to have earned the title of master, but that was not Quare's affair. He offered his congratulations, which the other man accepted as if they were no more than his due.

'But my dream,' he went on, lowering his voice but not his intense gaze, 'is to become a regulator like you, Mr Quare.'

'Someone has misinformed you,' Quare answered, glaring at Pickens, who smiled placidly in return. Only Master Magnus and Grandmaster Wolfe knew the identities of those inducted into the Most Secret and Exalted Order: not even the newly inducted agents themselves knew who their fellows were, and each took an oath to keep his membership secret, on pain of death. While in the course of his duties a regulator could expect to learn the identities of some, at least, of his fellows, that knowledge was subject to the same strictures of secrecy, and to the same harsh penalty. Quare suspected Pickens of being a regulator, but he had no proof other than the fact that the man expressed the same suspicion about him and had made a running joke of it.

'There! Didn't I tell you he would deny it?' Pickens demanded of Aylesford, thumping the table top with his open hand for emphasis.

The redhead nodded, as if Quare's denial constituted greater proof than even an outright admission would have done. 'I had hoped that report of my skill with a sword would reach the ears of Master Magnus, but despite my efforts, I have not been summoned to meet with that gentleman. Nor have I received the slightest indication that he is aware of my existence. Perhaps, Mr Quare, if you were to put in a good word . . .'

'Listen, Mr Aylesford—'

'Call me Tom,' Aylesford invited.

'All right. Tom,' Quare said testily. 'But the point is, Pickens here has been having you on. He knows damn well that I'm no regulator. I have no influence with Master Magnus or any of the masters, at least not in the way you mean.' He gave a sour laugh. 'In fact, just now a word from me on your behalf would likely do more harm than good. But, do you know, I believe there *is* a regulator among us.'

'Whom do you mean?' Aylesford asked eagerly, eyes shining.

Quare pointed with the slender, gracefully curving stem of his clay pipe. 'Why, who else but Pickens here?'

'Ridiculous!' scoffed the man in question.

'He names others to deflect attention from himself,' said Quare. 'What could be a more transparent ploy?'

'Sheer, unmitigated fantasy!'

Aylesford looked in confusion from one to the other as Mansfield and Farthingale sat back grinning. He pushed back from the table and stood, hand on the pommel of his sword. 'If either of you gentlemen thinks to make sport of me . . .'

'Whoa,' said Farthingale, leaning forward to grasp him by the elbow. 'Self-defence, old son. Self-defence.'

The redhead shook him off. 'I do not know about London, but in Rannaknok a man's honour is considered a thing worth defending.'

'Honour?' Quare laughed again, more sourly this time. 'How fortunate for you, then, that I was instructed on the subject only today, by no less an authority than the Old Wolf himself. It is a lesson I'm happy to pass along, if you'd care to hear it.'

Aylesford nodded warily, his hand still resting on the pommel.

'It's quite simple. Honour is superfluous in a journeyman. We are mere tools to be used by the guild leadership, flesh-and-blood automatons to be sent wherever they will, for whatever reason. What need has an automaton of honour? None. In fact, it's a positive hindrance. What counts for us is obedience. So relax, Tom. Sit down and drink with us. You have nothing to defend.'

'Grandmaster Wolfe told you that?' asked Aylesford, who had gone rather pale.

'Perhaps not in those exact words,' Quare granted, 'but his

meaning was crystal clear, I assure you. The only measure of honour a journeyman possesses consists in the thoroughness of his submission to the authority of the guild. I'm surprised the grandmaster didn't speak to you in a like manner about your duelling habits.'

'He did.' Aylesford slumped into his chair. 'Only I didn't understand until now. I guess I didn't want to.'

'Ah, there you are, darling!' exclaimed Mansfield, his ugly face beaming up at the blonde barmaid who had arrived at last, a tray with five brimming mugs balanced on one shoulder. She set the tray down on the table, providing a generous flash of cleavage as she dispensed the drinks. Mansfield snaked a hand into the folds of her dress, and she brushed him away without a glance, as if he were a bothersome fly. Then, retrieving the empty tray, she stood back out of reach and eyed them with a tired but not entirely unsporting expression on her plump, pretty face.

'Why do you treat me so cruelly, dear Clara?' Mansfield complained. 'Can't you see how much I love you?'

The barmaid rolled her blue eyes. 'I'm Arabella,' she said, and jerked her chin in the direction of the other blonde barmaid. 'That's Clara.'

Mocking laughter erupted from around the table, though Aylesford did not join in. Nor did Mansfield, who flushed crimson and attempted to rally: 'As the Bard has it, a rose by any other name would smell as sweet . . .'

Arabella sniffed. 'I do smell an odour, but it has little of the rose about it!'

Mansfield's colouring grew redder still, as if in emulation of that flower, and he developed a sudden interest in his ale.

'You journeymen of the Worshipful Company are all alike,' Arabella went on archly. 'Only interested in one thing.'

'And what might that be?' asked Pickens with a leer.

'Why, your clocks,' she said, not missing a beat.

More laughter, after which Pickens added: 'And our stomachs. We'll have another of your tasty pies, Arabella, if you please.'

At which Mansfield, who had already drained his mug, spoke up: 'And more ale.'

After Arabella had gone, Farthingale slapped the gloomy Aylesford on the back and returned to the earlier topic of conversation. 'Buck up, old son. Honour is vastly overrated. What is it good for anyway except to make people puffed up or miserable or dead? Take it from me, you're better off without it. Why, I'm a bastard, the whelp of a man who sits on an august throne, a man so far above the likes of you and me that there is more honour in one of his turds than in all the patrons of this fine establishment put together! And yet, which of us do you suppose is happier, eh? My right noble sire, whose every waking moment is spent in terror of some slight to his precious honour, who sees everyone in the world as his inferior, to be scorned or ignored accordingly, and who cannot publicly acknowledge the existence of his only son, or' – and here he laid a hand over his heart – 'that selfsame son, a humble journeyman so far below the notice of the great as to be invisible, a man who, having no honour, need never fear its loss, or risk life and limb in its defence, or say to himself that he cannot stoop to befriend this man or to bed that woman, who—'

'For God's sake, Prince Farthing,' cut in Mansfield. 'Must you drone on so?'

Farthingale was always rattling on about his royal father, much to Quare's annoyance. The man wore his bastardy like a badge of honour despite his disparagement of the term. But all bastards are not created equal, Quare had found. Farthingale at least knew, or claimed to know, who his father was – and did receive a regular allowance ... a liberal allowance. Quare, on the other hand, lacked all knowledge of his origins. Even the name of Daniel Quare had been given to him by a stranger, thrust upon him when he was a mere babe at the orphanage in Dorchester. Yet one day he would learn the truth. One day he would stand face to face with his father. On that day, he swore now for the millionth time, all debts between them would be paid, with interest, one way or another.

Farthingale, meanwhile, glared at Mansfield. 'Lucky for you I have no honour, sir, or I'd be forced to demand satisfaction!'

'Lucky for you *I* have no honour, or I'd be forced to accept!'

Pickens raised his mug. 'To dishonour!'

Quare lifted his mug along with Farthingale and Mansfield, his voice joining with theirs: 'Dishonour!'

There followed a pause, during which four mugs remained aloft and four pairs of eyes regarded Aylesford, who gazed back glumly.

'Come on, Tom, old son,' Farthingale coaxed, nudging him with an elbow. 'Forget your troubles. Drink up!'

Aylesford sighed, rolled his shoulders as if divesting himself of a great weight, and lifted his mug. 'To dishonour,' he echoed, albeit without enthusiasm. The same lack, however, could not be ascribed to his drinking, as he gulped down what seemed like half the mug's contents before lowering it from his lips, leaving a frothy moustache, which he wiped away with the back of one sleeve.

'Well?' prodded Farthingale after wiping away a moustache of his own.

'I begin to see the merits of your argument,' Aylesford admitted, and in fact the colour had returned to his cheeks, and his eyes shone.

'Keep drinking – soon you will be completely convinced!'

'Only until the effects of the ale wear off.'

'What of that, eh?' Mansfield scoffed. 'Is there a shortage of ale in London? Conviction, once lost, is easily regained.' He raised his mug. 'To conviction!'

'Conviction!' echoed four voices, of which Quare's was by no means the weakest.

5

Impossible Things

QUARE WOKE TO FIND HIMSELF NAKED IN AN UNFAMILIAR BED. AN unfamiliar body, also naked, was nestled familiarly within the curve of his own, facing away. Wisps of blonde hair, edged with gold in the fall of sunlight past a drab curtain, tickled his nose. He smelled sweat and sex, stale beer and tobacco smoke. His mysterious companion was snoring; he had no idea who she was or how they had come to be together. There was a sour taste in his mouth, as though he had vomited during the night. His head throbbed, and his brains seemed to have been reduced to a semi-liquid state: the slightest movement sent them sloshing against the walls of his cranium. Meanwhile, his bladder burned. To relieve the latter misery was to invite the former; he lay still, suspended in a murky zone of suffering in which the flow of time itself seemed to have, not stopped precisely, but rather encountered an obstacle. It circled sluggishly, like a backed-up eddy in a street sewer.

The previous night was a smear of colour and noise across his memory. He recalled a succession of toasts that spread from table to table until the whole tavern was taking part. Songs were sung to the accompaniment of the one-eyed fiddler and his dancing monkey. Eternal friendships were pledged and broken and tearfully pledged again. He remembered conversing with the red-haired journeyman, what was his name, Argyle? No, Aylesford. The two of them sitting with arms flung about each other's shoulders, commiserating over the sad lot of journeymen in the guild, the forfeiting of honour and other sacrifices that could only be alluded to . . . at least, Quare hoped he had gone no further than allusion. Surely he hadn't said anything about the Most Secret and Exalted Order, his recent mission to Wichcote House, Grimalkin, or the uncanny pocket watch in the possession of Master Magnus. He racked his brains but could think of no indiscretion. This was not entirely comforting, however, since so much of the night was a blur.

There had been a disturbance. A fight . . . The Pig and Rooster in an uproar, chairs and fists flying, swords unsheathed, the little capuchin, its turban knocked off, screaming as it leapt from table to table and took refuge at last in one of the wagon-wheel chandeliers, where it crouched gargoyle-like within the swaying circle of candles, teeth bared, eyes agleam, seeming to preside over the madness below like some savage demigod. That nightmarish image was the last thing he remembered.

He disengaged himself from his companion, careful not to wake her, and sat up with a groan at a sharp twinge in his upper back, between his shoulder blades, as if he had pulled a muscle during the night. He thought for a second that he might be sick, but nausea receded as his bladder reasserted its primacy. He got to his feet, shivering in the morning chill, espied the chamber pot tucked beneath a cabinet across the room, and set out for it as though embarked upon a journey of miles. Other aches and pains announced themselves with each step. The bandage on his thigh bore a dark stain, as if the wound had opened again ... though it didn't seem to be bleeding at the moment.

He recognized nothing in his trek across the shabby room save his own scattered clothing. He hooked the chamber pot out with his foot and relieved himself with another groan, this one expressing a pleasure almost sexual in its intensity. When he had finished, he turned and saw that the sleeping blonde was asleep no longer. She lay on her side, propped on one elbow and regarding him with amusement, as if she was not only aware of his confusion but enjoying it. A dingy bed-sheet draped the plump swell of one hip, leaving pendulous breasts the colour of rice pudding exposed. Both her face and its expression were known to him.

He cleared his throat and assayed a smile and a bow. 'Good morning, Arabella,' he said as if it were the most natural thing in the world to find himself here, stark naked.

Arabella smirked, tossed her blonde curls, and said, 'I'm Clara.'

At which he blushed from head to toe.

Her laughter was easy and forgiving. 'It's all right, love. You're not the first, and you won't be the last. Share and share alike, that's what I say.' She sat up, rearranging the sheet to cover her breasts. 'Where's Tom got to?'

'Tom . . .?' Quare's hands cupped over his cock, which, a bit slow on the uptake, had only begun to respond to the sight of her voluptuous body now that she had covered herself.

Clara seemed not to notice. 'Your friend. Redhead, looks about sixteen or so?'

'Aylesford.' He had no memory of coming here in his company. Or, for that matter, coming here at all. Wherever *here* was.

'That's the one.' Clara got to her feet, the sheet tucked about her, and approached him with short, mincing steps. He drew back to let her by. She looked back coyly over her bare shoulder. 'Can't a girl get a little privacy?'

He blushed again and turned away. 'Sorry.' What had happened last night? He retrieved his clothing from the floor and laid it out on the bed as, behind him, Clara's forceful stream rang against the sides of the chamber pot. There were some unsavoury-looking stains on his breeches and stockings, and dark splotches of what appeared to be dried blood on his shirt and coat . . . and, he now saw, more bloodstains on the sheets as well. A cursory examination of his body revealed some minor scrapes and scratches on his arms and chest, not enough to account for the stains. He supposed it must have been the wound that Grimalkin had given him. Or perhaps Clara had started her monthlies.

'What's your rush, love?' Clara called.

'I've an appointment.' According to his pocket watch, it was nearing eight-thirty, and nine-thirty was the time Master Magnus had set for their morning meeting. The actual time, he knew, must be somewhat later, as his watch bled minutes if not kept tightly wound, a duty he'd neglected to perform last night. He remedied it now. But even so, he had no idea what the true time was. The uncertainty only added to his sense of dislocation.

'But I haven't had a chance to thank you proper for last night.'

Quare turned. Clara was advancing towards him, bed-sheet cast aside. Gravity and time would bring those pert breasts low one day, but this, he noted, was not that day. Her creamy white hips and belly had the soft roundness of still-ripening flesh, and the hair between her thighs was so blonde and fine that he could see right through to the pink flower beneath . . .

at which point he, or rather a portion of his anatomy, decided that his meeting with Master Magnus was perhaps not so urgent, after all.

'That's more like it,' she said with a smile, her gaze rising to meet his own.

'I'm afraid I've bloodied your sheets,' he said, embarrassed.

'Your poor leg. But don't fret, love. What's a little blood between friends, eh?' Taking him in hand, she pressed him back onto the bed.

'Wait,' he said, though he offered no resistance. 'What did you mean about thanking me?'

She knelt on the edge of the bed. 'Why, you saved my life last night, Dan. You and Tom both. Don't you remember?'

'Well, er . . .' He shifted as she stroked his erection.

'There was a brawl, a big one.'

'I remember that. Or some of it, at least.'

'The worst I've seen,' she declared with relish, continuing to stroke him as she spoke, 'and the Pig and Rooster's had its share of nasty ones. I don't know what started it, but all of a sudden the whole place was a battlefield. Martha and Arabella and I tried to get away through the kitchen, but we got separated, like, and I was cornered by five blackguards with more than brawling on their minds. Said they was going to carve their initials into my pretty face, they did.' Her eyes widened as she produced – from where, he knew not, nor cared at the moment – a pig-bladder sheath, which she slipped over his manhood.

'That's to keep the brats off, love. A girl can't be too careful.'

Nor a man, he thought; he had been lucky in his amorous pursuits, never having contracted the pox, but he had witnessed enough of its effects never to enter the lists of love unarmoured. To say nothing of his determination to bring no more bastards into the world.

Clara straddled him and guided him inside her. 'I had a knife from the kitchen,' she went on breathlessly, 'but they had swords. Young noblemen, by the looks of them. Out for a bit of fun.'

'You're' – he gasped as she rocked above him – 'saying I stopped them somehow?'

'And Tom, yes. Came to my rescue like knights in shining armour.' She grunted and ground. 'He took one through the back before they even knew you were there.'

'What? Killed him, you mean?'

'All I know is that the villain went down and didn't get up again.'

'The damned fool!' He squirmed to get out from under Clara, but she redoubled her efforts, perhaps mistaking his panic for passion, or just not caring. Nor did his erection wilt along with his spirits, deciding, not for the first time, to go its own way regardless of his wishes. Quare's groan had more than just frustration in it. But his mind, walled away from his body, worked with the precision of a timepiece. A commoner drawing a blade against a nobleman was serious business. To wound one, or God forbid kill one, even in self-defence, was a death sentence. The Worshipful Company couldn't protect them from that. What had Aylesford done?

'After that, it come fast and furious,' Clara continued meanwhile, suiting her actions to her words. 'I wanted to run, but I was terrified. I couldn't hardly bring myself to look. I thought you and Tom was finished, outnumbered two to one. Then it would be my turn.' Clara gave a little scream, her breasts smacking against her chest as she climaxed, and he felt his own climax rise up in answer. Clara clung to him. But even then, her stream of words did not slow. 'Turned out to be the other way round. Your friend mightn't look like much, but he's a demon with a sword. Two clockmen plucking those feathered popinjays: it did my heart good to see!' She laughed, then at last took notice of his struggles. 'Why, what's the matter, love? Crushing you, am I?'

'Nothing personal.' Quare pushed her away and sat up. He pulled the sheath from his drooping member and let it fall to the dirty floor. He must have been drunk indeed to have drawn his sword against nobility, regardless of the provocation. No doubt the hot-headed Aylesford had acted first, and he'd followed suit, swept up in the excitement. But that wouldn't save him from punishment. That he remembered none of it only added to his anxiety. He wondered what had happened to Mansfield, Farthingale and Pickens. 'It was just the two of us, you say? No others?'

'That's right.'

He rubbed his throbbing temples and groaned. 'Then what happened?'

'Why, you cut down one man, and Tom took care of two.' Clara, sitting cross-legged beside him, pantomimed two quick sword thrusts to his chest. 'The last man tried to run, but the two of you got him before he'd taken half a step.' A third thrust illustrated the man's fate.

Clammy horror settled over Quare. 'We killed them all?'

'Nobody stopped to check the bodies,' she said with a shrug. 'The three of us beat it out the back door before the Charleys or the redbreasts could show up.'

Quare groaned again. If any of the men had survived, no doubt they'd already provided descriptions of their attackers. If, on the other hand, he and Aylesford had killed them all, it was possible that the Charleys – the city watch – didn't have any leads. But that wouldn't be the case for long. The watch – or, more likely, Sir John Fielding's red-waistcoated Bow Street Runners – would want to interview all those present at the Pig and Rooster last night, and the table of journeymen hadn't exactly been inconspicuous. With the exception of Aylesford, a stranger (who would have attracted notice for that reason alone), they were all regulars at the tavern, known by name. Sooner or later, the Charleys would hear of them and come looking. And when, inevitably, someone – perhaps Mansfield or one of the others – spilled the beans about Aylesford's penchant for duelling, the prickly redhead would find himself a wanted man. And if, as seemed likely, the two of them had been seen together during the fracas, so would Quare. He felt the remorseless logic of the situation closing around him like the bars of a Newgate prison cell.

'It's funny,' Clara mused meanwhile. 'The fight sobered Tom right up, but it made you even drunker. You could barely walk. The two of us practically had to carry you through the streets. I was afraid you'd been wounded, stabbed; there was blood on your coat and hands. But you swore you was fine. I didn't like to send you off in such a state, so I brought you here instead, both of you. My heroes.'

Quare still remembered none of it. She might have been talking about someone else entirely. It gave him an eerie feeling, as if his body had a life of its own, separate from his mind, and though he'd just had a vivid illustration of that very fact here in bed with Clara, what she was relating to him now went well beyond that momentary estrangement.

'I offered to take you on free of charge, however you wanted, one at a time or both together,' Clara went on, blushing like the innocent girl she must have been once upon a time. 'Tom was shy, said he was saving himself, but you were willing enough. He went out onto the landing to give us a bit of privacy, but we'd barely started before you jumped up, ran to the window and . . . Well, you can guess the rest, I'm sure, love, even if you don't remember. A blessing there. Afterwards, you came back to bed and passed out, like. That left Tom and me. I wanted to do something for him – to show my appreciation – but he brushed me off again, told me he couldn't even if he'd wanted to, that he was too tired to think of anything but sleep. I said he was welcome to share the bed with us, and so he did.'

'I wish he had woken me before he left,' Quare said. 'We could be in big trouble. We need to get our stories straight.'

At which Clara blushed more deeply than ever.

'What?'

'Nothing,' she said. 'It's just' – she shifted, averting her eyes, then looking at him again – 'I did wake up once last night and saw the two of you . . .'

'Yes?' he prompted.

'Mind you, I've nothing against it. Live and let live, I always say.'

'I don't have the slightest idea what you're talking about.'

'Don't worry, I won't breathe a word to anyone.'

Comprehension dawned. 'You think . . .?' He burst into laughter.

'I know what I saw.'

'And just what was that?'

'Tom was cleaving to you from behind, one hand clapped over your mouth. He saw me looking and winked at me over your shoulder, hissed at me to go back to sleep.'

'You were already asleep,' Quare said, disconcerted by the image. 'You dreamed the whole thing.'

She shook her head and repeated, 'I know what I saw.'

'And I suppose I slept right through everything?'

'Slept through it?' She gave a disbelieving laugh. 'Why, bless me, you were grunting like a pig the whole time!'

Quare's amusement had soured altogether. He got out of bed and began to dress. 'I think I'd remember if anything like that had happened.'

'Like you remember killing them men in the Pig and Rooster?'

That gave him pause. After all, what did he really know about Aylesford? The man was a stranger. Perhaps he *had* attacked him in the dark. But it strained credulity to think that he would have slept through such an assault as Clara had described. Quare considered himself a man of the world; his life as a journeyman had brought him into contact with men who loved other men, or who sought out both sexes. Though sodomy was a crime punishable by death, his philosophy, like Clara's, had always been live and let live. There had been furtive gropings in his boyhood with others his age, but those games had stopped even before his seduction, at the age of thirteen, by Emma Halsted, the wife of his master. But the whole thing was ridiculous. Surely there would be physical evidence of such an assault, and while his body bore its litany of cuts and scratches, aches and bruises, there was nothing to suggest he'd been raped. Either Clara had been dreaming, or, more likely, she'd misinterpreted what she'd seen. But what, then, *had* she seen? 'And afterwards? What did I do then?'

'Why, slept like a baby. But here's a laugh! Maybe you was done in, but Tom was just getting warmed up, like. Took me twice before he left, he did!'

'And I slept through that as well, I suppose.'

'Like a lamb,' she said.

'I never knew I was such a heavy sleeper.'

'A good rogering will do that. I'm feeling a mite sleepy myself,' she added with a giggle.

He sighed. 'Believe what you like, Clara. I'll not argue with you.'

'Why, it's nothing to be ashamed of, love. Don't I like it that way myself sometimes?' She turned onto her knees and waggled her fleshy backside at him, though whether in mockery or invitation he couldn't tell. 'No need to go rushing off,' she said, gazing over her shoulder with a wicked grin that seemed to settle the question.

But Clara's abundant charms were not as enticing as they'd been a moment ago. There was too much he didn't know about what had happened last night and what might be awaiting him this morning. Aylesford might have been taken already; the Scottish journeyman could have spilled his guts by now, blaming everything on Quare. He didn't think it likely, but it was certainly possible, and growing more so with every moment. There was no time to lose. He had to find Aylesford, and fast. If only he hadn't drunk so much last night . . . That had been his undoing. He pulled on his coat, searched the floor for his shoes. 'I've got to go, Clara. I need to find Aylesford before he's picked up. No doubt they'll question you as well. Don't tell them anything.'

She flounced on the bed. 'What kind of rat do you take me for?'

'Sorry,' he said with an apologetic smile. 'I know you're no rat.'

'Hmph.' She tossed her head. 'Under the bed.'

'What?'

'Your shoes.'

'Oh.' Sure enough, there they were . . . splashed with blood and other stains he preferred not to examine too closely.

Quare sat down on the bed and pulled the shoes on over his stockings, then stood.

Clara leaned forward. 'Give us a kiss before you go, love.'

He obliged. 'You won't be seeing me at the Pig and Rooster for a while.'

'You know where I live. Stop by sometime.'

'Maybe I will,' he said; he did not bother to inform her that he had no idea where he was at present – he would discover that soon enough. He paused at the door to belt on his sword. Then, drawing the blade halfway from its scabbard, he noted with a sinking heart that brown streaks of dried blood were clinging to the steel; he would have to clean and oil the weapon as soon as he got back to his lodgings. 'Have you seen my hat?' he asked, looking for his black tricorn.

'Another casualty of the night, I suppose,' Clara said from the bed. 'Here, take my cloak, love. You can't step out like that – you look as if you've just come from a murder.'

'I'm obliged to you.' He took the dark brown cloak that hung from the back of the door. Though short on him, it covered the worst of the previous night's leavings. He waved a last goodbye to Clara and hurried out into the morning.

As eager as Quare was to get to the guild hall, where Master Magnus was waiting, no doubt impatiently, to resume their conversation of the day before, and where he hoped as well to hear news of Aylesford and the others, he knew he needed to clean up and change into fresh clothes first. Wrapped in Clara's cloak, he kept to back streets and alleys as he made his way from her lodgings in Clerkenwell to his own in Cheapside; it made for a longer journey, but he met fewer people along the way, and those he did encounter seemed as shy of attention as he, keeping their heads down and their steps hurried, as if upon urgent business of their own.

It occurred to him that he was not the only one with secrets to hide; it was a peculiar sensation to imagine that everyone he encountered, young and old, rich and poor, had committed some crime or harboured some guilt that, if it were publicly known, would take them to the pillory or to Tyburn. He had often felt himself part of the London mob – known that joyful if also thrillingly perilous sense of belonging to something greater than himself, which buoyed him up and swept him along: a vigorous, industrious, prosperous, high-spirited throng. This was the obverse of that, furtive, skulking, mistrustful ... yet still, he realized, a true if heretofore unsuspected aspect of the city, the experience of which he would have gladly forgone. But London was always revealing fresh aspects of itself. He could live here a hundred years, he thought, and still not scrape the bottom of it.

He kept a wary eye out but saw no evidence of undue interest or pursuit from any quarter. So far, his luck was holding.

Guild masters and apprentices alike enjoyed free room and board at the guild hall in Bishopsgate Street, but journeymen were expected to fend for themselves. For the past year, Quare had taken lodgings at a comfortable if somewhat run-down house in Basing Lane, near Cheapside, that catered to journeymen of the Worshipful Company.

Quare surveyed the approach to this establishment from the shadows of an alley across the way. He watched carriages and wagons move along to the cracking of whips and curses as pedlars afoot sang out their wares, everything from candles to flowers to lemons and limes; saw ragged urchins darting quick as starlings up and down the walks, ignored by one and all, while overhead, like flags of battle displayed by a victorious army, ponderous painted wooden signs creaked as they swung, as if stirred by no other wind than that which arose from below, and higher still, from open windows along the street, women leaned out to shout down orders for whatever was needful: in short, all the normal colourful caterwauling that constituted life on Basing Lane or indeed any other London street.

The bells of St Mary-le-Bow began to ring out. Quare started then fished out his pocket watch, which displayed a time of nine minutes to ten. He wound the watch and adjusted the hands, gratified to see that the timepiece was still, as it were, within striking distance of the correct hour. Not that the bells of St Mary's were to be trusted, exactly, but for the moment they were no doubt a more accurate indication of the proper time than his own neglected watch. He wouldn't encounter a truly trustworthy timepiece until he reached the guild hall. But this would do for now. Amidst all the irregularities of the morning, and indeed the previous night, this small measure of certainty, however imperfect, was most welcome. Though the reminder that he was late and growing later for his meeting with Master Magnus was not.

Meanwhile, other bells had begun to chime in, adding their disparate voices to the hour. The monumental clocks of London, resident in cathedrals and churches, or presiding over public squares, did not keep a common time. They struck askew, filling the air, as now, with a cacophony made worse by the fact that, while the bells of each clock were tuned to produce a pleasant melody, no thought had been given to the effect of a number of pleasant melodies ringing out on top of each other – which, as it turned out, proved neither pleasant nor melodious. A clockcophony, Master Magnus called it. There had been talk of regulating the striking of the hours, so that only one clock's bells would be heard at a time, but the owners of the various clocks, who had spent large sums of money in building and maintaining their instruments, fought every proposal. Instead, they vied – with the assistance of the Worshipful Company available to all who could afford it – in making their particular clocks either the first or the last to strike, and this incremental competition, which had been going on for years now, with passions swelling in inverse proportion to the ever-smaller intervals of time involved, had served only to render the bells increasingly useless in what was, after all, their primary function: the imposition of a central temporal authority over the city and its environs. At least, so it seemed to Quare and his fellow guildsmen, whose sensitivity to such things was far more acute than that of even the most time-conscious curate or man of business, men who made use of time but did not, so to speak, inhabit it as Quare and his fellows did.

He could delay no longer. Telling himself that he was being foolishly suspicious, he took a deep breath and came out into the street. Though he felt as if a hundred hostile eyes were following him, he reached the boarding house without incident and entered, only to find himself face to face with his landlady, Mrs Puddinge, who drew back from the door with a small shriek of surprise, her face going as white as her apron. In her fifties, the childless widow of a master in the Worshipful Company of Clockmakers, she was a merry matchstick of a woman who took a lively maternal interest in her 'young men', as she called them.

'Merciful God in heaven, is it you, then, Mr Quare?' Mrs Puddinge's brown eyes narrowed beneath her cap as she took in his dishevelled state. 'Lord bless us, but he told me you were dead!'

'Dead?' Quare echoed, the surprise now on his side. 'What do you mean, Mrs P? Who told you?'

She pursed her lips, giving her face the aspect of a shrivelled prune. 'Why, your friend and fellow guildsman, Mr Aylesford. He told me there was a brawl last night at the Pig and Rooster. How often have I warned you young men against that den of iniquity?' Tears sprang to her eyes, and she wrung her hands in the folds of her apron. 'He told me you were all killed.'

'All?' Quare's brain was reeling.

'Mr Farthingale, Mr Pickens, Mr Mansfield and yourself.' She raised the apron to dab at her eyes. 'He said some young lords started it, and that they were killed as well. Made it sound a regular massacre, he did! And now here you are, a bit worse for wear but still among the living, after all! Why, 'tis a miracle! That's what it is. A blessed miracle. And the others? Are they also alive and well?'

'I-I don't know,' he stammered, trying to make sense of things. 'We were separated . . . When did Mr Aylesford tell you this?'

'Why, not half an hour ago! The poor lad was beside himself with grieving. Said he'd come straight from the guild hall, with orders to clear out your room before the city watch could trace you here. Seems the masters are afraid of scandal. They know where the blame will fall, with aristocrats and journeymen among the dead!'

An icy quiver ran down his spine. 'You let Aylesford into my room?'

'And why would I not? With you dead and him about the business of the Company?'

'But I'm not dead!' Nor, Quare was beginning to think, had Aylesford been about Company business – now or ever.

'Oh, aye, and God be praised for it. But how was I to know that at the time? Go up, Mr Quare, and surprise him! The poor lad will be overjoyed to see you, I'll warrant. Quite down-hearted, he was.'

'What, is he still here?'

'Unless he's gone out by the window. I— merciful heavens!'

Quare pushed past Mrs Puddinge with a hasty apology, mounting the stairs two at a time, then strode down the empty third-floor landing and flung open the door to his room.

It was as empty as the landing. His trunk was open, his things strewn across the floor. Quare crossed to the open window, which gave onto an alley behind the boarding house, but there was no sign of Aylesford below. Cursing under his breath, he turned back to survey the mess Aylesford had left behind . . . only to see the man himself step from behind the door, closing it with the heel of his boot.

'Mr Quare, as I live and breathe,' said Aylesford wonder-ingly, sword in hand.

'Not for long,' said Quare, shrugging out of Clara's cloak and drawing his own sword, 'unless you supply some answers, and quickly. What are you doing here? What happened last night? Where are Pickens and the others?'

'You have a lot of questions for a dead man.'

'You are overconfident, sir. You will not find me an easy mark.' Quare hoped he sounded more certain of that than he felt. Up until yesterday, he had never drawn his sword in earnest. Now, for the third time in as many days, he was facing an armed foe: first Grimalkin, a fight he had been lucky to win, much less survive; then last night, at the Pig and Rooster, a fight he barely remembered; and now, facing a man he felt sure was not what or who he claimed to be.

Aylesford gave a nervous titter. 'Why, I left you stabbed through the heart in that harlot's bed! I made sure of it. Are you a ghost, then? I'm not afraid of you! I'll send you straight back to hell!'

Yet he did not attack, or even step forward. And, Quare noticed, his sword arm was trembling.

But Quare did not move, either. He was trying to construe the man's words. He remembered what Clara had told him she had witnessed during the night, only it seemed, at least according to Aylesford, that what she had taken for an act of sodomy had in fact been murder. And yet, despite Aylesford's apparent confusion and fright in encountering him here, alive, Quare couldn't credit such an outlandish claim. How could he? Stabbed through the heart? It was preposterous, insane. He had no memory of being stabbed or of any struggle whatsoever. It made no sense. A man did not die and then rise again to walk among the living. But then how to explain Aylesford's seeming certainty or his evident fear? What kind of game was the man playing? 'You are no journeyman of the Worshipful Company,' he said, forcing his mind along more reasonable lines of inquiry.

'*Je suis de la Corporation des maîtres horlogers,*' Aylesford answered in Scots-accented French, giving the name of the Parisian clockmakers' guild, great rival to the Worshipful Company.

'So, you are a traitor to your country and your king,' Quare said with contempt.

'My country is Scotland,' Aylesford replied. 'And Bonnie Prince Charlie is my king.' This affirmation seemed to infuse the man with fresh courage, for now, circling his sword point with lethal intent, he came forward.

Quare advanced to meet him. In his rooftop clash with

Grimalkin, Quare had let panic overwhelm him, driving out his training in the art of swordplay. Now he resolved to keep a cooler head.

They came together in the centre of the room, a quick exchange of thrusts and parries, each man feeling out the defences of the other.

'Did you kill Pickens and the others?' Quare demanded, drawing back.

Aylesford smiled and circled, looking for an opening. 'With this very blade. In the confusion of the brawl, a quick thrust through the back, with no one the wiser.'

Quare pushed aside his grief and anger. They could not help him now. 'But why? What wrong had they done you?'

' 'Twas nothing personal. They were in the wrong place at the wrong time. I saw my chance, and I took it. Are we not at war?'

Quare had eaten and drunk with these men, laughed with them, worked beside them. This news of their cowardly murders stabbed him as surely as any sword. But it was hot anger, not blood, that spilled from the wound. He squeezed the grip of his sword as though it were Aylesford's scrawny neck. 'They were journeymen, not soldiers.'

'They were Englishmen,' Aylesford answered, as if that explained everything.

Quare snarled and struck at him, coming in with a high thrust and then disengaging the tip of his blade as Aylesford moved to parry. He flicked his wrist, bringing the point around in a cutting motion that slashed down the side of his adversary's sword arm. Blood bloomed against the white of Aylesford's sleeve. But even as Quare took satisfaction in the touch, Aylesford's sword point came flashing in towards his face, and his frantic parry was barely in time to slap the steel aside. The man was devilishly fast. He danced back, only then becoming aware of a burning along the shoulder of his sword arm, right through his coat.

'Behold, a ghost that bleeds,' said Aylesford with a wolfish smile.

Quare did not dare shift his eyes to take stock of the wound. 'And what of me?' he asked, continuing to circle his blade as he moved to Aylesford's left. 'Why did you not kill me with the others?'

'I would have,' Aylesford said, turning with him, his sword in line, 'but when I found you, you were facing down five men in defence of that harlot's honour – which, I feel sure, is more than she ever did. Still, a woman's a woman for all that, and no honourable man turns his back on a member of the fairer sex in need. Besides, it was a chance to add a fine gaggle of English lordlings to my night's tally. Then, once we had dispatched them, the arrival of the watch compelled me to postpone our reckoning again. And, I confess, when it became clear that the wench intended to reward our services with her own, I thought to myself, 'Why not give the poor sod one last happy memory?' Ah, my gentle heart will be the death of me! But from what the sow told me, you were too pissed to take advantage. She offered me her bed, and once she dropped off, I clamped one hand over your mouth and with the other drove my dagger between your shoulder blades and into your heart. Do you know, your struggles woke her! Yes, and the wench must have thought we were going at it fine and proper, for she smiled at me in the moonlight and giggled and turned her back to give us a bit of privacy. And what is more, the sight of her bare rump stirred me, sir, indeed it did! I left you dead as a doornail and had my way with her twice – God willing, I planted a Scotsman in her belly. Yet here you are, all lively and disputatious, bleeding like a stuck pig. I confess, I am at a loss to account for it.'

'You're a madman. And a murderer. There's your accounting.'

'I know what I know,' Aylesford insisted, and lunged.

Quare parried and counter-thrust. Aylesford knocked his blade aside with a snap of his wrist and riposted, and Quare, realizing a beat too late that he had fallen for a feint and was overextended as a consequence, had to scramble back for dear life. Aylesford came on, his sword a silvery blur. Quare, hard pressed, was backed towards one wall. Sweat poured off him, and he couldn't help but recall Aylesford's boast of having fought and won five duels since coming to London; that was one claim he found all too easy to credit. He had no breath left for idle speech, but Aylesford more than made up for the lack. He was one of those fighters who seeks to distract his opponent with words. Quare knew he shouldn't listen, that he could trust nothing of what he heard, yet the man's words were as deft as his sword strokes, and more difficult to deflect.

'Last night, in your cups, you mentioned a clock,' Aylesford said now, 'a most wondrous clock. And do you know, it was in quest of just such a timepiece that I was dispatched to London. Here I would find a clock, or so my masters told me, whose secrets, once unravelled, would confer so great an advantage upon whichever side possessed it as to all but guarantee victory upon the battlefield . . . and beyond. The mechanics of a clock, after all, differ merely in degree, not kind, from those of certain engines of war, and a device that can more accurately measure out minutes and seconds can more rapidly fling shot and more accurately hurl shell. Or perhaps the clock contained a solution to the problem of longitude at long last, conferring supremacy of the seas.

Whatever the truth, it was plain that this paragon could not be allowed to remain in English hands. Lord Wichcote had it in his possession until just two nights ago, or so my informants told me – but it had been stolen from him . . . and by no less a thief than the fabled Grimalkin, come out of retirement expressly for the purpose, apparently! Well, when Grimalkin steals something, it stays stolen. Everyone knows that. It seemed that my mission was a failure before it had scarce begun! So you may imagine my surprise and joy when I chanced upon you last night, sir. A most opportune encounter!'

All the while he spoke, his blade was never still. It darted like a needle, seeming to stitch an invisible net in the air, the strands of which inexorably tightened about Quare, constricting his possible counter-moves, like an attack in chess that does not succeed by a lightning strike of checkmate but rather by closing off every avenue of opportunity until only defeat remains, a defeat not so much inflicted as collaborated in. That Aylesford had not drawn blood again seemed less due to Quare's defensive skills than to a smothering intent which Quare could sense enveloping him but could not comprehend fully enough to escape. It was maddening. He was fighting tactically, Aylesford strategically. He knew it, but the knowledge was no help to him. His wounded shoulder was stiffening up, which was no help, either.

'From what you let slip,' Aylesford continued breezily, 'I realized that the clock must be in the guild hall, in the possession of that aptly named monstrosity, Master Mephistopheles. So, early this morning, with the guild hall in an uproar following news of the tragic deaths of four journeymen in a tavern brawl the night before, I took advantage of the confusion and went in quest of the clock.'

At that, Quare found his tongue again. 'If you've harmed him . . .'

'Oh, aye, what then?' Aylesford mocked. 'But 'twas not I who harmed him. I could not even find him in that blasted labyrinth! Yet it seems I was not the only one to seek him out. Some Theseus had threaded the maze before me. Or such was the rumour on every man's lips. Why, even those liveried corpses you employ as servants spoke of little else.'

'What are you saying?'

'Is it not clear? Master Minotaur is dead. Someone – I know not who; perhaps Grimalkin himself, or a man dispatched by Lord Wichcote to retrieve his property, or a patriot like myself, or a French assassin; or one of the Old Wolf's cubs; the man had no shortage of enemies who might wish him dead – visited the cripple in the night and slew him.'

'You lie,' Quare said, wishing it to be so but afraid in his heart that the man spoke the truth. Aylesford cast death about him the way other men cast a shadow.

'I merely report what I heard. I do not vouch for its truth. But with that avenue closed to me, I came here, thinking I might find some clue to the location of the clock, or to its nature, in your belongings, before the watch beat me to it. Imagine, then, my surprise, when I found myself interrupted in my search not by some bumbling Charley but by a man I had left for dead scant hours ago! Ah, well, I suppose I shall just have to be more thorough this time.'

And with that, before Quare could reply, or even react, Aylesford's blade spun through a dazzling series of moves whose result was to disarm him as easily as he might have plucked a wooden sword from the grip of a child. In the blink of an eye, or so it seemed, the tip of Aylesford's blade hovered at his throat.

'I do not think you will rise again from this death,' Aylesford said with a satisfied smile. 'But the priests do tell us that confession is good for the soul, Mr Quare. So may it prove for you. Tell me all you know of the clock, and I will make your end quick and painless. Perhaps I will even spare your life.'

'I would be a fool indeed to believe that,' Quare rasped, his mouth dry with fatigue and fear. 'And even if I did, I would not tell you anything. Perhaps you should have questioned me more closely last night, while I was too drunk to guard my tongue. You know – before, as you claim, you killed me.'

Aylesford winced. 'Aye, 'tis poor spycraft, I'll grant you, to kill a man first and then put the question to him. My masters tell me I am too impulsive, and I do acknowledge the fault. Clearly I should have made more certain of your demise. But I can't regret it, since I have the chance now to rectify my mistake. So, I'll ask you but once more before I begin carving – what do you know of this marvellous clock?'

'Go to the devil.'

'Let us see if—'

'Merciful heavens!'

This exclamation was followed by the sound of smashing crockery. Mrs Puddinge stood in the doorway, gazing at them in horrified dismay, her hands clutching the folds of her white apron. A serving tray and the shards of a teapot and cups lay on the floor at her feet. 'Mr Aylesford! Mr Quare! What is the meaning of this?'

Taking advantage of the distraction, Quare swung his arm to club Aylesford's sword point out of line. Before he could recover, Quare darted inside his guard, slamming his good shoulder into the other man's chest to shove him backward. Aylesford reeled, cursing, a panicky look in his blue eyes. For a moment it seemed he would fall, but somehow he managed to stay on his feet and bring his blade back into play. Yet by that time, Quare had retrieved his own blade from where it had fallen.

'Gentlemen,' cried Mrs Puddinge shrilly, her face flushed with anger beneath her white cap, 'put up your swords this instant! I'll have no bloodshed here! Why, the very idea!'

'He's a French spy,' Quare snarled out.

'A spy? Lord help us!' The landlady raised the hem of her apron to her face and peered wide-eyed over the edge of it as though looking on from behind the safety of a brick wall.

'Get help, Mrs P – I'll hold him here!'

'It will take a better man than you to do that,' Aylesford answered and rushed past the now-shrieking Mrs Puddinge. Quare started after him, but before he had taken two steps, Aylesford had thrown the hysterical woman into his path. She clung to him as fiercely as a drowning cat to a tree limb. In the moments it took him to calm her sufficiently to, as it were, retract her claws, Aylesford made his escape. As Quare moved to follow, she latched on to him again.

'Don't leave me, Mr Quare,' she begged, shaking like a leaf in a storm.

'I must make certain Aylesford has fled,' he answered, disengaging himself from her grasp. 'Stay here, Mrs P. You'll be perfectly safe, I assure you.'

She nodded, seemingly incapable of further speech.

Quare edged out through the doorway, alert for an ambush. The landing was empty. At this hour, all the lodgers would be about their business in the guild hall and city. He continued down the stairs and then out of the house, still meeting no one. The street outside, and the broad expanse of Cheapside beyond, were more crowded and bustling than they had been when he had entered the house just moments ago. There was no trace of Aylesford. London had swallowed him up, not caring a whit that the man was no friend to it or to England.

Quare sheathed his blade and made his way back to his room, where he found Mrs Puddinge seated on the bed, wringing her hands together. Her tear-stained face rose fearfully as he entered, and she sprang to her feet. 'What of Mr Aylesford? Is he . . .'

'No sign of him, I'm afraid,' Quare said. 'But I doubt he'll be back.'

'To think that one of my young men should turn out to be a spy,' she said.

'What, do you mean that Aylesford was lodging here?'

She nodded, drying her face with the edge of the apron. 'Since yesterday evening – Mr Mansfield brought him to me. Poor Mr Mansfield!' And the tears began flowing again. 'Oh, Mr Quare,' she said between sobs, 'do you suppose it was Mr Aylesford who killed him and the others?'

'I'm afraid it rather looks that way.' Quare moved to comfort her, patting her heaving shoulders as she wept into her apron. 'There, there, Mrs P,' he said. 'There, there. You must try to get hold of yourself.'

She nodded, drying her red-rimmed eyes. 'Such sweet young men,' she said. 'Not an ounce of harm in any of them.' She gave him a bashful, half-embarrassed smile that became a look of concern. 'Why, you're wounded, Mr Quare! Your shoulder . . . You must let me see to it at once!'

'I'm perfectly well,' he told her.

'Nonsense,' she said, already moving to divest him of his coat.

'There's no time for that, Mrs P,' he said, attempting no

more successfully than with Aylesford to keep her at bay. 'I feel sure the watch will learn of my presence at the Pig and Rooster and come looking for me here. I will speak to them, but not until I have spoken to my masters at the guild and warned them of the spy in our midst. And before I do that, I must have a quick look through Mr Aylesford's things. Will you take me to his room?'

'Oh, aye. Just as soon as I've seen to that shoulder. Do not struggle so, Mr Quare! I know you are pressed for time, but bleeding to death won't make things go any quicker. Now, sit down on the bed, sir. Sit, I say!'

Quare sighed grimly and gave himself up to her ministrations. In a flash, she had helped him out of his coat and waistcoat, both of which looked to be quite ruined with blood. The shirt beneath was in even worse shape. After her initial assertiveness, Mrs Puddinge appeared uncertain how to proceed, as if it had been a long time indeed since she had undressed a man.

'Can you . . .' She motioned with her hands, a blush rising to her cheeks.

Quare stripped off the shirt, wincing at the pain in his shoulder. Mrs Puddinge, meanwhile, had gone to a table across the room, where there was a wash basin and a pitcher of water, along with some folded cloths. She filled the basin, grabbed a cloth, and carried them both back to the bed. Setting the basin down beside him, she wet the cloth and began to wipe the blood away. He winced again at her touch, light as it was.

'There, there, Mr Quare,' she said as she cleaned the wound, seeming to have recovered from her earlier upset, as if caring for another was the best medicine for what had ailed her. ''Tis not so bad, after all. A nasty gash, to be sure, but not

a deep one. You'll not be needing a surgeon to sew it up. Here
. . . Press the cloth to the wound, just there – that's right. I'm
going to fetch some clean cloths to make a bandage. I'll just be
a moment.'

And with that, she bustled out of the room.

Quare got to his feet and crossed to the table from which
Mrs Puddinge had taken the wash basin. There was a fly-
specked square of mirror hanging frameless on the wall above
the table, and Quare now angled himself so as to be able to see
his back reflected in the glass. Specifically, the area between his
shoulder blades, where Aylesford said he had stabbed him as
they lay in Clara's bed.

The indirect light from the window, coupled with the
awkward positioning necessary to see anything useful,
defeated him. He groaned in frustration. But he could at least
examine his shoulder. Lifting the cloth, he saw a long, shallow
gash; a sluggish upwelling of blood accompanied the removal
of pressure. No doubt there would be a scar, to go with the
one that Grimalkin had given him. He had never imagined
that a career in horology would mark him so. He thought of
the grizzled old soldiers he had seen in taverns, swapping
stories and matching scars over glasses of gin. At this rate, he
would soon be joining them.

'Mr Quare, come back to bed this instant.'

He turned to see Mrs Puddinge glaring at him from the
door, her arms bearing enough cloths to swaddle a small army.
'A man would have to be foolish indeed to reject that
invitation,' he replied rakishly.

She blushed again, but couldn't suppress a smile. 'Get along
with you.'

Once he was seated on the edge of the bed, she tended to
his shoulder with practised efficiency, first cleaning the wound

again, then placing a folded cloth over it, which she secured with a long strip of cloth wound about his torso. He had intended to ask her to have a look between his shoulder blades, but, as it turned out, there was no need.

'Merciful heavens!' she cried out.

'What is it?'

'Why, another wound. A worse one. Much worse! Can you not feel it?'

'No. Or rather, a slight discomfort only between my shoulder blades, like an annoying itch I cannot scratch.'

'That would be the scab. Here, let me show you . . .' She fetched the mirror down from the wall and returned to the bed, where she held it at such an angle as to give him the clear view he had been unable to acquire for himself.

What he saw both shocked and fascinated; it felt strangely removed from him, or he from it, as though he were looking at someone else's body, or, as in a dream, gazing down at his own from a superior vantage like a ghost or angel. Nestled between his shoulder blades was a blood-crusted incision no more than an inch long. The skin to either side was as purple as the petals of a violet, yet also streaked with scarlet and yellow and a sickly, algal green. It was a wonder that his fight with Aylesford had not reopened the wound. A clammy sweat broke out on his skin, and he felt as if he'd swallowed a knot of writhing eels.

'Are you all right, Mr Quare?' Mrs Puddinge asked in concern at his sudden pallor.

He took a deep breath and looked away. 'I'm well,' he said, but the croak of his voice belied it. Obviously, Aylesford had failed to pierce his heart with his knife thrust in the dark. But even so, Quare felt sure that a wound such as this should have done more than merely itch. It seemed the sort of wound one might see upon a corpse. Yet there was not even a twinge of pain. His heart was beating strongly, rapidly, and his lungs had no difficulty drawing breath. He didn't understand it.

'I'm afraid that's beyond my poor skills,' said Mrs Puddinge, shaking her head. 'You'll need a surgeon to sew that up, you will.'

'I'll have it seen to at the guild hall,' he promised; now that he wasn't looking at the wound, he was able to think more clearly, though the nausea showed no sign of receding. 'Can you just bind it up for now?'

'I'll try, but God help you if it opens again.' She set to work. 'This is older than the one on your shoulder,' she observed as she twined a strip of cloth about his chest. 'You must've got it at the Pig and Rooster, a craven blow from behind, in the midst of the brawl.'

'No doubt,' he said. Perhaps it was the sensation of her hands upon the skin of his back, but he began to feel the stirrings of memory; or, rather, it was as if his body remembered what his mind could not. He began to tremble.

'There, there,' Mrs Puddinge repeated. 'Almost done . . .'

No, it was not memory. More like the way he had seemed, upon being shown the crusted wound, to separate from his own skin. So now did he see in his mind's eye the stark tableau, lit by moonlight, of himself and Aylesford pressed close on Clara's bed in a travesty of intimate congress. He seemed to feel the other man's body cleaving to his own, his hand clamped over his mouth; saw, or imagined that he saw, the wide eyes of Clara gazing at them, and then her knowing smirk as she turned away into shadows and tangled bed-sheets.

He rose to his feet and rushed to the open window, arriving just in time to spew the contents of his stomach into the alley below. Ignoring Mrs Puddinge, who, after an initial exclamation, had hurried to stand at his side, one hand stroking his arm, her touch like sandpaper despite her kindly intent, he leaned forward, arms bracing himself on the sill, closed his eyes, and let the cool city air – carrying its quotidian stinks of coal smoke and river stench and the waste of animals and human beings, odours that had sickened him during his first days and weeks in London, but which were now as familiar as the smells of his own body, and as reassuring – play over his face and torso. He was alive, damn it. Despite Aylesford's efforts. And he had work to do.

Taking a breath, he straightened and pulled away from Mrs Puddinge. 'I'd better have a look at Aylesford's room,' he said.

'Shouldn't I call for a doctor, after all?' she asked, concern in her voice and in her eyes.

He shook his head. 'Please, Mrs P. I've no time to argue.' He crossed the room and pulled a clean shirt from amidst the scattered pieces of clothing Aylesford had strewn about in the course of ransacking his trunk. 'There is more at stake here than one man's health. At any rate, as I told you, I'm perfectly well.' He turned away from her and drew the shirt over his head with a grimace, but schooled his expression to equanimity when he faced her again. 'Now, if you will lead the way . . .'

'Perfectly well, he says,' Mrs Puddinge muttered as she preceded him out of the room, down the still-empty landing and up to the fourth floor. 'With a hole in his back and a shoulder sliced open like a side of roast beef.' She stopped before a door, produced her ring of keys from somewhere beneath her apron, and glared up at him. 'You're not a well man, Mr Quare. Deny it all you like, but the longer you do, the worse price you'll pay. Heed your stomach, sir. It's wiser than you are.'

'The door, if you please, Mrs P.'

Scowling, she fitted the key to the lock. 'Why, it's unlocked!' She pushed the door open. 'Here you go, then, Mr Quare. I hope you find enough to hang—'

She broke off, and Quare pushed past her into the room, his hand on the pommel of his sword.

The room was empty, which was no more than he had expected. But it was not simply empty of Aylesford – it was empty of all trace of the man.

'Why, his things . . . they're gone!' Mrs Puddinge said from just behind him.

'What things?' he asked, turning to her.

'He had a small trunk that he carried in on his shoulder last evening,' Mrs Puddinge said. 'It was still here this morning – I'm sure of it. He . . . Oh, dear Lord in heaven!' She looked as if she might faint, and Quare reached out to steady her. 'There on the floor!' She pointed with the hand that held the keys; they rattled with her shaking. 'Blood, Mr Quare! He must've come back here after he fled your room! He must've come back here and waited until you had satisfied yourself that he was gone from the house! Then, when you returned to your room, he must have taken his trunk and crept out of here as quiet as a mouse!'

Quare felt close to fainting himself. Mrs Puddinge was right. The drops of blood on the wooden slats of the floor confirmed it. He'd assumed that Aylesford had escaped into the bustling streets, but instead he'd retired here, to this room, biding his time until Quare had given up the chase. Then – he could picture it as clearly in his mind as if he'd witnessed it himself – he'd hoisted his trunk onto his shoulder and left . . . along with any evidence that might incriminate him or shed light on his mission. Quare cursed – he had badly misplayed the situation. Master Magnus would not be pleased.

Master Magnus!

Aylesford had said the master was dead. Murdered in the night, like Mansfield and the rest. Quayle prayed to God that it was a lie, but he was forced to admit that everything Aylesford had told him this morning had thus far turned out to be true. He had to get to the guild hall.

Mrs Puddinge, meanwhile, was edging into hysterics. 'Why, he could have slipped back into your room while you were searching the street outside and slit my throat! Or when I went to fetch bandages, I might have met him in the hall or on the stairs, and what then? Oh, Mr Quare, he might still be lurking about, waiting for the chance to finish me off!'

'I'm sure he's not,' said Quare. 'He's gone to report back to his masters, just as I must do.'

'No,' she shrieked, grabbing hold of his arm. 'You can't leave me! He'll kill me, he will! Just as he did those poor young men!'

'Mrs Puddinge,' Quare said as forcefully and yet calmly as he could, 'Aylesford has no interest in harming you, I assure you.'

'Oh, aye, like you assured me I would be perfectly safe when you went gallivanting off after him!'

Quare felt his cheeks flush. Damn it, the woman was right. He had left her in danger. Once again, as in his confrontation with Grimalkin, he was forced to admit that he was ill-prepared for this game in which he suddenly found himself immersed right up to his eyeballs. He knew that he was lucky to have survived this long. And, no thanks to him, so was Mrs Puddinge. Nevertheless, he felt certain that Aylesford was long gone, and that Mrs Puddinge was in no further danger. 'It's me that he's after,' he told her now. 'But if it will set your mind at ease, I'll look for other lodgings as soon as I've spoken to my masters.'

'What, so that you can put some other innocent at risk? But even if you were to move out, Mr Quare, he still knows that I know he's a French spy,' Mrs Puddinge pointed out, not unreasonably. 'He'll still have cause enough to want me dead!'

'Once I've exposed him, the whole guild will know – and my masters will see that the news reaches the ear of Mr Pitt himself. Will Aylesford kill us all, then? Don't you see, Mrs P? The more people who know, the safer we are. Your surest protection lies in my getting to the guild hall!'

She pondered this for a moment, then nodded, a look of steely determination on her face, where, just a moment ago, he had seen only terror. 'I'm going, too, Mr Quare.' And, before he could object: 'I won't sit here all alone, waiting patiently for my throat to be cut. Say what you will, but you can't know for certain that he's not lurking about somewhere close by, watching and waiting like a cat at a mouse hole. As long as he sees that we're together, he'll not dare to strike. And if he sees us both go to the guild hall, he'll know the jig is up, and that it will avail him nothing to creep back here in the dead of night and silence me.'

Quare could not fault the woman's logic. 'Very well, but we must make haste. Give me a moment to clean myself up and finish dressing, and we'll go together.'

'I'm not letting you out of my sight,' she declared.

In the end, he prevailed upon her to allow him a modicum of privacy, standing with her arms crossed and her back to him just outside his cracked-open door. After dumping the bloody water out of the window and refilling the wash basin with the last of the fresh water from the pitcher, he undressed and hurriedly wiped the worst of the blood, grime, and sweat from his skin, shivering all the while. Then he dressed more quickly still, pulling fresh linen and clothes from the floor. He drew his hair back in a tight queue. His coat, if it were even salvageable, which he doubted, required more time and attention than he could spare just now, and so he wore only a waistcoat, once blue but now so threadbare and faded that it merely aspired to that colour. He tucked his spare hat, a battered tricorn, under one arm.

'Well?' he demanded of Mrs Puddinge at last. 'How do I look?' He did not want to draw unnecessary attention on the streets.

She opened the door fully and regarded him with a critical eye. 'I shouldn't care to present you to His Majesty,' she said at last, 'but I suppose it could be worse. Have you no spare coat?'

'Such luxuries are beyond a journeyman's purse, Mrs P.'

'Why, 'tis no luxury! Here, now, I've still got my husband's second-best coat – I buried him in his best, God bless his bones. I believe it will fit you very well indeed. Come along while I fetch it.'

So saying, she started off down the landing; her own rooms were on the ground floor of the house. Quare closed and locked the door to his room and followed her. At the top of the stairs, she paused and waited for him to catch up. 'I'll feel safer if you go first, Mr Quare.'

He nodded and slipped past her, descending with caution, his hand on the pommel of his sword. But, as before, he encountered no one. Mrs Puddinge unlocked the door to her private chambers, and again Quare preceded her inside, checking to make sure Aylesford was not hiding there. Only when he had searched every inch, including under the bed, did she deign to enter. Then, brisk about her business, she bustled to a trunk, threw it open, rummaged inside and drew forth a drab brownish grey monstrosity of a coat. This relic of a bygone age she unfolded and let hang from one hand while beating the dust from it with the other. Quare found it difficult to believe this garment had been anyone's second-best anything. He would have been embarrassed to see another person wearing it, let alone himself. It seemed to have been stitched together from the skins of dried mushrooms. He sneezed, then sneezed again more violently, as an odour reached him, redolent of the ground if not the grave.

'Here you go, Mr Quare,' said Mrs Puddinge, advancing towards him with the mouldering coat extended before her like a weapon. 'Not the height of fashion, I know, but sufficient unto the day, eh?'

He eyed the thing with something like horror. 'Er, I can see how much the coat means to you, Mrs P. As a keepsake of your late husband, that is. I couldn't possibly take it.'

'Stuff and nonsense,' she insisted. 'I won't have one of my young men walking about the streets without a coat. What will people think?' She pressed it upon him again, and, after setting his tricorn upon his head, he reluctantly took it.

'Got a bit of a smell,' he suggested, holding his breath.

'Beggars can't be choosers, Mr Quare,' she responded, as if offended by his observation.

Quare bowed to the inevitable with a sigh. He advanced his arms through the sleeves, half expecting to encounter a mouse or spider. Perhaps a colony of moths. The coat proved to be a trifle large, even roomy. It settled heavily across his shoulders, and the stench of it was like a further weight. He didn't think he could bear it. Yet before he could say another word, there came a sharp rapping at the front door of the house.

Mrs Puddinge shot him a fearful look.

'That must be the watch or, worse, the redbreasts,' he said in a low voice. 'Quick, Mrs P – you delay them, and I'll go out through the window. You can stay here; you'll be safe with these men.'

'I'll do no such thing!' Even as she spoke, she was crossing the room to a casement window looking out on the same alley as the window in his room above. She quickly threw it open, then turned to him as another round of hammering began at the front door. 'We've no time to argue, Mr Quare. Are you coming or not?'

Again he seemed to have no choice but to accede. Beneath her matronly exterior, Mrs Puddinge was a force to be reckoned with. Quare helped her over the sill and out of the window, then followed, pushing the glass-paned wings closed again behind him.

It was a chill, grey day, with more than a taste of encroaching autumn. Despite the lateness of the hour – nearly eleven by his watch – tendrils of fog snaked through the air, obscuring the sun and congealing in pockets along the cobbled pavement of the alley.

'What now, Mr Quare?' Mrs Puddinge asked, eyes shining beneath her bonnet, for all the world like a girl swept up in a childhood game.

'Now we make for the guild hall,' he said in a low voice. 'We'll go this way, up the alley, away from your house. Once we reach Cheapside, we'll blend in with the flow. Just act naturally, Mrs P. Don't hurry or do anything that might draw unwanted attention.'

'I confess I am rather enjoying this,' she confided as they walked up the alley side by side, avoiding as best they could the night's detritus thrown from upper storeys. The stench was enough to make him glad of the second-best coat, whose dank odour, however unpleasant, was preferable to that of offal and excrement. 'Why, it's as if it were five years ago, and Mr Puddinge still among the living! Many the morning I would walk him to the guild hall, he wearing the very coat you have on now, the two of us talking of everything and of nothing, happy as two peas in a pod!' As they reached the end of the alley and turned into the bustling thoroughfare beyond, she slipped her arm through his, giving him a warm smile, which he could not help but return.

But his own thoughts were far from dwelling on happier days of yore. Instead, they were all on what news he would find at the guild hall. Was Master Magnus really dead? He could not imagine a world without that outsized personality and quicksilver mind trapped in its stunted, misshapen body. As an orphan with no memory of his parents, Quare had been raised in a Dorchester workhouse, and from there, to his great good fortune, had gone in an apprenticeship to Robert Halsted, who had initiated him into the clockmaker's art . . . and whose wife, some years later, had initiated him into other, equally pleasurable arts. The couple had been kind to him, and generous, but he had at no point thought of them as substitutes for the parents he had never known yet often fantasized about, especially at night, when he lay abed unable to sleep, his fellow apprentice, Jim Grimsby, snoring and snuffling beside him like a hibernating bear. Then he would feel his loneliness most keenly and imagine himself surrounded by a loving family, or, in his more melancholic moments, as having been stolen away from his parents, a lord and his lady who had never ceased to search for him and would one day sweep him up in their arms and return him to his rightful place as heir to a title and the fortune that went with it.

Quare had given up such fancies long ago. He knew that no such life would be restored to him, even if he had once briefly possessed it – which, of course, he hadn't. He had long since come to accept that the only life he would have was what he made for himself, fashioned from the materials at hand with what skills he could master, assembling it piece by piece as if it were a kind of clock, one that would take an entire lifetime to finish. And in that respect, it was Master Magnus who stood in the nearest approximation of a father to him. Or, not quite a paternal influence, but an avuncular one. It was Master Magnus, not some mythical knight or lordship in shining armour, who had rescued him from Dorchester: a journey-man passing through town had brought the master a report of his horological skills, the master had come himself to inspect his work, and afterwards, Halsted had released Quare into his care. Master Magnus had struck him at the time as both frightening and comic, like a figure out of a fairy tale, Tom Tit Tot sprung to life. He hadn't realized then what a singular occurrence it was for Master Magnus to travel out of London to fetch a new apprentice, nor had he appreciated the agony the master had endured in the simple act of travelling the hundred-odd miles between London and Dorchester in a carriage that rattled his bones like dice in a cup. That Master Magnus was an orphan – to Quare's way of thinking, kissing-cousin to bastardy – constituted another bond between them. This was never talked about; indeed, sometimes months would pass in which he did not catch a glimpse of the man, much less exchange a word with him – even longer once he had attained the rank of journeyman. Yet Quare was always somehow aware that Master Magnus was keeping an eye on him and had his future in mind – as proved to be the case when, just over a year ago, the master had recruited him into the ranks of the regulators.

But it was not just gratitude for all that Master Magnus had done on his behalf that made Quare's heart ache with apprehension. He had embraced the master's plan without knowing its full extent, and now, like it or not, he was stuck in the middle of it, like a man crossing a flooded stream who finds himself in higher waters than he'd anticipated. It was too late to return to the safe shore from which he'd started; he could only press forward, into waters that might well sweep him away. He had lied to the Old Wolf, lost his place among the regulators, put his reputation and his hopes for advancement into the hands of a man who on the authority of a confessed murderer was now dead. And where would that leave Quare, who had always tried to cut an inconspicuous course through the treacherous shoals of guild politics? He feared that, without the master's protection, he would be expelled from the Worshipful Company or at best discarded, relegated to some backward sinecure, a small town far from London, where he would be permitted to open a shop but would never again taste the excitement of life so near to the centre of things. Nor, without the assistance of the master's intelligence network, would he ever learn the identity of his father.

And what of the watch he had taken from Grimalkin, the beautiful but deadly hunter with its bone-white workings and evident thirst for blood? Who else but Master Magnus could decipher its secrets? The mystery of it lay at the heart of everything that had happened. It was the reason Aylesford had been dispatched to London in the first place, the reason for the murder of his friends and the others Aylesford had killed, the reason Aylesford had lain close behind him in Clara's bed and slipped a knife between his shoulder blades. And it was the reason, too, that he had survived what should have been a mortal wound.

Quare knew this without question, deep in his bones. He had seen the hole punched into his back, the flowering bruise and scab. How, after the violation of such a stabbing, could he be walking now, heart beating, lungs drawing air? It was, he knew, a pure impossibility. Yet equally impossible was a pocket watch that derived its motive energy from blood and was capable of killing a roomful of cats in the blink of an eye. That these two impossible things should not be linked as closely as effect and cause struck Quare as a third, and even greater, impossibility.

Somehow, when the watch had drunk his blood, it had done something to him, changed his inner workings. There was no other explanation. Yet what the change consisted of, he could not say. Certainly it had not rendered him impervious to injury, as his wounded leg and shoulder both reminded him at every step. What then? It was a mystery as profound as that of the watch itself. Quare considered himself to be a man of science, of reason, but this went far beyond any science or reason that he knew of or could even imagine. It was as if objects had begun to fall upwards in his vicinity, the laws of Nature, and of Nature's God, suddenly and arbitrarily set aside. And what of Grimalkin, who sought the watch for her own purposes, and had tracked him down on the basis of some asserted sanguinary bond to demand or rather beg his assistance in stealing back the very object he had stolen from her in the first place? What had happened to her? Where had she disappeared to ... and why, if she were looking out for him, as she had implied, had she not helped him in turn, when he was most in need of it? The whole business was disturbing on a number of levels, from the physical to the metaphysical.

To Quare's relief, he and Mrs Puddinge arrived at the guild hall without incident. He had chosen a somewhat roundabout route for the journey, via Bread Street, Milk Street, Aldermanbury and Jasper Street, thence to London Wall and eastward to Wormwood Street, but approaching now down crowded Bishopsgate Street he had a good view of the venerable Gothic-style building with its broad front steps, thick wooden double doors, and, presiding over the façade from above, the great turret clock built by Thomas Tompion more than fifty years ago to replace the clock that had been there since long before the guild was founded, it having been decided around the turn of the century that the timepiece which was, as it were, the public face of the Worshipful Company should at least be seen to keep accurate time. Tompion's clock, known affectionately as Old Tom, with its hourly parade of fanciful figures from fairy tales, mythology, and the Bible, all somehow related to time – cowled Death with his hourglass and scythe; Joshua commanding the sun to stand still; the christening of Sleeping Beauty, with the twelve invited fairies, and the unlucky thirteenth, clustered around the cradle – presented a marvellous spectacle to the eye but was equally marvellous in what was hidden from public view: a double three-legged gravity escapement, one of the many horological innovations jealously hoarded by the guild – a secret technology which, even after more than half a century, had yet to pass into common knowledge. That, Quare thought now, and not for the first time, was a perfect allegory for the guild itself: a beautiful exterior concealing something wondrous made ugly – the avariciousness with which the masters sat atop their piled treasures like cold-blooded dragons coiled on heaps of stolen gold.

He did not advance straight to the hall but spent some

moments observing its environs from what he judged a safe distance, looking for any sign that men of the watch were lying in wait. He saw nothing that raised his suspicions, only the everyday hustle and bustle. Mrs Puddinge urged him forward, afraid that Aylesford might take this final opportunity to prevent them from reaching their goal, and at last he bowed to her impatience, and to his own, and led her across the crowded thoroughfare, weaving with practised ease through the noisy flow of pedestrians, carriages and carts, Mrs Puddinge clasping his arm with one hand while, with the other, she lifted her skirts above the appalling filth of the cobblestones.

Quare more than half expected to hear a shouted demand to halt, or to feel a hand clamp down on his shoulder from behind, but no one interfered as they climbed the steps to the front doors. The entrance of the hall was open to all, and thus there was no need to knock; he pushed one of the double doors open and strode into a gloomy, cavernous space, like the nave of a cathedral, in which stalls for the sale and repair of clocks and watches did a brisk business by candlelight and what drab illumination filtered through tall lancet windows high above, the glass of which, though daily cleaned by apprentices, seemed always coated with coal dust and grime.

A swell of murmurous voices echoed in the chill air. In lulls of conversation, Quare heard the ticking of a host of clocks, a welcome sound under the circumstances even though there was scant agreement between them, like a roomful of pedants talking past each other in urgent whispers. Here, too, the Charleys could have been waiting, but even if they had been – which did not seem to be the case – they could not touch him; the Worshipful Company had been granted certain privileges in its charter, prerogatives that it clung to as jealously as it clung to its hoard of secrets, if not more so, and by those terms it was the Worshipful Company, not the city watch, that, at least initially, exercised legal authority over its own members within the environs of the guild hall. Even had the watch been present, and tried to question him, the guild would not have permitted it. He was safe here, among his brothers, his family. He felt a weight slip from his shoulders.

'The moneychangers in the temple,' said Mrs Puddinge in a low voice beside him as they crossed the space to the far side, where another door barred the way to the inner reaches of the hall.

'I beg your pardon?' Quare glanced down at her, surprised at the vehemence in her tone. She was surveying the stalls with evident disapproval.

'That's what Mr Puddinge called them,' she told him with a self-conscious smile. 'He thought the guild hall should be free of commerce, that at least here, within these walls, the Worshipful Company should be more, well, *worshipful*.'

'Sounds like a man after my own heart, Mrs P.'

She gave his arm a companionable squeeze.

'Strange,' he said, dropping his own voice. 'Everything seems so normal, does it not?'

'Yes, I was noticing that,' she agreed. 'Do you suppose Mr Aylesford was lying about everything? That no one has died after all?'

'We shall soon learn the truth of it,' he said.

As they crossed the floor, Quare saw a number of journeymen and apprentices known to him, men and boys he would ordinarily have stopped and spoken to, for this antechamber of the guild hall was a great place for gossip and socializing. But now the urgency he felt in communicating what he had learned of Aylesford, along with his need to know Master Magnus's fate, impelled him past his acquaintances with nothing more than a nod and a searching glance. He found it odd, however, that not one of his fellows attempted to address him, and that few of them would meet his gaze . . . and when they did, there was an unaccustomed hardness in their eyes, a kind of reproach that filled him with misgivings. Behind them, he heard fresh whisperings, like dry leaves stirred up in the wake of a breeze. The skin at the back of his neck prickled. Mrs Puddinge seemed to sense it, too, for she grew silent and tightened her grip on his arm.

They drew up to the inner door, and Quare knocked – admittance beyond this point was reserved to guild members. The door opened, and a liveried servant asked him his business, his powdered face expressionless; even his voice seemed dusted with powder.

'I've urgent business with Master Magnus,' he said. 'He's expecting me.'

The man bowed and stepped aside. Quare could not tell if this action constituted an implicit refutation of Aylesford's claims or not. He made to enter; then, considering, paused on the threshold and turned to Mrs Puddinge. 'I'm afraid you can't accompany me any further, Mrs P,' he said. 'But if it will make you feel better, I'll ask the masters to send another journeyman to escort you safely home.'

'Very kind of you, I'm sure, Mr Quare,' she said, 'but I didn't come all this way just to turn back now. I mean to see justice done.'

'But—'

'I'm known here,' Mrs Puddinge stated. 'As the widow of a master, it's my right to enter the guild hall. Why, I'd like to see anyone try to stop me!' This with a challenging glare at the liveried servant, who showed as much reaction as if she had addressed a brick wall.

Quare shrugged and gestured for her to precede him, not at all convinced the servant would not step up to bar her way. But she bustled past the man without difficulty.

'Come along, Mr Quare,' she commanded, glancing back over her shoulder.

Marvelling, Quare stepped through the door.

At once, to his utter surprise and confusion, strong hands took hold of him. It was the servant, and another, indistinguishable from the first, who had been lurking, unseen, behind the door, which now swung shut with a bang.

'What is the meaning of this?' he demanded, too shocked even to struggle in the grasp of the two men. 'Release me at once! When Master Magnus hears of this—'

Mrs Puddinge interrupted him. 'Master Mephistopheles can't protect you now, Mr Quare.' Reaching forward, she deftly unbelted his rapier and its scabbard. Then, addressing the servants in an imperious tone he had not heard from her before: 'Fetch him along, you two. We mustn't keep Sir Thaddeus waiting.'

6

Gears Within Gears

QUARE FELT AS IF HE HAD ENTERED INTO AN OPPRESSIVE DREAM AS the two servants frogmarched him through empty corridors. Mrs Puddinge preceded them in frosty silence, navigating the maze of the guild hall with an assurance that bespoke considerable familiarity. Quare held his tongue as well; in truth, speech was beyond him. He'd walked these hallways just yesterday, feeling himself judged and found wanting by the dour-faced portraits looking down from the walls. Now that gloomy gallery seemed to regard him with outright hostility. So, too, the servants who had bent his arms behind his back and held them in a grip of iron as they impelled him – rather more roughly than necessary, he thought – in Mrs Puddinge's wake. What was happening? Why was he being brought to the Old Wolf in a manner more befitting a criminal than a journeyman of the guild? And how was it that Mrs Puddinge, of all people, had ordered the servants to lay hold of him . . . and been obeyed without hesitation?

Mrs Puddinge did not pause to knock at the door to Grandmaster Wolfe's study but pushed it open and strode inside. The servants bustled Quare across the threshold behind her. The room was as sweltering as ever, yet Quare perceived a distinct chill in the air.

The Old Wolf sat behind his desk as if he had not risen from it since Quare had last seen him. He took a long-stemmed clay pipe from his lips and exhaled a dense cloud of smoke, through which he gazed at Quare as balefully as a dragon. Mrs Puddinge, meanwhile, still holding his sword and scabbard, crossed the room to the Old Wolf's side and bent low to whisper into his ear. Quare felt his arms released; rubbing them briskly, he glanced back to see that the two servants had taken positions to either side of the now-closed door. They stared ahead like twin statues. Then the rumble of Grandmaster Wolfe's voice pulled his gaze forward again.

'Well, Mr Quare, it would appear that you've had quite a busy night and morning. What do you have to say for yourself, sir?'

'I-I've come to warn you,' Quare stammered, removing his tricorn and tucking it under his arm. He scarcely knew where to begin. He had so much to tell, so many questions to ask. Mrs Puddinge, standing beside the grandmaster's chair with her arms crossed over her chest – she had laid his weapon upon the desk – gazed at him inscrutably. He marshalled his thoughts. 'The French have sent a spy among us – a spy and a murderer. Aylesford, a journeyman claiming to be from Scotland, a man who—'

'Yes, yes, we know all about Mr Aylesford,' interrupted the Old Wolf, giving his pipe an airy wave. 'Master Magnus was not the only one with a network of spies and informants, you know.'

Mrs Puddinge gave a satisfied smirk.

But Quare was not concerned with Mrs Puddinge at the moment. 'Was,' he echoed dully. 'You said *was*. Is Master Magnus dead then?'

163

'Dead?' repeated Grandmaster Wolfe. 'Regrettably, yes.' Though if there was an iota of actual regret in his tone, Quare couldn't hear it. 'Murdered, in fact. But then, that is not news to you, is it, Mr Quare? Don't bother to lie – I can see right through you, sir.'

In truth, it was no more than Quare had feared – yet that fear hadn't prepared him for the reality. A kind of shudder seemed to pass through the floor, as if he were standing on the deck of a ship. Or perhaps the unsteadiness was his own. In any case, it was a moment before he felt in sufficient command of himself to reply. 'I had heard ... That is, Aylesford said . . .' He paused to clear his throat. 'Aylesford told me Master Magnus was dead. Said that he'd come to do the job himself, but that someone had beaten him to it.'

'I don't suppose he mentioned a name.'

'No. But tell me, sir, how did he die? Who found him?'

'You were working closely with him, were you not?'

'Indeed, we were very close. That is why I wish to know—'

The Old Wolf overrode him. 'You were present, I believe, at what the wits of the Worshipful Company have dubbed the Massacre of the Cats?'

Quare gave a wary nod.

'And that unfortunate event, unless I am gravely misinformed, had something to do with an unusual timepiece, a pocket watch – *this* pocket watch, in fact.' At which, with a triumphant flourish, he pulled from beneath the desk the silver-cased hunter that was at the centre of all that had occurred.

So, Quare thought with a sinking heart, despite all the efforts of Master Magnus to keep the watch out of his rival's hands, Grandmaster Wolfe had ended up with it anyway. And now, he realized further, his own role in deceiving the grand-master must come to light. He did not know what the repercussions would be, but he did not doubt they would be severe. This was not the time to mourn his master. Nor to solve the mystery of his death. His own life might well be hanging in the balance. He must weigh every word with the utmost care.

'Well, Mr Quare? Do you recognize this watch? It was found in Master Magnus's hand, clutched so tightly in death that, I regret to say, his fingers had to be broken in order to extract it.'

'I . . .' How much should he admit to? How much did the Old Wolf already know? 'I may have seen it before . . .'

'Do not fence with me, sir,' barked Grandmaster Wolfe. 'This is the very timepiece that you took from Grimalkin, is it not? The timepiece that originally belonged to Lord Wichcote?'

Quare sighed; it seemed he had no choice now but to reveal the truth – or, at least, that portion of the truth which was known to him. 'Yes, though I didn't realize it at the time. That timepiece – the one you are holding, I mean – was hidden within the one I took from Grimalkin. Or so Master Magnus told me.' He judged it best to say nothing yet of Grimalkin's gender.

'And what of the clock you brought to me, sir?'

'Master Magnus gave it to me.'

'And the story that went with it?'

'Master Magnus provided that as well.'

'I see. Both were counterfeit, then. I will hear the true story of what took place on that night from you, Mr Quare. But first, you will explain to me why Master Magnus took such extraordinary precautions to keep this watch from me. For I have examined it, and in truth I find it baffling. It seems no more than a model, a toy. Exquisitely crafted, to be sure. But useless as a means of telling time. Yet it was coveted by Lord Wichcote, Grimalkin, and Master Magnus – three men uncommonly well versed in the horological arts, whatever else one may say about them. The French, too, desired it, and dispatched Mr Aylesford to acquire it for them, by hook or by crook. Shall I tell you what I believe? If this hunter does not tell the time, then it must perform some other function – and somehow that function must be related to the Massacre of the Cats. It is, in short, despite its appearance, a weapon of some kind. A weapon with the potential to win the war for whichever side possesses it – for what may kill a cat may kill a man as well. Have I struck close to the mark, sir?'

'I do not know,' Quare answered. 'I cannot explain the purpose of that watch. I do not know the secret of its functioning. If Master Magnus knew these things, he did not share them with me.'

'You would do well to reconsider your loyalty to that man,' said the Old Wolf, frowning. 'He cannot protect you any longer – you must shift for yourself now, sir. Master Magnus had a duty to turn over this timepiece to me immediately. Yet he did not. What am I to think of that? What is Mr Pitt to think of it?' He held up a hand to forestall any response. 'Now you come to me with news of a French spy in our midst – Thomas Aylesford, to be precise. A man who is implicated in the murders of three journeymen of this guild, as well as in the deaths of some young noblemen who had the mis-fortune to be in the wrong place at the wrong time. You yourself are wanted for questioning in the matter of these killings. Yes, I know all about your disgraceful exploits at the Pig and Rooster. I will be blunt, sir. Some suspect that

Aylesford was not the only spy among us. That he had accomplices. Master Magnus, for one. And yourself, for another.'

'What? That's absurd!' Quare exclaimed in disbelief. 'Why, the man tried to kill me! Mrs Puddinge, you were there – you saw it!'

Mrs Puddinge shrugged and gave a tight-lipped smile, then addressed the Old Wolf. 'I saw the two of 'em fighting, true enough, Sir Thaddeus, but I don't know what caused the quarrel. I have only Mr Quare's word for that. Perhaps they had a falling out.'

'I didn't even know the man before yesterday,' protested Quare. 'I met him for the first time last night at the Pig and Rooster – Mansfield brought him. Yet you don't suggest Mansfield was a spy!'

'We are looking into Mansfield, never fear, as we are everyone who had aught to do with Aylesford. But Mansfield is dead. You, sir, are alive.'

'You say that as if it were a piece of evidence against me.'

'As well it might be. But surely you can prove your innocence, Mr Quare . . . if, that is, you are innocent as you claim.'

'I'm no spy,' he repeated. 'I'm a loyal Englishman. As was Master Magnus.'

'Are you so sure of that? Sure enough to bet your life on it? I do not think you are sufficiently aware of your position, sir. Five young noblemen were slain last night. Witnesses have placed you at the scene, in the very thick of the brawl. Already, powerful voices are clamouring for your death. It is only with difficulty that I have been able to protect you. But that protection cannot last for ever. Either you will tell me the truth now, or we shall see how you fare in the hands of the watch. You will find their methods crude, but quite persuasive.'

Now anger crept into Quare's voice. He was no less afraid, but he did not like being threatened. 'I've told you the truth, Sir Thaddeus. I do not know the secret of that watch. And if Master Magnus knew it, he did not reveal it to me. Nor do I know why he kept the watch from you, unless it was part of some scheme he had to take your place at the head of the Worshipful Company.'

'I can well believe that he sought my place. He was a brilliant man but also a vain and bitter one, always seeking to rise above his station and supplant his betters. But that is merely a slice of truth, not the whole pie. You can do better.'

'You don't want the truth,' Quare said as understanding dawned. 'You wish me to accuse Master Magnus. To testify against him. That is the price of my life, is it not?'

The Old Wolf sighed. 'You are not going to climb on your high horse again, are you, Mr Quare? How tedious. More is at stake here than you realize. The war is not going well. Even now, the French prepare an invasion fleet – a fleet that will make the Spanish Armada look like an afternoon boating party on the Thames. There are rumours that Bonnie Prince Charlie will soon land once more in Scotland, if he is not there already, to rally an army of rebels to his cause – a distraction His Majesty can ill afford at present. In the midst of all this, a watch comes into our possession – a weapon, rather – which, properly understood, promises to be of more value than a thousand cannon. Yet instead of turning this marvellous weapon over to myself or Mr Pitt, Master Magnus keeps it for himself. And, with the aid of an accomplice – that would be you, sir – concocts a story to cover his tracks. I ask you, are those the actions of a loyal Englishman?'

'He wasn't keeping it for himself,' Quare insisted.

'For whom, then? Aylesford? Or was he in league with Grimalkin after all?'

'You misconstrue my words, Sir Thaddeus. He merely wished to study it. To understand it before passing it on to Mr Pitt. What you call the Massacre of the Cats was an accident. The last I saw him, Master Magnus had no understanding of how it had happened. You see this watch as the answer to all our problems, a way to reverse the tide of the war. You think that it can be used to massacre men instead of cats. And you may be right. But consider this, Sir Thaddeus. That watch killed dozens of cats in the blink of an eye, by a means that neither Master Magnus nor myself could discern, let alone comprehend . . . and even less control. We did not direct its deadly effects; they could just as easily have struck us down. That watch is dangerous, sir. Too dangerous to be waved around like a loaded pistol.'

Grandmaster Wolfe's florid features blanched, and he lowered the timepiece to the top of his desk with one hand while the other replaced his still-smoking pipe in its stand. Mrs Puddinge's smug expression dissolved into a look of nervous apprehension, and she stepped away from the Old Wolf as if he had just laid down a hissing grenado.

'Are you saying that we could be struck down at any moment?' the grandmaster demanded.

Quare shook his head, once again remembering Grimalkin's warning, which seemed to be coming true with a vengeance. 'I'm saying I do not know. And that it is foolish to tempt fate by poking about in a science – if indeed it *is* a science – beyond our understanding.'

'You surprise me, Mr Quare. I thought you a man of reason. What is this watch, then, if not an instrument of science? Some kind of magic talisman, perhaps?' He gave a scornful laugh. 'Was Master Magnus dabbling in witchcraft?'

'Witchcraft?' echoed Mrs Puddinge with a little shriek. 'God preserve us! I always knew that horrid man was up to no good. Anyone with a pair of eyes in their head could see he was in league with the devil. Master Mephistopheles, indeed! Why, I'll wager he had hooves at the ends of those twisted legs. Yes, and a tail!'

'We are men of science here,' said the Old Wolf, shooting her a stern glance. 'We deal in facts, my good woman, not superstitions or old wives' tales.'

'Superstitions, is it?' she demanded. 'Old wives' tales? God knows I don't have the learning of men like yourself and Mr Quare, but at least I can recognize the devil's work when I see it! Spying is one thing, Sir Thaddeus, but I'll not put my immortal soul at risk by dabbling in witchcraft – no, not if His Majesty himself were to ask it of me!'

'Then by all means take your leave, Mrs Puddinge. There is no more that you can do here in any case. I'm sure I do not need to add that everything you have heard is to be held in the strictest confidence.'

Despite her words, and the grandmaster's dismissal, however, she appeared loath to go.

'Well?' asked the Old Wolf, raising his eyebrows. 'Your usual emolument will be waiting,' he said. 'With something extra added for your trouble and your diligence in bringing Mr Quare to us.'

'It's not that, sir,' she said, wringing her hands together, her combativeness gone as if it had never existed.

'What then?'

'Mr Aylesford,' she said in a whisper. 'He's still out there!'

'My good woman,' said Grandmaster Wolfe with the barely patient air of a parent schooling a child in the obvious, 'you may set your mind at ease on that score. Mr Aylesford is no doubt on his way back to France by now. His cover has been blown. He knows there is naught for him here but interrogation and the hangman's noose.'

'Oh, aye, very sensible, I'm sure. But I looked into his eyes, Sir Thaddeus! The man is not sensible. He is a fanatic. A madman! Ask Mr Quare – he'll tell you!'

Quare, who felt it was rather rich for Mrs Puddinge to be appealing to him now, said nothing.

The Old Wolf, meanwhile, sighed heavily. 'I am far from trusting Mr Quare's word on anything at the moment,' he said. 'But I will have a journeyman escort you home, Mrs Puddinge. And remain with you overnight. That should be sufficient to put your fears to rest.'

'Aye, and what about tomorrow, then?'

'I cannot guarantee your safety,' the grandmaster said. 'No one can. Why, just walking down Bishopsgate Street can be fatal. Not to mention the fact that you have chosen of your own free will to become involved in patriotic work that carries a substantial risk. This is something I told you at the outset of your service and have repeated many times since. But it would appear that my warnings have fallen on deaf ears.'

'I never saw no harm in keeping an eye on my young men like you asked of me, Sir Thaddeus. It were only good business, after all. But this is different. Mr Aylesford is different. He killed three of my young men! Who will want to lodge with me now?'

'Good Lord, madam, is that your concern?'

'All I have is Mr Puddinge's pension and that old house. Now no one will feel safe under my roof.'

'Why, our journeymen are not so squeamish as that. Besides, the murders took place at the Pig and Rooster – surely it is that establishment which will bear the brunt of any opprobrium, not your own. In any case, Mrs Puddinge, they'll lodge where I send 'em, and until you give me cause to do otherwise, I'll keep sending 'em to you. Do we understand each other?'

'I didn't mean nothing by it, Sir Thaddeus,' she said, bobbing a curtsy. 'A woman's got to make a living, ain't she?'

'Indubitably,' the grandmaster agreed.

Mrs Puddinge glanced at Quare and coloured. 'I hope as there are no hard feelings, Mr Quare. You was a good lodger. I only done my duty, and you can't blame a body for that, can you?'

'I would appreciate it if you sent my things on to the guild hall, Mrs Puddinge,' he replied. 'Once this matter is cleared up, I believe I will seek other lodgings.'

'There's no cause to get huffy,' she said, flushing more deeply still. 'Your things will be safe with me. I run an honest house, I do. But, not to put too fine a point on it, if it's a French spy you are, Mr Quare, why, then by law your things are rightfully mine, as it were me that nicked you. So if you don't mind, I'll be holding on to them for now.'

'I do mind,' he said.

'That's as may be. If, God willing, you're found innocent, then you can come and fetch everything – after payment of a small storage fee, of course. Good day, sirs.' With a stiff nod to Quare, and another curtsy to Grandmaster Wolfe, she left the study, escorted out by one of the servants.

'A formidable woman,' said the Old Wolf once she had gone. 'I sometimes think that if we could but ship a hundred like her across the Channel, the war would be won in no time.'

'Sir Thaddeus—'

'Have no fear for your possessions, Mr Quare. I have already dispatched agents to bring everything here.'

'Thank you for that, at least.'

'I have not done it for your sake, but so that we may examine your things with a fine-toothed comb. Once we are done, if you are judged to be a spy, then what is left – after the Crown has taken its share – will indeed go to Mrs Puddinge. That is the law. Now, sir. Let us return to the matter at hand.'

'I will not lie about Master Magnus,' Quare said. 'He suffered enough calumny while alive. I'll not add to it now, when he can no longer defend himself.'

'Noble sentiments, no doubt.' The Old Wolf leaned back in his chair – it creaked ominously – and regarded him for a moment, placid blue eyes unblinking. Then, seeming to come to a decision, he leaned forward again, to the accompaniment of further creaking, and placed his elbows on the desk, careful to avoid coming anywhere near the watch. 'You must consider the living, Mr Quare, and leave the dead to bury the dead. That is my advice to you. Now that Master Magnus is gone, I will be taking his place at the head of the Most Secret and Exalted Order. In these perilous times, it no longer makes sense – if it ever did – to divide the reins of guild authority between two men. I have already appointed Master Malrubius to assist me.'

Quare flinched at the name. Master Malrubius modelled himself upon the Old Wolf in his style of dress, his mannerisms, even his very girth; but the man was physically and mentally smaller than his model, and the contrast made him an object of ridicule and contempt among the apprentices and journeymen. But he was also an object of fear, for his dull wits did not preclude the frequent use of his fists, which were not at all dull. They struck with the force of small hammers.

Meanwhile, the Old Wolf had continued to address him. 'I do not yet know if Master Magnus was a traitor to his guild and his king – and do not imagine, by the way, that your testimony alone will acquit or convict him; you are not as important as all that, Mr Quare. It is the master's own writings that will testify most strongly to his guilt or innocence, and we have only just begun to sort through them; as you know, he was not what could be called an orderly man, at least not where his papers were concerned. But regardless of whether or not he was a French spy, it is already clear that Master Magnus used the regulators as a kind of private army, keeping secrets from me and from Mr Pitt alike, while pursuing an agenda of his own. You, sir, were a part of that agenda. And for whatever reason, when it came to this particular timepiece, the master chose to involve you, rather than a more experienced regulator. Now, however lax he may have been in the disposition of his books and papers, when it came to matters of horology and spycraft, the master was meticulous, as I think you will agree. Thus I conclude that it was not by chance or circumstance that he dispatched you to procure this timepiece. Nor, though the Massacre of the Cats may have been an accident, as you say, was your presence there accidental.'

This had not occurred to Quare. But he was quick to dismiss it. 'Master Magnus told me that all the more experienced regulators were on assignment. There was no one else close enough at hand to dispatch to Lord Wichcote's.'

'He told me the same, and I trusted him – I had no reason not to. Our rivalry was no secret, of course, yet I had always believed that, beyond these walls, we set our differences aside for the good of king and country. I know *I* did. But since his death – or, rather, since you came to me with that appalling and quite frankly fantastic tale of sparing Grimalkin's life out of a finicky sense of honour, a tale I did not believe for one instant – since that bit of uncharacteristic sloppiness on Master Magnus's part, as if events had taken an unexpected turn and forced him to a clumsy improvisation – I began to suspect that he had not been entirely truthful with me. I made inquiries. And so it proved. There *were* other regulators available that night, Mr Quare. Indeed, the master could have picked among half a dozen men with more field experience than you. And yet he chose you, a regulator still wet behind the ears, for a mission of, as it appears, extraordinary importance. Why would that be?'

'I-I don't know,' confessed Quare, taken aback by this information. He did not think the Old Wolf was lying to him. With Master Magnus, there had always been gears within gears. Not that his opinion of the man's loyalty had changed, but in this matter, he realized, he might have been too credulous. Loyalty, after all, did not preclude self-interest; aye, or the settling of old scores. 'The master intended for you to suspend me from the regulators,' he admitted. 'That was why he fabricated that story.'

'Now we are getting somewhere. You will tell me what truly happened between you and Grimalkin, Mr Quare. But first I will hear the reason that Master Magnus wished you suspended.'

'I don't know,' Quare repeated. 'He said he had some kind of special assignment in mind for me, one in which I would have more freedom if my connection to the Most Secret and Exalted Order was believed to have been severed, but he never had a chance to tell me what it was.'

'Perhaps we will find a clue in his papers,' mused Grandmaster Wolfe. 'But I think you yourself possess many if not most of the answers I seek, though you may not realize it.

Answers having to do with the nature and purpose of this watch, for one, and with Master Magnus's relationship to Aylesford and Grimalkin, for another. Either you are with-holding these answers to protect a perfidious scheme in which you are involved right up to your eyeballs, or, more charitably, out of misguided loyalty to a man undeserving of it, or you have simply failed to grasp the significance of certain details known only to you.'

'Sir Thaddeus, I swear—'

'Do not protest your innocence to me, sir. Or your ignorance. Mere words will not convince me of either. It is details I want. And details I shall have. Whether you provide those details willingly or require the persuasion of Master Malrubius is immaterial. Is that clear?'

Quare nodded. He did not see any alternative now to con-fessing everything: the fact that Grimalkin was a woman, along with her dire if imprecise warnings about the dangers of the timepiece – warnings that circumstances had borne out in such disturbing and incredible ways, from the discovery that the watch ran on blood, to the Massacre of the Cats, to his own unaccountable surviving of a wound that, to all appear-ances, should have been fatal. The watch was the key to all of these mysteries, and more, yet was itself, he felt certain, a greater mystery still. Its nature, its origin, its purpose – he knew none of these things, could not even begin to guess at them. He did not think he could convince the Old Wolf of what little he knew . . . or of how much he didn't know. He could, of course, offer to demonstrate the watch to Sir Thaddeus – could prick his finger and let his blood drip into its bone-white workings. But even if the hunter reacted as it had before, seeming to come to life with stolen vitality, Quare thought it entirely possible that such an action would merely light the fuse of some new and still more terrible manifest-ation of the object's parlous energies. 'Sir Thaddeus,' he began.

But the Old Wolf interrupted him again. 'I do not wish to hear anything more from you at present, Mr Quare. No, I think it best that you have some time to ponder your situation. To review all that you have told me . . . and all that you have not. Solitude, I find, can be a helpful goad to reflection, a pow-erful stimulus to memory.' He gave a nod, and Quare turned to see the remaining servant advancing upon him from his position beside the door. He backed away.

'This isn't necessary, Sir Thaddeus,' he protested.

'Oh, but I believe it is,' the grandmaster said. He had risen while Quare's back was turned, and now, moving with a swift-ness at odds with his bulk, he laid hands on Quare from behind. The man's aged, sweaty reek enveloped him. His grip was like iron, and Quare did not attempt to break free. The Old Wolf spoke low in his ear, his breath stinking of tobacco. 'Think on anything that Master Magnus may have revealed to you, whether in words or actions or otherwise, about the nature of this timepiece and his plans for it. Review your encounters with Grimalkin and Aylesford. Meanwhile, Master Malrubius and I will make a more thorough examination of the master's papers, and of your possessions as well. I think perhaps I will have him pay you a visit. I find he can be most persuasive. Be assured, if you attempt to mislead him, or hold anything back, I shall hear of it and take it as proof of your guilt, at which point I will not hesitate to turn you over to the watch – or to Mr Pitt himself, whose methods of interro-gation, I am given to understand, are more exacting still. Do we understand each other, Mr Quare?'

'We do,' he said tersely, trying not to breathe in the man's rank odours, as if they would leave a stain upon his insides.

'Good.' The Old Wolf released him, pushing him towards the servant, who did not take hold of him but gave every appearance of being prepared to do so should it prove necessary. But all the fight had gone out of Quare. He turned back to the grandmaster.

'Where . . .'

A satisfied smile lit the fat, florid face. 'You will be lodged with us, Mr Quare. We have rooms prepared for such occasions as this. Granted, it has not proved necessary to use them for some time, but they exist, and you will find them adequate, if, no doubt, lacking the amenities of Mrs Puddinge's establishment.' He nodded, and the servant spoke in the sepulchral tones cultivated by all his fellows.

'If you would come with me, sir.'

Quare glanced at the man. His powdered features might have been carved of stone, and his slate grey eyes gave no hint of the thoughts and emotions – if any – that were present behind them. Was he judging Quare now? Did he believe him to be a traitor to his guild, his country? Quare felt a deep-seated impulse to justify himself, to break through that impenetrable façade and evoke some kind of bare human acknowledgement, as if it were this nameless servant, not Grandmaster Wolfe, who would decide his guilt or innocence. But he said nothing, merely nodded his acquiescence.

Nor did the servant speak again. He turned about and strode to the door, opening it and then stepping aside for Quare to precede him. This he did, without another word to the Old Wolf, or even a backward glance. When the door closed, he felt as if he had left a portion of himself behind, along with his sword: and even if the sword were returned to him in the fullness of time, along with his other possessions, as he hoped would be the case, it didn't seem to him that the life those objects had ornamented would be as easily regained; indeed, that life seemed irretrievably lost to him, regardless of what happened next. Even if he were not expelled from the guild, he would never be elevated to the rank of master now. Instead, it seemed the best he could hope for was a beating from Master Malrubius, followed by an ignominious expulsion from the company.

He felt it likely things would go considerably worse.

It was in this morose frame of mind that Quare followed the servant down a series of candlelit halls and stairways clutching his tricorn as though it were a shield. They encountered no one. The only sound, other than the scrape of their footfalls, came from a bristling ring of keys that the servant held in one hand: a faint, discordant chiming that punctuated their progress. Every so often, he would pause before a particular door and without hurry or hesitation select a particular key from among dozens, unlock and open the door onto another hallway or staircase, wait for Quare to enter, then, after following him through, fastidiously lock the door again behind him before resuming the lead. All without a word. His grey eyes uninterested as mud.

At first Quare was equally uninterested, mired in his own muddy thoughts, but soon he began to take note of how, in their steady downward progress, the paintings and tapestries covering the panelled walls gave way to bare wooden panelling, which in turn gave way to stone, while, on the floor, tiles were succeeded by wood, then stone. The air grew cooler and damper, yet also cleaner, more pure. The candles in their wall sconces were set farther and farther apart, like stars in the night sky, so that the servant was finally obliged to lift one down and carry it before him to light the way. After this, whenever he had to unlock a door, the servant would pass the candle to Quare, then, on the other side, the door closed and locked again, take the candle back.

Quare felt as if he were descending through time as much as through space, traversing past iterations of the guild hall preserved intact like the chambers of a nautilus shell. How deep were the roots of this place sunk into London's rich soil? Who had walked here before him in years gone by? He shivered not only from the chill but from the sense that he might, at any moment, encounter the ghost of a Roman legionary or one of Boadicea's warriors; even the sight of a gnome did not seem out of the question.

But at last, without incident, they came to a section of passage lined with stout wooden doors, each, so far as he could tell in the meagre light, equipped with an iron grille set at eye level. Quare stopped in surprise and consternation. The servant had conducted him to a dungeon. He had not known, would not have guessed in a thousand years, that the guild hall even *had* a dungeon. Doubtless it was an atavistic survival of less civilized times, pre-dating the establishment of the Worshipful Company and perhaps the raising of the hall itself. Buried deep . . . but not forgotten. The Old Wolf had said that these rooms were kept ready, though they had not been used for some time. Quare wondered how long. Years? Decades? Who had been the last prisoner here, and what had been his fate? Such speculations were not helpful, yet he could not keep them at bay.

The servant, meanwhile, had stopped before one of the doors midway down the passage and was looking back at Quare. The raised candle imparted a ghastly cast to his powdered face, as if he were a shambling corpse. He did not speak but gave his ring of keys an eloquent shake.

Quare's heart quailed at the prospect of being shut up here for however long Grandmaster Wolfe chose to imprison him, but, really, what could he do? Even if he escaped from this servant, and managed to avoid the others who would surely be sent after him, he had no hope of finding his way out of this underground warren. He could no more retrace the route they had taken than he could flap his arms and fly. The servant shook his keys again, more vehemently this time, and Quare, taking a deep breath, obeyed the summons.

The servant handed the candle to Quare, who accepted it wordlessly, feeling not only helpless but humiliated to be thus rendered complicit in his own captivity. The lock clicked open, and the man gave the door a firm push; it swung inwards on well-oiled hinges, evidence that, indeed, the rooms had been well maintained. Beyond was a darkness that seemed loath to yield even an inch to the small candle Quare held in his trembling hand. But before he could put that to the test, the servant reclaimed the candle and stepped past him into the room. Once inside he ferried the flame to half a dozen fresh candles set in sconces on three of the four stone walls. Quare, continuing to hover at the threshold, watched as the darkness melted away, revealing a comfortably appointed chamber with a narrow pallet for a bed, a desk and chair, a chamber pot, and – taking up much of the fourth wall – a cavernous fireplace in whose deep recesses a fire had been laid. This the servant now brought to roaring life with another touch of the candle, the flames springing up with such alacrity that for an instant they seemed about to leap to the man himself, who, however, drew back unflappably and turned to Quare.

'I trust all is to your satisfaction, sir.'

'My satisfaction?' he echoed, disbelieving. 'And if it were not?'

'There are other rooms, though they are less well appointed.'

'I'm sure they are,' said Quare, and entered the room at last, looking about with wary interest. It was so far from the crude cell of his imaginings that, despite the bare stone walls and the scant, simple furnishings, he felt as if he had entered the bedchamber of a king. Already the heat of the fire was making itself felt. He tossed his hat onto the desk, then turned to the servant. 'It's not quite what I had expected.'

The servant raised an eyebrow. 'You are a journeyman of the Worshipful Company, Mr Quare, and as such entitled to certain amenities. Should that change, your accommodations will change accordingly.'

'Of course,' Quare said. 'How long must I remain here?'

'Why, until you are sent for, sir.'

'And how long might that be?'

'It might be any time at all, from hours to days. That is for the grandmaster to decide.'

'What am I to do in the meantime?'

'That is for you to decide. My suggestion, if you don't mind, sir, would be to spend your time in reflection, so that, when next questioned, your answers will prove more satisfactory. You will find paper and writing implements in the desk, should you care to avail yourself of them.'

'I see,' said Quare. He eyed the servant critically. 'Was it you who conveyed me to Master Magnus the other day? In the stair-master?'

The servant gave a slight bow. 'I had that honour.'

'I thought there was something familiar about you. See here – what's your name, my good fellow?'

'You may call me Longinus, sir.'

'Longinus . . . An unusual name.'

'Perhaps I am an unusual person.'

Quare let this pass without comment. 'What can you tell me of Master Magnus's death, Longinus?'

'Nothing at all, sir.'

'Why, you must have seen or heard something.'

'Indeed. What I meant was that I have been instructed not to tell you anything more about it than you already know. The grandmaster wishes you to probe your own memories, not mine or anyone else's.'

'Don't you care that he was murdered, Longinus? Aren't you at all interested in finding the killer and seeing justice served?'

'Most assuredly, sir. That is why I volunteered to serve as your jailer – for, make no mistake, despite the comforts of this room, you are a prisoner of the Worshipful Company. The sooner you realize that, the better off you will be, if you don't mind my saying so.'

Quare shook his head. 'You are unusually solicitous, for a jailer.'

'As I said, sir, so long as you are a journeyman of this guild, you are entitled to certain amenities.'

'I see. And if that should change . . .'

'Let us hope it does not come to that, Mr Quare. And now I must go. Either I or another servant will bring you food and drink this evening. Until then, I will leave you to your business.'

Quare said nothing until the man was through the door. Then he called out: 'I'm no traitor, Longinus. And neither was Master Magnus.'

The only response was the shutting of the door and the click of the key turning in the lock.

* * *

Alone, Quare felt the weight of all that had happened settle once again on his shoulders. As an orphan, he had known his share of hopeless moments, but nothing quite like this, with the threat of a hangman's noose staring him in the face. His friends and fellow journeymen were dead, murdered by a maniac who was still at large, perhaps even, despite what he had told Mrs Puddinge, still in the city. His landlady, whom he had heretofore thought of in maternal terms, had revealed herself as a spy – and what's more, a spy motivated not by patriotism but by avarice. Nor did it seem to him that his own motivations in that regard were any purer, any less selfish, for hadn't he become a regulator in order to advance his prospects in the guild, to acquire knowledge of horological innovations that would have been unavailable to him otherwise, and to learn the truth about his parentage? To ask the question was to answer it. No, he had no right to cast stones at Mrs Puddinge. He felt as if he had soiled his soul, and though Sir Thaddeus's suspicions of his loyalty were unfounded, he could not really claim to be innocent. London, he perceived, was a great murderer of innocence. But who could hold the city to account for its crimes?

Without noticing it, he had begun to pace the room like an animal in a cage. This was all Master Magnus's fault, he told himself bitterly. If only the man had not involved him in his schemes, he would not be here now, a prisoner of his own guild. And if the master had not been so damned curious, so fond of machinations mechanical and otherwise, he would very probably still be alive, for though Quare did not know who had killed Master Magnus, or how, he did not doubt that the man's death was related to his pursuit and investigation of the pocket watch he had sent Quare to retrieve from Lord Wichcote.

Could Lord Wichcote have engineered the master's death, having learned through his own sources of the master's interest in that timepiece, perhaps believing that Grimalkin was in the service of the guild, as was rumoured, and had therefore been sent to his house that night on the guild's business? It seemed possible. He was a wealthy and powerful man, used to living beyond the law. But Lord Wichcote was not the only suspect. Not by a long shot. There was Grimalkin, for one. And Aylesford, for another – despite his disavowal of the deed. Even the Old Wolf was not above suspicion; certainly he had wasted no time in turning the situation to his advantage by seizing control of the Most Secret and Exalted Order; after all, it was common knowledge that he had envied Master Magnus his leadership of that order and coveted it for himself. The same was true, to a lesser degree, of Master Malrubius, who nurtured not only his own ambitions but those of the Old Wolf as well. It sickened Quare to think that the Worshipful Company was so riddled with corruption and intrigue as to render the murder of one master by another an eventuality impossible to reject out of hand, yet, all things considered, he couldn't argue against it. Whether that was a result of his own predicament or an accurate reflection of the facts, he was unable to judge.

By now the fire had raised the temperature of the room a considerable amount. Quare had long since divested himself of the second-best coat; only with difficulty had he refrained from throwing the odious – and odiferous – garment on the flames, reminding himself that his prospects were uncertain, and that he might very well be glad of a warm coat soon enough. It lay like a heap of refuse on the floor in the furthest corner. Quare, tired of his circular perambulations, sat on the edge of the pallet and stared into the flames as if their dancing shapes held the answers to all the questions that plagued him. Yet he found no answers there, only further questions, not the least of which was whether the fire had been lit not for his comfort but as a preliminary to other, graver tortures. He could not help recalling that Master Magnus had threatened him with devices as wondrous in their way as the stair-master, only turned to a darker purpose. Now the decision to introduce him to any such devices rested with the Old Wolf and Master Malrubius. Quare could not be sanguine at the prospect.

He considered scattering the logs to diminish the blaze, but to do so would have required him to enter the cavernous mouth of the fireplace, which was so deep that it might almost have been a separate room. Besides, there was no poker at hand, and he didn't think his well-worn boots were up to kicking apart such a conflagration. He would have to wait for the fire to burn itself out. He wished now that he had thought to ask Longinus for water. When would the man return? How long had he been gone? Quare fished out his pocket watch: barely two hours had gone by since he'd left Mrs Puddinge's house. He would have guessed twice that, and he found the discrepancy unsettling; his two clocks, the inner and the outer, so to speak, were usually in closer agreement, and the fact that he should be so badly mistaken in his estimate now seemed due less to the finicky nature of time than to the radical upending of his life. He was running out of true, and he did not know how to put himself right again.

As Quare's anger ebbed, wilting in the heat, grief took its place – a grief that had been there all the time, biding beneath the agitated surface of his feelings. The faces of Farthingale, Mansfield and Pickens appeared to his mind's eye as he last remembered seeing them, flushed with drink and laughter in the smoke-filled confines of the Pig and Rooster. Try as he might, he could not recall anything of the fight that had ended the night . . . and their lives. His memories cut off so abruptly that it was as if they had been surgically excised, and he wondered if the cause had less to do with the amount of alcohol he'd consumed than the watch that had somehow, or so he believed, protected him from what should have been a fatal wound.

The trio of grinning faces seemed to reproach him now – for what, exactly, he didn't know. Perhaps for having survived. He mourned them, and in doing so mourned something in himself. He prayed for the repose of their souls.

His grief for Master Magnus was of a different order, mixed as it was with anger, guilt, gratitude, and a host of other emotions he felt keenly but could not put a name to. He well remembered his first sight of the man. It had been six years ago, in Mr Halsted's Dorchester shop, late on a Saturday morning in June. Mrs Halsted, who usually manned the front desk, was busy in the kitchen, while Master Halsted and Quare's fellow apprentice, Jim Grimsby, were in the back room that served as both a workshop and sleeping quarters for the two apprentices.

Quare had been examining a mantel clock brought in for repair by Mr Symonds, the vicar, who stood on the other side of the desk, gazing down at the disassembled timepiece spread out between them, an anxious look on his face as though it were a sickly living creature, a beloved pet, perhaps, and not a mechanical device. Elsewhere in the shop, the vicar's wife and his beribboned young daughter, thirteen-year-old Emily, a vivacious blonde-haired girl whose bright blue eyes were of more interest to Quare at present than the insides of her father's clock, were examining a case of pocket and pendant watches: Mrs Symonds with unfeigned interest, while Emily's blue eyes kept rising to meet Quare's gaze, then darting away, a pretty blush colouring her cheeks. This heated if innocent flirtation, which had been going on between them for months now despite, or perhaps because of, the fact that the participants had not spoken more than a handful of times, and then only to exchange platitudes in the constraining presence of their elders, had made for as diverting a morning as Quare could desire, but he knew at once, upon looking up at the jingle of the bell announcing a new customer, that things were about to get a lot more diverting.

Bustling into the shop like a fairy-tale figure sprung to life was a humpbacked dwarf dressed all in black who pulled himself along with a pair of slender but stout walking sticks, pivoting with each 'step' on twisted legs that, wrapped in metal braces, seemed more like clever machines than appendages of flesh and blood. He was lean as a whippet, with a head whose wild mane of white hair made it seem even larger than it actually was, as out of proportion to the stunted body beneath as the heavy head of a sunflower to its stalk. And as the head to the body, so the nose to the head: a carbuncled, tuberous growth that appeared to have usurped the place of a nose; and upon that prodigious organ, nestled there like a black and gold insect, a pair of spectacles so darkly tinted that it seemed impossible anyone could see through them.

Yet see through them he obviously could, and did, for the man – the apparition, rather, since fifteen-year-old Quare could scarcely credit what his own eyes were showing him – had stumped across the shop floor, bringing all conversation to a halt. Even Mr Symonds drew back from the new arrival as he came to stand beside him. Without so much as a by-your-leave, the man tilted his leonine face up at Quare – he scarcely topped the desk; yet Quare realized that the man was not in truth a dwarf, but only so hunched over as to be indistinguishable from one – and demanded, in a voice that had more than a touch of the lion in it as well, 'Are you Quare?'

Quare gazed back open-mouthed.

'Well?' the man continued. 'It seems a simple enough question. Are you or are you not the apprentice Daniel Quare?'

At that, he found his voice. 'I am, sir. If you would but wait a moment, I will be with you as soon as I finish with this gentleman.'

'I would see your master,' said the man as if he hadn't heard. He struck the floor with one of his sticks for emphasis, like a goat stamping a hoof, at which Quare started and Emily gave a cry from across the room. Quare glanced at her and saw that the poor creature was white as a sheet and close to tears, at which indignation rose in his breast.

'See here, my good sir,' interjected Mr Symonds before Quare could speak, recalled by his daughter's distress to his paternal and churchly authority. 'There is no need to be so brusque. Young Mr Quare is having a look at my clock, and—' He got no further.

'Clock?' interrupted the man. 'You call that a clock?' He seemed amused and affronted in equal measure. 'Why, I would wager that object is more accurate in its timekeeping now than it ever has been!'

'More accurate?' the vicar echoed, uncomprehending. 'But it is broken, as you see.'

Quare rolled his eyes. 'The gentleman refers to the fact that even a stopped clock is right twice a day.'

'Ah,' said Mr Symonds. 'Why, bless my soul, so it is . . .'

Again the petulant stamp of a walking stick. Again a girlish cry.

Quare felt himself losing the reins of his temper. He looked to Mr Symonds, but the man appeared to be engrossed in contemplation of the horological profundity just revealed to him. Perhaps, Quare thought, he was considering how best to work it into a sermon. At any rate, the task of dealing with this unpleasant little man had now fallen to him.

'I ask you again to wait your turn,' he said as politely as he could manage. 'And to refrain, if you would, from upsetting Miss Symonds' – this with a significant look in Emily's direction.

The grotesque creature swivelled its body to regard the young lady in question, who burst into tears. 'My pardon,' he said, though there was nothing apologetic in his tone, 'if my appearance has upset you, Miss Symonds.' And here he sketched a bow, or something redolent of a bow; Quare could not decide if he meant the gesture to be as much of a mockery as it appeared, or whether his deformities, and the sticks and braces meant to correct them, rendered his movements, regardless of the intent behind them, naturally – or, rather, unnaturally – graceless and parodistic. 'I am but as God made me.'

Mrs Symonds seemed to have no difficulty in deciding the question. 'Come, Emily,' she said, throwing an arm about her daughter's shoulders and shepherding her, sniffling behind a handkerchief, from the shop, all the while staring daggers at Quare, as though he were somehow responsible. 'Henry,' she called from the doorway, at which Mr Symonds emerged from his trance.

'Ah, yes, dear,' he said, giving Quare a distracted smile. 'I trust the clock will present no difficulties, Mr Quare?'

'None at all,' Quare affirmed. 'It will be ready on Monday.'

'So soon?' queried the vicar. 'I would not have you working on the Lord's day, Mr Quare, not on my account or any man's.'

'We keep the sabbath in this shop, vicar,' said Quare.

'I am glad to hear it,' said Mr Symonds and turned to the dwarf, who was watching this exchange with unconcealed impatience, lips twitching in his eagerness to speak. 'Good day to you, sir.'

'And to you, vicar,' he growled. He did not even wait for the man to exit the shop before importuning Quare again, once more accompanying his words with a thump of his stick. 'Now, Mr Quare, if it would not be too much trouble – your master, if you please.'

As if on cue, Mr Halsted poked his bald head through the door leading from the workshop. 'What is that c-confounded noise, Da—' He broke off upon catching sight of the dwarf. 'G-good g-gracious,' he stammered, stepping into the room, his ruddy complexion blanching to the paleness of a sheet. 'As I live and b-breathe. M-master M-magnus.'

'How are you, Halsted?' the man inquired. 'Glib as ever, I see.'

Quare's master had a fierce stammer that emerged whenever he was flustered or excited; the neighbourhood street urchins mocked this impediment ruthlessly, both behind his back and, the better to elicit it, to his face, but Quare had not thought to find such cruelty in an adult.

Making a visible effort, Mr Halsted calmed himself, or tried to – with scant success, however. 'Daniel, this g-gentleman is one of the g-great masters of our g-guild, come all the way from L-London, or so I imagine.'

'You imagine correctly,' said Master Magnus. 'And a

damned uncomfortable journey it was, too, with more bumps and jolts in the road than are to be found even in one of your utterances, Mr Halsted.'

'I am sorry to hear it. M-mayhap you will take refreshment here. My home is yours. Daniel, c-close the shop. Oh – my apprentice Daniel Quare, m-master. A m-most promising young m-man. Mr Quare, M-master M-magnus.'

'An honour, sir,' said Quare, and meant it: though he was only fifteen, it had long been apparent to him that Dorchester was a backwater, horologically speaking, and that the only place for an ambitious and talented young man like himself was London. The journeymen who passed through town had whetted his appetite for years with stories of the great guild hall of the Worshipful Company and the masters who ruled it, led by Grandmaster Wolfe. Halsted had his own tales to tell, for he had travelled to London for his investiture as a master of the guild, and had returned twice, for brief periods, in the years since Quare had become his apprentice, lodging each time at the guild hall, and each time coming home full to bursting with the wonders he'd seen and experienced there. Now one of that august company stood before him in the flesh. And not just anyone, but Master Magnus – or Mephistopheles, as the journeymen had called him – a man they had variously termed a genius, a terror, a monster, a freak of nature, and whom Master Halsted, in hushed tones, as if he feared being overheard even at such a distance, had once compared to a spider in its web. Quare studied the man with fresh interest, wondering what secrets he could impart, what lessons he could offer; Quare had already absorbed everything Halsted could teach him, and his horological skills now outstripped those of his master. 'I apologize for not recognizing you at once, Master Magnus.'

'And how should you recognize a man you have never seen?' came the sharp inquiry.

'Why, your reputation precedes you, sir,' Quare answered, ignoring Halsted's cautionary glance. 'The journeymen who stop by our shop on their travels speak of you as a man of great learning and application.'

'Do they now?' mused the master. 'Are you quite sure, Mr Quare, that it is not the size of my body, rather than the size of my intellect or accomplishments, that precedes me?'

Quare saw too late the trap he had fallen into, for in fact the journeymen who had recounted Master Magnus's accomplishments with awe had also spoken fearfully of his temper and sensitivity to any perceived insult or slight on account of his size or other handicaps.

'C-close up the shop, now, Daniel, as I t-told you,' Halsted interjected, coming to Quare's rescue.

This Quare moved to do, blushing fiercely as he came around the counter.

'To what do we owe the p-pleasure of your visit, master?' Halsted continued, seeking to shift the conversation to safer ground. 'If you had but n-notified me that you were c-coming, I would have received you with m-more ceremony.'

'Bah, I require no ceremony, Halsted, as you should know very well.'

'Still, I feel sure, after your long and d-difficult journey, that some refreshment would not c-come amiss. C-come into the k-kitchen, sir, and do me the honour of meeting m-my wife . . . and, of c-course, my other apprentice, James G-grimsby.'

'A cup of tea would suit me very well,' Master Magnus admitted.

Halsted conducted the older man through the door that led to the workshop and, beyond it, the kitchen, while Quare closed up the front of the shop. By the time he had joined the others, Master Magnus was seated at the kitchen table in a chair that accommodated him as well as it would have done a child of ten – less well, in fact, for his metal-caged legs did not bend at the knees but instead stuck out parallel to the floor. His chin barely overtopped the table, where a steaming cup of tea was set on a saucer, beside a plate of biscuits and butter; it did not escape Quare's notice that Mrs Halsted was using her good china. His walking sticks were propped against the edge of the table, close to hand.

Standing opposite him on the far side of the table were Mr and Mrs Halsted, along with Grimsby. Halsted and his wife regarded their visitor with some apprehension, nervous smiles plastered on their faces, as if he were not entirely tamed and might be set off by a wrong word or gesture, while the freckled, red-headed Grimsby, who had listened, along with Quare, to tales of mad Master Mephistopheles from the journeymen who lodged with them on their way through town, gawped in open-mouthed astonishment. Everyone, save Grimsby, turned to Quare as he entered the room.

'Mr Quare, thank the Almighty,' said Master Magnus. 'Sit you down, sir.' His gesture encompassed the entire kitchen. 'All of you, sit, please. You are making me feel like a baboon on display at Covent Garden. And Mr Grimsby, pray close your mouth, lest what little wit you possess escape entirely.'

Grimsby flushed to the roots of his red hair and shut his mouth with an audible snap. Mr and Mrs Halsted wasted no time in seating themselves, followed, seconds later, by Grimsby, which left but two chairs for Quare, one on either side of Master Magnus. He took the nearer.

A tense and expectant silence filled the kitchen, punctuated only by the regular ticking of a small tower clock situated above the hearth – an exact replica of Master Halsted's master-piece, in fact, the original of which resided, as did all masterpieces, in the vaults of the Worshipful Company; this modest timepiece was the pride of the house, horologically speaking, though it was, in Quare's considered opinion, barely adequate as a specimen of the clockmaker's art.

Master Magnus, as if oblivious to the strained atmosphere, reached with some difficulty for his tea, which he sipped noisily and with apparent relish, holding the china cup in both hands; the steam rising from the liquid testified to a heat that should have communicated itself to the cup, but Master Magnus gave no sign of discomfort, though he did blow, between sips, upon the top of the tea, as if to cool it. Quare noticed both the suppleness of the man's hands and fingers and the fact that they bore a multitude of small scars, as if from a lifetime of nicks and cuts; later he would learn that the master's hands, for all their dexterity, had not escaped the general blighting of his body: though able to discriminate by touch among gradations of pressure and texture too fine for Quare's rough senses to perceive, his fingers were entirely numb to pain.

Master Magnus drank until the cup was empty, at which he smacked his lips and, once again contorting his body, replaced the cup on its saucer with a rattle that brought a look of distress to Mrs Halsted's blue eyes, though her polite smile never wavered. 'An exquisite brewing, Mrs Halsted,' the master said graciously.

'I try, sir,' she answered, blushing beneath her white cap. 'I do try. We do like our tea in this house, sir.'

'You do more than try, madam. Why, it is plain that this house is blessed with two masters. Indeed, I would go so far as to suggest that you might dispense with clocks entirely and open a tea house instead.'

This barbed and backhanded compliment left his hosts speechless. Smiling, with the air of a guest fulfilling his conversational duties, Master Magnus turned his dark spectacles towards Grimsby, who actually flinched back in his chair.

'Steady, Mr Grimsby – steady on, sir,' he said as if to comfort the apprentice, who was Quare's junior by two years. 'I have read the reports of your work dispatched to me by your good master here. Amidst so much tedious verbiage, one word leaps out, and I find it so apt that I have already employed it in reference to you myself and am about to do so again. That word, if you cannot guess it, is *steady*. Your hands are steady, your mind equally so; in short, you are as dependable and dull as a bullock, destined, I have no doubt, for a life of plodding but honourable labour in the fields of time, much like Master Halsted himself. Of such as you is the backbone of our guild – and, indeed, our country – constituted, and I salute you, sir, most sincerely, in your majestic mediocrity.'

Grimsby's face bore an expression of intense concentration, as if he were attempting, without notable success, to untangle *majestic* from *mediocrity*. 'Er, you are too k-kind, Master Magnus,' he said, seeming to have caught Master Halsted's stammer.

'Not at all,' the master rejoined and turned now to Quare, who just managed to keep from flinching as Grimsby had done under that blank, reflective gaze, in which he saw himself not merely reflected but belittled. 'Your master has written to me of you as well, Mr Quare. It is a duty I require of every master in our company, for how else am I to separate the wheat from the chaff, as it were, crippled as I am and able to leave London only with the greatest difficulty and inconvenience?'

'Yet you have come to Dorchester now, master,' Quare observed.

'Quite,' said Master Magnus, and without further ado removed a pocket watch from within his black coat. This he laid upon the table, then pushed over towards Quare. 'Do you recognize this, Mr Quare?'

Quare shook his head, mystified.

'Go on,' said Master Magnus. 'Have a closer look.'

Quare picked up the watch. He was struck at once by the plainness of it: no lid covered the glass; the hands were simple stark pointers; the black numbers on the white face had been painted without embellishment; the silver backing was bare of any engraved mark or design. He held it to his ear and heard a steady ticking.

'Well?' asked Master Magnus.

The others looked on with mystified expressions.

He was being tested; that much was clear. But as to the purpose of the test, let alone its consequences, he had no idea. 'It is very plain,' he said, weighing his words with care. 'But it seems well made for all that. I would need to open it up before I could venture anything more.'

'Then do so,' the master said, inclining his head.

Quare always carried a small tool kit with him; in a moment, he had prised the back of the pocket watch open. The inner workings of the timepiece did not match the drabness of its outer appearance. There were a number of small but significant innovations to the mechanisms that powered and regulated the watch. This in itself was unexpected; he knew very well – what apprentice did not? – that the Worshipful Company took a dim view of innovation, confiscating or destroying outright any timepieces that departed from what had been officially sanctioned. So it came as a surprise to have such a watch handed to him by no less an authority of the guild than Master Magnus. Surprise turned into something approaching shock a moment later when he recognized the innovations as his own. For some time now, Quare had been keeping a notebook that he filled with sketches of improvements to the mechanisms he worked upon each and every day in Master Halsted's shop. But he had not yet found the courage to actually translate one of his sketches into reality. Nor had he shown the notebook to anyone. Yet here was a watch that incorporated not one but a good half-dozen of his ideas. It seemed impossible.

'I ask again,' said Master Magnus. 'Do you recognize anything about this watch?'

Quare glanced up, surveying the faces that were regarding him in turn. With his eyes hidden behind his dark spectacles, Master Magnus's expression was inscrutable. Grimsby's mouth had fallen open again. Mrs Halsted's blue eyes shone with a tender concern he blushed to see: the look of a fond mistress. Halsted looked away, his cheeks flaming, and Quare wondered if the man suspected what his wife and his apprentice got up to when he was away.

'Well?' Master Magnus prompted.

Quare swallowed, mouth gone dry. He felt as if he'd been manoeuvred into a trap. Just a moment ago, Master Magnus had spoken of reports he'd received from Master Halsted; he realized now that those reports must have contained copies of his sketches. He felt a sharp sense of betrayal – ridiculous, as he had betrayed his master's trust in a more tangible fashion: but feelings are not reasonable things, and he felt what he felt regardless. Apprehension, too, crept along his veins, for he did not doubt that his sketches alone could result in a stiff sanction from the guild, if not outright expulsion. And then where would he go, with no family and no trade? Yet despite this, one other feeling surged through him, stronger than the others.

Pride.

Though he had not cut and filed the parts of this watch with his own hands, nevertheless they were realizations of his designs. Something that had existed only on the page and in his mind had been made real and tangible. And, at least as far as he could tell from such a cursory examination, the mechanisms worked as he had anticipated. How could he deny this thing he had created? To do so would be to deny himself.

'I didn't make this watch,' he said, 'but I suppose you could say that I designed it.'

'Daniel, I—' Halsted began, but Master Magnus, lifting a hand, overrode him.

'So, you admit that the watch is based on your designs?'

'Yes.'

'By keeping those designs to yourself and not showing them to your master, so that he, in turn, could forward them to me for review, you have failed in your obligations as an apprentice of this guild. Do you dispute that?'

'No. I don't dispute it.'

'Very well.' Master Magnus nodded in satisfaction . . . or so it seemed to Quare. 'I will tell you, sir, that the small improvements you have made were known to us already. This watch was not crafted to your specifications. I made it myself when I was a mere apprentice, more years ago than I care to admit. Nor is it the only such example in our archives. So you see, you are not as clever as you may think, Mr Quare – not by a long shot. You are not the first to have had these insights. Others have been here before you. Still, I won't deny that you have talent.'

As soon as he had registered what the master was telling

him, Quare had turned all his attention back to the watch. And indeed, now that he looked more closely, he could see that the various parts of the watch that reflected his sketches did not do so with the fidelity he had at first thought to find there. In some cases, it seemed to him that his design was the more elegant; in others he saw that, on the contrary, he had not found the best solution. But the truth was plain: the sketches he had struggled over in solitude, the innovations he had dreamed would revolutionize horology and win him acclaim and riches, were no more than instances of reinventing the wheel. Yet though he was disappointed, he was not as crushed as he might have imagined; instead, it was as if an unexpected vista had opened out before him. Who could say what wonders were to be found there? He seemed to see them in the distance, glittering like the gold-leafed spires and towers of a fabulous city: a city built entirely of clocks. At the same time, he feared that he would be denied entrance to that city, permitted only to glimpse its wonders from afar. He looked up at Master Magnus. 'I assume I am to be punished?'

'Oh, indeed,' said the master. 'Most dreadfully punished. To begin with, you may consider your apprenticeship with Master Halsted over.'

Again Master Halsted began to speak. Again Master Magnus silenced him with a gesture. No one else said a word.

So that was it, then. It was to be expulsion. Now, indeed, Quare felt crushed, the very breath squeezed out of him.

'You will be coming back to London with me,' Master Magnus continued. 'You will continue your apprenticeship there, at the guild hall, under my supervision.'

'I . . . what?'

'Go and get your things ready, Mr Quare. We leave within the hour.' He turned towards the others as a dazed Quare rose to his feet. 'Mr Grimsby, your presence is no longer required. Perhaps you can assist Mr Quare in packing.' Grimsby nodded, looking as dazed as Quare, and stood.

As Quare left the room, Grimsby trailing behind him, he heard Master Magnus's voice: 'If I might trouble you for another cup of tea, Mrs Halsted, your husband and I will work out the transfer of Mr Quare's indenture.'

In the workroom, he hurriedly packed his things as Grimsby pestered him with questions he scarcely heard and in any case could not answer. His life had been turned upside down in an instant, and his thoughts, divided between what he was leaving behind and what awaited him in London, had no purchase on the present. In what seemed the blink of an eye, he was shaking Mr Halsted's hand as his master – *former* master! – stammered out an awkward goodbye, then embracing a tearful Mrs Halsted, who pressed him to her ample bosom with more-than-maternal zeal, or so it seemed to Quare, though no one else appeared to find the embrace remarkable. Nor were his own eyes empty of tears; he was, after all, leaving the closest approximation to a family that he had ever known.

Then he was seated across from Master Magnus in a jolting carriage that bore the arms of the Worshipful Company – a great golden clock showing the hour of twelve, surmounted by a crown and cross, itself surmounted by a plumed silver helmet, which was in turn topped by a banded sphere of gold; the whole supported on one side by the figure of Father Time with his scythe and hourglass, and on the other by a monarch with a golden sceptre, and beneath it all, as if inscribed on a flowing scroll, the words of the guild's motto: *Tempus Rerum Imperator*. Time, Emperor of All Things.

Quare watched the familiar sights of Dorchester pass by the open window of the carriage. Streets and buildings he had seen a thousand times without emotion tugged at his heart like burrs that had become fastened there without his knowledge and now came away grudgingly and not entirely without pain.

'Dry your eyes, Mr Quare,' commanded his companion, who even now, in the dim confines of the conveyance, wore his dark glasses. The man's perch on the padded bench was a precarious one; each bounce and swerve threatened to throw him down and doubtless would have done so already were it not for a strap that was bolted to the bench and which he had drawn about his waist and torso upon first clambering onto the seat – 'My own invention,' the master had explained in response to Quare's inquiry.

'After a day or two in London,' he continued now, 'Dorchester will seem no more than a childish fancy, a dull dream from which you will be glad to have awoken. Your real life is about to begin, sir. It will not be easy, but you will have a chance to put your talents to their best use, I assure you.'

'I can scarcely credit all that has happened to me today, Master Magnus,' Quare said. 'I hope I don't seem ungrateful or ignorant of the honour you have shown me. I will do my best to be a good apprentice to you and assist you in all your labours.'

The master laughed. 'You mistake me, sir. I do not require your assistance. Perhaps one day, if you are diligent and obedient, and progress to the rank of journeyman, I will make use of you. But that day will not come for years, and to be frank may never come. "Many are called, but few are chosen", Mr Quare.'

'Then whose apprentice will I be?'

'Why, on paper, my own. But I have many such apprentices. Do not consider yourself a special case. I had other business in

Dorchester, and it was convenient to fetch you at the same time; otherwise a journeyman would be conveying you now. Once settled in London, you will not serve a single master but will instead be placed at the disposal of all the masters of the guild hall. Your day-to-day training will be overseen by journeymen – more than that, I cannot say; I find such details tedious and leave them to others.'

'What . . . what is London like, master?'

'London? She is a painted strumpet – loud, boisterous, full of frantic energy, beguiling seductions, and desperate schemes. She will stroke you with one hand and pick your pocket with the other, and leave you with the pox besides. She is life itself, Mr Quare – and death. And the Worshipful Company of Clockmakers is a microcosm of that city. Life within the guild hall could not be more different than the cosy situation you are leaving behind. We are a brotherhood, true enough, yet Cain and Abel were also brothers, were they not? But you will discover all this for yourself soon enough, as I did. You may not believe it to look at me, Mr Quare, but I was once much like you.'

'Indeed, sir?' he inquired.

Again the master laughed. 'I, too, came to the city full of dreams and ambitions, burning to make my mark on the world and to unravel the secrets of time. Like yourself, I have known the tender embrace of the workhouse – the memory is engraved on my bones, on my very soul. And like you, I escaped that hell on Earth and found refuge within the guild.'

'Why, are you an orphan, too, sir?'

'As good as. I know nothing of my parents – they abandoned me as soon as they had a good look at me. I suppose I can't blame them; indeed, I am grateful they didn't smother me in the cradle.'

'Have you made no attempt to find them?'

'To what end? A tearful reconciliation? I leave that to the scribblers. Nor has the prospect of revenge ever interested me. No, I consider my parents dead, and myself an orphan, as I said. It is simpler that way for all concerned. But what of your own parents?'

'They died in a fire when I was but a babe,' Quare said. 'Or so I have been told. I have no memory of them.' This was not quite true; in fact, Quare possessed certain vague memories – impressions, rather – that he associated with his parents. From time to time, most often as he was lying in bed, on the verge of sleep, a warm peacefulness would settle over him from he knew not where, all the strength would ebb from his limbs, and he would feel himself enveloped in a kind of tender, loving regard that he knew at no other moment in his waking life. As far back as he could remember, he had associated this feeling or mood with the presence of his parents, as if they were watching over him from beyond the grave. But he would not divulge such a private solace to Master Magnus or anyone.

'I was raised in an orphanage,' he continued, 'and from there, at the age of seven or eight – to this day, I am not certain of my exact age – was sent to the workhouse, where I remained until, quite by chance, when I was ten, or perhaps eleven, I made the acquaintance of Mr Halsted, who often, out of Christian charity, hired some of us children to help in his workshop. He encouraged my interest in timepieces and, as my aptitude for the work became plain, arranged to take me on as an apprentice. I owe that gentleman everything. He was like a father to me, and more – like an angel, sir. A guardian angel.' Indeed, as if the truth of that statement had not been manifest to him until he had spoken it aloud, Quare felt his throat constrict with emotion. He dried his burning eyes with the cuff of his coat and looked again out of the carriage window.

They had left the city of Dorchester behind and were travelling along a dusty road past open fields of rolling farmland. In the distance, under blue skies, he could see the glint of the sun off the River Frome. It was the furthest Quare had ever been from home.

'What if I were to tell you that you are not an orphan?'

Quare's head whipped back round to face his companion. 'I beg your pardon?'

'An orphan is a child deprived by death of father and mother. It's true your mother is dead – she perished giving birth to you. That is in the parish records. But your father remains very much alive, or so I believe.'

It took Quare a moment to gather his wits. 'My father . . . alive?'

'I have found no evidence to the contrary.'

'Why has he not come for me? Why has he allowed me to believe I am an orphan for all these years?'

'Because he does not wish to acknowledge you, sir. He does not wish to know aught of you, and he desires even less that you should know aught of him.'

'But why?'

'Is it not obvious? You are no orphan, sir, but a bastard. Some man's by-blow.'

'How do you know this?' Quare demanded, his hands squeezed into fists at his sides.

'I make it my business to learn what I can about every apprentice.'

'But then who is my father?' A sudden foreboding came over him. 'Is it you, sir? Is that why you have come to fetch me?'

At this, Master Magnus threw back his head and roared with laughter while Quare turned the shade of a beet. When the master had composed himself, he answered: 'No, I am not your father, young Quare. Have no misapprehensions on that score.'

'Then Mr Halsted! Perhaps that is why he was so kind to me.'

'Nor is Halsted your sire. Put such thoughts from your mind.'

'Then who?'

'Why, I do not know,' Master Magnus confessed with good humour. 'What I have related to you is no more than any man could have found at any time simply by perusing the parish records. Your mother's name was Mary Trewell. A milkmaid. No doubt seduced and cast aside. A common enough tale, though a sad one, I grant you.'

Quare was reeling; he felt as though he had slipped into a kind of dream. 'Did . . . did Mr Halsted know this?'

'Who do you think it was that examined the records? He dispatched the information to me. A boy, Daniel Quare, born to Mary Trewell, father unknown. Your name, sir, is a witty reflection of that fact, from the Latin *quare*, which is to say "from what cause".'

'I . . . I scarcely know what to say, what to think,' Quare mumbled, passing a hand before his eyes. 'Why have you told me this?'

'Should I have kept it from you? Surely a man has the right to know the truth of his own parentage.'

'But you have told me a half truth, no more. Now I must wonder at who my father may be. Does he yet live? And if so, does he dwell close by or far away? Have I seen him, all unknowing? Does he know of me? Perhaps he does not, and would acknowledge me if he but learned of my existence. I must find him! Sir, can you not help me?'

'I might look for years and never find him. No doubt the trail has gone quite cold. And who is to say that he wishes to be found? A man might very well know that he has a bastard son and yet desire no more intimate acquaintance with him.'

'Please, sir. I should like to find him anyway.'

'And what would you do then? What would you say to him?'

'I . . . I do not know.'

'You are no longer a boy, Mr Quare, yet neither are you a man. Wait a while, sir. Complete your apprenticeship. Acquit yourself well in all that is asked of you, and then, in a few years, when you have attained the rank of journeyman, ask me again, and perhaps I will be disposed to assist you.'

'Thank you, sir. Do you know, I was angry at Mr Halsted for sending you my sketches. But now I see that I have to thank him as well.'

'Not everyone would be so thankful to learn themselves a bastard.'

'My whole life, I believed myself an orphan – that is worse. You and Mr Halsted have given me back my father, or hope of him. I will work hard, sir. You shall see! I will acquit myself well – and come to my father as a man he will be proud to acknowledge.'

'An admirable plan, young Quare. I hope you are not disappointed. But life has a way of disappointing bastards, I have found.'

'I will pray to God that it may be otherwise, sir, and trust in his providence.'

'Why, do you imagine that God cares a fig for bastards? Surely he has more important things on his mind.'

'I . . . I don't know, sir. I mean, yes, sir, I suppose he does. Have more important things on his mind, I mean.'

The master's leonine head nodded approvingly. 'What sorts of important things?'

'I'm sure I don't know.'

'Then I shall tell you. Time, Mr Quare. Time is the mind of God in motion. His thought, His intent, His very essence. We horologers, as much as or even more than the clergy, are doing His work, for every timepiece is a microcosm of the universe the Almighty created and set in motion. In making and repairing clocks and watches, we of the Worshipful Company expunge the errors and anarchies of the Adversary, restoring a small but significant measure of order to the world, without which the time appointed for the return of our Saviour might be indefinitely delayed, or never draw nigh at all. Do you think I exaggerate? Have you not felt the truth of it? In repairing a damaged timepiece, do you not also repair a part of yourself, some damaged spring or coil or counterweight of the soul, and, in so doing, for a while at least, draw closer to the master of clocks and men?'

Now it was enthusiasm rather than embarrassment that brought a flush to Quare's cheeks. 'Yes! I have felt that, or something like it – and . . .' He paused, groping for the right words.

'Go on.'

'Well, as if, in drawing closer to Him myself, I bring some measure of the world along with me. I know that sounds foolish – to think that my small labours can influence the entire world . . .'

'But why should they not? The workings of a clock teach us how even the smallest part or movement can influence the greater whole. In life, as in horology, everything is connected, even if we lack the discernment or wisdom to perceive the nature of the connections. But do not doubt that they exist. Perhaps neither men nor clocks can be made perfect, young Quare, but they can both be made less imperfect, approaching, with each small improvement, in a kind of ceaselessly worshipful striving, ever nearer to that ideal of timeless perfection forever beyond the grasp, though not the aspiration, of mortal hand and mind. Each refinement in the measurement of time brings the world nearer to God, and to the moment, ordained since before the beginning of time itself, when we shall be ransomed from the prison of time and admitted at last into the hallowed precincts of eternity. Such, at any rate, is the belief of our guild, the consummation towards which we struggle.'

'Mr Halsted never spoke to me of such things.'

'I should be surprised to hear otherwise. In the guild, as in the wider world, there are gradations of knowledge, strata of understanding. Greater and lesser truths, if you will. Horology is a practical science, but it also has its mystical, or perhaps I should say esoteric, side. Just as the journeyman knows more than the apprentice, and the master more than the journeyman, so, too, do the elect of the Worshipful Company know more than the common herd. I have spoken to you now as I have, young Quare, because I judge that you possess the potential to be one of the elect – your designs proclaim it. Whether you realize this potential is another matter. That is up to you. I have but cracked a door open to give you a glimpse of the secret knowledge shining on the other side like the piled treasure of a dragon's hoard; now I must pull that door shut, and I will not open it for you again. When the time comes, if it comes, you shall open the door yourself.'

'I . . . I don't understand, sir.'

'It would be a wonder if you did. For now, it is enough that you reflect upon all that I have told you, and that you keep the memory of it in your thoughts in the weeks and months – indeed, the years – that lie ahead. One more piece of advice I will give you: to the extent you may reasonably do so without causing offence, keep your own counsel. Do not let yourself get tangled in the petty cliques and Machiavellian intrigues that have come to infect the guild under the leadership of our present grandmaster. Steer a middle course, young Quare, for as long as you can. That course, I make bold to say, will lead to mastery in the end. Aye, and to your father as well, like as not.'

'Why, is he a master horologer, then? Is that what you mean?'

'I know not what he is, nor who, as I have said. But if you would have my help in finding him, then you must apply yourself as I have suggested. That was my meaning, no more and no less.'

'I will do my best,' he answered, and so he had . . . and now found himself in a prison cell deep beneath the guild hall. Had all the choices he had made, the actions he had taken, or not taken, led him inevitably to this moment, this place? The past could not be changed – but what if the same were true of the present and the future, and all the events of a man's life were as if carved into stone from the day of his birth, or earlier still, set down by the hand of the Almighty at the beginning of time? Choice, then, would be an illusion, and the course of each man's life would be as fixed as the movement of a clock. Perhaps there was some comfort in this view – useless, then, to struggle, to regret, to dream. Whatever happened, happened in accordance with God's plan, and each human being merely played the part assigned to him or her. Yet

Quare's spirit rebelled against this comfort and the attitude of supine passivity it encouraged. He rejected them both. Illusory or not, he would act as if his actions mattered, as if the future were not set in stone.

And how could it be, really? He himself was the proof of it – or, rather, the wound he bore, which by all rights should have been fatal: an assassin's knife thrust between the shoulder blades and into the heart. Yet when death had come for him, somehow, by some means he did not understand, he had escaped. And if that prison had not been able to hold him, how could this one? He resolved that when Longinus or another servant returned, he would not sit meekly by and wait for whatever fate was in store for him. He was not help-less; he was a regulator, after all. It was time that he started acting like one.

Quare rose from the pallet and crossed the room to the desk. Heedless of the noise, he lifted the wooden chair and, holding it by the back, swung the legs against the wall until, with a loud crack, one splintered; this he prised loose, and as quickly as that held a rude club in his hand. If he could knock whoever came to check on him unconscious, he could take the man's keys, lock him in the cell, and try to make his way out of the guild hall. It was not much of a plan, but it was the best he could come up with under the circumstances. No doubt, once he was out of the cell, other opportunities would present themselves.

Then, once he was free, he would have to clear his name. Until he did so, he would be a hunted man. But better that than to be hanged as a scapegoat for crimes he had not com-mitted.

He retrieved Mr Puddinge's foul-smelling coat and arranged it on the pallet to give the impression of a curled and sleeping body. His hat he placed where his head might have been. Then he went to the door, standing to one side, so that, when it was opened, he might surprise whoever entered. He waited, listening for the sound of approaching footsteps and watching for a telltale glimmer of torchlight behind the iron grille set into the door.

Some moments passed. The only sound was the crackling of the fire. Quare's eyelids began to grow heavy in the stuffy, overheated atmosphere of the room.

'Waiting for someone?'

The voice came from behind. Quare started then spun to face the speaker.

'Longinus?'

The servant standing in front of the fireplace nodded, a wary eye on the club in Quare's hand. In his own hand was a belt and sheathed rapier: the very belt and weapon that Mrs Puddinge had taken from Quare and left with the Old Wolf.

'Put that down,' Longinus said. 'We've no time for such foolishness.'

Instead, Quare hefted the club and stepped forward. 'How did you get in here? What are you doing with my sword?'

'I've come to free you,' Longinus answered. 'But I would prefer not to receive a knock on the head in thanks for it.'

At that, Quare stopped short. 'You're letting me out?'

Longinus nodded, and for the first time, Quare noted that the servant's normally fastidious appearance was anything but: his powdered wig had been knocked askew, and the powder on his face was streaked with sweat; his clothes were torn in places and spattered with what looked like blood – whether his own or someone else's, Quare couldn't say.

'The Old Wolf has made his move,' Longinus said. 'He's been preparing this for a long time, but I did not think he would strike so soon after Master Magnus's death. Something must have forced his hand – I know not what.'

'What do you mean, made his move? What's going on out there?'

'A purge,' Longinus said, and grimaced. 'A bloody purge – that's what's going on. Every regulator loyal to Master Magnus is being hunted down and killed by the Old Wolf's men. I barely got away with my life . . . and your sword. Here.' He tossed the belt to Quare, who, shifting the club to his other hand, managed to catch the sheathed weapon. Longinus, meanwhile, continued speaking. 'You're on the list, too, Mr Quare. Apparently the Old Wolf has decided that you're worth more to him dead than alive. There's not a moment to lose: we have to get out of here now. Master Malrubius is on his way here to kill you.'

'How can I trust you?' Quare asked. 'How do I know this isn't a trick?'

'Because I know about the hunter and what it can do,' Longinus replied. 'I know that it drinks a man's blood – and I know, too, that it killed Master Magnus.'

'What? Killed him? How?'

'As soon as we are safely away from here, I'll tell you everything I know, I swear it. But for now, you'll have to trust me. Master Magnus never had a chance to tell you, but he intended for the two of us to work together. Surely you recall his promise to assign a more experienced regulator to assist you. I am he.'

'You? A regulator?'

'Retired,' Longinus said, and sketched a bow. 'Now, Mr Quare, if you don't mind, save your questions and follow me.' With that, he turned and entered the fireplace, leaping as nimbly as Jack of the nursery rhyme over the burning logs to vanish into the back of the cavernous space. 'Oh,' came his voice from out of the cavity, 'you might want to bring that appalling coat of yours.'

This was a turn of events Quare had not anticipated. He didn't trust Longinus, but neither did he want to take the chance that the Old Wolf really had dispatched men to kill him. With all that had happened, he found that he could not discount the possibility.

The decision was made easier by the sound of voices and hurried footsteps in the corridor outside. It seemed that Quare was about to have visitors.

'Quare!' hissed Longinus from behind the flames.

Quare rushed to the pallet, snatched up the coat, which he bundled into his arms, along with his tricorn, and, leaving the makeshift club behind, but clutching his sword and belt, ducked under the cowl of the fireplace.

'Jump,' came Longinus's voice from out of the shadows. 'It is quite safe, you shall see.'

He heard the click of the lock turning in the door behind him. Without a backward glance, Quare closed his eyes and jumped over the burning logs, feeling the heat of the flames lick across his shins.

'Good man.' Strong hands took hold of him and pulled him forward, out of the heat and the smoke.

Opening his eyes, Quare found himself in a small, square room with a bell pull in one corner and a railing that ran horizontally, at waist height, around each of the three walls; each wall bore a sconce with a burning candle. 'Why, it's the stair-master,' he breathed in wonder.

'Quite,' said Longinus even as the door to the chamber slid shut, cutting off the shouts of consternation from the cell Quare had just vacated. 'You would be surprised, I think, to learn just how widely the stair-master may travel throughout the guild hall. Or perhaps not, knowing Master Magnus as you did. He was a man who prepared for every eventuality save one: the bizarre circumstances of his own death. But who in this world could have prepared for such a demise? Who could have imagined that such a timepiece could exist?' He gave a sharp tug to the bell pull, and the chamber began to move, lurching backwards so suddenly that Quare nearly fell, righting himself only with difficulty by dropping his coat, hat and sword belt and grabbing hold of the rail with both hands.

'Wh-where are we going?' he gasped out.

'Up,' said Longinus. And, as if that had been a signal, or rather a command, the stair-master jerked to a halt and then shot upwards. Quare's stomach lagged behind, and his knees almost buckled. 'Steady on, Mr Quare,' said Longinus. 'I hope you are not afraid of heights.'

Quare shook his head, speech beyond him for the moment. He noted that Longinus had belted on a sword, and also that two large cloth bundles, each black as pitch and secured with an assortment of leather straps and clasps, were leaning against one wall of the now smoothly ascending chamber. The bundles looked unwieldy and lacked, as far as he could see, any shoulder straps. He could not imagine what purpose they might serve. Longinus wore a hint of a superior smile on his face as he regarded Quare, who continued to cling to the rail.

'How high are we going?' he asked, for, as the seconds ticked by, it seemed impossible to him that they had not yet reached the apex of the guild hall ... assuming that was indeed their destination.

'Why, all the way to the top, of course,' said Longinus, and again, as if his words had served as a signal, the stair-master jerked, less violently than before, then glided to a stop. The door slid open upon a moonlit rooftop wreathed in drifting tendrils of fog; Quare had not realized how much time had gone by since his incarceration.

'Buckle on your sword belt,' Longinus instructed. 'Gather up your coat and one of those bundles, and follow me.' He had already lifted one of the bundles himself, which he proceeded to carry out of the stair-master.

Quare buckled on his belt, picked up his coat and hat and the remaining bundle – which was heavier than it appeared, and covered with an unfamiliar substance that clung to his fingers – and followed Longinus onto the rooftop. From this height, Quare could see much of the surrounding roofscape of London, though indistinctly, as a mass of bulky shadows and spindly shapes in which, here and there, like the stars above, tiny flames winked without providing much illumination. To the south, through tears in the curtain of fog and coal smoke, he saw the dull shine of the Thames, a length of tarnished pewter. He was reminded of his rooftop pursuit of Grimalkin – had it really been only two nights ago? But the difference was that the roof of the guild hall was substantially higher than the surrounding buildings, and Quare saw no way to leap from their present perch to an adjoining one, as he had done while scrambling after Grimalkin. They were trapped. Did Longinus mean to betray him?

'Stop gawking and come over here,' said Longinus. 'You will have plenty of time later to admire the view.' The servant – though Quare supposed he could no longer think of him in that way – was kneeling beside a brick wall some distance away. He had his bundle open and spread out before him. As Quare approached, he saw that there was a large metal canister near by, from which a tube extended into the midst of the opened bundle. There was a hissing sound, as of escaping air.

'What are you doing? What is that thing?'

'Lay your bundle down there,' Longinus replied, pointing to the wall where the canister stood.

Quare placed bundle, hat and coat where Longinus had indicated, then turned, his hand on the hilt of his sword. 'I want answers, Longinus. And I want them now. Why have you brought me here?'

'You fool!' the other hissed. 'We don't have time for this! Even now the Old Wolf's men are climbing towards us – they will not let us escape if they can help it.'

'Escape? Why, there is no escaping this rooftop – not unless we can sprout wings and fly!'

Longinus laughed and got to his feet. 'We shall do the next best thing. Behold another of Master Magnus's wondrous inventions: the Personal Flotation Device. It will lift us from this rooftop and carry us safely through the air.'

Quare's mouth dropped open. 'Are you mad?'

'You know as well as I what Master Magnus was capable of. This canister, which is connected to a substantial reservoir beneath the roof, is filled with flammable air, a gas that is lighter than the air around us – so much lighter that it provides sufficient buoyancy to lift a heavy object . . . a person, in this case. The device itself consists of a leather harness and a sphere of sailcloth coated with the sap of a Brazilian tree – the natives call it *caoutchouc*, or so I am told. This sap holds the gas within, while permitting the bladder to expand. Once airborne, the device can be manoeuvred by dropping carefully calibrated weights – packets of sand of varying sizes – and by releasing controlled bursts of flammable air from the sphere.'

'You *are* mad!'

'I have used the Personal Flotation Device many times, Mr Quare. It is quite safe, over relatively short distances.'

'Right. Safe, is it? I suppose that's why the gas is called "flammable air". Because it is so much safer than ordinary air. You know, the non-flammable kind.'

'The gas is dangerous only if it comes into contact with a spark or flame.'

'Oh, that's very comforting. And if it does?'

'Then, Mr Quare, we shall both go out in a blaze of glory. But if you would rather return to your cell or remain here on the rooftop to await the arrival of Malrubius and his men . . .'

Quare grimaced. 'I take your point. How does the damned thing work?'

'There is not sufficient time to train you in its operation, unfortunately, so I am going to tether us together. Once you are aloft, touch nothing, do nothing, unless at my direction. Is that clear?'

'As crystal,' he replied.

'Put on your coat,' Longinus directed. 'You'll be glad of the warmth, believe me.'

Quare did so, donning his hat as well. Then Longinus fitted him into the leather harness, strapping it snugly about his thighs and across his torso and shoulders. All the while, the sailcloth bladder expanded, retaining its spherical shape; it was bigger than he had realized, perhaps twice his own size, if not more. Soon the sphere rose gently off the roof and into the air, a dark moonlet seeking its rightful place in the sky. Quare could feel it tugging at him. By that time, moving with practised efficiency, Longinus had opened the second bundle and spread it out, attaching a second tube – or 'umbilical', as he put it. As the device began to inflate, he strapped himself into its harness, spurning Quare's offer of help.

'You would only hinder me,' he said, 'or fail to secure the straps properly, and, in your ignorance, however well-meaning, kill us both.'

The whole operation did not take more than a few minutes, objectively speaking, yet all the same, Quare felt as if time had slowed to a crawl. He kept expecting to see armed men burst onto the rooftop, and so fixated was his anxious stare on the trap door that gave access to the roof that he was taken by surprise when, in a gust of wind, the sphere to which he was attached raised itself higher still, pulling him off his feet in the process. There he remained, dangling in the air above the rooftop like a puppet from its strings, secured only by the taut umbilical and the tether with which Longinus had bound their harnesses together. His hands clung to the ropes of the harness that rose from his shoulders to the sphere above as if by doing so he might somehow pull the device back to earth. It was all he could do not to scream. Then another gust of wind snatched the tricorn from his head, and he cursed loudly at the loss of it.

'A moment more,' Longinus said. He, too, would have risen into the air were it not for a pair of cables running from his harness to moorings set into the roof. His sphere bobbed below Quare like a cork.

Seeming to strain with the effort, Longinus bent over the canister and turned a small wheel there. Then he slipped the cables from the moorings. Both inflated spheres sprang upwards, carrying their human cargoes along. The umbilicals, pulled free of the spheres, fell back to the rooftop; even amidst his terror, Quare retained sufficient presence of mind to marvel at Master Magnus's ingenious design, which must have included some sort of self-sealing mechanism.

'*Allez-houp!*' cried Longinus.

Quare contributed an incoherent cry of his own as the bladders zoomed up and away – and not a moment too soon, for even as the rooftop receded dizzyingly below them, the trap door opened. 'Longinus!' Quare shouted, hoping his voice could be heard over the rush of the wind.

If Longinus responded, Quare didn't hear it. He watched in near-panic as the men on the rooftop – four of them, as small now as dwarfs, and a fifth, seemingly smaller still: Master Malrubius, nearly as spherical as the inflated bladder that had swept him aloft – raised what could only be pistols and seemed to follow their progress through the air, tracking them with steady hands. Quare felt as if he must loom as vast and ungainly in their sight as an airborne elephant. He cursed as a cluster of bright flashes marked the flintlocks' firing and strove to somehow make himself smaller. He recalled very well what Longinus had told him about the result should the flammable air in the bladders encounter a spark or flame, and he wondered what effect the strike of a ball would have. Even if the gas in the bladder did not ignite, it was a long way down.

But the bullets did not find their marks – at least in so far as Quare could determine. Certainly he had not been struck, and it didn't seem that the bladder carrying him ever higher and farther away had suffered injury, either. Nor did it appear that Longinus or his Personal Flotation Device had been hit. And their attackers could not reload fast enough to fire again. Quare watched in amazement, his heart aflutter like a frantic bird, as the men dwindled into insignificance, soon swallowed by shadows and the night.

They had done it. They were free.

A giddy exhilaration swelled in his breast, as if he had just swallowed a dram of strong liquor; under its influence, he could not forbear from shouting in triumph. Even his terror at dangling in mid-air like a mouse caught in the talons of an owl contributed to his sense of having escaped not only his prison cell and the fate Sir Thaddeus had planned for him but the laws of nature itself, as if it were an enchantment and not the application of scientific principles that had lofted him high above the city.

Here the air belonged to a colder season. For once, Quare was glad of Mr Puddinge's coat, for despite its stench – which the wind of their swift passage kept at bay – it provided some welcome insulation from that same wind's icy probings. Still, the exposed flesh of his hands and face soon began to sting, and his eyes to water; his mouth had grown so dry that he clamped it resolutely shut.

Longinus soared ahead of him, a dark shape visible against the softer coal of the night sky, where a ceiling of high cloud was silvered with moonlight, suggesting nothing so much to Quare at this moment as the surface of a great sail carrying the entire planet shiplike through the ether. That sail was torn in places, and through the ragged gaps he could see the glimmer of stars far brighter, it seemed, than he had ever perceived them from the level of the streets, even on moonless nights, and the moon, too, though not yet full, seemed, as it drifted behind the clouds, a brighter presence than he had known, a place it might, perhaps, be possible to travel to by this same method. What a journey that would make! What wonders might he find there!

But there were wonders nearer to hand. A wider rent had opened in the clouds, and in the plangent wash of moonlight the whole of London was revealed, extending as far as he could see. From his unaccustomed vantage, it seemed a different city than the one he had come to know, a fairy metropolis spun out of shadow and suggestion, of soft, silvery light and slate-grey webbings of fog, insubstantial as a dream. He passed over a weird terrain of rooftops and spires, chimneys belching smoke, deep valleys of streets, and squares in which the occasional torch flickered like a lonely star reflected in the mirror of a placid lake. There was no sound from below, only the rushing of the air, as noisy – and cold – as if he had plunged his head beneath a freezing cataract. Perhaps they had reached the moon after all, and this was no earthly city but the capital of some lunar country . . .

The undulating thread of the Thames, stitching in and out of the darker fabric of the night, gave Quare the means to orient himself, and he realized with a shock of recognition that he was passing almost directly above his lodgings – former lodgings, rather. Below him, Mrs Puddinge was no doubt enjoying the slumber of the just. What would she think if she looked up and saw her dead husband's coat flapping overhead like a ragged spirit condemned to an eternity of restless wandering?

That errant thought reminded him of more recent deaths, of spirits that clamoured for justice and revenge, if only in the court of his own conscience. Was the murderer Aylesford still at large in London, seeking the timepiece that, in some fashion Quare did not understand, had both saved his own life and killed – at least, according to Longinus – Master Magnus? Sir Thaddeus had the hunter now, and Quare shuddered at the thought of what might occur as the Old Wolf subjected the device to a thorough examination. Grimalkin's warning had been amply borne out, it seemed to him, and he wished that he had thought to question her more closely on the subject when he'd had the chance. He would have given a lot to see her again; she was as intriguing as she was beautiful, and he did not doubt that she could supply answers to many of the mysteries that had so thoroughly entangled him.

As the vertiginous sensations of flight lost their novelty, Quare realized that he and Longinus were not at the mercy of every capricious breeze. They were moving with steady intent, like ships that hold to their course despite the vagaries of the wind. None of this was Quare's doing. Tethered to Longinus, he could only follow where the other man led; though at times it seemed that he was leading and Longinus following as the two Personal Flotation Devices performed a drunken minuet, each seeking to rotate about the other in a freewheeling demonstration of pendular motion that would have engaged Quare's mind had it not been so upsetting to his stomach. More than once they collided in mid-air, pushing themselves apart with grunts and curses before the lines of their harnesses could become fouled.

It seemed impossible that the mere manipulation of sand and gas, as Longinus had described to him, could bring their flight under control. But such was the case. Though there was not sufficient light to observe Longinus, Quare marvelled at the visible results of the man's unseen actions. Small, purposeful alterations in trajectory, height and velocity nudged the two devices in a particular direction, cutting westward across the city, angling closer to the Thames. Quare felt as if he had been caught up in a waking dream, or come under the influence of a magic spell. All his senses were heightened. He was drunk with wonder and fright.

Then, after an interval that could have been seconds or hours for all his ability to judge it, they began to descend. The city rose to meet them, surfacing out of fog and shadow like a leviathan bestirring itself after a long slumber. Someone – confederates of Longinus, Quare supposed – had set a ring of torches burning atop a particular roof, and it was towards this marker that Longinus steered them now. But how did he mean to set them safely down? It occurred to Quare that landing might prove to be even more dangerous than flying. He watched apprehensively as – far too swiftly, it seemed – the Personal Flotation Devices came swooping in.

He cried out, certain that he was about to die, but then a handful of figures ran into the torchlight, scurrying over the roof as if chasing something too small for Quare to see. Even as they passed above these men, who, he noted, wore the livery of servants, a strong jerk thrust him against his harness, driving the breath from his lungs. Urgent cries rose up from below. When he could breathe again, he saw that the men were holding tightly to ropes that Longinus had let drop from his harness. The servants had caught these ropes in mid-flight and tied them to moorings set into the roof. Now the men were hauling them in hand over hand. Quare smiled at his saviours with a gratitude that bordered on love. They did not spare him a glance, intent on their work, and he loved them all the more for it.

'That wasn't so bad, eh, Mr Quare?' came Longinus's voice.

Quare could only grin stupidly.

But his grin faded as he took in the details of the roof. He knew them very well. There was the chimney behind which he had concealed himself two nights ago. There the skylight from which, wreathed in grey smoke, Grimalkin had emerged.

Longinus had brought him to Lord Wichcote's house.

He was betrayed.

7

Lord Wichcote

WHAT SECONDS EARLIER HAD SEEMED LIKE SALVATION TOOK ON A very different aspect as the men on the rooftop – there were at least a dozen – reeled Quare in like an eel dragged from the Thames ... though that hypothetical eel would have had a better chance of slipping the hook than Quare of escaping his harness. Longinus had liberated him from one jailer only to deliver him, snugly trussed, to another. Perhaps Lord Wichcote did not want him dead, as the Old Wolf did – though it occurred to Quare that he had only Longinus's word on that – but his lordship was no friend of the Worshipful Company. Lord Wichcote would not have had him brought here out of benevolent philanthropy. He wanted something.

The flickering torchlight imparted a hellish cast to the frantic activity below. Red-glazed hands reached up for him, taking hold of his legs and pulling him roughly down. Even before his feet touched solid ground, other hands were busy at the straps and buckles of his harness. Nearby, Longinus was being similarly attended to. The servants were well practised at this work, and in less than a minute had extracted both men. The Personal Flotation Devices were dragged to the far side of the roof; Quare surmised that the bladders could not be vented near the torches owing to the danger of an explosion. But that was the least of his worries.

The servants had not taken away his sword, as he had feared they would. Nor did they make any attempt to restrain him. In truth, it was all he could do to remain upright. His legs seemed to have become unfamiliar with the ground . . . either that, or the ground had grown less stable in the time of his absence from it. He would have liked nothing better than to lie down on the rooftop and close his eyes until the world stopped wobbling and his queasy stomach settled. But this was no time to give way to weakness. A grinning Longinus was striding towards him. He had lost his wig in the flight, and his bare scalp gleamed in the torchlight, putting Quare in mind of a vulture. He drew his sword.

Longinus stopped short, smile vanishing. 'I confess I had expected a warmer thanks for having saved your life, Mr Quare.' He motioned with one hand for the servants to stay back.

'Take another step and you will find it hot indeed, I promise you,' Quare said. 'Why have you brought me to Lord Wichcote's house?'

'Ah, so you recognize it, then. Good.'

'Lord Wichcote was no friend to Master Magnus, and he is no friend to the Worshipful Company, either.'

'In that you are quite wrong,' Longinus said. 'His lordship has long been a benefactor of the Worshipful Company and a close associate of Master Magnus – I will not say a friend, because that gentleman, God rest his troubled soul, was not capable of genuine friendship with any creature besides a cat. But the two men, for all their differences, had a genuine respect for each other and worked together often, if behind the scenes. They did not always see eye to eye, but when it came to the interests of guild and country, there was no space between them. Only, it suited them to have the world believe them enemies. A secret ally is often of more value than a friend whom all the world can see, as this night has amply demonstrated. So put up your sword, Mr Quare. You have nothing to fear from Lord Wichcote.'

'I think not,' said Quare, his glance shifting to the surrounding servants, all of whom were watching intently. Yet not one of them made a threatening move in his direction. It seemed that Longinus had some authority over them.

'A shame,' Longinus said meanwhile, and, moving faster than Quare would have guessed possible in a man of his age, drew his own sword.

The next few seconds were a blur to Quare. He had thought Aylesford a skilled swordsman, but Longinus was in another class altogether. Quare managed two weak parries before the sword was wrenched from his hand as if by an invisible force; it clattered to the ground, where one of the servants picked it up. Quare, clutching the wrist of his now empty hand, which had been rendered numb and useless by a blow he had not seen coming – or going, for that matter – could only gape in astonishment as Longinus sheathed his sword.

'Your technique is woefully inadequate,' the man remarked with a sad shake of his head. He did not appear in the least winded. 'I see that I will have my work cut out to make a respectable regulator out of you, as Master Magnus wished me to do.'

'And what of Lord Wichcote's wishes?' Quare demanded. 'He is your true master, is he not? How much did he pay you to betray me?'

'Why, nothing at all.'

'I think I shall call you Judas rather than Longinus. The name suits you better.'

'I prefer Longinus. But if you would call me something other, then my true name will suffice for now. Josiah Wichcote, sir, at your service.' He gave a small bow.

Quare's mouth gaped wider still. 'L-lord Wichcote?' he stammered at last.

'The same.' As he spoke, it seemed to Quare that the man stood taller, straighter; it was as if he had cast off a subtle disguise. 'No doubt you have many questions,' he continued. 'I will answer them as best I can. But first, I intend to change out of these clothes and enjoy a hot bath. I invite you to do the same. I will have you shown to your rooms; fresh clothes and anything else you may require will be brought to you there. Then, sir, we shall dine together, and I shall tell you everything I know about the circumstances of Master Magnus's death . . . and other things you will, I dare say, find equally incredible.'

With that, Longinus – Lord Wichcote, rather, if his assertion could be believed – bowed again and took his leave. Surrounded by a bevy of servants, he strode across the roof and descended through a trap door some distance from the skylight with the ease of a much younger man. Most of the remaining servants busied themselves with the Personal Flotation Devices and harnesses, but a pair of them – including the one who had picked up his sword – presented themselves to Quare.

'If you please, sir,' said the one holding his sword, 'we will conduct you to your rooms now.'

'Is that really Lord Wichcote?' he couldn't help asking.

'Oh, indeed, yes,' the servant replied with a note of pride in his voice. 'His lordship is quite the swordsman, is he not?'

The feeling was only just returning to Quare's hand. 'The

best I have seen,' he answered, flexing tingling fingers; it seemed to him that Lord Wichcote would be a match even for Grimalkin. And yet, he reminded himself, Grimalkin must have bested the man two nights ago, when she had stolen the hunter. Of course, that was no proof of superior swordsmanship, for he, in turn, had bested Grimalkin. Luck and surprise went a long way.

'If you please, sir,' the servant repeated, gesturing towards the trap door.

'I am your prisoner,' Quare said. 'My pleasure has nothing to do with it.'

'Our guest, rather,' said the other servant, who had been silent until now. 'His lordship has charged us to see to your comfort. We are at your disposal, Mr Quare.'

'I am glad to hear it,' Quare said. 'In that case, I will have my sword back.'

The servant holding the weapon did not hesitate; he passed it back to Quare, hilt first.

Quare accepted it warily, fearing a trick. But the two servants regarded him placidly as he held it. For a long moment, their eyes met, and Quare considered then rejected the idea of fighting his way out; he suspected a second attempt would end no better than the first, and quite possibly worse. The return of his sword had not made him any less a prisoner; if anything, it had made him more conscious of his helplessness. Still, he felt better for having it. He sheathed the weapon. 'Lead on,' he said.

Later, as he basked in the waters of a hot, perfumed bath, taking care to keep his bandages dry, Quare reflected that there were jails and then there were jails. His cell in the guild hall had been spare but comfortable, with a pallet to stretch out on, a desk and writing implements, even a roaring fire. But the luxury of his present confinement beggared all comparison. Upon entering the rooms, he had caught his breath at the sumptuousness of the furnishings and other appointments; he had never seen their like, not even in the guild hall. Everywhere was colour and the shine of metal in candlelight; he felt like a savage stumbled into the midst of a civilization he could only marvel at without understanding. There were some objects here he had no name for and whose purpose was as far beyond his grasp as the moon, though their beauty was equally evident. Even the many things he did recognize – the oil paintings and tapestries on the walls, the gold-embroidered curtains hanging before the tall windows, the trompe l'oeil scene of receding clouds and cherubs upon the ceiling, the silk-upholstered chairs and settees, the great four-poster bed – seemed different from similar items in his experience not just in quality but in essence, as if he had entered a realm of Platonic ideals.

After descending through the trap door in the rooftop, he had found himself in a different part of the house entirely from the attic workshop that had been his destination two nights ago. This confused him, but he kept his questions to himself, trying to take everything in as the two servants Lord Wichcote had assigned to him bustled him down a set of stairs, along a sequence of branching corridors and thus into the rooms that, he was told, had been prepared for him; though whether that meant Lord Wichcote had always planned to bring him here, the men would not say.

He could hear them now, moving about behind the flimsy Chinese screen that did not confer privacy so much as the illusion of it. The unfolded panels depicted a vertiginous, mist-shrouded mountain landscape whose gentle colours and sinuous lines appeared drawn from dream rather than nature. It seemed to Quare, made drowsy by the scented waters of the bath, from which tendrils of steam rose like extrusions from the painting itself, that he might, by some small effort of will, drift across whatever boundary separated this world from that one, and thus make his escape. He closed his eyes and imagined himself standing upon those lofty crags, gazing into the fog-patched depths of a strange country.

But though the illusion was a pleasant one, he could not long sustain it; the noise of the servants as they arranged things in the room, and the gradual cooling of the water, kept Quare from entering fully into the peaceful reverie that lay almost but not quite within reach. At last, after he heard the servants leave the room, he rose from the bath. A towel had been laid on a nearby table; he took it and rubbed himself dry, in the process returning welcome heat to his body. He could see from the state of his bandages that his wounds had not started bleeding again.

Wrapped in the towel, he stepped from behind the screen. A fire blazed in the hearth, and fresh clothes had been laid out for him on the four-poster bed; of his old clothes, including Mr Puddinge's mangy second-best coat, there was no sign. There were a number of clocks in the room – what he had seen so far of the house suggested a quantity and variety of timepieces that rivalled the collection of the guild hall. However, no two were in agreement; each kept its own time, and Quare felt a strange disorientation as he crossed to the bed, as if he were traversing a score of tiny intersecting universes in which different measures of time held sway. Parts of his body seemed to be surging ahead or falling behind; more than once on that epic journey of a dozen feet or so he had to pause and catch his breath, wait for his head to clear.

He had intended to dress himself and go to demand answers of Lord Wichcote, but when he reached the bed, he fell into it, and was at once deeply asleep.

Quare woke with a start, shivering atop the bed. The candles in the room had burned low, and the fire was a feeble flickering. His thoughts were thick and muddled, as after a night of drinking. Yet he had not had a drop ... which led him to wonder if he had been drugged somehow. His deep and dreamless sleep had not been a natural one, or so it seemed to him now. And how long had he slept? The clocks in the room gave no answer, or, rather, too many answers, impossible to interpret. A gauzy light shone through the curtains that hid the windows. Drawing them aside, he saw that it was morning; his window overlooked a large green garden that, like the house itself, was filled with an abundance of timepieces. It reminded him of the time garden at the guild hall, but seemed even more capacious ... and, if possible, capricious, for the variety of horological devices on display, even judged by outward appearance alone, surpassed anything in his experience, ranging from the primitive to the sophisticated to the downright incomprehensible, and, rather than being set aside for study and contemplation, as in the guild hall, the devices here were overgrown with vegetation, like ancient ruins peeking out from a resurgent wilderness. Whatever the truth of Lord Wichcote's relationship to the Worshipful Company, Quare reflected, his relationship to time was an eccentric one.

He dressed in the clothes that had been laid out for him. His watch he found tucked into a pocket of the waistcoat; it had stopped running and thus was of no use in determining the hour. Still, the familiar heft of it gave him courage, like a friendly talisman amidst so much that was strange. Even more reassuring was the continued presence of his sword, which he now strapped to his side.

Dressed in clothes that were finer than he had ever worn, and that fitted better, too, than anything in his late and lamentable wardrobe, as though Lord Wichcote had known his measurements and had had the clothes tailored for him, Quare felt ready to confront his host. He half expected to find the door locked, but it opened freely. The hallway beyond was empty, lit by tapers set in gleaming sconces at intervals along the walls. Of his two minders from the night before, there was no sign. Quare paused, uncertain which way to go. But he supposed it didn't matter. He wasn't going to retreat to his rooms and wait there to be summoned. With a shrug, he set off down the hall, his mind on exploration rather than escape.

Closed doors lined both sides of the hall; he stopped before them in turn and listened, but heard nothing from within; when he essayed one, he found that it was locked. Pushing on, he reached a stairway and followed it down; on the next landing, he again chose a direction at random. All the while, the only sounds were his own footsteps and the busy ticking of the many clocks set on the walls or upon shelves or small tables, all of them out of step with each other. His earlier impression had been of a sort of temporal anarchy, with every clock face displaying a different hour and the audible beat of the mechanisms following no common measure, like the mindless clamour of insects crowding a hot summer's night, but now it struck him that there was order here, too, for it must take considerable effort to ensure that the clocks did not agree in any apparent way. The cumulative effect was claustrophobic; Quare felt hedged in on all sides, as if he were pushing his way through a dense, thorny thicket. The farther he went down the hall, the worse this sensation grew. The air itself seemed resistant to his progress. Was he actually moving more slowly? He halted and took a breath, trying to steady himself and clear his head.

A sharp edge was laid across his throat. A hand had snaked from behind to press a blade there; at its touch, his perceptions cleared, though he did not dare to so much as twitch a muscle. The voice of Longinus – Lord Wichcote, rather – sounded low in his ear.

'Tick-tock, Mr Quare – you're dead.'

Quare swallowed.

The knife lifted, and Quare turned – measuredly – to face the man who had either rescued or abducted him . . . he wasn't quite sure which. Perhaps both.

'''Tis worse even than I thought,' the older man said as he appraised Quare from over the tip of the knife like a butcher examining a side of beef to determine how best to flense it from the bone. Like Quare, he had changed his clothes; but it was more as if he had changed his very skin, for there was no trace of the servant in the man who faced him now, dressed in the bright finery of a foppish aristocrat, complete with white-powdered skin and wig, and a dark beauty mark on his left cheek. Yet Quare, whose experiences of the last few days had given him a new perspective on such things, wondered if this was as much of a costume as the servant's garb the man had worn earlier – chosen to facilitate the playing of a role. 'If I had been your Mr Aylesford, you would have been dead now, Mr Quare. And you call yourself a regulator?'

'I . . . I would have answers, my lord.'

'Would you indeed?' Lord Wichcote tucked the blade into the sleeve of his coat, sliding it hilt-first under the cuff as if this were the natural repository of such objects. 'First you must get into the habit of calling me Longinus, not Lord Wichcote or my lord or any other such advertisement of identity or rank. I assure you, I shall take no offence. Our lives may depend upon it.'

'You make demands on me, sir, but you do not give reasons. You rescue me, for which I am not ungrateful, only to drug me – for I can only assume that some drug was placed into my bath last night, so precipitately did I fall asleep afterwards. And now you put a knife to my throat. You promised me answers. I will hear them, or I will take my leave . . . and you may try to stop me if you like.' He laid his hand on the hilt of his sword but did not draw it.

'I think we both know how that would turn out,' Longinus said with a dismissive shrug. 'Even if you made it past me, which is highly unlikely, you would not last for long on the streets outside, with both the watch and the Old Wolf's agents looking for you. You are correct about the drug. I will not apologize for it. You were in need of a good night's sleep. As for the knife, I wanted to test your alertness, your reflexes. Even I should have had difficulty in creeping up on a properly trained regulator. Yet you showed not the slightest awareness of my presence until the blade touched your skin.'

'I am still not fully recovered from the drug you administered. My senses are somewhat clouded, as I told you. These infernal clocks of yours – the noise of them . . .'

'Indeed? You interest me more and more, Mr Quare. Come, sir: let us eat and drink. You must be famished.'

'What is the time?'

'Why, any time you like,' Longinus answered, gesturing at the clocks that lined the hallway. 'You may have your pick of the time in this house.'

'I would prefer to know the true time.'

'True? If there is such a thing, a timepiece will not tell you.

You slept through the night; it is now morning – let that suffice. Come, let us break our fast together. There is much you need to know.' He gestured Quare forwards.

Thoughts all awhirl, Quare complied, keeping hold of his sword hilt and his questions. His host led him down another flight of stairs and into a dining room where a buffet had been laid out. Large windows looked out on the garden he had seen from his room; the day was bright and clear, at least by London standards. Quare took in the side table laden with fillets of beef, fish, mutton cutlets and poultry, along with sausages, omelettes and soft-boiled eggs, assorted varieties of bread, jams and orange marmalade, plates of cut fruit, and cold game pies. Liveried servants were waiting to pour tea or coffee or chocolate. Here, too, an assortment of clocks kept their sundry times.

'I like a country-style breakfast,' commented Longinus, nodding to the servants as he led Quare to the dining table and gestured for him to sit down. A footman had already pulled a chair out for him and was waiting, like an automaton designed for the purpose, to slide it back.

'Will others be joining us?' Quare asked as he sat. The table could have accommodated thirty, and there was food enough for twice that number.

Longinus walked around the table to take a seat opposite him. 'I thought an intimate breakfast might be just the thing to get us off on the proper footing,' he said as he settled into the upholstered chair another footman had pulled out for him. Already plates of food were appearing on the table. 'What will you have to drink, Mr Quare? I like a strong cup of coffee in the morning,' he added as a man stepped forward to pour him one.

'Coffee will serve,' said Quare, and found this instantly

supplied, as were all his other wants. Still, he did not sip from the cup, nor eat any of the food.

Longinus, who had begun eating, looked up at Quare.

'I'm afraid I don't entirely trust you, my lo— er, Longinus. I can't help but wonder if you are feeding me some other drug or even poison.'

'Yet you must trust me, Mr Quare. We need not be friends, but we must not be enemies. Partners, rather. We need each other. And England needs us.'

'That is all very well. I hope I am as patriotic as the next fellow. But actions speak louder than words. You expect me to trust you, yet what do you offer in return?'

'I have already given you your freedom.'

'Am I free? Could I get up from this table and walk out of that door and leave this house?'

'I have explained to you why that would be most unwise.'

'Yes. But would you seek to prevent me from leaving if I should nevertheless choose to go?'

'I would.'

Quare nodded. 'So, we understand each other. I remain your prisoner, though my accommodations are certainly improved, and for that, at least, I do thank you.'

'I promised you answers, and you shall see that I keep my promises. As for the food – you may do as you like. I cannot force you to eat. But speaking as an old soldier, it is wise to eat when one can while in the midst of a campaign.'

Quare's misgivings were grave as ever, yet he could not ignore the promptings of his belly, nor the tempting smells of the food. He needed to eat, if only to keep up his strength. Once he began, he could not stop; he had not realized he was so famished, and the food was delicious. He ate everything the servants put in front of him. For some time, he was too busy to ask any questions, or, for that matter, to think of them. But at last his mind and stomach regained their equilibrium, and he sat back to regard Longinus, who was watching him in turn. His host had finished with his own breakfast and was on his third cup of coffee. Quare cleared his throat. 'That was very good, my l— that is, Longinus.'

'My cook is first-rate,' he replied.

'I have so many questions, I scarce know where to begin.'

'That is understandable.' Without looking away, Longinus made a gesture of dismissal, and Quare watched as the servants stopped whatever they had been doing and trooped from the room. When the last of them had gone, closing the door behind him, their master leaned back in his chair and said, 'Ask me whatever you please, and I will answer as plainly and forthrightly as I can.'

'Anything?'

'Anything at all.'

'Why are all your clocks out of step with each other?'

'I beg your pardon?'

'Your clocks, sir. Each reflects a different time. It was the same in the workshop of Master Magnus. I used to think that disorder a reflection or product of the master's unruly genius, but now I suspect there is something else at work.'

'You are correct,' Longinus answered. 'Your question cuts straight to the heart of the matter. Here, sir. Examine these.' And so saying, Longinus drew from his coat no fewer than five pocket watches of various designs, which he set on the table and pushed towards Quare.

Quare picked them up one by one. Each registered a different time. Which, if any, was correct, he had no way of knowing. He slid the watches back towards Longinus, who restored them to their original places on his person.

'Why do you carry those?' asked Quare, baffled. 'What possible use can they be?'

'They protect me.' He gestured to encompass the room. 'As do all these other timepieces.'

'Protect you? From what?'

'What is time, Mr Quare?' Longinus asked in turn. 'What do we measure with our clocks and watches? Is it some ethereal substance, akin to the grains of sand that dribble through an hourglass or the drops of water that power a Chinese clock? Is it, rather, an exhalation, a product of some reaction invisible to us, like the smoke that rises from a burning candle? Or is it simply the creation of man, an illusion that has no objective existence at all? I would be most interested to hear your thoughts on the matter.'

'Master Magnus once told me that time is the mind of God in motion.'

'Yes, I have heard him say so. But alas, I do not believe in God any longer, and so I have had to formulate my own understanding of the matter. Does that shock you?'

'It baffles me, rather. The proofs of God's existence are all around us; it seems to me that one would have to be blind not to see them.'

'Perhaps I am blind. But I hope you will grant that a man may learn to navigate his way through the world without sight. Why, I have known blind men – and women, too – whose other senses have, as it were, become all the sharper in compensation for the lack of it. One of the keenest horologists I ever met was a blind man able to repair time-pieces by touch and hearing alone. So it may be with a man like myself, blind to what others take for granted. Certainly I do not mean to disparage the genius of your late master. His insights into time and horology were profound, and I never met a quicker, more fertile mind, one better able, moreover, to turn its fancies into facts. And what wondrous facts! Nor did our differences of opinion on this and other matters prevent our long partnership from being, on the whole, a happy and successful one. I mourn his passing, sir, and honour his memory: truly, I do. And I will have more to say about that in due course. But I have pursued my own researches into the nature of time, and I think it fair to say that I have come to an understanding no less profound than your late master's.'

'I should like to hear it,' Quare said.

'I believe that time is another dimension. A fourth dimension, if you will. It is like a river in which we find our-selves, a great river stretching into the unknowable distance of the future and the irretrievable distance of the past. Yet we know only an infinitesimal portion of this river. Of its depths we can say nothing. Nor do I believe that we are afloat upon its surface; that is an illusion of perspective. Rather, it surrounds us on all sides, and the heights to which it extends above us are as infinite as the depths below. What we perceive as the passing of time, the steady beat of seconds and minutes that we measure out with our clever clocks, the signs of aging that we recognize with dismay upon our faces and the faces of our loved ones, which testify to the briefness of our earthly lives, the progression of the seasons, which, like a rolling wheel, both repeats its revolution and moves forward towards some culmination we cannot know, are but visible indications of an invisible force, just as the rustling of leaves in a tree signifies the passing of a breeze we cannot otherwise perceive. In this great river – or ocean, if you prefer – of time, we are but bits of debris carried along by the current. We mistake, in our ignorance and arrogance, the flow of that current for our own movement, and flatter ourselves that we give shape and direction to our lives by our actions and beliefs. But in fact, the vast majority of us are quite helpless, and all our vaunted intelligence is lost on inconsequential ephemera, bubbles and rainbows, rather than on the mysteries of this wondrous medium that surrounds us.'

'An interesting theory,' said Quare.

At which, as if acknowledging the scepticism behind Quare's politeness, Longinus gave a bark of laughter. 'It gets better, sir. Imagine, then, a great sea, in which we humans are carried along on a particular current, just as, in our own seas, ships may travel from one place to another simply by catching a certain stream. But would it not be strange if, in this sea of time, there were not other currents? And would it not be stranger still if there were not other creatures also living in this sea – just as, in our own watery seas, there is an abundance of life – life, moreover, that is not captive to one current or to any of them, but may move with freedom and purpose throughout the entire medium?'

'What sort of creatures do you mean?'

'Call them what you like: gods or angels, demons or dragons. Fairies, even. Creatures of myth and legend, though quite otherwise than those myths and legends paint them. Names are unimportant; what matters is that they exist. Some are mindless, some harmless, but others are as intelligent as we, or more so, and far more dangerous. These creatures can take many forms. What they look like in their own realm we cannot even imagine; we see them as they choose to appear to us, within the bounds of what our senses are equipped to perceive. Their own senses are quite different from ours, as you might expect, and their perceptions of time far more complex and acute. To some of them, the regular ticking of a clock has a scent as well as a sound – you understand that I am speaking metaphorically – a scent that attracts them to us, as the scent of blood in the water will attract a shark. That is why I keep all the timepieces in my house and on my person out of step. To muddy the waters, so to speak, and thus keep these predators at bay.'

'I see.' Quare did not know what to make of the man before him. Was he a lunatic? His words were almost absurdly fanciful . . . yet not without interest. 'What of a workshop like Sir Thaddeus's, where an army of clocks marches to the same drummer?'

'Such a place is like a beacon in the dark. A veritable light-house. Whether he knows it or not – and I believe he knows it very well – Sir Thaddeus has been visited by these creatures. Indeed, I believe he has been suborned by them.'

'To what end?'

'Nothing good. They would use him to extend their influence among us, to make our dimension, into which they cannot fully enter, or long remain, a subsidiary of their own – or such is my belief. In short, they war against us. They are a deadlier enemy than the French, more powerful, more subtle . . . more to be feared. Because they are not human.'

'And you have proof of this, I suppose?'

'There are many proofs. You have held one of them in your hands.'

Quare felt a chill. 'The hunter.'

'Yes, the hunter.'

'What did you mean earlier when you said that the hunter had killed Master Magnus?'

At this, Longinus pushed back his chair and stood. He began to pace alongside the edge of the table, his hands clasped behind him. When he reached the far end of the table, he turned and started back. Not until he had drawn level with

Quare did he speak again. 'I wish that damned device had never come into my possession. In truth, part of me was glad to surrender it. And yet, now, I would give anything to have it back. Once he had that watch, Magnus turned the whole of his formidable intellect upon it. He was convinced that, properly understood, it would give us the means to defeat the French for good and all. Especially after the slaughter of his cats, he became obsessed with it. I tried to warn him, but, scornful as ever of my theories of time, he would not heed my entreaties. He was, to the last, a man of science and reason, and he had faith that science and reason would unlock the secrets even of a mechanism whose very existence flouted both. Faith, Mr Quare, is a dangerous thing. Faith in God, faith in reason – each is blinding in its own way. That is why I strive to be as free of it as I can. I recommend the same approach to you, sir. A regulator, above all other men, should take nothing on faith. His life, no less than the success of his mission, depends upon it. But I digress. Magnus knew that blood was the fuel that drove the engine of the thing, but how that was possible, and to what end, he did not know. And it was this that he was determined to discover, using his own blood to power the device while he experimented upon it. After what had happened to the cats, you will understand that I had no desire to be present during those experiments.'

'Quite,' said Quare. Even now the memory of his experience with the hunter was fresh enough to make his blood run cold.

'We had arranged that I should monitor his progress and his safety at regular intervals,' Longinus continued. 'Every half an hour, I would send a signal to him via bell pull, and he would signal back the same way. Thus did we continue through that day and into the night. At last, early in the

243

morning, at two-thirty, to be precise, there came no response to my signal. I rushed back to his workroom, and there I discovered my friend stretched upon the floor, on his back, his glasses knocked askew and the eyes behind them open wide and staring sightlessly at whatever horror it is that doomed men see. In his hand was clutched the foul mechanism, glowing cherry red and pulsing like some loathsome organ. Even as I watched, the glow faded, and the thing returned to its former pale appearance – but no paler now than the man who held it, drained of every last drop of blood and stone cold dead.'

Quare could not repress a shudder.

'I was not eager to touch the thing. Nor did I have the chance to do so. Before I could act, a half-dozen of my fellow servants burst into the workroom – men, I saw at once, loyal to Sir Thaddeus. There was nothing I could do against so many, not without revealing myself, and so I stood aside as they gathered the notes that Magnus had been writing upon his desk and, with a callousness that injured my heart to see, wrested the timepiece from my poor friend's fingers – which, strangely, were already locked in rigor, though I do not believe he had expired more than ten minutes before my entry. Nonetheless, such was the case, and to free the timepiece from his frozen grasp the servant had first to break those supple fingers, which, as you well know, sir, were as beautiful and well-made as the rest of him was stunted and grotesque – the hands of an angel affixed to the body of a gargoyle. I felt as if I were witnessing a desecration, and I confess I had to look away, though I do not believe I shall ever be able to forget the sounds of his bones snapping like twigs. But forgive me – I did not mean to cause you distress!'

And indeed, Quare had found Longinus's account of

Master Magnus's end distressing, but not entirely for the reasons the other assumed. Now he too stood, leaning over the table to demand of Longinus: 'Did you say two-thirty?'

'Yes. Why? Is there something significant about that time?'

Quare sighed, shoulders drooping. 'You could say that. It was approximately the time of my death.'

'I beg your pardon?'

'There is a particular detail of my brief acquaintance with Mr Aylesford that I withheld from Sir Thaddeus, for reasons that will become obvious. Following the brawl at the Pig and Rooster, Aylesford and I took refuge at the lodgings of one of the barmaids. I was all but insensible – I realize now that I had been drugged; indeed, I believe that the assassin slipped something into all of our drinks that night, to facilitate his cowardly butchery, but for some reason the drug was slower to act on me than on my unfortunate fellows. My last memory of the night is staggering through empty streets, supported by Aylesford and Clara. When I awoke the next morning, Aylesford was gone, and Clara reported having woken during the night to find Aylesford and myself engaged in an act of sodomy – though in fact, what she witnessed was a crime far worse. Murder. For as I discovered shortly thereafter, I had been stabbed in the back – a wound angled towards the heart, sir, and deep enough to have reached it. Yet there was little blood, no pain to speak of, and, obviously, no death. You may imagine the look of shock on Aylesford's face when I surprised him later at my lodgings! Because I could not account in any rational way for having survived such a wound, I looked to the irrational, and fixed upon my experiences with the hunter earlier that day, when the device had drunk my blood; it seemed to me that the two events must be related. Somehow, though I could not guess by what means, the watch had saved me – had restored me to life, or, rather, taken away my death. I do not know the exact moment that Aylesford slipped his knife into my heart, but it was early in the morning by Clara's testimony. Surely the fact of Master Magnus's death at approximately the same time can be no coincidence – not with that infernal watch involved. Just as, earlier, it had taken the lives of all those cats, so, too, or so I must believe, it transferred my death to Master Magnus, and, perhaps, his life to me.' Quare slumped back into his chair. 'It was I who killed Master Magnus. Not the hunter. His blood is on my hands.'

'That . . . that is most interesting.'

'Interesting? Is that all you can say?'

'Your pardon. I understand your feelings. Yet you must not blame yourself. How were you to know what would come of handling that watch? Magnus himself did not comprehend it, nor did he forbear from risking his life to unlock its secrets.'

'How did such a thing come into your possession in the first place?'

'I will tell you. But first – what of your wound? Has it healed?'

'Honestly, I have been afraid to look.'

'Let us look now.'

'Are you a physician, sir?'

'I have some small skill in physic.'

'Very well.' Standing, Quare removed his coat and then his waistcoat and shirt, laying them over the back of the chair. Longinus, meanwhile, had come around the table to stand beside Quare, who now turned away from him, displaying his back. Quickly, using the dagger in his sleeve, he cut away the bandages.

'Extraordinary.' Longinus more breathed than spoke the word.

'What is it? What do you see?'

'It is as you said. There is a puncture below the left shoulder blade. I confess, I should expect to see such a wound upon a corpse, not a living and breathing man. There is no blood; the wound is quite clean. The flesh shows no sign of infection or of healing. And you say it does not pain you?'

'There was some pain at first, but now it merely itches, like the bite of a bedbug.'

'Most extraordinary,' Longinus repeated. 'May I examine it more closely?'

Quare nodded. He heard the rattle of metal from the table behind him and turned to see Longinus holding up a butter knife.

'I do not have my instruments to hand, but this should serve admirably as a probe.'

'I am not a scone, sir.'

'That had not escaped my notice. Try to relax, Mr Quare.'

'That is easy for you to say.'

'I will stop the instant there is any pain.' He motioned for Quare to turn.

Sighing, Quare complied and braced himself. He felt the cold but gentle touch of the butter knife at his back, then an altogether unsettling sensation as the flat blade slipped under a flap of skin and entered the wound. He shuddered, gasping, hands fisting at his sides; the knife halted but was not withdrawn.

'Mr Quare?'

'I cannot say it is pleasant,' he answered through clenched teeth, 'but there is no pain.'

The progress of the knife resumed, accompanied by an outbreak of cold sweat upon his forehead. His insides spasmed most unpleasantly, and he felt his gorge rise – less from the sensation of the intrusion than the unnaturalness of it. 'Take it out,' he said at last, when he could stand it no longer.

Longinus did so at once. 'I apologize for any discomfort,' he said.

Quare's body was trembling beneath a sheen of sweat. Speech was beyond him. He held to the back of the chair to keep himself standing. Spots swam before his eyes.

'You had better sit down,' came Longinus's voice; and then Quare felt the man guiding him into the chair. 'Put your head between your knees.'

Again, Quare complied. It did seem to help.

'Here.'

He raised his head to see Longinus offering him a tumbler filled with a dram of amber liquid.

'Brandy,' he said.

Quare took the glass and drained it at a swallow. The liquor flushed new vigour through his limbs. 'Thank you,' he said.

'You're most welcome. I think I could do with one myself. Can I get you another?'

Quare shook his head and stood. He lifted his shirt from the back of the chair and began to dress. 'Well? What is your diagnosis?'

Longinus, who had crossed to the side table to pour himself a glass of brandy, tossed it back before answering. 'Diagnosis?' he echoed, setting down the empty glass. 'Asclepius himself could not diagnose your condition. You are a walking dead man, sir. A living and breathing impossibility. That is my diagnosis.'

'But . . .'

'I do not doubt that your surmise is correct, and the hunter is holding your death at bay by some mechanism unknown to me. Whether permanently or temporarily, I cannot say. It would be interesting to learn if you are proof now against all mortal injury – in short, whether the watch has conferred a kind of immortality upon you. Unfortunately, I can think of no way to test this hypothesis without risking your life.'

'Yes, most unfortunate, that,' Quare said, shrugging into his coat.

'You asked how the watch came into my possession,' Longinus said. 'Come, Mr Quare. A turn in the garden will do you good, I think. And I shall tell you as we walk.'

Longinus crossed the room and opened a glazed door leading out to a terrace. He gestured for Quare to precede him. The morning air was cool and refreshing, the sun bright, the garden green and flowering, woven through with meandering white gravel paths and sequestered behind high brick walls that screened off the neighbouring houses. The two men set off along a path, the crunching of their footsteps over the crushed stones and shells loud and vigorous in the hushed air. The bustle and clamour of London seemed miles away.

'Are we safe in the open like this?' Quare inquired. 'Won't the Old Wolf send his regulators against us?'

'Not even Sir Thaddeus would dare to trespass here,' Longinus replied with confidence. 'My royal cousin, His Majesty, would look most unkindly upon any such intrusion, as the Old Wolf knows very well indeed. No, you may set your mind at ease on that score, Mr Quare. As long as we remain behind these walls, we are untouchable – at least, by Sir Thaddeus and his minions. Of course, we have other enemies to worry about. Nor can we remain behind these walls for ever. But I think we are safe enough for now. Besides, we are both armed, are we not? And though you cannot see them, rest assured that my own men are present, watching over us.'

Quare glanced about but, indeed, could not detect another soul. 'They are very well hidden.'

Longinus inclined his head. 'Now, as to the watch. I have been an avid collector of timepieces for many years, even before my partnership with Magnus. At first it was the exteriors that attracted me: I admired the richness and beauty of ornamentation lavished upon certain clocks and watches, caring nothing for the refinement of their inner works or even how accurately they kept the time. But gradually my interest shifted, and, as I began to pursue my researches into the nature of time, I sought out timepieces of advanced or eccentric design – it was this which brought me to the attention of Master Magnus. He viewed me as little more than a dilettante at first, a mere dabbler, but he did not scorn my wealth and influence, which he perceived, quite rightly, could benefit the Worshipful Company. In exchange for my patronage, I insisted that he take me on as an apprentice – and this he did. Our association was a secret one; not even the Old Wolf knew of it. But from that time, we proceeded in parallel, Magnus and I, our respective researches mutually reinforcing despite their obvious differences. In truth, we learned from each other. My experiments became more rigorously scientific, while he learned to be less scornful of the more esoteric branches of horological inquiry. When my apprenticeship was complete, I joined the ranks of the regulators, just as you did, though, again, the association remained secret, and I functioned more along the lines of a special agent, continuing to undertake my own investigations and acquisitions alongside the occasional mission that Magnus did not wish, for one reason or another, to entrust to the common run of regulator. And so it was, some twenty-odd years ago, that I first began to hear rumours of a timepiece like no other, a clock or watch –

opinions varied on this point – that was to other timepieces as the philosopher's stone is to these stones beneath our feet. Though "rumours" may be putting it too strongly – hints, rather, of something strange and anomalous, of a clockmaker who might as well have been a wizard out of some old fairy tale. When I mentioned them to Magnus, he dismissed them out of hand and advised me against chasing phantoms. Needless to add, I did not heed him. In those days, Mr Quare, I was young and fit – well, younger and fitter – and liked nothing better than a good adventure; my fortune allowed me the luxury of chasing whatever phantoms I pleased. I was absent from England for a number of years, and my quest took me throughout Europe, into Russia, and farther east, to Mongolia, China, and Japan, and thence to India, the Holy Land and Africa, and finally back to Europe again. Such marvels I encountered in my travels, horological and otherwise, that we might walk from here to Edinburgh before I had related even a tenth of them. Yet always the object of my search remained tantalizingly out of reach; the rumours, as it were, seemed to recede before me, drawing me ever onwards. And such, I concluded, was the case – I was being led a merry chase.'

'By whom?' asked Quare.

'Why, the wizard himself – or so I convinced myself. It seemed that wherever I set foot, he had preceded me and left behind traces of his presence designed less to throw me off the track than to entice me farther along it. There was something flattering about it. I felt as if I were being tested like some knight of old, that I must prove myself worthy before I should be permitted to find the grail which I sought.'

'That being the watch, I assume.'

'I did not know it at the time. But patience, Mr Quare – you shall hear all. Indeed, you shall be the first to hear it. Not even Magnus knew the whole story. He would not have believed it. I did not fully believe it myself for many years, although it happened to me. I thought much of it a dream. And perhaps it was. But dreams, too, can be real. Never doubt it, sir.'

PART TWO

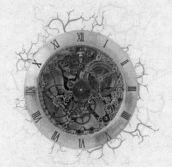

8

Wachter's Folly

I REACHED MÄRCHEN WITH THE LAST ECHOES OF THE HOUR STILL haunting the air. Snow was falling, as it had done on and off during my ascent of Mount Coglians. I was exhausted, hungry, chilled to the bone. My rucksack seemed to weigh a thousand pounds. Even my hat was heavy. Yet I was in high spirits. I had been back in Europe for some months, having sailed from Africa to Italy, then made my way up the peninsula and across the Italian Alps into Austria. Winter was drawing nigh, and I was glad to be away from the oppressive heat of the climes in which I had spent much of the last year. I was travelling incognito, in the guise of a journeyman, following the clues – or riddles, rather – left by that nameless horologist whose footsteps I had dogged halfway round the world. Wherever I went, I found evidence that he had preceded me. Among the timepieces brought to me for examination and repair in each new town or city, I would find one or two that bore the unmistakable signs of his touch – strange, capricious-seeming alterations whose only purpose, as far as I could tell, was the introduction of random inaccuracies.

By random I mean simply that they were not regular, as, for example, the loss of a certain number of minutes in a day, but rather unpredictable from day to day and even moment to moment. A clock might run fast and then slow, then speed up again, for instance, all within the space of an hour. Needless to say, the mechanisms responsible for such variation were impressive, and quite often beyond my understanding – I sent drawings back to Magnus, and he incorporated many of them into subsequent inventions of his own. Always there would be a clue concealed somewhere in the timepiece itself, or in its altered functioning, that, once divined, led me to my next destination. And this was true, by the way, regardless of the type of timepiece. Not just mechanical clocks driven by springs or weights but clepsydrae and other water clocks, hemicycles, hourglasses, even gnomons. Nothing, it seemed, was beneath the interest, or beyond the expertise, of my quarry.

I did not expect to end my quest in Märchen. Indeed, I was not even aware of the town's existence until, travelling on foot across the lower slopes of Mount Coglians, I happened to hear, from out of the cloud-steeped heights above me, the tolling of bells that struck an hour at odds with what my pocket watch assured me was the correct time. I paused to examine my map but could find no trace of a town anywhere near by, save for the place I had spent the previous night. Of course, I could have been hearing the echo of a clock from elsewhere: the peaks and valleys of the mountains had a way of playing tricks with sound. Still, I decided to investigate. Over the next five hours, as I picked my way up the side of the mountain, following trails that seemed better suited to sheep than men, the clock struck thrice only. And not once did the tolling of the bells – one tone overlying the next, echo building upon echo to extend across the frozen surface of the air, then dispersing by an equivalent subtraction until no trace remained – coincide with the true hour.

Märchen turned out to be a small village; it almost had to be, perched so high, in the shadow of an immense glacier. All the way up the mountain, amidst snow flurries, I had watched the sun progress towards that distant upthrust dagger of ice until, at last, it seemed to impale itself there. Now, in the waning light, skirls of snow and ice crystals unfurled from the glacier's jagged edge like blood from a wound in the sky. I topped a ridge, and as quickly as that, with a suddenness that took my breath away, I found myself on the outskirts of the village. Even at the time, it seemed strange to me that there had been no warning, no sign that I was drawing near to a place of habitation. No rubbish such as one might expect to find at the edge of a settlement, no pastured animals, no stray dogs, not even wagon tracks. I looked back the way I had come, but all was lost in mist and snow; I might have been in a different world altogether from that in which I had started.

The few people I saw on the streets were bundled against the weather and hurrying to be out of it; they did not stop to talk, shooting me curious but not unfriendly glances. I nodded as I passed by, taking note of their simple but well-made clothing. The houses and other buildings of the town shared these qualities. There was nothing ostentatious about them; everything I saw bespoke the quiet confidence of long-standing prosperity, as if the bloody tides of war that had surged back and forth across the lands below had never risen high enough to splash Märchen's well-kept streets.

Street lamps glittered through the snow, which had increased, whipped by a biting wind that made me clutch my cloak to my throat. Upon reaching what I took to be the central square, I saw a lone, dark-cloaked figure kindling the lamps around its periphery from a sputtering flambeau. The man was scarcely more than four feet tall and required a stepladder to perform his task; he carried this implement with him, slung over one shoulder, which gave him a hunchbacked appearance as he trudged from post to post with an uneven gait, the flickering torch held before him, his dark cloak flapping behind. For an instant, I thought I was seeing Magnus, and that, by some incomprehensible circumstance, my friend and former master had preceded me here.

At the centre of the square stood the clock tower, a square, monolithic structure about fifteen feet to a side that rose to a height of perhaps thirty feet. Such monumental clocks are usually part of a town hall or prominent church, but this one stood alone in the middle of the square – where I would have expected to find a statue or fountain – as though proclaiming its independence from all secular and religious authority. The façades of the surrounding buildings, as far as I could make out, were clockless.

I approached, the chill forgotten. I think I knew already – and not just from the evidence of my eyes, but on an instinctive level, by the pricking of my thumbs, as it were – that I was in the presence of a horological masterpiece, and, moreover, an eccentric one. This impression was bolstered by the tower's appearance, which, though it revealed nothing of the mechanism within, nevertheless confirmed my sense of an idiosyncratic personality at work, for it more than made up for any lack of ostentation in the other structures I had seen so far. I did not doubt for an instant that I had found another example of the wizard's work – the purest example yet, for this was no mere addition to something made by a lesser craftsman, as was the case with the other timepieces I had encountered in my travels: this masterpiece could only have come from the hands of the wizard himself, or so I imagined.

The ragged pulse of lamplight and shadow through the curtain of falling snow imparted a semblance of activity to the figures that covered the tower's exterior. I couldn't tell at first if they were castings or carvings, nor if they were painted; they seemed to sprout from every inch of the façade and came in a variety of sizes: the smallest no larger than my finger, the largest as big as life, or bigger. Men, women and children were represented, but also gargoyles that mixed human and bestial aspects, winged devils and cloven-footed demons, as well as angels, and skeletal figures, too, wielding scythes or hour-glasses that seemed no less dangerous. Twining through and about them all was the coiling body of an immense serpent . . . or perhaps a dragon, though it lacked wings as far as I could see. Never had I beheld the sufferings of the damned depicted so persuasively, for such, it appeared, was the artist's subject. The crowd of tormentors and tormented blurred before my eyes into a single undifferentiated mass, as if those inflicting pain and those seeking to escape it suffered alike the agony of exile from God's presence even as they remained subject to His will, fixed in place for ever by a judgement that permitted neither escape nor appeal.

As I gazed at the tableau, a feeling of horror stirred in my breast, and I shivered beneath my cloak. Despite my admir-ation for the artistry, or what I could discern of it, I found myself hesitant to undertake a closer examination. Indeed, I felt an impulse to step back, as if I were in the presence of something dangerous or vile, and though I stood my ground, I did not draw any nearer.

The decorated portion of the tower rose to a height of fifteen feet or so, where an opening gaped, wide and dark as the mouth of a cave: daylight would no doubt reveal a recessed stage there, across which, at the stroke of some predetermined hour, figures emerging from within would progress along inlaid tracks in jerky pantomimes of living movement. I had seen such parades of dolls and automatons hundreds of times in my training and my travels, and knew them inside and out, but I felt certain that whatever display emerged from this particular tower would be like nothing I had witnessed before.

Above the proscenium, the pale clock face floated in mid-air like some smaller sister of the moon seduced down from the heavens. I tried to make out the time, but I couldn't see the hands clearly, much less the numbers to which they pointed. Rising out of the mix of snow and shadow, in which feathery black flakes seemed to be falling alongside the white, was the apex of the tower: a campanile open on all four sides. Clustered within, dimly visible, were the pear-shaped silhouettes of five bells. The two largest hung motionless, but the three smaller ones were swinging slowly back and forth, each following a rhythm of its own. Though there was no sound of striking clapper, faint pings and clicks reached my ears through the keening of the wind – a forlorn music.

'*Tempus Imperator Rerum*,' rasped a voice from behind me in German-accented Latin.

I jumped, startled; lost in reverie, I had not heard the man's approach. Turning, I saw the lamplighter looking up at me with a sly expression, as if pleased to have surprised me. This close, there was no mistaking him for Magnus: he was younger, for one thing, with a full and vigorous reddish-brown beard (in which snowflakes winked and melted), a bulbous red nose and glittering blue eyes beneath a battered brown tricorn. Unlike Magnus, he was a true dwarf, his head disproportionately large for the rest of his body, as were his hands. Yet he might almost have been a dwarf of legend.

'I beg your pardon?' I said.

In one gloved hand, the man held the knotted end of a hempen rope by which the ladder was slung over his shoulder; in the other, like a club, he carried the flambeau, now extinguished. '*Tempus Imperator Rerum*,' he repeated. And then, in an English that bore the same accent as his Latin: 'Time, Emperor of All Things. Is that not the motto of your guild?'

'What guild would that be?' I asked in turn.

He laughed aloud, flashing teeth as white and large as those of a horse, or so it seemed to me. The combination of physical exhaustion and mental stimulation made everything dreamlike and unreal. 'Come now, lad,' he chided, although he did not appear any older than I. 'Do you think I don't know a member of the Worshipful Company of Clockmakers when I see one? Why try to hide it?'

'I'm not hiding anything,' I replied. 'I'm merely curious as to how you came to that conclusion, as I carry no badge or mark of identity.'

'Do you not?' he asked, still grinning. 'Who else but a clock-man would be standing here in the middle of a snowstorm, oblivious as a pilgrim in a cathedral? And you are English, as I deduced from your manner of dress, and as your speech confirmed. Finally, you recognized the Latin motto. Thus, you are an English clockman. Thus, you are a member of the Worshipful Company. *Quod erat demonstrandum*.'

'You are here,' I pointed out. 'You speak English and are acquainted with the motto. Does that make you a member of the guild?'

The man gestured with the charred flambeau. 'I have to be here, don't I? No matter the weather, the lamps must be lit. But now my work is done, and I'm for the hearth and home. You'd best come along, before you freeze to death.'

I confess I was taken aback at the invitation. 'That's very generous of you,' I said, 'but if you could just direct me to a good inn . . .'

Again he laughed, expelling gouts of steam from the thicket of his beard. 'Why, where did you think we were going? To *my* hearth and home? The missus would have my head on a platter!' Chuckling, he started off across the square, moving with the lurching gait I had noticed earlier, as if the ladder slung over his shoulder was a lot heavier than it looked.

'What's your name, clockman?' the man inquired once I had caught him up.

I gave him my alias. 'I am Michael Gray.'

'Adolpheus.'

I wondered whether this was a first or a last name. No clarification was forthcoming.

'Come to fix our clock, have you, Master Gray?'

'I'm no master,' I told him. 'Just a journeyman. But yes, I'd like to try.' That seemed the safest way to answer the question.

'Climbed all this way, did you? Afoot, with no horse to bear you?'

'That's right.'

'You're fortunate. Each spring we find the frozen bodies of those who stray off the track in some snowstorm or other.'

'I didn't realize it was so dangerous.'

Adolpheus grunted but said no more. He led me through a maze of steep and narrow lanes, all of them deserted, past closed-up shops and dwellings whose curtained windows glowed warmly through the falling snow, which had increased in intensity, along with the wind. If it didn't qualify as a snow-storm yet, it would soon do so.

At last, following my guide around a corner, I found myself

facing a two-storey dwelling whose windows were ablaze with light. The inn – or so I judged it to be from the clapboard sign that hung above the door, which depicted a dog lying curled before a fire and was flapping vigorously back and forth as though determined to break loose and fly away, a creature tethered against its will – seemed to promise more than mere hospitality, as if every species of earthly delight were to be found within.

'The Hearth and Home,' Adolpheus said, bustling forward. He unslung his ladder and leaned it against one wall, where snow was already piling up, then laid the dead torch across the top rung. Motioning for me to precede him, he flung the door open.

A wave of warmth and conversation rolled out. Smells of wood smoke, tobacco, cooking meat, mulling wine and cider, and spilled ale mingled with the steamy odours of wet garments drying in the heat of a roaring fire. I paused on the threshold, dizzy, dark spots and bright sparks dancing before my eyes. A hush descended, not hostile, but not welcoming, either. A dog barked once, sharply.

In my travels, I had of necessity become a connoisseur of silences. Being able to judge them correctly can mean the difference between life and death to a stranger entering a place whose customs and language may be other than his own. This silence was made up of curiosity and suspicion in equal measure. I guessed that more than one of the hushed con-versations had concerned my identity and purpose – news of a visitor spreads fast in small towns, along with the wildest of rumours. In such cases, it is imperative to make the proper first impression. People are ever eager to believe the worst.

I removed my hat, but before I could say a word, Adolpheus pushed me forward and entered behind me, slamming the door against the wind. 'Bless all here,' he said in German, vigorously brushing the snow from his beard.

Voices chorused a welcome: 'Doooolph!'

'I've been known to look in from time to time,' he confided to me in English with a wink and a grin as he tugged off his gloves.

My eyes had cleared, the dizziness lifted, and now I saw that there were a dozen or so men seated at tables in the inn's common room, and an immensely fat, middle-aged woman who stood behind a long and unoccupied bar. All their eyes were fixed on me through a drifting bluish haze, but I sensed no animosity in their regard; thanks to Adolpheus, I had been accepted, accorded the provisional status of guest rather than intruder. I nodded a generalized hello, and the buzz of conversation resumed.

A medium-sized but rotund brown and white terrier, which I assumed was the same dog that had barked at my entrance, came waddling up like a sausage with legs, and Adolpheus chuckled and scratched behind the animal's foxlike ears. 'Hello, Hesta, old girl.'

The dog had but a single eye; the other, to judge by the scars surrounding the empty socket, had been lost in a fight. She wagged her stubby tail, basking in the attention, then gave my outstretched palm a sniff and allowed herself to be patted on the head before retreating, satisfied, to what was plainly her accustomed spot before the fire.

'It's she who truly owns the place,' said Adolpheus, tucking his gloves into the pockets of his cloak. 'The great Frederick himself couldn't stop here if Hesta didn't approve.' He unfastened the cloak and shrugged it off, then handed it to me, indicating with his eyes a row of wooden pegs along one wall, above his reach, where other cloaks were hanging, dripping onto the wooden floor. 'Would you mind?'

'Not at all,' I told him in my rough German. At his raised eyebrows, I added, 'You see, I am as adept in your language as you are in mine.'

'Then perhaps we can misunderstand each other equally,' Adolpheus replied – in German – with a laugh. He had taken off his hat and tucked it beneath his arm, revealing a full head of hair the same reddish-brown as his beard.

I hung the cloak on an empty peg, then hung my own beside it. I shrugged out of my rucksack and stamped clinging snow and ice from my boots, toes tingling as they began to thaw. Meanwhile, the woman from behind the bar came forward to greet us. I tried not to stare, but I had seldom seen a woman – or man, for that matter – of such prodigious girth. Her bare arms were the size of hams; her neck and chin were lost in rolls of rosy pink flesh; the movement of her bosom beneath the tent of her blue and white smock, with its colourfully embroidered designs of mountain wildflowers, was positively oceanic. Seeing her across the room, I had assumed she was in her mid-to-late forties, perhaps somewhat older, but up close she appeared younger than that – or, no, not younger, but as if the range of her possible ages was wider than I had at first supposed, just as she herself appeared to widen as she approached, glowing with health and vigour. Her cheeks were like firm red apples, her eyes were blue as gentians, and thick brown braids, like wreaths of fresh-baked bread, curled about ears that were translucent, pink, and incongruously small, like souvenirs of a dainty girlhood otherwise unimaginable.

'Well, and who's your handsome friend, Dolph?' she asked in German, appraising me with a frank and, or so it seemed, flirtatious stare. She was nearly my own height, but she must have outweighed me by two hundred pounds or more. She smelled like beer and bread. What would it be like, I found myself wondering, and not entirely without interest, to bed such an enormous woman?

Adolpheus introduced me as Michael Gray, a journeyman of the Worshipful Company. The woman's name, I learned, was Inge Hubner.

'A pleasure to meet you and enjoy such warm hospitality,' I told her with a gallant bow. I spoke in German, and the rest of our conversation took place in that tongue; indeed, unless I mention otherwise, you should assume that all the conversations I report to you were conducted thus.

Inge laughed, her chins jiggling. 'You're a long way from home, Herr Gray. But I'll bet I can guess what brings you to Märchen. You've come to try your luck with Wachter's Folly, haven't you?'

'She means the clock,' Adolpheus put in. 'That's what we call it hereabouts, after its maker, Jozef Wachter.'

'I should very much like to meet him,' I said.

'Why, you should very much *not!*' Inge said. 'The man is dead and gone almost half a century now, with that old clock, his monument, growing crazier by the year . . . by the day, I sometimes think. Can you set it to rights?'

'With God's help,' I made modest answer.

'Worshipful indeed!' Her blue eyes twinkled with a teasing good humour that brought a blush to my cheeks – and even in those days, I was not a man given to blushing.

Adolpheus chuckled. 'You're embarrassing the lad, Inge.'

'Nonsense.' She winked at me, and for a moment I was afraid that she was going to reach out and give my cheek a pinch. 'Have I embarrassed you, Herr Gray?'

'Not at all, Fraülein—'

'Herr Gray!' interrupted Inge with a little shriek, as though scandalized; she held up her hand to display a fat gold band around a sausage-sized finger. 'I'm a married woman!'

'My apologies, Frau Hubner.'

'Just call me Inge; everybody does. Now, I suppose you'll be wanting a room? At this time of year, you can take your pick. Six pfennigs a night; eight, with meals included. You'll do no better, I promise you.' She grinned; her teeth were small and white, like kernels of Indian corn. 'The Hearth and Home is Märchen's only inn.'

'And a fine one, by the looks of it,' I said, nor was I flattering my hostess. The common room was clean and comfortably appointed. It had an atmosphere of cosy geniality, from the fire roaring in the large stone fireplace, to the mugs lined up above the mantel, to the oil paintings – of pristine Alpine vistas full of tumbling waterfalls, stark precipices, stands of pine, verdant meadows dotted with wildflowers, and wide, blue skies – hanging on the oak-panelled walls; all affirmations of the town's prosperity. The men gathered companionably at their tables gave me the impression of belonging nowhere else, and the steady murmur of conversation and laughter that rose from them seemed as intrinsic to this place as the crackling of the fire. There was even a cuckoo clock behind the bar; its hands indicated eighteen minutes past the hour of seven. Fishing out my pocket watch, I was surprised and impressed to find only a small, but quite acceptable discrepancy between them.

'Not every timepiece in Märchen is in need of repair,' remarked Adolpheus. 'Herr Gray, I'll leave you in Inge's capable hands. Once you've got him settled, Inge, I'll have a cup of your excellent mulled wine.'

'I'm grateful to you, Adolpheus,' I said. 'You must let me buy that wine.'

'With pleasure.' He gave me a smart bow, which I returned. Then the little man moved off towards one of the tables, still walking with his lopsided gait. Only now did I perceive that he was crippled; one leg was shorter than the other, and his right shoe had been built to correct the defect, which it did but imperfectly.

'I'll take you upstairs,' said Inge. 'Don't worry about your cloak; it's safe where it is. You'll find no thieves in Märchen.'

I followed the ponderous sway of Inge's massive hips up the creaking stairs and down a passage lit by the candle she held before her. She unlocked a door at the end of the corridor and went in, hips squeezing past the sides of the frame. After a moment, the tremulous light within grew stronger, and she called my name. Was it my imagination, or did she press herself against me as I entered the small room? It was impossible in any case to avoid her. As I brushed by, breathing in her yeasty smell, I had the sense that, if she chose, she could engulf me like rising dough swallowing a raisin. The image, however ridiculous, was not entirely without appeal. Again, I felt myself blushing. Nor was that the only physical response she had provoked. I like women with meat on their bones, yet I had never imagined that my tastes ran to such an extreme.

I turned away as soon as I could, embarrassed by an attraction I couldn't account for, and set my rucksack on the wooden floor, leaning it against the wall to one side of the door. Inge gave no sign of having noticed anything amiss. Perhaps she, too, was embarrassed.

The room may have been small, but it was neat and snug, with a narrow bed along one wall, a painted cupboard whose insides smelled of cedar and saxifrage, a boxy ceramic stove so hot that the air around it shimmered, making its diamond-patterned red and white tiles seem to undulate, and a table upon which sat a wash basin, a covered pitcher of water, and an upside-down glass, along with a folded towel and an oil lamp that cast a shivery light. There, too, Inge had set her candle. The chamber pot, she told me, was under the bed. Outside the window, the snow was coming down so thickly that I couldn't make out the street below, only the smudged glow of street lamps that might have been wrapped in muslin.

'Quite a blizzard,' I commented, taking the opportunity to place my damp hat upon the edge of the table nearest the stove.

'Blizzard?' Inge scoffed. 'Why, this is but a flurry!'

'Will it last long?'

'A day, a week; who can say? Perhaps it will be over by morning. Perhaps not until spring.' She gave me a wink. 'You may be with us for a long while, Herr Gray!'

I confess I hadn't considered the possibility of becoming trapped here. The prospect was worrisome. 'Surely there must be means of transport up and down the mountain.'

Inge shrugged. 'We're self-sufficient here. We have to be. For us, winter is a siege. All summer long, we lay up supplies. Then we sit tight and wait the winter out. But if someone wants to tempt fate and go down the mountain, who can stop them?' She twisted the front of her smock in her beefy hands. 'Sometimes people go a little . . . mad. The shadow of the glacier falls across their souls. A desperation fills them, a desire to be gone from the endless snow and ice, the howling winds, that clock that keeps its crazy hours. It's a sickness, a fever. Some flee suddenly, in the dark of night; others plan obsessively, in minute detail, before setting out. Either way, few who descend the mountain in the dead of winter reach the bottom alive.'

'How horrible! Does it happen often?'

'Often enough. Herr Hubner, my husband, disappeared seven winters ago. His body has yet to be found.'

'I'm sorry. It must be terrible not to know what happened, whether he's dead or alive. I suppose that's why you still wear your ring: a token of hope that he might return one day.'

Inge laughed, her teeth glinting like seed pearls. 'The explanation is not so romantic, Herr Gray! I wear my ring because I can't get it off my finger – I was but skin and bones all those years ago, when I first put it on. Besides, in my profession, a wedding ring is an asset. It lends a certain . . . respectability. But truthfully, if my husband were to walk into Märchen tomorrow, I'd kill him myself, the swine. He robbed me, you see. Emptied the till when he left – took every last pfennig. I know what you're thinking. How can it be robbery when it was all his own property?'

'I'm no lawyer, thank God,' I told her, for I had not been thinking any such thing.

'He left me nothing,' she insisted. 'Only debts. I would have lost this place if not for Herr Doppler, the burgomeister.' Inge shook her head as if reluctant to let go of the subject. 'Never mind. He won't be back. He didn't make it down the mountain.'

'If his body was never found, how can you be sure?'

'I saw it in a dream.'

'And do you always believe your dreams?'

'You may be an educated man, Herr Gray, but you don't know everything. I watched Hans fall; I saw him lying broken at the bottom of a crevasse. He wasn't dead, either; not yet he wasn't. Just paralysed. Eyes aglitter with pain and terror, he was gazing up as the snow fell down, covering him like a shroud. That was my dream.'

'It sounds more like a nightmare.'

'I'm not ashamed to admit that I woke up with a smile,' Inge said, and for just a second, or so it seemed to me in the shifting light, her eyes became coals of feral satisfaction, like a cat's. 'It was the answer to my prayers, that dream. Haven't you ever had such a dream?'

'I have many dreams,' I told her. 'In some I fly. In others, beautiful women desire me. Once I took a journey to the moon! Alas, none of them are real.'

'Perhaps they are more real than you know.'

I laughed. 'Do you suppose I visited the moon after all?'

'Or the moon visited you. Some believe dreams come from there.'

'The moon is a globe of rock, Inge. I have examined its bleak surface through a telescope. It is a dead place, a battered wasteland, as though a great war.was fought there long ago. A war that left no survivors.'

'I didn't say *I* believed it,' she answered. 'Still, I don't suppose you'd deny that God can send us true dreams if He wishes it.'

'By all means. But why should He wish it? Is there some flaw in His design that requires personal intervention?'

'I wouldn't know, Herr Gray. I'm a simple woman. I only know what I saw.'

'But then why not go to the spot you dreamed of and dig up the body? Get your money back?'

She wagged a finger under my nose. 'Now you are teasing me. The dream didn't supply me with a map. I saw a crevasse, one of hundreds. Every year there are avalanches. Crevasses fill up. Others open. Should I waste my time searching for something that might not even exist any more? No, I have an inn to run.' She picked up the candle from the table. 'Now, shall I have some supper sent up, or will you eat downstairs?'

'I'll be down in a moment,' I said. 'I'm starving.'

'A bowl or two of my stew will fix that.' Inge removed the key from the door and handed it to me. 'As I said, you'll find no thieves in Märchen, but if there are any valuables you'd care to safeguard, purely for your own peace of mind, I keep a strongbox.'

'Just my tools,' I told her, glancing towards the rucksack. 'But I carry them with me at all times. And this as well.' I patted my hip, where I wore a long dagger in a leather sheath.

'Och, you'll not need that pigsticker here,' Inge protested.

'I'm sure I won't, but I feel safer with it just the same.'

'Well, as long as you keep it sheathed. I don't want you waving a blade around under my customers' noses!'

'Not unless someone's waving a blade under mine.'

'Then we'll have no trouble, Herr Gray. I'll leave you to get settled in now.' Executing a curtsy, Inge withdrew, shutting the door behind her. The floorboards trembled to her retreating footsteps.

I strode to the door and locked it. I thought it odd that my hostess would confess to having been robbed, albeit by her own husband, and then assure me that there were no thieves in town. But then, Herr Hubner wasn't *in* town, was he? Whether his corpse lay entombed in ice at the bottom of a crevasse, or, more likely, he was enjoying a new life, with a slimmer wife, somewhere far away, the man was not to be found in Märchen. And if he knew what was good for him, I thought, remembering the fierce look that had kindled in Inge's eyes, he never would be.

Alone, I performed my ablutions, then poured a glass of

water and gulped it down. The water tasted pure, ambrosial; so cold, despite the heat of the room, it made my teeth ache down to the roots. Drawn, no doubt, from some pristine mountain spring. I poured a second glass. The contents glittered in the lamplight and went straight to my head like a liquor distilled from glacial ice, frozen instants aged to a ravishing potency. I leaned into the table, steadying myself against the prickly aurora that crystallized behind my eyes. It melted away in a slow, shimmering ebb, leaving me dizzied, breathless. My heart tolled in my chest.

A dazed weariness stole over me, all those miles I'd climbed catching up at once. That, and the stifling heat. I made my way to the bed, intending to sit for a moment before return-ing to the common room for a bowl of Inge's stew, but the downy mattress had other ideas, seeming to pull me in as I had imagined Inge herself doing. I let myself fall back into its embrace, closing my eyes, in my ears a soft hissing that, already half asleep, I attributed to snowflakes expiring against the windowpanes over my head rather than to the efficiency of the stove.

I awoke to a faint, persistent rasping, as of something heavy being dragged across the floor. Someone was in the room. But the lamp had gone out; I couldn't see a thing. I listened as the sound continued, seeming to draw nearer by slow inches – drag, pause, drag, pause – until it reached the foot of the bed. Then it fell silent.

I held my breath. The only sound was the hissing of the stove. Had Inge sent a man to murder me, intending to steal my possessions? Such crimes were not unheard of. Or was the purpose of this visitation to administer a beating, a warning from the wizard I had been following to meddle no more in his affairs? Either way, I would not be an easy victim. I drew back against the headboard, pulling my dirk from its sheath. 'Who's there?' I growled. 'I'm armed, I warn you.'

A light kindled, like no earthly light I had ever seen. This was no enemy of darkness, no flame of lamp or candle to send shadows scurrying like bedbugs or blind my eyes. It was as though a star had drifted down through the ceiling, shining with a cool, silver-blue radiance that penetrated the dark without dispelling it, revealing the bed, the cupboard, the blade I held in a trembling hand . . . which shook not just from fear but because the temperature had plunged in an instant. Only, there was no star, nor any other single source of light. Rather, the light seemed to be an inherent property of the objects themselves. It covered their surfaces in a frostlike rime whose glow radiated outwards like a visible manifestation of the cold I felt so keenly that my teeth had begun to chatter. Even the stove seemed a font of frigidity now, and the fog of my breath glimmered as if with crystals of ice. It was beautiful but also terrible, like a glimpse into some wintry netherworld.

Beautiful and terrible, too, was the woman who stood at the foot of the bed, gazing at me with eyes of smoky green, like malachite. Her skin was pale as alabaster, her lips the blue of lapis lazuli, her long hair blacker than the darkness that seemed not just her rightful habitation but her sovereign domain. And indeed, she wore a gown such as the queen of midnight's kingdom might wear, of deep, wine-dark velvet and white, diamond-studded lace that bloomed around her slender neck in intricate latticework patterns and tumbled in frothy swathes from her shoulders and arms like abundant drifts of snow. Had I been standing, I would have fallen to my knees; as it was, my nerveless fingers could not retain their grip on the dirk, and it fell into the bed-sheets beside me.

Surely, I thought, I was in the presence of an angel! Feelings of worshipful awe came streaming into my heart, filling its chambers, stretching its walls. Yet so exquisite was the pain of this ravishment, so unreservedly did I give myself up to it, that I yearned for the process to go on and on, even if it meant my swollen heart must burst. Or, no, I *wanted* it to burst, ached to lose myself in a blissful annihilation . . .

But the explosion, when it came, involved another organ. I felt the first shuddering spasm and looked down, only then realizing that my member was as hard as iron. I had never spent myself so violently, so prodigiously. I groaned as much in shame as in ecstasy, for the feelings kindled by the sight of my visitor had been pure, exalted, spiritual in the highest sense, and yet some faulty mechanism of my body had translated those feelings into the grossest sort of animal display. But I couldn't cover the spreading stain, couldn't move so much as a finger. And this was just from the mute aura of her presence. If she should speak or touch me, I felt that I would expire . . .

I raised my eyes to her face, expecting to see disgust and anger written there, afraid I had committed a sin for which the punishment would be swift and of utmost severity, though the gravest punishment I could think of was the loss of her. Instead, she was smiling, and her green eyes seemed kind, alive in a way they hadn't been before, as if I'd made her a rich offering, a tribute that she accepted not just as her due, but with true gratitude: because it was needful somehow, precious to her despite its base origin . . . or, perhaps, because of it. I didn't know. I only knew that I would do anything to please her, to keep her looking at me that way.

'Please,' I whispered. 'Please . . .'

She seemed about to speak, but then she gave a start, as if

at a noise only she could hear. Alarm and fear rose in her features. This shocked me, for how could such a perfect being be afraid . . . and of what? I realized at the same time that she was younger than I had thought: was, in fact, younger than I. Had she always been so? A rosy blush infused her skin; her lips glistened as if with the juice of blueberries; the green of her eyes was no longer that of cold stone but a shade at once more vibrant and more fragile: an audacious springtime green. She seemed to be in the throes of a transformation, as though something frozen in her had begun to melt; and even as I had this thought, tears welled up in her eyes, spilling down her cheeks.

'What is it?' I asked, pierced to the heart by this evidence of vulnerability and filled with a fierce desire to protect her; indeed, at that moment I would have laid down my life for her without question or hesitation. 'What are you afraid of?'

She answered in a breathless voice that was nothing like I had imagined it might be – beautiful, yes, but humanly so . . . which made it seem even lovelier, and made her seem lovelier, too, nearer to me, not an angel but a woman. 'He approaches.'

'He?'

A booming shudder passed through the bed, the inn, the world. And then another. Like the rolling thunder of an avalanche. Or the footsteps of a giant.

'My father,' she said, her voice little more than a whisper. 'If he should find me here . . . I must go!'

'But who are you? I don't even know your name—'

Another footstep, much closer, as if from just outside the window behind me. I turned, but could see nothing through the glass, which was thoroughly befogged. The whole room, in fact, was filling with fog, and when I turned back to the girl, I saw that the source of it was her gown. The air had grown warmer, and I heard the steady hissing of the stove again. Or not the stove, but the gown itself, the icy fabric melting, dissolving, turning translucent as it thinned, so that I could see the outline of the body within, willowy and white, the pink buds of breasts visible for an unforgettable instant before, raising one arm to cover herself, the girl turned with a cry and fled the room.

'Wait,' I called, but she was gone, vanished into the billowing mist. As I moved to follow, I felt the unmistakable sensation of being observed, and so powerful was this intrusive presence that I turned back to the window, afraid that I would see a gigantic eyeball pressed to the glass. But the swirling fog was too dense. Whatever was out there, watching me, I could not see it, though the force of its dreadful regard immobilized me, held me in its grasp so that I could not even breathe.

Then the pressure withdrew. I coughed, sucking air into my lungs as I heard and felt the ponderous footsteps drawing off. I was limp with relief, drenched in sweat. Yet I could not forget the girl was out there, pursued by a father (for so she had named him) that she feared. I was afraid as well, I won't deny it, and a part of me wanted nothing more than to pull the sheets up over my head and, like a trembling boy, take refuge in a cosy darkness of my own making. But I would not be ruled by fear. I paused only to pick up my dirk before plunging into the already dissipating mists after my beautiful visitor. She would not face her father alone and unprotected.

She proved easy to follow: her melting dress had left a wet trail across the floor that glowed with a silvery-blue phosphorescence. I lost my footing once and almost fell as I hurried down the stairs and into the common room . . . which was empty save for the hound, Hesta, asleep before the glowing coals of the fire, her fat old body twitching in the throes of some doggy dream. Curtains of fog made slow undulations in the air. I wondered how late it was, how long I had slept, but I couldn't make out the face of the cuckoo clock. Nor did I linger for a closer look or check my pocket watch. Instead, I hurried out of the inn.

The snowstorm had grown worse. I did not think even Inge would have baulked at the word *blizzard* now. Driven by the wind, icy flakes smacked into my face from all sides, like an insect swarm. I sheathed my dirk and pressed forward, my hands raised in a useless attempt to ward off the snow. I managed a few stumbling steps before halting, overwhelmed, in a snowdrift that reached to mid-thigh, so disoriented I wasn't sure I could find my way back to the inn. The sweat had frozen upon my body, so that I felt rimed in ice, and the seed I had spilled was so cold against my skin that it almost seemed to burn. Perhaps I should have given up then, or at least returned to the Hearth and Home for my cloak, but then a fresh blast of wind tore the white swarm asunder long enough for me to pick out the trail again: a shimmering path that twined across the mounds and swells of snow like the track of a sledge. All at once, at the end of that trail, I saw the girl rise into view as if emerging from out of a hole in the ground; she was far away, a small glowing figure that skimmed over the snow like a skier. I cried out, but the wind tore my words away, and then she swerved around the corner of a building and was gone.

I pushed after her. The trail I had seen was a narrow path of ice whose thin crust stretched unbroken by so much as a foot-print over the new-fallen snow. It did not bear my weight as it had hers, and I felt rough as an ox as I lumbered in her wake through drifts that reached to my hips, fighting the wind every step of the way, pulling myself forward with my arms as if wading through a river.

After a time impossible to measure, I saw what I took to be crows or ravens flapping frantically inside glass cages, and I stopped, aghast at the strangeness and cruelty of the sight, wondering at its purpose. But then I realized that I was looking at the street lamps Adolpheus had lit earlier, their flames so black it was as if darkness itself had caught fire. This seemed even stranger than my first, mistaken impression, and I felt my courage quail. But though I no longer heard or felt the earthquake footsteps of the girl's father, I believed she was still in danger, still in need of my help.

Redoubling my efforts, at last I turned the corner where I'd lost sight of her. The clock tower loomed ahead. *Wachter's Folly*, Inge had called it. Like everything else except the flames of the street lamps, it glowed a spectral blue . . . only the light appeared more intense than elsewhere, as if I had found its source. I hadn't thought the night could get any colder, but now, as I approached the tower, the temperature dropped further, and the air actually seemed to grow denser, as if in transition from gas to solid. The wind, too, opposed me, pushing back until I was no longer advancing but struggling just to hold my ground.

The girl's trail led straight to the base of the tower, a good ten yards away . . . and vanished. Had she entered the structure somehow? Or climbed its intricately adorned surface, seeking shelter from the blizzard and her father in the recess of the upper platform or among the bells of the campanile? I glanced up, shielding my eyes, and saw that the hands of the clock were spinning wildly, out of all proper relationship to each other, as if following different measures of time. The hour hand flew by the minute hand, which was itself turning at an abnormally fast speed.

This was no malfunction. I had seen enough examples of the wizard's work to know that the clock was operating as it had been designed to do. I was convinced that I had found what I had been searching for – if not the wizard himself, then a timepiece built by his hand, or to his specifications. I needed to get closer, to get inside the tower, where I could examine the machinery. I would need no lamp or candle in the otherworldly blue light, which did not fall from without but instead seemed to have its mysterious origin deep within each object, a radiance arising from the heart of all matter. Then it struck me. And shook me to my soul. For what else could be the source of this eldritch light but time?

Surely, I thought, this was how God and His angels apprehended the world! Within this clock tower, preserved like a corpse within a glacier, lay the secret for which I had been searching, the grail I had followed halfway round the world: a mechanism by which time itself could be mastered, transcended. I was sure of it. And the same intuition that told me the end of my quest was waiting within the tower assured me the girl was a part of it all . . . and, what's more, always had been: that without ever suspecting it, I had been searching for her as well as the wizard. I did not know who – or even what – she was: whether woman or angel. I only knew she was essential to me, that I would never possess the secret of this clock until I possessed her. She *was* the secret, I sensed, or a facet of it, a part inseparable from the whole. To gain one was to gain the other.

By now the spinning hands had lost their individuality, melting into a silver-blue blur that seemed distinct from the clock itself, detached from it, a cloudy, pearlescent sphere hovering in the air before me like a cyclopean eye. I shuddered, feeling that I had come once again under the scrutiny of whatever had observed me earlier, in my room at the inn. The girl's father, whose footsteps had shaken the ground like an avalanche and sent her fleeing in terror. But where was he? *What* was he? I could not tear my eyes away from the floating orb, could not move so much as a finger.

And then, with mounting horror, I perceived that the orb was not merely *like* an eye but was in fact that very thing, and the tower likewise was no tower but a serpentine body coiled tightly upon itself. The campanile was the crest of a huge head, and what I'd taken to be a recessed platform, a stage across which automatons would parade in stiff, mechanical pantomime, was a cavernous mouth that could swallow me at a gulp. As I could see only a single eye, I assumed at first that the beast was peering at me sideways, its vision monocular, like a snake's. But then the great head stirred, rose, and came gliding towards me without haste, inescapable as fate, and I realized that the dragon was staring at me full-on and that there was just the one eye, the other socket empty, as if the eye once housed there had been put out long ago by the lance of a questing knight. Its breath washed over me, redolent of hot metal and oil, and for a second, deep in the monstrous gullet, I saw a silvery glimmer, like a chain of stars. Then what might have been a cloud of bats came winging towards me from out of that long tunnel, hundreds, thousands of flickering shadows. I quailed, remembering the black flames trapped in their glass cages. But there would be no caging these flames, no escaping them. Paralysed with terror, I awaited incineration.

It did not come. No fire shot from between the gaping jaws. Instead, a pleasant warbling filled the air, as if, despite its size and appearance, what faced me was nearer to bird than dragon. Sweet music tumbled over me, an avalanche of pure, ringing tones . . .

It had been, of course, a dream, as I realized the instant I came awake, bolting upright to a cascade of carolling bells. My heart thumped, and sweat clung to my skin in the over-heated room. Outside, Wachter's Folly was tolling some no doubt outlandish hour. In the strong and shifting winds, laden with their cargo of snow, the sounds seemed near one second and far off the next, as if the tower were being blown about like a kite on a string. But those winds couldn't touch me here, claw as they might at the windows, rattling the panes. The lamp on the table across the floor glowed a warm, welcome yellow, and its steady light illuminated the furnishings and other objects it fell upon, just as proper light should do. The stove sighed contentedly in its corner.

I rubbed my eyes, wondering how long I'd slept. According to my pocket watch, it was well past midnight. Dream images fluttered through my mind. I recalled the head of the dragon drawing near, the baleful effulgence of its solitary eye. And the girl . . . How beautiful she had been! Majestic, like a queen of ice and darkness . . . yet vulnerable, and all the more desirable for it.

Desirable indeed, for as I rose from the bed, a certain intimate dampness testified to one way, at least, in which the dream had not been entirely a thing of fancy. Succubus-like, the girl had ravished my body even as she seduced my mind.

I made my way to the table, where I laved water from the basin over my face; though lukewarm now, it brought me fully awake. My stomach rumbled, reminding me that I hadn't eaten all day. I turned to leave the room, intending to go in search of food, perhaps some of that stew Inge had mentioned . . . and froze, hackles rising.

Water was puddled on the floorboards at the foot of the bed. A trail of smaller puddles led to the door.

Someone had entered my room, tracking in snow from outside, and stood at the foot of the bed, watching as I slept. I assured myself that my purse had not been cut, thinking with a shiver that it was fortunate I was such a deep sleeper; had I woken, it could very well have been my throat that was cut. But some intimation of the intruder's presence had reached me nonetheless, insinuating itself into my dream. The girl, the menacing sense of being observed, even the tread of footsteps . . .

The thought of my tools intruded, and I crossed to where I'd left my rucksack. It was, I saw at once, open; I knelt and rummaged through it, cursing under my breath as my worst fears were realized.

My tools were gone. Stolen.

9

Herr Doppler

ONLY A FELLOW HOROLOGIST CAN GRASP THE MEANING OF SUCH A loss. To anyone else, a clockman's tools might seem no more than mute instruments of metal and wood, but to us they are repositories of knowledge and experience, imbued with memories, with hopes and dreams. More than mere possessions, they are expressions of who we are, extensions of our deepest selves. Some of those tools were my own inventions. Others had come to me from Magnus himself. I felt their loss most keenly. Without them, my examination of Wachter's Folly would be perfunctory, all but useless.

So much for Inge's assurances! And yet she'd invited me to place my valuables with her for safekeeping. Had she, then, known or suspected that I might be visited by a thief? Had she been trying to warn me?

I would confront her, of course ... but shouting and accusations would accomplish nothing. I had to practise tact, diplomacy. I was a stranger in Märchen, a foreigner; I didn't know whom to trust. The law was on my side, but that didn't mean I could count on the burgomeister's help. Märchen was isolated by the mountains and further cut off by the snow-storm; thus, I reasoned, the tools must still be somewhere in town, and it should be possible, with the proper inducement, to procure their safe return. A generous reward . . . though it galled me to think that I would be paying a thief's ransom.

Returning to the table, I lit a candle from the lamp there and then went back to the door. To my surprise, it was locked. What kind of burglar picks the lock to an occupied room, slips inside and performs his thievery, then, upon leaving, takes the time to lock the door behind him? I didn't see the sense of it. But for that matter, I didn't understand why the burglar hadn't taken the trouble to ensure that he didn't leave a trail of puddled snow-melt behind, either. If the crime had been committed by a fellow guest at the inn, the trail might very well lead me to him.

I unlocked the door, swung it open, and stepped out into the empty passage. Then paused, the candle upraised as though I might hear better by its light. The wind howled outside, and the inn groaned around me like a ship riding out a tempest. Someone was snoring near by, but I heard nothing from the common room below. I started forward, following the watery trail, then stopped and turned back to lock the door – not that there was anything in the room worth stealing now . . . or that a locked door would afford any protection. Still, the sound of the key turning in the lock was reassuring. Then, feeling like a thief myself, I crept past the closed doors of other rooms to the end of the passage and descended the creaking stairs to the common room.

It was eerily like my dream; all that was missing was the fog. Aside from my candle, the only light came from the still-smouldering fire, which illuminated the sleeping form of Hesta, curled beside the hearth. I started at what seemed at first a gathering of silent, hooded figures by the door, like some grim convocation of monks, then recognized my cloak hanging in the company of several others. At least that had not been stolen.

Someone had taken a mop to the floor, splashing water about . . . and covering the thief's tracks. So much for my hopes of following the trail to his door. Meanwhile, though, I was hungrier than ever. I crept towards the kitchen, not wanting to awaken the dog, who would in turn awaken the rest of the inn with her barking. But it was no use; her ears pricked and her head came up, followed by the rest of her. She yawned, shook herself from nose to tail-tip, then ambled over to me, toenails clicking across the stone floor. But she did not bark or growl. Instead, tail wagging, she looked up at me, seeming almost to grin.

'Poor old Hesta,' I whispered and reached to scratch behind her ears. 'Not much of a watchdog, are you, with just one eye? Are you hungry, girl? Let's see what we can scrounge up to eat around here.'

The dog followed as I slipped behind the long wooden bar, past the cuckoo clock, and through a swinging door that led, or so I assumed, to the kitchen.

It did. The floor had been mopped here as well, and the smooth but uneven stones held pockets of water that glittered like scattered coins in the candlelight. The tables were clear and clean; metal pots hung from hooks in the walls and in the beams overhead. Dishes, glasses and silverware had been set out to dry beside a sink that was larger than some bathtubs I have seen. A huge black cast-iron stove radiated a moderate heat, while orange coals glowed like watchful eyes in the depths of a fireplace that dwarfed the one in the common room. Suspended there by thick chains was a cauldron from which savoury aromas of stewed meat and vegetables spilled.

'Looks as though we're in luck, old girl.'

Hesta wagged her tail, eye bright with anticipation.

Setting the candle on a table, I took a bowl from the dishes laid out to dry. Then I crossed to the fireplace, Hesta at my heels. The cauldron was covered, and the heat rising from the lid discouraged me from removing it with my bare hands. But after a moment's search I found a rag that provided sufficient insulation for the task. A steamy exhalation of mouth-watering odours accompanied the lifting of the lid. I set it down, leaning it against the stones of the mantel. I took a copper ladle from a hook near by and filled my bowl; then, after replacing ladle and lid, made my way back to the drying dishes and silverware. All the while, Hesta's eye was fixed upon me, as if she hadn't eaten in days, and though that was plainly not the case, I was moved to set the bowl down on the floor for her. Magnus's weakness was cats, but I confess I cannot resist the importuning of a dog, provided it is politely done.

'Ladies first,' I told her. As she dug in, I fetched a spoon and another bowl, which I filled and brought to the table where the candle was burning. I pulled up a stool and followed Hesta's example, albeit in a more civilized fashion.

The stew was delicious. I do not think I have ever tasted better. There were chunks of tender beef, potatoes, tomatoes, carrots, peas and chopped onions, as well as an array of spices that ranged from the recognizable to the mysterious, all blended with sublime skill. Almost as miraculous as the use to which they had been put was the mere fact that fresh and exotic vegetables should be obtainable in Märchen at this time of year. I wolfed down the contents of my bowl nearly as fast as Hesta did hers, then went back for seconds.

After another spoonful, it occurred to me that a bit of ale would not come amiss. I pushed back the stool, picked up the candle, and left the kitchen through the swinging door. When I returned a moment later, it was with a foamy moustache affixed to my upper lip and a mug brimming with ale from the tap behind the bar.

I stopped short at the sight of a stranger sitting at the table and eating from a bowl of stew. *My* bowl of stew. The man must have entered through a back door, though I had heard no one come in and Hesta had raised no alarm. Snow clung to the contours of his cloak and, melting, dripped to the floor around the stool on which he sat. His boots, too, were shedding puddles. A large tricorn, capped with snow like a miniature model of the glacier that presided over the town, lay on the table beside a pair of yellowish leather gloves. A lantern had been hung from an iron hook on the wall beside the fireplace, and it shone with a buttery yellow light. As for Hesta, she was stretched on her side next to the fireplace, soaking up its heat; the dog lifted her head as I entered, then lowered it again, unconcerned. I confess I did not share her equanimity.

The stranger appeared to be in his mid-sixties or so, but robust. Despite the inclement weather and the lateness of the hour, he wore a silver club wig whose long tail reached his broad shoulders. With his bristling white moustache, mottled red complexion, and fierce dark eyes, now glaring over the top of the wooden spoon raised partway to his lips, he put me in mind of certain old soldiers I had encountered in my travels, men unable or unwilling to relinquish the habits of military life long after their separation from the service.

'So,' he said in heavily accented English, 'you are the thief who has been making himself at home in Inge's kitchen.'

I replied in German. 'I am a guest at the inn. Who are you?'

The man smiled, but did not appear any less menacing on

account of it. 'Who am I?' He, too, spoke in German now. Setting down the spoon, he removed a white handkerchief from within his left sleeve, dabbed the ends of his moustache, then tucked the handkerchief back in place. 'You say you are a guest; that makes me your host.'

My confusion deepened. 'You're Inge's . . . husband?' A shiver ran through me, as if I were conversing with a ghost, a revenant crawled from out of an icy tomb.

He laughed, and Hesta's tail thumped at the sound. 'His successor . . . though not in the matrimonial sense. I am Inge's business partner, co-owner of the Hearth and Home. And you are Herr Michael Gray, journeyman of the Worshipful Company.' Seeing my surprise, he added, 'There are no secrets in our little town, Herr Gray!'

'You have me at a disadvantage, Herr . . .'

'Doppler.' The man rose, stepped to one side of the stool, and clicked the heels of his boots together while inclining his torso in a crisp, fractional bow, eyes never leaving my face. His movements shook the last clumps of snow from his cloak. 'Colonel, retired. I'm the burgomeister here.' He gestured towards a nearby stool. 'Please, join me.'

This, I perceived, was not a request. Herr Doppler was a man used to being obeyed. Nor was I, as a stranger precariously situated, inclined to challenge his authority. I settled my candle and mug on the table, pulled up the stool, and sat.

Doppler remained standing. He gazed down the length of his nose at me, a sardonic gleam in his eyes, which I saw now were of a strikingly deep blue, almost purple. 'I apologize for poaching on your supper, Herr Gray. I'm afflicted with insomnia, and when I cannot sleep I like to walk about the town, making sure everything is as it should be – even on a night like this. Inge knows of my nocturnal perambulations and will often leave me a bite to eat, so when I saw the bowl of stew, I assumed it was intended for me.'

I did not believe he was sharing the entire truth. It seemed to me that it would take more than insomnia to send a man out into the middle of a blizzard. Had I interrupted a tryst? Was the setting out of food a prearranged signal between Inge and Doppler, alerting him that the door to his business partner's bedchamber would be unlocked? 'You're welcome to the stew,' I said. 'And I was stealing nothing, by the way. I would have told Inge in the morning, so she could add it to my account.'

'No doubt, no doubt,' Doppler said dismissively. He flipped up the back of his cloak and resumed his seat. 'I was speaking in jest when I called you a thief. I knew who you were the instant I laid eyes on you, though I confess I didn't expect to have the pleasure of meeting you tonight.' As he spoke, he produced a silver pocket watch from within his coat, glanced at it, and placed it beside him on the table with the lid open. 'Or this morning, I should say.'

My gaze was drawn to the timepiece; it seemed ordinary enough, the silver case monogrammed with a design I could not make out in the candlelight: Doppler's initials, perhaps. 'While we're on the subject of thieves, Herr Doppler, I'm afraid I've been the victim of one.'

The spoon halted halfway to Doppler's mouth. His gaze turned hard – or, rather, harder. 'Go on,' he said.

'My tool kit was stolen as I slept.'

'Are you sure you did not simply mislay it?'

'Quite sure,' I told him and explained the circumstances, though I said nothing of my dream. 'I hate to accuse anyone, but the locked door, the trail of melted snow . . .' I shrugged and took a sip of ale.

'Yes, yes, it's all very suggestive,' Doppler agreed. He pushed the half-finished bowl of stew to one side as if disgusted by the taste of it. 'Damn her eyes!'

'Are you referring to Inge?' I asked.

'Inge?' Doppler plucked at one end of his bristling moustache. 'No, not Inge. My daughter, Corinna. I'll lay odds on it, the incorrigible minx!'

'But why should your daughter want to steal my tool kit?' I asked in perplexity. 'And for that matter, how could she have done so? My door was locked. Is she an accomplished burglar, Herr Doppler?'

He chuckled and shook his head, his anger as swift to wane as it had been to wax. Now he appeared amused, flush with a father's indulgent pride. 'The how is easy enough, Herr Gray. My daughter helps out here at the inn. She has access to all the keys. As to the why, well, I'm afraid she was present when Adolpheus came to tell me of your arrival. Corinna is quite attached to our wayward clock. All of us are, but my daughter especially so. She sees it as a kindred spirit. Certainly, she can be equally mercurial in her moods and actions, as this latest misadventure demonstrates only too well.'

'But I don't understand,' I said. 'Does she think I mean to harm the clock?'

'Do you not?' Doppler demanded. 'Can you deny that the journeymen of your Worshipful Company are charged with the collection and, if need be, suppression of horological curiosities?'

'I don't know what you mean.'

Doppler's wolfish smile returned. 'Please, Herr Gray. Do me the courtesy of an honest reply. I have been to England. I know the ways of the Worshipful Company of Clockmakers.'

'I won't deny that we must sometimes take action to

protect the patents of our guild,' I admitted, choosing my words with care. 'We have every lawful right to do so. Our authority in these matters, as you must know, derives from the king himself. However, we are not in England, sir. I am a visitor to your country, bound by your laws and the obligations of a guest.'

'Yes, but you remain an Englishman for all that. You do not change loyalties, I think, as easily as you do languages. And old habits, so they say, are hard to break. Harder to break than clocks.'

'But your clock is already broken, Herr Doppler. I have seen it but once, briefly, and from the outside only. It is undeniably impressive: a masterpiece, without question. It would be a crime to destroy such a clock. A sin. Once my tool kit is returned, I should like to try my hand at repairing it.'

'The clock does not require repair. It is in perfect working order.'

'I would hardly call it perfect, Herr Doppler! I realize I haven't been in Märchen very long, but all the same, I have not heard it strike the correct hour once in that time.'

'I would be surprised if you had,' he said. 'As far as anyone knows, Herr Gray, not once in all the time the clock has been running – more than fifty years now – has it indicated the correct time, either by peal of bells or position of hands. That is a record of perfection as extraordinary in its way as a clock that has never once been wrong, for as you know, a timepiece that runs slow or fast will eventually mark the correct time, if only briefly and, as it were, in passing. Even a stopped clock tells the correct time twice a day. But our clock, to the extent it has been observed, has never, ever been right.'

'Not once? For that to be true, the hands would have to move backwards as well as forwards!'

'And so they do, back and forward and back again, as if time were as capricious as the wind. The minute and hour hands often move in opposite directions, at disproportional rates. Have you ever encountered such a marvel, Herr Gray?'

'I confess I have not.'

'Surely you can see that to repair such a clock would be tantamount to destroying it.'

'I don't agree. To impose order upon this chaos would be—'

Doppler interrupted, leaning towards me intently. 'But there is already order here, Herr Gray.'

'If by *order* you mean the clock's record of being consistently and invariably wrong, I suppose I must grant you the point in a philosophical sense. But it is an impractical sort of order, to be sure.'

'Are all things to be judged by their practicality? What about a painting, a statue? Does not a different standard apply to such works of art, one of beauty rather than utility?'

'Even beauty has its uses, Herr Doppler, if only to give us pleasure. But the highest art unites beauty and utility. What, after all, is more beautiful and useful than a well-made clock? An accurate clock is beautiful in its functioning, regardless of the trappings in which it is set. A timepiece that embraces inaccuracy, however beautiful in appearance and impressive in design, is a perversion of the true clockmaker's art, which, after all, seeks but to reflect with ever-greater precision the divine ordering that men call time.'

'A pretty speech,' Doppler replied. 'But have you considered the possibility that this clock reflects that divine order more accurately than any other?'

I laughed. 'Now you are being absurd, Herr Doppler!'

'To human senses, time seems to flow in one direction only,

by a progression of discrete intervals, like grains of sand through an hourglass. But to the Almighty, whose senses are infinite and omnipresent, surely time is something quite different. An eternal instant in which past and future are equally perceptible, equally accessible. Equally real. Have I shocked you?'

'The concept is interesting, but hardly shocking,' I replied. Yet in truth, my hand trembled as I raised the mug to my lips and took a deep swallow, though less from shock than from excitement. I remembered how everything had shone with a peculiar blue light in my dream, and how I had associated that radiance with the sacred essence of time. What Herr Doppler was saying resonated with that dream epiphany, confirming my intuition that the clock had much to teach me, if only I could examine it.

'No doubt you are well versed in all manner of horological speculation,' Doppler continued. 'Like Papist Inquisitors, the journeymen of the Worshipful Company of Clockmakers are more knowledgeable about heresies than the heretics themselves, eh?'

'Are you a heretic, then, Herr Doppler?'

'One can hardly live in proximity to Wachter's Folly without developing a unique perspective into the nature of time.'

'That much I'll grant you. Who was this Wachter? Did you know him?'

'I was a boy when he disappeared.'

'Disappeared?'

'Herr Wachter was not a native of Märchen. He arrived one day with his daughter. No one knew whence they had come. He was a clockman, a master of the Worshipful Company, or so he said.'

'You had reason to doubt him?'

'Not at first. He took rooms here, at the Hearth and Home, and began to ply his trade with such skill that no one thought to question his claims. He did not merely repair the timepieces that were brought to him, Herr Gray: he improved them. So it was that when he approached the burgomeister – that is, my father – with plans for a tower clock that would make Märchen famous throughout the empire, a monument to the piety of our town, he was listened to with respect and, finally, refused with regret, for he was an eloquent and persuasive man. My father allowed me to be present, and believe me, when Wachter spoke of the clock he had in mind to build, it was as though your own Shakespeare had penned the words. But Märchen was then just as you find it today: a humble town, prosperous enough but far from wealthy. We could not bear the financial burden of such an ambitious project.'

'And yet the clock was built,' I observed.

'When my father conveyed his refusal, Herr Wachter made a generous counter-offer. In retrospect, suspiciously so. But at the time, we thought him merely eccentric. We had ample proof of his genius; we had no reason to doubt his sincerity.'

'What was the offer?'

'If the town agreed to provide for all the daily wants of his family, he would pay for the clock himself out of his personal fortune, for he was – or so he said – a wealthy man.'

'And you believed him?' I laughed outright. 'Did your father not stop to wonder why a rich man would require the support of the town?'

Doppler gave me an angry scowl. 'As I said, we thought him eccentric. Wealthy men often are. And so, for that matter, are clockmen.'

'I suppose we clockmen have a certain reputation for eccentricity, not entirely undeserved,' I was bound in all honesty to admit. 'But we have no great reputation for wealth. A tower clock is a huge expense, as you know. I doubt even the grandmaster of my guild, by far its wealthiest member, could finance such a project.' This was of course not entirely true. My own fortune, for example, was and is sufficient to build a hundred such towers. But that Herr Doppler did not need to know.

'Even assuming Herr Wachter possessed sufficient funds,' I continued, 'why should he dip into his own pocket? The services of a master clockman are widely sought after and well recompensed. If Märchen could not afford to finance the clock, surely there were other, wealthier towns and patrons to whom Wachter could have applied with every expectation of success, whether here in Austria or in some other country – France or Russia, for instance, if not in England herself, which perhaps more than any other nation holds horology in high esteem. A man with Wachter's talents could have won the patronage of kings and emperors . . . if, that is, he was what he claimed to be: a master of the Worshipful Company of Clockmakers. But I'm afraid this Wachter of yours was nothing of the sort. His actions prove it. I suspect he was an amateur, immensely gifted, to be sure, but also – if, as you say, the clock was intended to function in the manner that it does – more than a little mad.'

'Mad? Perhaps – though the line between madness and genius is a thin and permeable one, I find. But you're right that he did not belong to your Worshipful Company. After Wachter vanished, my father wrote to London. The guild had never heard of him.'

'He should have written sooner.'

'No doubt. But there was no evidence that Wachter was not exactly who and what he claimed to be. During the time he was with us, he laboured steadily on the tower clock and continued repairing our timepieces, as well as building new ones, all of which functioned perfectly.'

'And how long was he with you?'

'Nearly ten years,' Doppler answered, then added defensively: 'A tower clock is not built in a day.'

'Still, Herr Doppler, do you mean to tell me that in ten years, no one in Märchen suspected there was anything odd about the tower clock going up right in their midst?'

'How could we suspect? We are not experts in such things.'

'The first true clockman to pass through town would have exposed him as a fraud.'

'No doubt you are right, but no clockman did pass through. Those were unsettled times, Herr Gray. All of Europe was at war. Men did not wander so far off the beaten track as they do today.'

'Yet Märchen couldn't possibly have supplied him with all the necessary materials for such a project. Orders must have been placed, supplies delivered.'

'Even in dangerous times, men will seek profit. Especially in such times.'

It was strange, but though Doppler's answers to my questions were quite reasonable, I nevertheless felt myself becoming suspicious of them ... and of him. His answers were *too* reasonable, if you see what I mean. Every objection I raised was so smoothly deflected that I couldn't help wondering what he was hiding. 'Go on,' I prompted.

'There is not much more to tell,' he said with a shrug. 'As agreed, we built him a fine house and provided him with everything he needed to live among us in comfort, if not luxury. The years passed as I have told you. Herr Wachter became a fixture of the town, as did his daughter, who grew to young womanhood among us – with no shortage of suitors, I might add, though she showed them scant encouragement; Wachter, like many widowers, was a stern and jealous father. Yet they both seemed content enough here. And one day, at long last, the tower was finished. A ceremony was set for the next day, at which the clock would be blessed by the minister and set to running. But Märchen was awakened before dawn that very morning by the bells of the clock, and I'm sure it will come as less of a surprise to you than it did to us that the hour being tolled so beautifully by those bells was not the same hour we saw registered upon our household clocks, many of which had been made by Wachter. A crowd gathered before the clock tower, where it was discovered that the hands of the clock were moving willy-nilly, as if they possessed a life of their own. But it wasn't until Wachter was sent for that we received the biggest shock of all: he and his daughter were gone, vanished in the night. He must have planned their escape for a long time, using all the genius he employed in his clock-making endeavours, for no trace of them was ever found.'

'Perhaps they perished, fell into a crevasse like Inge's husband.'

'Perhaps.'

'She told me earlier that he was dead – Herr Wachter, I mean.'

'A logical enough assumption, but not personal knowledge. Wachter was fifty-two years old when he disappeared. He would be over a hundred today. I suppose it's possible he might still be alive somewhere, but it hardly seems likely.'

'And he left behind no explanation for his strange actions?'

'Only the clock itself. It explains everything ... and nothing.'

'Why in the name of heaven didn't your father have the clock repaired at once, when the extent of Wachter's mischief was apparent?'

At this, Doppler tugged at one end of his moustache. 'He tried, Herr Gray. He wrote to our own Clockmakers' Guild in Augsburg, requesting that someone be sent to us. A journeyman was duly dispatched.'

'It proved beyond his skill?'

'Beyond his sanity, rather. He entered the clock tower and remained inside for a day and a night. At last, the bailiff went in after him. The man was found lying in one corner, his eyes wide open and unblinking, his body stiff as a corpse. But he was not dead, merely cataleptic.'

'My God – what happened?'

'A significant shock to mind and body, or so said the apothecary. After a few days, the man was able to move again, after a fashion, but his mind never recovered. I won't trouble you with his ravings. They were utterly without sense. Some time later, the guild sent a master clockmaker. The result was identical. No further attempts were made. The entrance to the tower was bricked shut; no one has entered since.'

'Why, I suspect you are telling me a fairy tale, Herr Doppler!' I could not forbear from exclaiming.

'It is the gospel truth, I assure you.'

'And I suppose you will have a ready answer as well for why the clock was not destroyed after all this?'

If Doppler took offence, he didn't show it. In fact, he seemed more amused than anything. 'That was supposed to happen, Herr Gray. My father received an order to that effect from the guildmaster in Augsburg; such orders, as you may not be aware, being a foreigner, carry the weight of imperial writ. He wrote back stating that he had complied. That ended the matter. As far as the Clockmakers' Guild is concerned, Wachter's Folly is no more.'

'Was your father in the habit of disregarding imperial decrees?' I asked.

'Hardly,' Doppler replied with a tight smile. 'But in this case, or so he told me later, he felt that disobedience was the lesser betrayal.'

'I'm afraid you've lost me.'

Doppler glanced at his pocket watch, lying open on the table. He picked it up, snapped the lid shut. 'I will show you.' He got to his feet, sliding the watch back into his coat. Then he lifted the candle. 'Come with me.'

'But where . . . ?'

'Not far. Come.' He walked to the swinging door and held it open.

Intrigued, I stood. Hesta, too, bestirred herself. Toenails clicking across the stone floor, she preceded us both through the door. Doppler motioned for me to follow her, which I did, and he brought up the rear. Then, holding the candle before him, he stepped past me and alongside the wooden bar, once again motioning me to follow.

He stopped opposite the cuckoo clock that hung on the wall behind the bar. By the light of the candle, which Doppler placed on the bar, I saw that it was just shy of one o'clock.

'In a moment, Herr Gray,' Doppler said in a hushed voice, perhaps afraid of waking Inge, whose room was downstairs, or so I gathered, 'you will have the answer to your question. Or the beginnings of an answer.'

I had noticed the clock earlier but hadn't examined it closely. Now that I did, I recognized Wachter's craftsmanship: there, in miniature, carved into the dark walnut housing, was the same hellish scene depicted upon Märchen's tower clock.

Only here the crowd of the tormented and their tormentors was roughly done, like a study for the larger and more complex composition outside. The figures were blocky, ill-defined, their faces possessing crude features, like marks gouged by a hasty knife, or no features at all. They seemed to be engaged in a struggle to keep themselves from losing definition and sinking into each other, into the wood itself, as if it were the nature of hell to dissolve all distinctions, on every level, mixing matter into a primordial soup of suffering from which, by some supreme effort of stubborn will, or an impulse of pain impossible to imagine, the old body reshaped itself for a time, to undergo again, and yet again, into eternity, the stripping away of flesh from bone, of bone from spirit, of self from self. I wondered what remained after such a scouring. Was it the soul? Or could that, too, be unravelled and reknit, broken down and built up again for ever and ever?

Across the bar, the minute hand of the cuckoo clock jerked upright. A whirring commenced within the housing. I leaned forward, resting my elbows on the bar, intent not to miss anything of whatever was about to occur.

The small doors at the top of the clock flipped open, and out popped the strangest-looking bird I had ever seen. But even as it spread glimmering bronze wings, I realized that it was no bird at all. It was a dragon.

The automaton – no bigger than my thumb – was exquisitely crafted. Its metal wings were supple in their flexing, and its barbed tail lashed from side to side in the manner of a cat's. Arching its neck in a sinuous movement, the mechanical dragon cocked its horned head to one side and seemed to regard me with curiosity through jewel-like eyes. The craftsmanship was extraordinary; I could almost believe I was looking at a living creature. Then the mouth opened, revealing rows of silvery, needle-sharp teeth and a tongue the colour of cold iron. A loud hiss emerged, as from a boiling tea kettle, and I stepped back, reminded of my dream. Even as I did so, a jet of flame gushed from between the mechanism's jaws. It extended no more than an inch, but so unexpected was the display that I gave a start and cried out as though I had been scorched.

Doppler laughed with childlike glee as the automaton was pulled back into the housing. The tiny doors snapped shut behind it; the minute hand jerked forward.

'Tell me, Herr Gray,' he demanded, 'have you ever seen such a wonder?'

I could truthfully admit that I had not – not in all my travels.

'Here it is no exception,' Doppler stated. 'Just one of many marvels left to us by Herr Wachter.'

'I should like to examine the workings,' I said.

'As to that, you must ask Inge. The clock is hers.'

'I have read of such marvels,' I mused. 'It is said that the court of Byzantium was filled with automatons all but indistinguishable from the birds and animals they resembled. But those secrets were lost with the city.'

Doppler shrugged. 'Perhaps they survived. Or Herr Wachter rediscovered them.'

'And you say there are more clocks like this one?'

'Not precisely the same as this, no, but many others are as distinctive in their way. Herr Wachter lived among us for ten years. He was not idle.' Doppler slipped out his pocket watch and laid it on the bar. 'Go on, take it.'

I did so with alacrity.

'You are holding Wachter's personal timepiece,' Doppler told me with pride. 'My father admired it so often that

Wachter finally presented it to him as a gift. And my father passed it on to me. Go on – open it.'

I complied. There, on the face, I saw strange and indeed incomprehensible shapes standing, as it were, in place of numbers, and hands that had the shape of a dragon. Herr Wachter, it seemed, had been obsessed with dragons.

'Hold it to your ear,' Doppler directed.

I did so under his expectant gaze. But I heard nothing of interest. In fact, I heard nothing at all. 'It's stopped,' I said.

'Indeed, it has not.'

'I hear no ticking.'

'There is none to hear.'

'But when you wind the watch, how—'

'It is not wound,' Doppler interrupted. 'The stem is merely decorative.'

I gave the stem a gentle twist. It did not budge. 'Then how is the watch powered?'

'I do not know. But it has never run down in all these years. My father did not permit the casing to be opened, fearing that to do so would destroy the mechanism within, and I have followed his wise example.' He extended his hand; with regret, I laid the watch in his palm.

After Herr Doppler had put away the watch, I pressed him again for permission to examine the tower clock.

'Imagine,' he replied, 'that we were in England, and thus under the jurisdiction of your guild. What do you suppose your masters in the Worshipful Company would make of our tower clock, or the other timepieces you have seen here?'

I knew the answer only too well. They would not permit such unique timepieces to exist. Every last one would be dis-assembled, stripped of its secrets, and destroyed. But to admit that would have been to scuttle my chances. 'I cannot say,' I told him.

'You are being disingenuous,' he returned. 'We both know what their verdict would be. What your verdict, as their faithful representative, must be. You have already made your judgement, Herr Gray. Do not bother to deny it.'

'How can I judge what I do not understand?'

'You judge *because* you do not understand. That is the way of your Worshipful Company, and indeed of our own Clockmakers' Guild.'

'That is not my way,' I insisted. 'I left England to search out just such timepieces as these. I wish to learn from them, not destroy them.'

'You wish to plunder them, rather, to take their secrets for your own. Can you deny it?'

'I am a scientist, Herr Doppler. I proceed by experiment and observation. By reason. How can the science of horology advance unless such marvels as the timepieces of Märchen become part of the common stock of knowledge available to all horologists?'

He laughed. 'Ah, so you are an altruist, then. You would share your knowledge with the world and not keep it for the advantage of your guild and country. Forgive me, sir, but I am not so naïve as to believe that.'

'For more than two years now, I have been on a quest of sorts,' I told him. 'A quest that has taken me halfway around the world and finally brought me here. I had not heard the name Wachter before yesterday, and yet I have known of him – indeed, I have seen his handiwork in my travels, hints and clues that pointed towards something grander, more fully realized: that pointed, in short, to Märchen. Perhaps you will think me deluded, but I believe that someone – call him

Wachter if you like – has led me here for a purpose. I am meant to examine these timepieces.'

'So you think that Wachter is still alive, do you?' Doppler mused. 'You think that he has somehow been a step ahead of you in your travels, leaving behind examples of his craftsmanship like a trail of breadcrumbs for you to follow. And you accuse *me* of telling fairy tales?'

I confess I blushed at that. 'I know it sounds far-fetched,' I admitted. 'Yet I also know what I have seen. Wachter – or some horological wizard with intimate knowledge of his work – has brought me here. There is something I am supposed to learn. Something I am supposed to do . . .'

'I think perhaps it is a good thing that my daughter took your tool kit,' Doppler said. 'She acted rashly, precipitately, as she is wont to do, but her instincts were sound. You are a dangerous man, Herr Gray.'

'You think me mad?'

'Worse – sincere. You are determined to examine our timepieces regardless of the risk to them . . . and to yourself.'

'Is that a threat, Herr Doppler? Am I to be arrested? Expelled from town? Or will I simply vanish, swallowed by the snows like Inge's husband?'

At this, Doppler's white whiskers seemed to bristle like the fur of a cat. 'Do you think we are barbarians, criminals? We are civilized people! I am concerned for your welfare, Herr Gray. Recall the fate of your predecessors who ventured inside the clock tower.'

'I am willing to take the risk. I would promise to touch nothing, simply to observe, if you would allow me to enter the tower – or to examine the workings of any of the timepieces here.'

'As to the tower clock, that is off-limits. But you are otherwise free to ply your trade.'

'You will return my tool kit, then?'

'We are no more thieves than murderers, Herr Gray. Of course your property will be returned.'

'And then?'

'Why, that is up to you. By all means, advertise your services. Make your ambition known. Who can say? Perhaps one of our citizens will bring you a clock or watch made or enhanced by Wachter. Or you may persuade Inge to let you examine her cuckoo.'

I confess I blushed at that, for it seemed to me that Herr Doppler was alluding to something other than the clock whose operation we had just witnessed. I remembered the yeasty smell that had emanated from the corpulent woman, as if she were a loaf of bread freshly removed from the oven, and how that smell had stirred a hunger in me to lose myself in her flesh – a hunger that had, or so I believed, somehow transmuted itself into the succubus-like figure that had invaded my dream. I was a younger man then, and such wayward expressions of desire embarrassed me. I still had much to learn of life and of love. 'And you will not impede me from plying my trade?' I asked Doppler.

'As long as you do not attempt to force the issue, no.'

'For that I thank you.'

Doppler inclined his head. 'I have no doubt that you will abide by our agreement,' he said. 'Your tool kit will be returned tomorrow. And now, Herr Gray, I must bid you good night. I do not have far to go, but the snow will make my journey home a tedious one, I'm afraid.'

'Why not remain here, at the inn? Surely Inge has an extra room.'

'Are you a father, Herr Gray?'

I shook my head.

'Then you will not understand. But I find I cannot sleep a wink if I am not under the same roof as my daughter. She is all I have left, you see, since the loss of her mother.'

'I am sorry.'

'Ach, it was years ago,' he said, making a dismissive gesture with one hand. 'In truth, we were badly matched, she and I. It amazes me still to think that such an ill-suited union could have produced a treasure like Corinna. I hope you will not hold her indiscretion against her, Herr Gray. She is a good girl at heart.'

'I have no ill feelings,' I assured him, 'and shall tell her so when I meet her.'

'She will be relieved to hear it, I am sure,' he replied and took his leave.

10

Corinna

IT WAS SNOWING HARDER THAN EVER WHEN I AWOKE THE NEXT morning. Outside the window of my room, in the pale morning light, I could catch only fleeting glimpses of the street and hints of buildings across the way. It was as if the town were flickering in and out of existence, suspended in time.

As best I could tell, I'd had no further nocturnal visitors, either in dreams or reality. I performed my morning ablutions and went down to breakfast. The common room was deserted, no doubt because of the snowstorm. There was no sign of Inge or anyone else at the bar; nevertheless, the fire had been built up again, and the room was warm and welcoming. I took a seat at the bar opposite the cuckoo clock, which indicated a time of approximately seven forty-five. As I pulled out my pocket watch and wound the stem, I thought of Doppler's watch, its ordinary appearance hiding a secret I would have given much to know. A watch that needed no winding, that had not stopped or slowed in more than fifty years, if the man was to be believed. When I'd held it up to my ear, I'd heard nothing at all, as though it were hollow inside. Or solid all the way through. But of course there had to be a mechanism within, some source of motive power. But what?

I looked up at the sound of the kitchen door swinging open. Inge emerged in a cloud of fragrant smoke.

'Why, good morning, Herr Gray,' she said, wiping her beefy hands, white with flour, on her apron. She seemed to have grown stouter overnight. Her plump cheeks, flushed from the heat of the kitchen, glowed like ripe tomatoes.

'Good morning, Inge.'

'I heard what happened last night,' she said, lowering her voice to a whisper as she drew abreast of me on the other side of the bar although we were alone in the room. 'I'm altogether mortified. The girl will be punished. You'll get your tools back, never fear.'

'So Herr Doppler assured me,' I said.

'Och, that girl gives herself airs. She thinks that I work for her and not the other way around.'

'I'd like to speak to her. Is she here?'

'So early? Not that one! It's a rare day she's out of bed before noon. Thinks she's a princess. And her father, bless his tender heart, doesn't do anything to correct the impression. What that family needs is a woman's hand. A mother for the girl, a wife for the father.'

It sounded as if Inge had aspirations to both positions. 'He's a widower, I understand.'

'Lost his wife the same time I lost my husband.' She leaned across the bar, her yeasty smell once again working its disconcerting magic. Her breasts swelled beneath her apron, seeming about to spill over the top of her blouse. I shifted on my stool as she continued, her voice again dropping to a whisper. 'They ran off together, Herr Gray, the two of them. I'm telling you because you would have heard it sooner or later, the way the folk of this town gossip. So you see why I wasn't exactly distraught when I learned of my husband's fate.'

'Your dream, you mean.'

She nodded. 'I saw her there with him, lying broken at the bottom of the crevasse.' Her smile of fond reminiscence sent a chill down my spine.

'Of course, it's not Corinna's fault that her mother was no better than a common whore,' Inge continued, sounding as though she believed the opposite was in fact true, 'but blood tells, you know. The girl needs to be treated firmly, not with the indulgence her father lavishes on her, encouraging all her worst tendencies. I do my best, but I'm afraid my efforts aren't always appreciated as they should be.'

This I could well imagine. I found myself feeling un-expected sympathy for the motherless girl who had stolen my property.

'Ach, no matter,' said Inge, straightening. 'You're here for breakfast, not to listen to my troubles. But wouldn't you prefer to sit at a table, Herr Gray?'

'I'm right where I want to be,' I told her. 'Close to your remarkable clock.'

Inge turned to the side, crossed arms nestling her ample bosom, and beamed at the timepiece on the wall behind the bar. 'Yes, it's something, isn't it?'

'I saw it strike the hour last night with Herr Doppler. He said I might ask your permission to examine its workings.'

'I'm afraid that's out of the question,' she replied without hesitation.

'But—'

'No, Herr Gray. What if you should break it? Who could fix it again? Could you?'

'I believe I could,' I answered. 'Clocks are mechanical devices, no more and no less. Even such a marvel as this one. Herr Wachter's secrets, once studied, can be understood, and once understood, replicated. I've encountered many wondrous clocks in my travels, and I've never found one beyond my abilities to repair.'

'You're not lacking in self-confidence, I'll say that for you. Yet sometimes your duty is to destroy, not repair, isn't that so? At least, that is the case with the journeymen of our own Clockmakers' Guild.'

'It is the same with us,' I admitted. 'A sad duty.'

'Sad or happy makes no difference,' Inge said with a shrug. 'The result is the same either way. Perhaps you are correct, and you possess the skill to examine my clock without disturbing its workings, or, failing that, to repair it successfully, but what if, instead, you should find something that compelled you to destroy it?'

'My guild has no authority outside England,' I answered, choosing my words with care. 'Indeed, one of the reasons I left England was to escape its authority, so that I would no longer have to put the parochial interests of the guild above science. Destroying clocks is not something I enjoy. It's abhorrent to me. Besides, I'm a guest here, and it's a rude guest who damages or destroys the property of his host! Really, if you think about it, I could be a godsend to this town, an English horologist at once beyond the reach of his own guild and unbound by the strictures that would govern the actions of any Austrian clockman. I discussed all this with Herr Doppler last night. He told me I might advertise my services freely and repair or examine any timepiece I cared to – with the owner's consent, of course.'

'You make a strong case, Herr Gray. But you must understand, my clock is special. It is Herr Wachter's finest creation . . . after the town clock, of course. In some ways, it's even finer.'

'It is marvellous,' I agreed.

'I'll tell you what,' she said. 'I will not be your first customer, but if you can find someone else willing to let you examine their timepiece, I'll consider giving you a peek at mine. Don't look so discouraged, Herr Gray – I haven't set you an impossible task. Herr Wachter made many timepieces during his years here. You won't find a household in Märchen without at least one.'

'I'm not at all discouraged,' I told her. 'I'll make inquiries around town today.'

'Just one other person,' she reiterated with a broad wink, 'and my cuckoo is all yours.'

As with Herr Doppler the night before, I had the sense that Inge's meaning was twofold. But before I could manage a reply, she turned and made her way into the kitchen, the back of her dress swaying voluminously from side to side with the quiet tolling of her hips. The sight put me in mind of my visit to the clock tower the day before, when I'd watched the bells of the campanile swinging soundlessly in the falling snow. I felt an incongruous stirring of passion, as if the mechanism of desire had become unbalanced in me. As I said, I like women with meat on their bones, but this was beyond anything I had ever experienced. What would it be like to sink into those rolls of flesh, I wondered, to scale the soft mountain of that massive body?

A familiar whirring sound shook me from my reverie. What followed was as extraordinary as I remembered – perhaps even more so, for I was fully awake now and, not taken by surprise as I had been the night before, able to register details that had escaped me when the room had been illuminated by a single candle instead of bright lamps and a roaring fire.

The little coppery dragon that emerged from the clock was the most natural-seeming automaton I had ever seen. Yet it was also the most *un*natural, for no matter how realistic it appeared, how lifelike the glimmer in its eyes, the sinuous curling of its barbed tail, the ripple of tiny muscles under sleek scales, there are no such things as dragons. They are, are they not, no more than superstitions, myths, the stuff of dreams. As the little fellow vented its finger-length of flame, I recalled my own dream of the immense one-eyed dragon and how it had swivelled its grizzled head towards me and opened wide its jaws. I remembered the dark flickerings in its throat, as of a vast colony of bats stirring in the depths of a cave. A wave of dizziness swept over me, and I clung to the bar like a drowning man to a piece of wreckage.

Then the minute hand jerked forward, and the dragon retreated into its sanctuary, the tiny door snapping shut behind it. There was a last, fading whir, then a silence broken only by the regular knocking of the pendulum. The longing that pierced me at that instant was so pure that it was physically painful. I knew then that my assurances to Herr Doppler and Inge were meaningless.

I would do whatever it took to get inside that clock.

I spent the next hours calling on townsfolk in their homes and places of business. The blizzard was still in full force. Narrow pathways had been shovelled along the streets, with side passages leading to individual buildings to allow for ingress and egress. To prevent these paths from filling up again, they had been lined with wooden frames that joined together to form covered corridors, lit by lamps at regular intervals. The mazelike passages thus formed were narrow, cold and draughty but preferable to being exposed to the elements.

While I slept, the town must have been hard at work erecting these frames. I had never heard of such a thing, but the people of Märchen assured me that otherwise they would be snow-bound for months on end, trapped in their homes. This way the life of the town could go on even in the depths of winter, while storms raged that made this one appear a mere dusting. It struck me as a peculiar but ingenious solution to the problem set by nature, and I was not surprised to learn that, like the timepieces that so interested me, it, too, was an innovation of Wachter's.

I found that I did not have to introduce myself: everyone knew who I was and why I had come. The townsfolk were friendly, if somewhat formal. They invited me into their homes, offered me food and drink, a place by the fire, and asked for the latest news of the wider world. I obliged, con-cealing my impatience with their questions and the comments they exchanged among themselves, which scarcely varied from house to house. Maddeningly, these mundane conver-sations almost always took place with one of Wachter's creations in plain view, hanging on the wall or sitting on a nearby table. But at last the moment would come when my hosts would turn to the reason for my visit.

In this, Inge had not exaggerated: every shop and house-hold possessed at least one timepiece of Wachter's manufacture. These their owners presented for my admir-ation, hovering at my side as if afraid I might attempt to steal them right out from under their noses. Yet I kept a pleasant demeanour, praising with perfect sincerity the timepieces and the care with which they had been maintained over the years. Each was a masterpiece. In some places I was given no more than a quick glance; in others, I was allowed to hold these beautiful and eccentric creations, which moved me with feelings of wonder, excitement and sadness, as if their secrets lay not merely out of my sight but beyond my understanding, and would remain so even if I should look upon them more closely. I would have had my notebook with me in order to make preliminary notes and sketches, but since my tool kit was still missing, despite Herr Doppler's assurances that it would be returned, I had judged it best to approach the towns-folk empty-handed, hoping to put them at ease. Nevertheless, my requests for permission to perform a more thorough examination later were everywhere rebuffed.

It struck me after the first hour or so that I hadn't seen a single timepiece that didn't show evidence of Wachter's touch. Inquiring about this, I was told that while Wachter had repaired every clock and pocket watch that was brought to him, he refused to accept new commissions unless his prospective clients first destroyed every other timepiece in their possession. I couldn't help thinking of the policies of the Worshipful Company and the Clockmakers' Guild, which would have seen all of Wachter's timepieces destroyed; here the opposite had occurred, and that had been the fate of the ordinary, run-of-the-mill timepieces. Thus, over the years of his residence, such timepieces had vanished from Märchen altogether, replaced by Wachter's original creations, or by timepieces he had not just repaired but altered to such a degree that they were, to all intents and purposes, original creations as well. And in the years since his disappearance, no new timepieces had appeared; indeed, the townsfolk, by common consent, kept them out. My own watch, for example, was looked upon with outright suspicion, as if it might carry some sort of plague, and I soon learned to consult it in private only.

By mid-afternoon, discouraged but not defeated, I returned

to the Hearth and Home for supper. Easier said than done, as I soon lost my way in the warren of dimly lit passages, none of which was marked; doubtless the townsfolk had no need of signs to direct them, as sure of their routes as rabbits or rats, but I was not so fortunate. Nor was I able to ask directions, for I seemed to be the only one out and about. It was disconcerting, to say the least, as if the men and women I had just been visiting and speaking to had vanished off the face of the earth, leaving me alone, trapped in this strange place. The farther I roamed, the more I felt cut off from the outside world. The passages down which I made my way, scarcely wide enough for two people to squeeze past each other – Inge would have been stuck like a cork in a bottle – might have been miles beneath the surface of the ground, cut deep into the bowels of the Alps. I began to be aware of a great weight pressing down from above, more than could be accounted for by the snow, and I felt the first stirrings of panic, as if the ceiling were about to collapse on top of me, or as if I had strayed somehow beyond the borders of the town.

It was then that a gust of icy wind blasted past me from behind. The lamps guttered and went out, plunging me into a darkness more absolute than I had ever known. I carried a tinderbox, of course, but it was not easily accessible, and was difficult to use in such draughty conditions. But I did not lose my head. Laying my hand along one wall, I pressed on in the direction I had been going, reasoning that sooner or later I would emerge into another lighted area or come upon a side passage leading to a house where I might request assistance.

Neither proved to be the case. In the dark, it was all too easy to imagine that I had slipped between the cracks of the world, as if I might fall at any moment, like Inge's husband, into a crevasse where I would lie helplessly until death claimed me. I lost track of time – for a clockman, a most disturbing sensation. Finally I swallowed my pride and called out for help, but there was no answer.

Or, rather, the answer that came was less welcome than the silence that had preceded it. For what issued from out of the darkness at my back was a sound that had nothing human about it. A harsh chuffing, as of some bestial exhalation. I froze, hackles rising. It came again, closer now, and I felt a shudder pass through the ground, as if whatever was back there was heavy as a bull. I felt as if I had re-entered my dream of the night before – or, rather, that the dream had entered the waking world, pursuing me. I ran. I had no light, no weapon save my dirk. But I did not imagine it would afford any protection against this unseen foe.

Was this some plot of the townsfolk? Had Herr Doppler arranged to have the lamps extinguished, then introduced some large and angry animal into the labyrinth? I didn't know what to think; I barely retained the capacity for thought. More than once I struck a wall or other barrier that sent me reeling or even to my knees, head spinning, but I pressed on every time, certain that my pursuer, whatever it was, would strike at any moment. I sensed its presence at my back, felt the hot wind of its breath; I could have reached out and touched it, had I dared – which I did not.

Then a last collision . . . and I was outside. I fell to my knees in the midst of howling wind and snow. After my immersion in darkness, even the wan light of the day was blinding, an explosion of white and grey that seemed as much inside my head as outside it. I was exhausted, spent; I knelt there in snow up to my waist, shivering, clutching my dirk with one hand, my hat with the other, ready to fight but with no idea of what I was fighting or from which direction an attack might come.

But no attack did come. After a while, my eyes adjusted to the light – though the blizzard still made it difficult to see – and I was able to rise to my feet. Looming out of the gloom before me I saw the outlines of a building, and I made for it as though my very life depended upon it.

As I drew closer, I recognized the distinctive shape of the clock tower and heard, tangled in the keening of the wind, a raw and random music: the muffled chiming of storm-buffeted bells. I could barely make out the campanile; as for the bells within and the clock face below, I could not see them at all, and the proscenium seemed less a potential shelter from the snow and wind (assuming I could somehow climb so high) than the source of both, like a cave from whose frigid depths winter was exhaled upon the world.

A shovelled passage led to the base of the tower, which struck me as odd: according to Doppler, the entrance had been sealed, and it seemed a waste of effort to shovel a passage that led nowhere. Unless, of course, the burgomeister had lied to me in order to discourage me from seeking the entrance on my own. But at that point, all I cared about was getting out of the storm and away from whatever had been pursuing me – and might still be, for all I knew.

Upon reaching the foot of the tower, I saw that the passage branched left and right, as if circling the structure. Rather than following it in either direction, I stepped up to the wall, where snow was nestled in the niches and hollows created by the ornamental figures I'd noticed upon my arrival the day before. Most of them were buried now, but here and there arms and hands and heads emerged from the snow as in some macabre representation of an avalanche, or, rather, the aftermath of one. Even the great snake or dragon depicted there was all but submerged . . . yet the way its coils broke free of the snow only to plunge out of sight again made it seem to be sporting amidst the corpses like a sea serpent frolicking amidst the carnage of a wreck.

I swept the snow away with my hat and then groped among the contorted shapes, which I saw now were metal castings, looking for evidence of a door, perhaps a hidden mechanism that, once triggered, would cause the façade to swing open and admit me. But there was nothing – at least, nothing that my fingers, clumsy within gloves that provided scant protection against the cold, could detect. I wondered if I could climb the façade, use the castings as hand- and footholds to reach the shelter of the proscenium, and gain entrance to the interior from there. But I did not like my chances in such a climb. The façade was slick with snow and ice, and the gusting winds would make any attempt even more hazardous.

I considered turning back, looking for an alternative route to the Hearth and Home, or seeking shelter from one of the townsfolk, but I wasn't ready to give up on the tower yet; this close, my curiosity was rekindled: it was no longer just the need for shelter that drove me. When, I asked myself, would I find a better opportunity to examine the tower unobserved? Hunching my shoulders against the wind and snow, and jamming my hat back onto my head, I set off down the left-ward-branching passage.

I hadn't gone far when the bells of the tower began to peal in earnest, striking some arbitrary hour. I ducked my head and pressed myself against the base of the tower as clumps of snow and ice, dislodged from above, fell around me. The metal figures of the façade poked into my back, and through them I felt a deep, slow, rhythmic thrumming: the inner workings of the great clock. I hadn't felt the slightest vibration earlier when I'd groped among the castings; now, with the tolling of the bells, an internal mechanism had been set in motion, and I knew at once what it must be.

I ran back to the front of the tower and peered up through the falling snow. The icy flakes stung like chips of stone, and indeed the sky, or what I could see of it, was as grey as clouded marble, like the roof of a vast domed chamber, so that, for a moment, as I gazed into the hollow arch of the proscenium, it seemed to me that I was not looking into an enclosed space but rather *out* of one, and though I could not see even a glimpse of what lay beyond the snowy curtain, I sensed a presence wider than the world I knew. The vivid force of this perception staggered me, and I felt again, as I had the day before, an impulse to step away from the tower, to retreat out of range of its uncanny influence. But my curiosity outweighed my fear, and I held my ground.

Though the bells were still tolling, they had lost all semblance of musicality. Now they came crashing down like thunder. I flinched with every peal, each louder than the one before, until the very ground seemed to tremble beneath my feet. Once again I recalled my dream, how the girl had fled from footsteps that shook the ground in just this way.

I would have turned then and fled myself, curiosity be damned, if the first automaton hadn't appeared from out of the snow-blurred depths of the proscenium. At first, I couldn't make sense of what I was seeing. Something angular, tall and dark, like the prow of a ship, came gliding into view. The prow of a second ship seemed to pass it on the outside, as if some ghost armada were sailing out of the clock tower. But then my mind made an insane adjustment of scale, of perspective, and I realized that I was seeing a pair of legs scissoring through the snow. The legs alone were far larger than could be contained within the tower; they seemed to rise up for ever. But of course they did not: no more than mountains rise for ever. Yet it might have been a mountain that I was seeing – a mountain in the shape of a man.

My legs folded, depositing me on my knees. Then, as the earth resounded like the skin of a drum to each impossible footfall, I toppled onto my side, gazing up at the colossal figure. Another strode behind it. And another behind that. They moved slowly, effortlessly, it seemed, through the blizzard. The tower was still present, its dimensions unchanged. Though the figures overtopped it by hundreds of feet, they continued to emerge from its depths, nor did their weight crush the stage across which they filed, nor, for all the vastness of their strides, had the first of them yet reached the opposite side. It was as though the laws of nature were in abeyance, and categories of perception that could or should not coexist in a sane mind were suddenly thrust together. I felt the gears of my reason grinding against each other. I suppose I must have screamed.

At that, the figures halted. The bells fell silent. There was only the howling of the wind. I tried to get to my feet and run, but it was useless. I was like a dazed rabbit scratching for shelter in the snow. Then came a sight that stilled even those feeble movements. A hand was reaching for me, dropping through the blizzard like a dark cloud, like the fall of night. There was no escaping it – not even if I'd been able to run. I had no doubt but that I was about to die. In that moment, a dreamlike clarity possessed me. I felt intensely present yet at the same time detached from what was happening; I watched the fingers of that immense hand open to grasp me, and in those seconds, which seemed to stretch into hours, it struck me with the force of revelation that these were not automatons I was seeing – no mechanical constructs could possibly be so large – but rather living creatures, giants such as the Bible speaks of, and the pagan myths, too. It occurred to me then that Wachter's Folly was not a clock tower but instead a kind of portal, a gateway, so to speak, between our world and another, and that these giants had crossed some un-imaginable distance to come here. Had Wachter summoned them with his wizardry, compelled them to parade in single file across the stage of his extraordinary clock? And if so, for what purpose? I did not think I would learn the answer to these questions, or any others, as the gigantic fingers closed around me, blotting out the snow, the light, the world.

When next I opened my eyes, I was in bed in my room at the Hearth and Home. The light of a candle illuminated the startled face of a girl seated in a chair between the bed and the hissing stove. She gave a cry and sprang to her feet, rush-ing from the room before I could say a word. I heard her calling for Frau Hubner from the hallway. I winced and raised a hand to my throbbing head . . . only to encounter a bandage. Pain flared, and I jerked my hand away with a groan.

I sat up, and the covers slipped to my waist. I was shirtless; in fact, I was naked. I had no memory of what had happened to my clothes . . . or, for that matter, to me. The room was toasty warm; the curtains were drawn over the window, so I had no idea what time it was or whether it was still snowing. The girl, meanwhile, had left off calling for Inge, though she had not returned to the room, and now I heard – and felt as well – the landlady's heavy tread as she mounted the stairs. It was no more than a faint trembling compared with the earthshaking footsteps of the giants, yet the terror I'd felt as I lay helpless in the snow took hold of me again. Shivering like some palsied ancient, I groped for the covers and pulled them to my chin.

Inge squeezed into the room, her round face flushed red. 'So, you are awake at last, Herr Gray! But what are you doing? You're in no condition to get out of that bed!'

'Indeed, I am not,' I agreed. 'Where are my clothes?'

'I was going to ask you the same question,' she replied as she bustled over. I flinched, thinking that she was going to push me down – weak as I was, a child could have done it. But instead she touched the back of her hand to my forehead, then reached past me to fluff the pillows into a backrest. Her yeasty scent enveloped me, and had its customary effect, which I endeavoured to hide by shifting beneath the covers.

'There,' she said at last, stepping back to survey her work with satisfaction, her thick arms crossed over the shelf of her bosom, 'all nice and comfy.' I had the impression that she was rather enjoying my helplessness. 'You gave us quite a scare, Herr Gray! Ach, what possessed you to pay a visit to the clock tower in such weather? And what happened to your clothes?'

'Do you mean to say I was naked when you found me?'

'It was not I but Adolpheus who found you,' Inge said. 'Lying in the snow at the base of the clock tower as naked as the day you were born!'

'I lost my way in the storm,' I told her, 'and found myself at the clock tower. The bells began to chime, and I saw the most incredible display . . .' I trailed off, afraid that she would think me mad if I said any more. 'That is all I remember.'

'Lucky for you I happened by,' Adolpheus remarked, entering the room with his lopsided gait. Hesta trotted in behind him, tail wagging. The dog went straight to the stove, where she circled once before curling up on the bare floorboards.

'I found you at the foot of the tower,' Adolpheus

continued. 'It seems you were struck on the head by a piece of falling ice.'

I raised my hand to the bandage again, but stopped short of touching it, remembering the pain that had ensued the last time I did so.

'Big as a cannonball it was,' my rescuer stated, demonstrating the size of the ice chunk with his hands. 'Blood everywhere! I thought you were dead at first – if not from the blow to the head, then from the cold, for you weren't wearing so much as a stitch of clothing. I covered you with my cloak, lifted you in my arms, and carried you here. I may be small, but I am strong as a bull.'

'But my weapon . . . my watch!'

'As for your dirk, I saw no sign of it. Perhaps it is buried under the snow. Your watch, however, was clutched in your hand; indeed, I had some difficulty prising your fingers apart to remove it! It's there, beside the bed.'

And so it was, on the nightstand. The sight of it was immensely reassuring for some reason; even more so was the familiar heft of it in my hand. But I didn't know what to think. Had it all been a dream? Everything had seemed so real! Yet I remembered how, when the bells began to toll, chunks of ice had fallen from the tower. Perhaps one had indeed struck me – knocked me, dazed and bleeding, to the ground. And from there, before I blacked out, I had gazed up and seen the automatons emerging from the tower; from that perspective, they might have loomed large as giants. Yet that did not explain what had happened to my clothes and my dirk.

Inge, meanwhile, had poured a glass of water from the pitcher on the table beside the stove, and this she brought to me now. 'Here, Herr Gray. You must be parched.'

I accepted the glass and took a deep swallow . . . then began to cough – racking coughs that made my ribcage ring like iron and left me aching in every muscle and bone. Only when the fit was over, and I lay back weakly against the pillows, gasping like a fish out of water, a cold sweat clinging to my skin, did I notice that Inge had taken the glass from me before I could spill it over the bedclothes.

'You must take things slowly at first, Herr Gray,' she admonished, shaking her head sternly, chins jiggling like vanilla puddings.

With a sense of things clicking belatedly, dreadfully, into place, I asked her how long I had been in bed.

'Adolpheus found you six days ago,' came the reply.

Six days! I didn't remember a moment of even a single one of them. Yet I had no trouble recalling my last moments at the clock tower. They might have taken place just hours ago, they were so fresh in my mind. 'And was I unconscious all that time?' I demanded.

'As good as,' said Inge. 'You were feverish. Burning up. You raved, ranted. We took turns sitting with you. Tending you like a newborn baby. Adolpheus, the girl and I. Even Herr Doppler.'

'I'm grateful,' I told her. 'And sorry for any trouble I caused.'

'Ach, what trouble?' Inge replied. 'The important thing is that the fever has broken at last. You're on the mend now.'

'You'll be up and about in no time,' Adolpheus seconded, grinning through his beard.

'But you need to build up your strength,' said Inge. 'Do you think you could eat something?'

'I feel as if I could eat a horse,' I told her.

'I'm afraid that's not on the menu at the Hearth and Home,' she replied with a smile.

'You could have fooled me,' interjected Adolpheus.

She ignored the gibe. 'I doubt solid food would agree with you just now. Better to start with some nutritious broth. I'll send up a bowl.'

'Thank you, Inge. You, too, Adolpheus. I'd be dead if you hadn't come looking for me.'

'As to that, I may have found you, Herr Gray, but it wasn't from looking. No, I was about my duties, keeping the pathways clear and the lamps lit, when I spotted you. Didn't know whether to dig you out or finish burying you!' He chortled. 'But what happened to your clothes, Herr Gray?' He tapped the side of his nose with one finger. 'An afternoon tryst, perhaps, interrupted by a husband unexpectedly returned home?'

Before I could deny it, Inge broke in.

'Leave off your teasing, Adolpheus. Can't you see how tired he is? It's time we took our leave. You, too, Hesta.'

And in fact, my eyes had drifted shut while Adolpheus spoke. I wasn't sure if it was a lack of strength or inclination that kept me from opening them again as my visitors left the room. I *was* tired – I could not remember ever having felt so drained . . . yet my mind would not stop racing, presenting me with nightmarish images of what I had seen, or hallucinated, and wondering, too, at the mystery of my missing clothes. It seemed that someone must have found me before Adolpheus, and removed them . . . perhaps wanting me to freeze to death. But who would feel threatened enough by my presence to commit murder? Could it have been Doppler after all?

My musings were interrupted by the sound of my name. I opened my eyes to see once more the girl who had been watching over me when I first awoke. Perhaps I had dozed off, for I hadn't heard her come in. She was sitting in a chair drawn up close to the bedside and leaning towards me with an anxious expression, as though eager to wake me yet fearful of it, too. A fine gold chain encircled her neck, and dangling from the end of it was a glittering gold ring, like a wedding band. The girl was young – no more than sixteen or seventeen, I thought; surely the ring could not be her own, or she would be wearing it . . . unless it had belonged to a husband now deceased. Beneath a pale blue kerchief, two wings of blonde hair fanned to either side of a snowy white forehead whose worry lines added an appealing touch of vulnerability to features that were otherwise flawless. Those lines deepened as she blinked hazel eyes and drew back slightly.

'I-I brought you this,' she stammered, and raised a steaming wooden bowl from her lap in a flustered motion that sent a portion of the contents spilling over her skirt . . . at which, to my astonishment, she burst into tears, twisting away from me in the chair.

'Here now,' I said, sitting up with alacrity, 'what's wrong? Are you burned?'

She shook her head.

'Then why are you crying?'

She faced me, her cheeks rosy in the candlelight. She was like a figure in a painting, present yet remote, beautiful and sad, and I ached to know the cause of her distress, and to assuage it if I could. She wiped her face with the back of one sleeve, first one cheek and then the other, reminding me of a cat grooming itself, and gave me an embarrassed smile. 'Because you will hate me,' she said.

'Hate you?' I was flabbergasted. 'I don't even *know* you.'

Her gaze faltered at that, dropping to her lap, then rose again, resolute now. 'I took your things,' she said.

'You mean my clothes . . . ?' But then, as her blush

deepened, comprehension dawned. 'My tool kit! You're Herr Doppler's daughter.'

She nodded, fresh tears welling in her eyes. 'You *do* hate me!'

I assured her I did not. 'I'm just glad to have my tools back,' I said. 'You *did* bring them back, didn't you?'

She nodded again, sniffling. 'They're in your rucksack, where I found them.'

I heaved a sigh of relief, sinking back against the mound of pillows. 'Thank God. And thank you, Fraülein.'

'Then . . . you're not angry?'

'Your father told me that you took my tool kit to keep me from destroying the tower clock or any of Herr Wachter's other timepieces. Now that I've seen them for myself, or a number of them, anyway, I can appreciate your concern – not that I approve of what you did. Nor was there ever any danger of my doing what you feared.'

'My father doesn't understand anything,' she confided with more than a hint of bitterness, her eyes shifting towards the closed door as if she expected him to come barging in at any moment.

'Then I'm afraid I don't, either,' I said.

'Clockmen never stay in Märchen for long,' she said. 'They arrive one day and leave the next. I thought that if I stole your tools, you'd be forced to stay.'

'I would have been forced to stay in any case, thanks to the blizzard.'

'But I didn't know that. When I came to your room, the snow had only just begun to fall. I saw you lying there in bed, sound asleep, and I thought you looked so young, not much older than me, and kind, so that you wouldn't mind if I sneaked a peek at your tools. Once I had the kit in my hands,

I couldn't stop myself from taking it. I know it was wrong, Herr Gray, but I was afraid you'd leave the next morning if I didn't do something.'

'But why should it matter to you whether I go or stay?'

'Because' – and her gaze went to the door again, or perhaps to my rucksack, which was no longer on the floor but hanging from a wooden peg on the back of the door – 'because I want to be like you. A clockman.'

So unexpected was this answer that I burst out laughing. 'A clockman? You?'

The look she gave me was not tearful but angry; my laughter shrivelled in the fierceness of her gaze. 'Why not?' she demanded. 'Do you think me too dull to understand your arts?'

'No,' I answered, drawing out the word as I considered how best to proceed. I recalled how Herr Doppler had spoken of his daughter's mercurial nature, and the way she was clutching the bowl in her lap made me suspect that my next words would determine whether or not I received a faceful of hot broth. 'It's just that neither my guild nor any other of which I am aware accepts apprentices of your sex.'

'Yes, that's just what Papa says. But I don't need to join a guild. *You* could teach me, Herr Gray!'

I would have liked to dismiss it all as a joke, but there was no mistaking the girl's seriousness and determination. 'Look, Fraülein,' I began.

She interrupted. 'Please, Herr Gray. Call me Corinna.'

'And you must call me Michael,' I said, 'for I hope that we can be friends.'

Her face lit up in a smile, and I felt a stirring in my heart.

'Then you'll do it?' she demanded. 'You'll instruct me?'

'Why are you so interested in clocks?' I asked in turn.

She laughed. 'Living in Märchen, how could I not be?' She seemed to take belated notice of the bowl in her lap and, blushing again, offered it to me. 'Frau Hubner says you are to finish this broth – every last drop.'

I took the bowl from her, feeling a tingle where our fingers brushed. The beefy smell of the broth made my mouth water. There was a wooden spoon in the bowl, and I raised it to my lips and sipped. I had never tasted anything so delicious; warmth and vitality coursed through my body in dizzying waves.

'Slowly, Michael,' the girl admonished as I slurped down the broth. After a moment, she returned to the subject of clocks. As she spoke, she toyed with the ring on her necklace, turning it in the fingers of one hand, and I found myself wondering once again about the story that no doubt lay behind it: felt, too, a twinge of jealousy at the thought that some other man, living or dead, might have a claim on her affections.

'When I was young, our timepieces seemed like magic to me. But as I grew older, I began to wonder at how they functioned. I longed to take them apart and see for myself what it was that drove the hands in their orbits and regulated their progress around the dial. But as you have discovered, it is impossible to get permission to open any of Herr Wachter's creations. Of course, that didn't stop me. I can't tell you how often I tried in secret to gain access to my father's pocket watch or one of the other timepieces of the town. And how often I was caught and punished. But despite my efforts, I never managed to open a single one. As for the tower clock, I've searched and searched for a way in, even climbing to the campanile itself, but without success. Yet I haven't been completely defeated. Over the years, I managed to find a few old timepieces tucked away in attics – clocks and pocket watches from before Wachter's day – and these I studied thoroughly, dissected and put back together as best I could, with tools I fashioned myself out of cutlery and anything else that came to hand. But I have reached the limits of what I can learn on my own. I require instruction, a teacher. A man like you, Herr Gray . . . that is' – and she blushed again – 'Michael.'

Finished with the broth, I returned the empty bowl to her and lay back against the pillows. A vast and sleepy well-being pervaded me. I felt light-headed, almost drunk. I had no desire to argue with this pretty and spirited young girl. 'I should like to see some of those tools of yours, Corinna,' I said.

Her blush deepened. 'I would be ashamed to show you.'

'Ashamed?'

'I didn't simply take your tools, Michael. I studied them. What beautiful things they are! So cleverly designed, so lovingly crafted. By comparison, mine are crude, laughable, ugly.'

'I received most of my tool kit when I became a journeyman. Over the years, like many clockmen, I've added some implements of my own design. But to do what you have done, without benefit of a master's guiding hand – that is truly impressive.'

'Papa doesn't think so. He finds my interest in timepieces unladylike. I'm afraid I couldn't show you my tools even if I wanted to, for he confiscated them from me after learning that I had taken yours. But he's done so before, and it hasn't stopped me yet.' She flashed a conspiratorial smile. 'I just make new ones.'

'I've never met a girl quite like you, Corinna,' I told her. 'And yet I almost feel as if we have met before . . .'

'Why, that's not surprising,' she said. 'After all, I helped care for you during your sickness, even if you don't remember it.'

'For which I'm grateful.'

'Grateful enough to teach me something of your art?'

It occurred to me that I had been manipulated into acknowledging an obligation, but somehow I didn't care. 'I doubt your father would approve.'

'He doesn't have to know,' she said. 'It can be our secret. At least for the next few days, while you're getting your strength back, you could teach me. What harm could it do?'

'I'll think about it,' I told her. After all, what would be the harm in showing her a few things? Nor was it lost on me that Corinna could prove a valuable ally in my efforts to convince her father, the burgomeister, to grant me the permission I sought. And if all else failed, perhaps I could enlist her as an accomplice, get her to bring me one of Wachter's timepieces; she had already proved herself an adept thief. Besides, the notion of spending more time with Corinna was appealing for its own sake.

'Thank you, Michael,' she said, breaking into a wide and dazzling smile.

'I haven't agreed to anything yet,' I cautioned.

'But you will,' she said. 'I know it.' At which, to my surprise, she leaned forward impulsively and planted a kiss on my cheek. A jolt shot through me at the touch of her lips, and the scent of pine enfolded me, rich and resinous, as if I were walking through a mountain forest in springtime.

Just then, a voice thundered from the doorway: 'What is going on here?'

Corinna drew back with a gasp. 'Papa!'

Herr Doppler marched into the room, his bushy white moustache bristling like lightning, his face an ominous shade of red. He wore a colonel's uniform and a powdered club wig the colour of pewter.

Corinna rose and went to him before I could say a word, laying a hand on his arm. 'Calm yourself, Papa, dear. I was merely making Herr Gray more comfortable.'

He glared at her. 'Were you indeed, madam? It appeared to me that the rascal was stealing a kiss.'

'Papa!' she chided him. 'Our poor patient is too weak to steal anything.'

Doppler gave me an appraising glance. 'He looks feeble, I'll grant you, but looks can be deceiving . . . as can daughters.'

Doppler was now the recipient of the same fierce look that had been directed at me a moment ago. He withstood it no better. 'That is,' he said, 'these footloose rascals can lead innocent girls astray with their wild talk.'

At which Corinna stamped her foot. 'Honestly, Papa! Do you take me for a simpleton? I swear to you on my honour that Herr Gray did not steal a kiss.'

'Is this true?' the burgomeister demanded of me.

I nodded, impressed with Corinna's sangfroid.

'There, you see?' The girl stood on tiptoes to plant a kiss on her father's ruddy cheek.

The man fairly glowed. 'Forgive me, my dear,' he said, then addressed me once more. 'I beg your pardon as well, Herr Gray. With such a treasure, a father cannot be too careful.'

'Your daughter has been my ministering angel,' I told him, struggling to keep my expression serious and my voice level as, behind Doppler's back, Corinna blew me another kiss. 'I would not repay her in such a base fashion.'

'Such sentiments do you credit,' said Doppler. He turned back to his daughter. 'Frau Hubner has need of you. I will tend to the patient for a while.'

'Yes, Papa,' she said demurely. 'I will see you later, Herr Gray.'

'Thank you again, Fraülein,' I replied.

Smiling, she curtsied and left the room.

As soon as she had gone, Doppler's manner underwent a stark change. Crossing to the bed, he seated himself in the chair that Corinna had vacated and took hold of my upper arm, squeezing so that I gasped in pain.

'Let us speak as men,' he said in a low voice that was all the more threatening for its icy calm. 'Should I discover that you have trifled with my daughter, Herr Gray, you will wish that Adolpheus had left you buried in the snow. Nay, do not speak. I know how it is with you wandering rascals. Clockmen? Cockmen, more like! Do not trouble to deny it, sir! I have been a soldier. I know what it is like to be young and footloose, far from home, with pretty wenches set before you like dishes at a banquet. You try a taste of this one, of that one. Where's the harm? Come, sir! Do I have the wrong of it?'

I stammered out some excuse or other.

His vice-like grip tightened. 'We are both men of the world. Pray do not insult me.'

I wrenched my arm free. 'What do you wish me to say, sir? Yes, I have had dalliances in the course of my travels. You imply that you did the same as a younger man. It is, as you say, the way of the world. But that does not mean I have no honour, Herr Doppler. No gratitude. And you speak of insult? It is you who have insulted me!'

Herr Doppler's blue eyes widened during this outburst. At the end of it, he sat a moment as if stunned, then broke into hearty laughter, slapping his knee. 'I like you, Herr Gray; indeed, I do,' he said at last, wiping his eyes. 'In truth, I meant no offence. I merely wished to impress upon you that my daughter is precious to me above all things.'

'You might have done so in a less literal manner,' I

muttered, examining my arm, where the imprint of Doppler's fingers was purpling to a bruise.

'It will not have escaped your notice that there is a greater span of years between us than might normally separate a father and daughter,' he went on, arranging himself more comfortably in the chair. 'I was already in my fifties when I met and married Corinna's mother, the youngest daughter of a fellow officer. Maria was scarcely older than Corinna is now when we became man and wife. She was loveliness itself, but fragile as a springtime flower. And our life together was as fleeting as that season. The rigours of childbirth proved too arduous for her delicate constitution, and the effort of bringing Corinna into the world ushered her out of it.'

'I'm sorry,' I said, while reflecting that this story was quite different from what Inge had told me of the fate of Corinna's mother. One or both of them was lying. Which, and from what motive, I did not know. But perhaps I could find out, and make use of that knowledge. It is always wise to learn the truth behind the lies that people tell each other, and themselves. Such knowledge is like a dagger up the sleeve; sooner or later, you will be glad to have it close to hand. 'Then, the ring she wears about her neck . . .'

'Her mother's wedding ring,' Doppler affirmed. 'I sometimes think there must be an ineffable law, as absolute as that which governs the movement of celestial bodies, preventing two creatures of such sublime beauty from existing simultaneously on Earth, and it was in obedience to that law that Maria was taken from me. For Corinna has grown into the very image of her mother, and there are moments, Herr Gray, moments when I could swear to you that it is Maria herself who stands before me, miraculously restored to life, or never having left it at all, the last seventeen years nothing more than a dream from which I have suddenly awakened. Like Wachter's Folly, the heart does not recognize the ordinary flow of time, and what the mind knows to be an impossibility the heart embraces without hesitation or reserve. And so my love for Maria remains as fresh today as on the day we married, and my grieving as profound as on the day she died. Add to that a father's natural affection for his only child and you will understand why I am perhaps a trifle indulgent with Corinna, and at the same time so ardent in safeguarding her welfare.'

I replied that she was fortunate to have such a father, though in fact I pitied the girl, not just for the loss of her mother but for the enduring legacy of that loss, thrust upon her by her surviving parent, to be both daughter and wife to him . . . or, rather, part-daughter, part-wife, neither one thing nor the other. It seemed a heavy burden to impose on a child, as unhealthy as it was unfair. Growing up without a parent is difficult enough already. The ring she wore about her neck, the mystery of which had so tantalized me, now seemed as much a token of a father's obsession as it was the symbol of a daughter's devotion. No wonder the girl was rebellious, head-strong. How else could she insist upon her uniqueness, demonstrate to her father – and, indeed, to herself – that she was more than just the image of the mother she had never known?

Doppler, meanwhile, stroked his moustache and smiled. 'She does not always recognize that fact, I'm afraid. In beauty, she takes after her mother, but she has also inherited her father's martial spirit, and the promptings of that spirit some-times make her forget her filial duty, not to mention the natural modesty that is the most becoming ornament of her sex.'

'I found nothing immodest about her,' I protested, feeling compelled to come to her defence even as I savoured the memory of her impulsive kiss.

'I know my daughter,' Doppler replied. 'Doubtless her apology in the matter of your tool kit was so charming that you have by now completely forgotten the theft that occasioned it.'

'No, but I have forgiven it,' I said.

'Have you? I'm glad to hear it.' Doppler glanced towards the door with a furtiveness that reminded me of Corinna's movements earlier. 'I should like to ask a favour of you, Herr Gray.'

'By all means,' I told him, curious.

'This must remain between us.'

'Of course.'

Doppler seemed at an uncharacteristic loss as to how to proceed. He cleared his throat, shifted his position on the chair, smoothed his moustache. Then he blurted out: 'My daughter is obsessed with horology. She nurses the ambition of becoming a journeyman like yourself, and one day even a master. When she was younger, her interest in timepieces was amusing, and I indulged it. I thought she would grow out of it, but instead her interest has only grown stronger with the years. I mean no disparagement to your profession, sir, but it is not suitable for a lady, as I am sure you will agree.'

I nodded for him to continue.

'It was this fascination, this obsession, that led her to steal your tool kit, Herr Gray.'

'She has confessed as much to me already,' I told him. 'Indeed, she told me that she has made tools of her own, and has taught herself the rudiments of horology. Can this be true?'

'I'm afraid so,' Doppler confessed shamefacedly.

'Quite remarkable,' I said. 'The influence of Herr Wachter, no doubt.'

'She requires a more salutary influence now,' Doppler told me. 'I have found, as her father, that my efforts to curtail her enthusiasms in this regard only have the opposite effect. Thus I am turning to you, Herr Gray.'

'To me?'

'Yes,' he said. 'I know it is an imposition, but I would consider it a great favour if you would take my daughter under your wing, as it were.'

'You want me to teach her?' I could scarcely believe my ears.

'I want you to discourage her,' Doppler clarified, 'under the guise of teaching her. You will be outwardly encouraging but meanwhile set her tasks beyond her abilities, the better to convince her that she lacks the aptitude for horology, that her talents lie in more . . . feminine directions. Could you do that, Herr Gray?'

'Let me make certain I understand you, sir. You wish me to deceive your daughter, to invite her trust and then – subtly, to be sure – betray it.'

'For her own good,' Doppler said defensively.

'She will not like it.'

'If you are skilful enough, Herr Gray, she need never know.'

'And if I succeed?'

'Why, you will have earned the gratitude of an anxious father.'

'I am not in the habit of deceiving young ladies, Herr Doppler. Certainly not at the invitation of their fathers.'

'And if I were to offer you a more tangible measure of gratitude?'

'Go on,' I said.

'Dissuade my daughter from her unseemly interest in time-pieces, and I will permit you to examine my pocket watch – which, you may remember, once belonged to Herr Wachter himself.'

'I should want to remove the casing,' I told Doppler.

'Of course.'

'And make detailed sketches of the workings.'

'Naturally.'

'I might even need to dissassemble the mechanism, or at least portions of it.'

I watched a struggle play out on Herr Doppler's features. But at last he gave a terse nod. 'Acceptable,' he grunted, and I could see that it had cost him much.

'You surprise me, Herr Doppler,' I confessed. 'When last we spoke, you were adamant in refusing to let me examine the watch. Yet now you agree to everything I asked of you that night, and more.'

'You see how much my daughter means to me,' Doppler replied. 'More even than the oath I swore to my father when he passed Wachter's timepiece on to me. Above all else, I wish for Corinna to be happy, yet as long as she harbours these dangerous fantasies, she will never be content. If she cannot find what she so desperately desires here in Märchen, sooner or later she will look for it farther afield . . . and find something quite different, as we both can imagine only too well. So I ask you to dispel her illusions, Herr Gray, as gently but firmly as you can, to spare her a more grievous awakening at less gentle hands. Once resigned to her proper sphere, she will find fulfilment as a dutiful daughter, and later as a wife and mother, as God and Nature intended.'

I did not share Herr Doppler's conviction on this point. The fanatical gleam I had seen in Corinna's eye would not be so easy to extinguish. Yet I agreed to his proposal, for it promised to deliver not only Herr Doppler's pocket watch, but Inge's cuckoo into the bargain. Nor was that my only reason for accepting the offer. Someone had attacked me. Knocked me out, robbed me of my clothes, and left me to die in the snow. I was determined to learn the secrets of Wachter's timepieces, but I was also determined to learn the identity of my would-be murderer, and my efforts in that regard would be hindered, it seemed to me, if I made an enemy of Herr Doppler. 'When shall I begin?' I asked him.

'The sooner the better,' he answered, rising from the chair. We shook hands, but he prolonged the clasp, fixing me with his steely gaze. 'If I find you have betrayed my trust, Herr Gray, and used this opportunity to seduce my daughter, I will kill you. Is that understood?'

'I am interested in another prize entirely,' I assured him.

And what's more, I believed it.

11

A World Newly Born

MY EXPOSURE TO THE ELEMENTS HAD LEFT ME WEAKER THAN I realized, and it was some days before I was able to rise from my sickbed and take even a few tottering steps across the room. In that time, Inge and Corinna took turns caring for me like ministering angels indeed. True to my agreement with Herr Doppler, I began to teach Corinna the rudiments of the horologist's art. At first, as promised, it was with the intent of discouraging her. But it soon became apparent to me that she would not be discouraged. Every task I set her she accomplished with ease. She was a natural. Her mind was quick, her fingers clever and dexterous. The tools she had made for herself – which I had asked Herr Doppler to return to her – were as effective as they were ingenious. In truth, she had already passed beyond the rudiments. More than once, as we bent together over one of the timepieces she had brought to me – the ones that pre-dated Wachter's arrival – and my own pocket watch, I thought of my own apprenticeship and found myself wondering what Magnus would have made of this prodigy. I think he would have been as scandalized by her sex as he was impressed by her skill.

When I summoned up the courage to tell her of the

bargain I had struck with her father, she laughed and replied that she'd guessed as much from the first, and had been waiting to see if I would play her false and try to dampen the fires of her enthusiasm. But, she said, knowing me for an honourable man, she had never doubted my intentions. I felt ashamed at hearing her say so.

I suppose I had already fallen in love with her. Any man would have, for she was beautiful, kind and brave – as well as having more natural ability than any horologist I had ever seen, with the exception of Magnus. Under other circumstances, she might have rivalled Wachter himself. Her grasp of horology, entirely self-taught, was extraordinary, as was her mechanical genius, evidenced not only in the timepieces she had at first dissected, then repaired, and finally improved, but in small automatons she had crafted, cunning little creatures that were nearly as lifelike as Wachter's creations. I remember in particular a metal mouse that, when wound with a key, would scamper up and down the sides of an old clock like the rodent in the nursery rhyme, or run along her arm like a tame pet.

But did she return my feelings? How could I dare even to hope it? I was her teacher, her friend. But that was as much as I aspired to. The snows had continued to fall, and by now it was clear that I would be stuck in Märchen until the spring thaw. It would have been foolish – not to mention, with Herr Doppler's threat hanging over me, suicidal – to attempt a seduction.

Nevertheless, Doppler realized soon enough that things were not going according to his plan. I explained to him that Corinna had proved to be more gifted than I had expected, and that it was taking longer than anticipated to discourage her. Rather than disappointing him, the news puffed him up with fatherly pride, and he told me to take as much time as necessary. After all, he said with a laugh, I didn't have any other pressing engagements.

Corinna broached the subject of 'borrowing', as she put it, one of Wachter's timepieces for me to study, but I told her at once that such a course would be too risky. Instead, I suggested that the two of us collude in making it appear that she had reached the natural limits of her abilities and was at last growing discouraged. By the terms of my agreement with her father, he would then yield up his pocket watch for my examination, and Inge would follow with her cuckoo. I would, of course, share the fruits of my investigations of these timepieces with Corinna. She was willing, but preferred to wait until she had learned more of what I had to teach. I agreed. Herr Doppler was right, after all. I had no pressing engagements, and to be trapped for months in Märchen without the solace of Corinna's company would have been unbearable. The hour we spent together each day, talking of horology and other things, was like gold to me, an interval of time no clock, not even one of Wachter's, was fit to measure.

Meanwhile, life went on. As the days and weeks passed, snow continued to fall, until it reached and then overtopped the second-storey window behind my bed. No one had thought to wind my pocket watch as I lay in the grip of fever, and by the time the fever had broken, the watch had long since stopped. Herr Doppler had assured me his own watch was accurate, and Inge insisted the same of her cuckoo, and though it was true that the two timepieces agreed with each other, I found it impossible to fully trust any timepiece built by Wachter. I reset my watch, yet for the rest of my stay in Märchen I felt untethered, cut off from the outside world, as if I had entered a kind of bubble where time was not the dependable constant of my experience but instead something as variable as the wind. It sometimes seemed to me that the only clock I could rely on was the rising and setting of the sun. At other times, even that seemed suspect, for I saw so little of the sun, hidden as it generally was behind a thick scrim of grey cloud or snow. Yet I kept my watch wound, and carried it with me everywhere, not only because I needed some yardstick against which to measure the day, however arbitrary or inaccurate in an absolute sense, but because it made me feel safe, protected. I suppose it had stopped being a timepiece exactly and become a sort of talisman. Perhaps that is all our ingenious watches and clocks really are, when you come right down to it.

I had no more strange dreams, no more terrifying visions. In fact, I stopped dreaming altogether – it was as if I were living a dream, and thus had no need for fantasies. Once I felt strong enough, and had replenished my depleted wardrobe, I resumed the visits that had been cut short by my illness. As before, the townsfolk, though friendly, refused to grant me access to their timepieces. Soon my perambulations had made me familiar with the labyrinthine network of passages that was now the only means by which Märchen could be navigated without snowshoes or the danger of becoming lost and freezing to death. Of course, the passages had their own dangers. Occasionally the weight of the snow would cause a section to collapse, but the townsfolk seemed to have a second sense about such things, for I never heard of any deaths or injuries, and either I came to share their sensitivity or was just lucky, as I, too, escaped harm. In the aftermath, the able-bodied men of the town, led by Adolpheus, would gather to clear and repair the damage, and I joined with them whenever I could, hoping to win their trust more completely, to the point that they would give me what I sought. But though they seemed appreciative of my efforts, standing me drinks at the Hearth and Home, even inviting me into their homes on occasion to share a meal, they remained adamant in their refusals – though they did not seem angry or annoyed at my persistence. In truth, after a week or so I had resigned myself to the idea that only with Corinna's help would I ever gain access to the secrets that lay within Wachter's timepieces.

The only place I did not visit once I had recovered sufficiently to leave the Hearth and Home was Wachter's Folly. The mere thought of it left me trembling with fear, an irrational terror that had seeped into my very bones. You may protest that there was nothing irrational about it. After all, I had nearly died there. I had been struck a blow to the head, stripped of my clothing, and left to freeze to death in the snow. And the man – or woman – responsible was still at large, perhaps awaiting the opportunity to finish what they had started. Yet it was not that which turned my will to quivering jelly but the memory, which haunted my waking hours, of the parade of automatons I had seen: those titanic figures, like forgotten gods from ancient days, that I had witnessed emerging from a space too small to contain them. The whole world seemed too small for them. I could not forget how one of them had reached for me, its hand closing over me as if snuffing out a candle. All it took was the chiming of the bells for those memories to rise up and overwhelm me, and for a weight of darkness to descend over my eyes, as if the shadow of that hand was once again engulfing me. And the bells chimed with perverse frequency now, far more often, or so it seemed, than they had previously, as if the clock, no less than I, had been changed by our encounter – as if it sensed my fear and sought to exacerbate it, toying with me like a cat with its prey. Or like a dragon. For I could not forget, any more than I could the giants, the dragon I had seen. I felt its malevolent intent focused upon me like a second sun: a dark sun.

Corinna noticed everything, of course. Though I tried to hide my distress, ashamed to be so unmanned by a mere memory, I was with her too much, and she was far too attentive a pupil, for her to be deceived. Earlier, in my weakness, I had told her what I had seen, though I had not confided in anyone else.

'Let me accompany you to the Folly,' she offered at last. 'Two may face together what one cannot.'

'I have no desire to visit that clock again,' I assured her. 'Nor to see what might emerge from it.'

'Why, what better way to lay your fears to rest than to see for yourself that what comes out of the clock, however fanciful, is nothing to be afraid of? What you saw – or, rather, thought you saw – was due to the blow you received. How could it be otherwise? Even Wachter, for all his genius, could not create such automatons! No mortal could, but only God Himself. In any case, I don't believe you when you say you have no desire to go back. You are like me, Michael. We cannot so easily extinguish the curiosity that burns in our hearts, stronger than any fear. You know that I am right.' She reached across the table to take my hand.

We were in my room, where, with Inge's blessing, I had set up a small workshop for my daily sessions with Corinna. In the course of those lessons, our fingers had brushed a hundred times, our hands had touched, our eyes had met and exchanged silent understandings – or so I had fancied. Yet we had said nothing of our feelings, and the kiss she had given me, whose warm imprint I could still feel upon my cheek, had not been repeated. But now, as she laid her hand atop mine and looked into my eyes, I felt something shift in me, in us both. In the world itself. That shifting drew us together, until it was not just our hands but our lips that were joined. And our hearts. For I knew at once that this was no dalliance of the sort I had admitted to Herr Doppler. This was much, much more. At that moment, I understood for the first time that there is something greater than time in the world. The motto of our guild refers to time as the emperor of all things. But that is wrong. It is love that is the true emperor, for time is helpless against it, and though love exists within time, so, too, does it transcend it. In my mind, that first embrace we shared, that first kiss, has not ended; it will never end. But that is all I will say of it. To speak of such things is to dishonour them.

Afterwards, we sat side by side, our hands clasped, her head resting on my shoulder, our hearts too full for speech, basking, as it were, in a world newly born. Then, as if it had long been decided, we began to talk of the future, of how, when spring came, and the snows melted, and the paths were clear once again, we two would leave Märchen, embarking on a life together here in London. It all seemed so simple, so obvious. I wished to do the honourable thing and ask Herr Doppler for his daughter's hand, but Corinna forestalled me.

'That you must not do!' she said, gripping my hand, her gaze locked with mine. 'Far from giving his consent, he would banish you at once . . . or worse. You must promise me that you will not ask him!'

'I am not afraid of him,' I told her.

'You should be,' she replied. 'I have learned to be. In this, you must let me be your tutor, dearest Michael.'

How it wrung my heart to hear that false name so lovingly on her lips! Yet I did not tell her who I really was. In truth, I was afraid to. Afraid that I would lose her if she realized I was not the man she thought I was – not the man she had fallen in love with but an imposter, a liar. I told myself that there would be plenty of time to confess everything in the weeks ahead, that it would serve no purpose to reveal myself now. Instead, I promised that I would be instructed by her in this and in all things.

That earned me another kiss – a sweet reward for a base betrayal. But I did not spurn her lips on that account. On the contrary. Their velvet caress absolved me of all my sins . . . for a while. As I breathed in the fragrance of her breath, which seemed to contain the springtime we had just been speaking of, I swore to myself that if I did not yet deserve the love of this goddess, I would merit it one day by my words and actions.

But rather than drawing nearer, that day seemed to recede into a hazy future. As our closeness grew, the lie at the heart of it became all the more difficult to expose. To do so would have put everything at risk: Corinna's love, Wachter's secrets – they were too tangled in my mind to allow any easy unravelling. To lose one was to lose the other. It was the pursuit of those secrets, after all, that had brought us together, that sustained us in a common purpose and gave us hope of a shared future.

From that point on, our daily lessons had little to do with horology. We put aside clocks and watches and all the finely calibrated instruments of our craft and instead devoted ourselves to the study of each other. Not our bodies alone but our minds, our very souls – always excepting that kernel of untruth which, hard as I tried, I could not forget about for long, however deeply I buried it. Corinna approached these investigations in the same bold and insatiable spirit of inquiry that had characterized her pursuit of horological knowledge.

I will say no more of what we shared – it is enough that she became my wife in every way that mattered to us, if not to the rest of the world. I have taken no other wife in all the years since. I never shall.

We took care that we should not be discovered, though we had some close calls, with Inge especially, for she was always looking in on us. But her size made stealth impossible; one could always hear her coming. Doppler might have done better, but he made no effort to surprise us. On the contrary, he seemed pleased with the reports I gave him, content with the pace and progress of Corinna's lessons – though of course there was little truth in what I told him.

Corinna, meanwhile, continued to press me to visit Wachter's Folly, and at last I gave in, unable to refuse her anything and wanting as well to be rid of the unreasoning fear that had all but paralysed me in this matter. Besides, I did not want her to think me a coward – the more as I knew myself to be one.

'But how shall we determine when to go?' I asked. 'The automatons only emerge when the clock strikes, or so your father informed me, and it strikes randomly, at no set or predictable interval. I have no wish to stand out in the bitter cold for what could be hours. Yet if we wait until we hear the bells begin to ring, the whole display could well be over by the time we reach the Folly.'

'You need not worry about that,' she replied. 'Over the years, we townsfolk have developed a second sense about when the timepiece is going to strike. There is a tension in the air, like the onset of a thunderstorm. And not only in the air. We feel it in our bones, in our hearts, a vibration that cuts right through us.'

'It sounds painful,' I told her.

She shrugged. 'We are used to it.'

'But how extraordinary!' I continued. 'How long does it take to develop this sensitivity?'

'No time at all,' she said. 'We are born with it, you see.'

I did not see. Nothing in my knowledge of horology or natural science could explain how the workings of a clock might impress themselves into the bones and sinews of a single human body, much less an entire town. Not that I doubted her. Thinking back, I realized that I had witnessed the truth of her assertion many times over in fleeting expressions that passed across the faces of the townsfolk in the moments before the bells of the clock began to peal, looks of anxious anticipation, as if at some signal I could not discern, followed by smiles and sighs indicative of release. These quirks of behaviour had puzzled me, but I had not inquired into them, thinking them related somehow to my presence. I felt no such connection myself. In truth, I envied it. It did not seem right that these people, who knew nothing of our art, should manifest a deeper affinity to the flow of time than even the masters of our Worshipful Company could lay claim to.

Thus it was that Corinna and I made our way early one afternoon to Wachter's Folly. When we emerged from the lamplit passage into the open, the glare of sunlight reflecting from the mounds of snow and ice that had more than half buried the town left me blinded. Even after my vision cleared, I stood frozen in place, dazzled by the stark beauty of the scene. I do not think I had ever seen a sky so blue; it made my eyes ache, and still does, in memory. The jagged peaks of the surrounding mountains, and the upthrust dagger of the glacier that seemed to stand guard over the town, glittered as if encrusted with diamonds. The air sparkled with ice crystals swept up in a biting wind that blew without pause, piercing my clothes, my skin, all the way to the bone. I shivered, still weaker from my ordeal than I had realized until that moment. It was the first time in weeks that I had stood under an open sky.

Corinna put a steadying arm around my waist and asked if I wanted to return to the Hearth and Home. I shook my head and told her no. 'Then we must hurry,' she said. 'The bells are about to strike.'

I swear that I could feel, through her touch, the same thrumming vibration I had felt weeks ago when I had laid my hands upon the figures decorating the tower's façade. Those figures were less visible now, buried more deeply beneath fallen snow; even the great dragon that coiled about the tower was lost to view, only bits and pieces of its serpentine length exposed, like the gnarled roots of an immense tree.

The pathways shovelled into the snow, by which I had approached and half circled the clock on my last visit, were still in place, well maintained despite the mountains of snow on either side, a testament to the industry of the townsfolk, and especially that of Adolpheus, who, as I had seen, tirelessly laboured to keep the paths shovelled, the covered passages repaired, the lamps lit.

Corinna led me forward. The bronze hands of the clock were in motion, the hour hand creeping slow as molasses in a clockwise direction while the minute hand drifted in retrograde. I could hear, above the whistling of the wind, muffled sounds of activity from within the edifice as the mechanism governing the automatons engaged. As before, I felt a kind of trepidation or wariness, a hesitation to come too close that grew stronger as I drew nearer, until my heart was thumping in my chest and a sheen of sweat broke from my skin, chilling me further. Once again I saw, in my mind's eye, those gigantic legs scissoring across the proscenium. Though I more than half believed it had all been a vision, or at best a memory stretched out of recognition by the blow that had felled me, as if I had glimpsed the legs of my assailant before I had lost consciousness, on a visceral level I was crawling with dread. It was all I could do not to pull out of Corinna's grasp and rush back to the safety of the passage. But, again, I did not want her to think me a coward.

She seemed to be in the grip of sensations as intense as my own, though different, for, rather than resisting an urge to flee, as I did, she appeared to be fighting an opposite inclination, as if she were being drawn towards the tower by a force I could not feel. At last, by a mutual if unspoken decision, having reached a point of equilibrium between our conflicting desires, we stopped, each of us holding the other, and, still silent, waited for the bells to ring. We were the only ones present; the townsfolk had grown so accustomed to the marvels in their midst that they no longer recognized them as such; Wachter's creations had become ordinary. In a way, that seemed the most incredible thing of all.

I felt a shudder pass through Corinna and heard the catch of her breath. Then, with no more warning than that, the bells pealed out. The clock itself might have been wild and without sense in its timekeeping, but the carillon – though I had heard it crash like thunder, or wail like a pack of banshees – now produced a music as clear and bright and cold as the day. It echoed from the buildings around the square, until the sounds seemed to be coming from everywhere at once, produced not by the bells but by sunlight striking the ice and snow. At the first chime, my apprehension shattered like glass, and I felt the shards of it falling inside me, soft as snow but sharp enough to draw blood, like feathers from an angel's wing, so that I shivered now not from cold or fear but in a kind of exquisite agony.

'Do you feel it, too?' Corinna asked in a whisper.

Before I could reply – if I could have used my voice at all – the door on one side of the proscenium swung open with a clap, and the automatons began their parade. Corinna had been right. There were no giants now, no impossibilities of scale. Just a succession of child-sized mechanical figures moving through their ordained paces as the echoes of the bells faded away. Soon the only sounds were the keening of the wind and the whirs and clicks that rose from within the clock and from the figures themselves as they pantomimed the actions of living men and women out for a stroll: knees rising and falling in a parody of locomotion, heads turning, eyes moving, as if to take in the view, arms rising in greeting or farewell, yet all with a stiff and jerky artificiality, like wooden puppets moving without the benefit of strings, that could not have been more different from the smooth counterfeit of life I had witnessed in the operation of Inge's cuckoo clock and certain other timepieces of Wachter's that I had seen. Even Corinna's mechanical mouse was more lifelike. Relieved as I was at the absence of the giants, I was disappointed as well. I had expected more.

Yet it seemed a further revelation of the eccentricity of the clock and its maker that there should be no angels or devils, no figures of Father Time with his scythe and hourglass, no saints or martyrs, none of the garish and fantastical crew such clocks always feature. Instead, what emerged from within the clock was what I had already found outside it: nothing larger than life but rather life itself, in all its mundane variety, as if Wachter, or whoever had crafted the automatons, no doubt at his direction, had used ordinary townsfolk as his models.

Burghers, farmers, tradesmen and -women. All roughly, even crudely executed, as if they had been carved in a fit of inspiration, or at the last moment, and painted with equal haste. Yet their slapdash quality, which spoke of enthusiasm more than skill, somehow gave them a vitality more meticulous representations might have lacked; they seemed, as it were, in their rude expressions and painted-on clothes, to aspire to the lives they mimicked. Their small size only added to this impression, as of a parade of children dressed in the clothing of adults.

As I watched, it struck me that certain of the figures looked familiar, as if I had glimpsed them somewhere before, but I ascribed this at first to their caricature-like quality. Until, to my astonishment, I saw Adolpheus emerge from the tower, a stepladder strapped across his back. Indeed, I thought at first that it was the man himself playing a trick on me, though a closer look dispelled my confusion, as he, or rather it, was as crudely rendered as the others. But there could be no doubt that the automaton was modelled on Adolpheus. Why, it even incorporated his limp, and the handicap that caused it! Nor was this the only shock in store for me. Behind him came Inge, with her flour-dusted apron and apple-red cheeks, a loaf of bread in her hands and Hesta jumping up again and again at her feet, as if begging for crumbs. She was followed by Herr Doppler, stiff and stern in his colonel's uniform, white whiskers bristling as if sheathed in ice, a sword buckled at his side, which he drew and flourished, then sheathed again, over and over, as he marched, looking neither to the left nor to the right. Following him like a dutiful daughter was Corinna, eyes downcast, steps slow and hesitant, as if she were yoked to him by an invisible leash and was being led off to some altogether unpleasant fate.

I turned from my contemplation of the painted wooden

figure to the flesh-and-blood original at my side. 'How is this possible?' I demanded.

Corinna only shook her head, her gaze fixed on the unfolding tableau. The expression on her face was one of surprise and, or so it seemed, horror, as if the display was as new and unexpected to her as it was to me . . . though I did not see how that could be.

'Corinna,' I insisted, 'is this your father's work? Is he playing some kind of twisted game?'

As if in answer, she gasped and raised a hand to her mouth. I looked back at the clock, and there, trailing the figure of Corinna like a lovesick bumpkin, Sylvius vainly importuning cold-hearted Phoebe, I saw what could only have been intended as a mocking representation of myself. But it was the mere fact of the thing's existence, rather than its satirical intent, that left me reeling; I felt as though my reality had been called into question, as if I should look into a mirror and see reflected there the chiselled features of a marionette leering back at me. For the thing wore my stolen clothes and hat, or so it seemed to me.

By the time I had collected my wits, or at any rate enough of them to feel in command of myself again, my doppelgänger had completed more than half its journey across the proscenium; already the figure of Adolpheus had left the stage, disappearing into the interior of the clock through a door opposite the one from which it had emerged, and my own figure came at the very end of the parade – soon it, too, would vanish, and the door would close.

Impulsively, I pulled my hand free of Corinna's and ran towards the clock, ignoring her shouts for me to stop. Slipping and sliding over the icy ground, I reached the bristling façade and without hesitation flung myself upon it, finding hand- and footholds amid the ice-and-snow-crusted figures there, hauling myself upwards like a mountain climber. Earlier I had rejected the idea of just such a climb, judging it too perilous to attempt, but now I flew up the slick surface, surprising myself with the sureness and ease of my ascent. Before I knew it, I stood bare-headed on the proscenium, my hat lost in the climb. Only then did it strike me that the space was free of snow and ice, and I wondered, at the back of my mind, if Adolpheus were responsible, for though it was some-what sheltered from the elements, it was open to the wind. But there was no time for such puzzles.

To my left, the figure of Corinna was re-entering the clock. Below me, the real Corinna was yelling at me to come down. I paid her no heed. With a cry, as if I might thus command the procession to halt, I hurried forward, reaching out for my counterfeit's painted shoulder as I would for some urchin cut-purse overtaken on a London street. Indeed, I felt that something had been stolen from me, though I could not have said what. I half imagined that the mannequin would turn to face me when I laid hold of it.

But I never did. Instead, a wrenching pain in my ankle brought me to a sudden stop; my boot had become wedged in the track that carried the automatons across the proscenium. I felt the grinding of bone as the train continued to move, carrying me along with it willy-nilly, and my cry now had nothing of command in it, only pain. It was no more effective in stopping the mechanism.

The image is a comical one, I will grant you, like some allegorical study: 'The Clockman Caught by Time'. But I confess the humour escaped me at the moment. All I could think of was the likelihood that my foot would be mangled in the gears of the train. Yet try as I might, I could not tug my boot free. Overriding the pain, panic filled me as I watched my diminutive double disappearing through the door and into the dark insides of the clock. I would be next. Earlier I had wished more than anything to be privy to the secrets hidden away there, but this was not the way I had imagined myself gaining access to them. What had beckoned with the promise of untold riches, like the treasure hoard of a dragon, now seemed forbidding, hostile. Some tardy instinct warned that to enter the clock in this manner would mean my death, and I did not doubt it for a second. I resumed my efforts to pull my boot free, or, failing that, to extricate my foot from the boot before it was too late. But the motion of the train, disturbed by my interference, was no longer as smooth as it had been; it had grown as jerky as the movements of the automatons, and in attempting to keep my balance and remove my foot, I accomplished neither, falling onto my backside, from which undignified position, more or less of a height with my wooden double, I saw him swallowed by the darkness behind the door that was now swinging shut, even as I continued to be drawn towards it. I say darkness, yet from out of it there shone, like a scattering of stars, glints of silver that I would have taken for reflections of sunlight from metal or ice were it not for the fact that grey clouds had once again spilled over the jagged tops of the mountains and begun to drop their heavy loads of snow, quite obscuring the sun that had just moments before had the sky to itself. So swift was this change that it seemed as much a mechanical effect as the tolling of the bells and the parade of automatons, as if the influence of Wachter's Folly extended even to the heavens.

But my attention was on lower things. I saw that the door would shut before I was drawn through it, yet not before my trapped boot was carried over the threshold. The door looked substantial, and I had no doubt that the mechanical force behind it would be sufficient to crush my foot. I redoubled my struggles, in vain. I could neither free myself nor, from my prone position, on my back now, my free leg extended to push against the closing door, employ sufficient leverage to stop or even slow its progress. I cried for help, but there was no answer from Corinna. I closed my eyes and braced myself for what was to come.

But instead of the agony I was expecting, I felt myself lurch to a sudden halt. Opening my eyes, I beheld Adolpheus. His appearance was so sudden and unheralded that it was almost as if he had emerged from the clock. The dwarf had used his stepladder to prevent the door from closing, and this, in turn, had stopped the train – though I could feel it straining beneath me, its motive force frustrated for the time being but still exerting itself, like a trapped behemoth flexing against its bonds, building towards an explosive escape. Perhaps only another clockman would credit it, but at that moment my apprehension was not for myself but for the well-being of the timepiece. I feared it would suffer some irreparable harm.

'This is getting to be a habit, Herr Gray,' said Adolpheus, a grin flashing through his rusty beard. 'If Corinna hadn't found me, you'd be shorter by a foot about now.'

'My boot is caught,' I told him. 'I can't get it out!'

He gave my leg a tentative tug, at which I gasped as pain shot through my ankle. 'Ach, you're wedged in there good and proper,' he commented as though admiring a fine bit of carpentry. 'Looks as though I might have to cut the boot away . . .'

'There's no time for that,' I replied. 'The clock is going to damage itself – can't you feel it?'

'What do you suggest?'

'Why, pull it out, man! You've got the leverage.'

Adolpheus grinned again. 'It's going to hurt.'

'Best hurry then,' I replied.

He nodded and stepped aside to take hold of my leg with his gloved hands. 'Ready?' he asked. 'On three. One . . . two . . .'

There was no *three*. Adolpheus yanked with what seemed the strength of a giant, and my boot came free – but with such a surfeit of pain that I screamed as if, rather than liberating my appendage, he had torn it off. I rolled away, howling and clutching my leg below the knee; my boot had been shredded in the gears of the train, and I saw a dark stain of blood on the leather, and splashes of crimson glistened on the proscenium. Meanwhile, Adolpheus must have removed his stepladder, because I felt a lurch as the stalled train resumed its course, and the door did likewise, clapping shut with a bang, after which the train stopped again, this time by design.

'Can you walk?' Adolpheus asked.

I could not speak, but only shook my head.

He bent down and, before I could protest, lifted me as if I were no more than a child and slung me across his broad shoulders. The movement brought another stab of pain to my ankle, and everything went dark.

12

The Cogwheel Sun

THE NEXT THING I KNEW, WE WERE ON THE GROUND AGAIN, AT the base of the clock. I was lying with my back propped against the stepladder, gazing into the concerned faces of Adolpheus and Corinna as snow continued to fall around us. Corinna knelt at my shoulder, cushioning my head against her arm, while Adolpheus squatted by my foot, which he appeared to have been examining while I was unconscious. My ankle throbbed in time to the beating of my heart: two perfectly synchronized timepieces.

'Are you all right, Michael – er, Herr Gray?' Corinna asked. Her face was pale with worry, though a faint blush coloured her cheeks as she corrected her use of my Christian name – but not before Adolpheus had taken note of the slip, as I saw from the sharp glance he gave her.

'Not the smartest thing I've ever done, Fraülein,' I admitted with an attempt at levity, both because I wanted Corinna to think me brave and because I didn't want Adolpheus to report back to Herr Doppler that she and I were in the habit of addressing each other so informally. One intimacy might lead to another, after all . . . at least, in the mind of a father so determined to guard his daughter's innocence. But the sight of my foot – or, rather, the torn and bloody boot that covered it – wiped even the hint of a grin from my face, and all bravery from my heart. What would I find beneath that mangled boot? The thought of it made me sick with apprehension.

'Hard to tell how bad it is without cutting off the boot, or rather what's left of it,' said Adolpheus. 'Let's get you back to the Hearth and Home, and we'll see where things stand. And speaking of which, I don't suppose you can – stand, that is.'

'I should not like to try,' I answered.

'Then I will carry you,' he said. 'I will be as gentle as I can.'

Again he lifted me effortlessly, cradling me against his chest. What a ludicrous sight we must have made as he bore me back to the Hearth and Home! A dwarf carrying a man almost twice his own height! But there was no one to witness my humiliation. The square was deserted, as were the covered passages. Corinna followed us, the stepladder slung over her shoulder by its rope, which she held in both hands, bent forward to better distribute the weight of the ladder, as if she bore a load of kindling on her back. Though she said nothing, her concern for me was palpable.

True to his word, Adolpheus was gentleness itself. Not once did he bang my injured foot against the sides of the corridors, which, though spacious enough for two people to pass abreast, were yet not very much wider than my own length. Even so, the trip was a torturous one, and it took all my self-control to keep from crying out when, as was inevitable, some movement jostled my foot, or, as happened despite Adolpheus's care, my boot brushed against a wall as he turned a corner.

'Herr Doppler will not be pleased when he hears of this,' Adolpheus remarked as we neared the inn.

This seemed so self-evident as not to require a reply.

Besides, I feared that if I opened my mouth to speak, I might whimper like a beaten dog.

But Corinna spoke up from behind. 'Oh, must you tell him, Adolpheus? The only harm done was to poor Herr Gray. Surely there is no reason for my father to know.'

'I have never lied to your father,' Adolpheus answered without slowing or looking back, 'and I do not mean to start now. I am the watchman of this town, and it is my duty to report such transgressions. Herr Doppler has been indulgent where you are concerned, Fraülein – what father would not be? But I do not care to tempt his wrath by dissembling. I will tell him what I know. In any case, the story would soon come out. The injury, after all, speaks for itself.'

'Then let it,' she returned pertly.

'I will tell what I know,' he repeated.

'But what *do* you know, after all? Only that his foot became caught in the train. You do not know how he came to be in that position.'

'It seems clear enough. He sought entrance to the clock – which he promised your father not to do. Is that not the case, Herr Gray?'

Corinna replied before I could. 'He climbed to the proscenium because I asked him to. What happened is my fault entirely!'

At this I protested, of course. 'She's lying,' I ground out between clenched teeth.

'I'm not,' she insisted. 'Herr Gray is only trying to protect me by taking the blame onto himself, as any gentleman would.'

'Protect you from what?' Adolpheus demanded. I confess I was curious to learn this as well; looking back at her over the dwarf's shoulder, I saw her raise an admonitory finger to her lips. Clearly, she had something in mind, though I could not guess what it might be. But I held my tongue.

'The truth is – you will think me wicked, Adolpheus – but the truth is that I teased him mercilessly, challenged him again and again to scale the tower. Every boy in Märchen has made the climb, I told him. Are you, a grown man, afraid to match them? I don't know why I did it; I try to be good, but there is something in me that likes to stir things up, some devil that delights in mischief.'

'I'm disappointed in you,' Adolpheus said. 'And in you as well, Herr Gray. To allow a young girl's teasing to provoke you into breaking a solemn promise. You should be setting this one a sober example, not encouraging her waywardness.'

Again Corinna spoke up before I could. 'He didn't want to go,' she said. 'He wasn't going to, no matter what. But then I promised that I would reward him most handsomely if he scaled the tower and returned to the ground before the automatons had completed their course. I was only teasing, I swear it, but up he went like a jackrabbit. You know the rest.'

'What did you promise him?' Adolpheus asked. 'That is what I would know.'

At this, Corinna burst into tears, or seemed to, letting the stepladder fall behind her as she turned towards one wall and buried her face in her hands. 'Oh, I cannot say. Do not ask it of me, Adolpheus! I am too ashamed.'

Needless to say, this had the effect of encouraging rather than deflecting Adolpheus's curiosity. He stopped and half turned to look behind him at the weeping Corinna – in the process grazing my boot against the wall, so that I had to bite my lip to hold back a cry. 'If you will not tell me,' he said to her, 'I will require it of Herr Gray. He, I feel sure, will know his duty.'

'No,' she said, seeming to dry her eyes, though she would

not meet Adolpheus's demanding gaze – or my own un-comprehending one. 'I will tell you. I promised him . . . a kiss.'

Now, indeed, a cry escaped my lips, but of surprise rather than pain. Yet I don't believe Adolpheus heard it, for he had thrown back his head and was roaring with laughter. 'A kiss!' he managed to gasp out. 'Bless you, a kiss!'

This response provoked Corinna to anger. 'Yes, why not a kiss? What is so funny about that, I should like to know! Am I so hideous, that no one would want to kiss me?'

But Adolpheus did not reply. Still laughing, he turned and continued towards the inn.

Corinna followed, furious now. 'Answer me, Adolpheus! Adolpheus!'

He paid her no heed. As for me, I was at a loss to explain why she had concocted such a story to account for my presence upon the proscenium. Adolpheus might find it amusing, but I felt sure her father would have a different reaction. That she had some scheme in mind was obvious – but what? I grasped that she had not wanted me to reveal what we had seen, yet I could not guess her reasons. Indeed, I could scarcely credit my own eyes. That the automatons should resemble the townsfolk of Märchen seemed possible – though it meant Herr Doppler had been less than truthful when he'd told me that no one had touched the inner workings of the clock since Wachter's day. But that someone could have prepared an automaton to resemble me in the relatively short time I'd been there – why, that was beyond credulity. I supposed a skilled craftsman work-ing diligently from the moment I'd set foot in town could have made such a thing, but why? For what purpose? Howsoever I racked my brains, no answers came – at least, no sane ones.

My return to the Hearth and Home was a humiliating one. Corinna, looking daggers at Adolpheus, held the door open for him to carry me through. The taproom was crowded and noisy, much as it had been the night of my arrival. And, as had been the case that night, all conversation ceased at my entrance. But unlike that night, the silence was followed by raucous laughter as the spectacle of a dwarf carrying a full-grown man in his arms registered on the patrons.

'Behold,' shouted one wit, 'the watchman bears the clockman!'

'Got too much time on your hands, Dolph?' contributed another.

'Quiet, you dolts,' Adolpheus roared. 'Can't you see the man's been hurt? Someone fetch the doctor!'

At that moment, Inge entered from the kitchen with a tray of glasses. Seeing us, she gave a little shriek and dropped the tray. The sound of shattering glass provoked greater mirth from the denizens of the taproom, which in turn set Hesta, already roused from her slumber by the hearth, to barking.

With a growl of annoyance, Adolpheus carried me across the room and up the stairs. Inge, recovered from her surprise, bustled after us, bombarding Adolpheus with questions that, for the moment, he ignored. Corinna followed her, and, last of all, came a still-barking Hesta. I had the uncanny sense that this, too, was but a grouping of automatons. Shakespeare wrote that all the world's a stage, but at that moment it seemed to me a clock.

The door to my room was locked, and though I had the key in my pocket, I could not get to it easily from my current position, and so Adolpheus stood to one side as Inge used her master key. The dwarf's arms were like bands of iron; despite the distance he had carried me, I could not feel even a tremor in his muscles. It seemed that he could bear my weight for hours more if need be.

'Ach, Herr Gray,' Inge said as she pushed the door open, letting a heavy exhalation of heat roll from the room, 'what have you done to yourself now?'

'The fool climbed the clock tower,' Adolpheus answered as he shouldered his way past her.

'Lord bless us!' Inge responded, entering the room behind him. 'Did he fall?'

'I simply wished to examine the automatons more closely,' I explained, tired of other people speaking for me, 'and my boot became caught in the mechanism.'

'You're lucky to be alive,' the landlady stated. 'That clock has ways of defending itself.'

'That's ridicu— holy Christ in heaven!' A wave of pain over-whelmed me as Adolpheus none too gently, whether from weariness or exasperation, deposited me onto the bed.

'Apologies, Herr Gray,' he said cheerfully.

'Adolpheus, you clumsy idiot!' cried Corinna, who had followed Inge into the room. 'Are you trying to kill him?' She rushed to my bedside as though to protect me from a murderer. Ignoring the hurly-burly, Hesta went straight to the simmering furnace and flopped down onto the floor in front of it.

'That's enough from you, young lady,' Inge said sharply. 'Herr Gray left in your care, and see how he returns!'

'Are you saying it's my fault he was hurt?' Corinna demanded, pulling up short and turning to face the landlady, an incredulous look on her face.

'Isn't it?' Adolpheus asked. 'After all, he would not have climbed the tower had you not tempted him with a kiss.'

Corinna flushed, and whatever she had been about to say went unsaid; in the heat of the exchange, she had, or so it seemed to me, forgotten what she had told Adolpheus earlier, but now the memory of it left her quite unable to speak.

'What?' cried Inge at this news. 'Why, you shameless hussy! A kiss, indeed! Your father shall hear of this, I promise you.'

'But Frau Hubner . . .' Suddenly she looked near tears. Real ones this time. Corinna's customary self-possession had the effect of making her seem older than her years, but now that façade was stripped away, revealing her youth and innocence. It wrung my heart to see, yet what could I say? She had invented the story of a kiss to stop me from telling Adolpheus the real reason for my climb; for whatever reason, she wished to keep what we had seen a secret, and I had no sense now that her wishes had changed, even if circumstances had taken an unforeseen turning.

'But nothing,' Inge said. 'Get downstairs with you this instant. You're late for work as it is, and that crowd of drunks is probably robbing me blind.'

'But—'

'I said now! You, too, Adolpheus – Herr Gray is not a sack of potatoes to be thrown down so roughly. He requires a woman's touch.'

Corinna, after a plaintive glance at me, eyes brimming with tears, turned and left the room, her posture one of abject defeat. Adolpheus followed almost jauntily. 'Well, clockman,' he said in the doorway, 'I'll look in on you later, assuming there is anything left of you after Herr Doppler is through.' He shook his shaggy head and chuckled. 'A kiss indeed. That girl is a menace.'

'She is innocent,' I responded.

'And all the more dangerous for it, as you are about to discover.' He jerked his chin in my direction and added, 'If the lesson hasn't sunk in already.'

'Ach, don't pay him any mind,' Inge said after Adolpheus had departed. 'He is just jealous.'

'Jealous?' I exclaimed.

'Of course jealous,' she answered. 'Do you think anyone has offered to kiss him lately? Or ever?'

I had to laugh.

Inge smiled, her apple-red cheeks dimpling. 'That's more like it. Don't worry about Herr Doppler. He knows his daughter's tricks and fancies. You are not the first she's led astray.' The landlady leaned over the bed, her abundant breasts seeming about to spill out of the top of her blouse like ripe fruits from a cornucopia. The heady aromas of the kitchen wafted from her as if from an open oven, and once again they proved to have a stimulating effect, which I shifted my position on the bed to disguise, though I could see by Inge's glance that my condition had not escaped her notice. 'Your poor foot,' she said, laying a massive hand on my leg, above the knee; I could feel the heat of her through my clothing, as if she and not the tile stove were the source of the room's excessive warmth. 'Can I do anything to ease your pain until the doctor arrives?'

I had the distinct impression that she was not referring to my foot at all. But just at that moment, the gentleman in question knocked at the open door. He was a small man, though of course taller than Adolpheus, but slight as a reed and pale as parchment, as if he had no more than a trickle of blood in his veins. He peeked into the room, blinking owlishly behind a pair of spectacles. He was dressed in black, which made his skin seem all the paler; his powdered grey wig, of a style long out of fashion, was tilted askew, as though he had jammed it onto his head while rushing out of the door. I did not think I had seen him before, though there was something familiar about him.

'I was sent for,' he said defensively, as if afraid his presence would be questioned.

'Come in, sir, come in,' said Inge, straightening and stepping back, her hand sliding from my leg in a kind of caress. 'Your patient awaits.'

The doctor entered, holding a small black bag very much like my own tool kit before him in the manner of a shield. 'How do you do, sir,' he said with a somewhat convulsive bow in my direction.

'Not too well, I'm afraid,' I replied, indicating my foot.

'This is Herr Gray, Doctor,' Inge said.

He repeated his bow. 'I am Dr Immelman.'

'A Jew,' Inge added in a stage whisper, as if this fact were significant.

'A convert,' the doctor was quick to amend, as if this, too, were significant, indicative of superior, if not occult, knowledge.

'It is your medical rather than your religious practices that concern me,' I told him with an attempt at levity that appeared to fall flat.

'We may be a bit out of the way here in Märchen, off the beaten track so to speak,' he said as he approached the bed with that same tentative air, 'but I think you'll find my skills more than adequate.'

'I have no doubt of it, Herr Doctor,' I assured him. 'It was merely a joke – a poor one.'

'Ah,' he said, nodding sagaciously. 'A joke. Of course.'

The concept seemed foreign to him.

'Well, Dr Immelman,' Inge broke in, 'will you need my assistance? Is there anything I can get for you?'

By now Immelman had reached the bed. He settled his black bag upon the edge of the mattress and adjusted his spectacles as he looked me over. His bloodless face and pale, high forehead were slick with sweat; he almost seemed to be melting, as if made of wax or ice. 'That boot will have to be cut away,' he said. 'I will need hot water and bandages, Frau Hubner. And a bottle of schnapps for the patient, to dull the pain.'

'I'll have them sent up at once,' she replied. 'I'll leave you in the doctor's capable hands for now, Herr Gray. Later I will bring some food and sit with you awhile. Come, Hesta,' she added, and the dog rose from the floor and followed her out of the room.

Dr Immelman pulled up a chair and sat down near the foot of the bed, facing me but keeping his gaze fixed on my boot. 'You will let me know if there is any pain,' he directed, reaching out with long, slender fingers, like those of a pianist.

I swore as he began to manipulate my ankle; his touch was gentle enough, but even so the pain was severe. He drew back at once.

'Is it broken?' I asked him.

He withdrew a handkerchief from within his black coat and mopped his perspiring face, then tucked it back inside. Now his gaze did meet my own, but only, as it were, glancingly. 'I cannot say for certain without removing the boot. It seems likely, however.'

I swore again.

'How were you injured, Herr Gray?' Immelman asked. 'I was told only that my services were required.'

'I climbed the clock tower, and my foot became lodged in the train along which the automatons move.'

Now his gaze returned to my own, and this time it did not waver. 'Why would you do such a foolish thing?'

I shrugged but did not look away. 'It seemed a good idea at the time.' I didn't want to say anything more concerning the automatons, not only because of Corinna's apparent desire that I should keep quiet about their resemblance to the people of Märchen, but because I was convinced that I had seen the good doctor – or, rather, his wooden counterpart – among them. Yes, I remembered the sight of him quite clearly; he had preceded Adolpheus in the parade, that black bag of his held before him in the same fashion he had held it just moments ago, before setting it down on the bed. The recollection made it impossible to view the man with equanimity; despite his timidity, there was something uncanny, almost sinister, it seemed to me, about his presence now, and I experienced once again, more intensely than I had in the taproom, a sense of – how to describe it? – *misalignment*, as if I no longer fitted properly into the world, or as if the world had undergone some subtle change, one that had left it less friendly to me, less, well, like home. The sensation was all the more troubling in that it was so inchoate, a pervasive wrongness I could neither explain nor explain away.

'You are the English clockman,' Immelman said. 'You have come to learn the secrets of our timepieces, no?'

'I hope to be permitted to study them,' I allowed.

'You have a strange way of going about it, climbing the tower like that. It is not the sort of behaviour likely to be rewarded by Herr Doppler.'

'I suppose not.'

'I think it was no idle action.' Immelman glanced to the door, then leaned towards me, his voice a confiding whisper. 'I think you saw something that . . . astonished you. Something that provoked you to make the climb.'

'On what do you base your diagnosis?' I asked. 'Have you yourself seen something astonishing?'

'I have seen many such things in my time here,' Immelman replied, once again casting a nervous glance towards the door.

He licked his thin lips. Then, as if coming to a decision, he addressed me in English. 'Sir,' he said, pitching his voice lower still, 'you are in grave danger. Märchen is not what you think. Nothing here is what you think. You must be on your guard if you ever wish to leave this place alive.'

I confess I was too taken aback to make an immediate reply. It was not only the shock of being addressed in my native tongue, but the warning thus conveyed, which, though it had come out of the blue, was uttered with such conviction that I did not doubt the man's sincerity. But of course sincerity is no guarantee of truth. No one, after all, is as sincere as a madman.

'They have tried to keep us apart,' Immelman went on, his words spilling out in a breathless rush. 'This is not your first injury since you arrived in Märchen, yet only now have I been given the task of treating you. Do you not find that strange?'

'They? Who is this *they*?' I found my voice at last.

'Herr Doppler and the rest. They are afraid I will warn you, as indeed I have. Afraid I will help you escape, as I should like very much to do. Yes, and go with you, away from this cursed place for ever! They wish to keep you here, Herr Gray. They have need of you. Just as, years ago, when I was as young a man as you, they had need of me.'

The disarray of the doctor's clothes and wig, which I had at first taken as evidence of a certain absentmindedness often to be met with among medical men, now began to suggest a more troubling interpretation. Inge had told me that the long months of isolation imposed by Märchen's heavy snowfalls sometimes induced a kind of mania in the townsfolk. Was that the cause of Dr Immelman's odd behaviour? His eyes had a wild cast behind his spectacles, and his skin glistened with sweat; he looked sickly, feverish. I responded reasonably, hoping to calm him. 'If my skills are required, Herr Doppler need only ask. Instead, he has denied my every request.'

'He has his reasons, of that you may be sure. But it is useless to try and puzzle them out. They do not think as we do, Herr Gray. They are not—'

He broke off at the sound of approaching footsteps, turning to the door as Inge entered, carrying a tray on which she had balanced a steaming jug, a bottle of schnapps with a small glass turned upside down beside it, and a pile of folded white cloths. 'What is the prognosis, Doctor?' she inquired.

Dr Immelman blanched at this innocuous question and, switching back to German, stammered out his diagnosis of a broken ankle.

'I am sorry to hear it,' said Inge, shaking her head in sympathy as she crossed the room to us and set the tray on the bedside table; her bosom strained against her blouse as she leaned down, but somehow, as before, failed to overspill it. That was as astonishing as anything else I had seen, I assure you. When I tore my eyes away from the display of ripe pink flesh, it was to find her gazing at me with what I can only describe as hunger, as if I were a feast spread before her. At that moment I felt an answering hunger, as though, were it not for the presence of Dr Immelman, each of us could have devoured the other. I felt ashamed of my feelings, and guilty, as if by having them I was being unfaithful to Corinna, but I couldn't ignore them, either. Inge smiled, seeming to divine my thoughts. 'I shall take good care of you, Herr Gray, never fear.'

The spell was broken as Dr Immelman once again manipulated my ankle, this time without the gentleness he had displayed earlier. I cursed more loudly than ever, and the doctor apologized profusely. His hands were shaking.

'For God's sake, Doctor,' Inge erupted, 'can you not be more careful? Pull yourself together!' She fetched a chair from across the room and sat beside him. 'Come, I will assist you.' She poured a small portion of schnapps into the glass and handed it to him. 'Here, this will steady your nerves.'

'Thank you,' he said and gulped it down. Then, by what seemed an immense effort of will, Dr Immelman asserted control over his trembling hands. He opened his black bag and began to lay out his instruments. The routine of it seemed to calm him further. Yet the sight of those instruments only increased my apprehension.

'Now it is your turn, Herr Gray,' said Inge meanwhile, filling the glass from the bottle and offering it to me. 'Drink it down, now, all of it.'

I did not need any encouragement. I drained the glass as if it held water. I have never been fond of schnapps – I find its sweetness cloying. Give me a good English port any time. Yet this was like no schnapps I had ever tasted. When I had first arrived in town and secured my room at the Hearth and Home, I had poured myself a glass of water – a glass that had seemed, instead, to contain a most potent liquor, cold and sharp as an icy needle to the brain, which, upon melting, had diffused its numbness through my body, sending me into a sleep so profound that Corinna's presence at my bedside had not awakened me, but had only, as it were, become transmuted into the stuff of dreams. This draught of schnapps was like that, except more so: it was as if I had swallowed a magical elixir, the ambrosia of the gods, something too strong for mortal senses, as far beyond normal schnapps as that water I had tasted was beyond normal water. The sleep that claimed me was beyond sleep, and if I experienced any dreams, they were beyond the grasp of my memory, for I have never, in all the years since, been able to recall even a glimmer of what passed through my mind from the time I swallowed the schnapps until I opened my eyes again to find the room lit by candlelight and, instead of Inge and Dr Immelman, Herr Doppler himself seated at my bedside.

'The sleeper wakes,' he said, closing the thin leather-bound volume he had been reading and setting it on the mattress.

I was too groggy and disoriented to reply, but merely lay there, half reclining against the headboard, trying to situate myself.

'Here, Herr Gray, allow me to assist you,' Doppler said, getting to his feet. He poured me a glass of water and, with an arm behind my neck, helped prop me up to drink it. I sipped; the water was cold but not intoxicating – invigorating, rather. It brought me fully awake. As if sensing this, Herr Doppler set the glass down on the bedside table, plumped the pillows behind me, and resumed his seat. 'How are you feeling?' he inquired. 'Any pain?'

I shook my head. I lay on top of the covers, fully dressed save for the absence of my boots. One foot was in its stocking; the other was wrapped in pristine white bandages and elevated upon a pillow. It was twice the size of its fellow. Beneath the bandages, I could feel nothing at all. 'Where is Dr Immelman?' I asked, recalling his warning to me.

'Downstairs, eating his dinner. I will call for him in a moment, never fear.'

'I cannot feel my foot,' I told him. 'It is as numb as a block of wood.'

Herr Doppler chuckled at this. 'Calm yourself, Herr Gray! The good doctor knows his business. I arrived in time to watch him at his work – a steadier hand I have seldom seen. Why, he cut away your boot as if he were peeling an orange, then set your ankle so smoothly that you did not so much as twitch in your sleep. Then he applied some kind of poultice – a numbing agent, he called it, to keep the pain at bay while the break begins to heal. He can explain it better than I, and will do so, I am sure – but first, you and I must have a chat, sir. I dare say you can guess the subject.'

'My head is somewhat fuzzy,' I temporized. 'If you would enlighten me . . .' It seemed safest to let him take the lead.

'Ah, Herr Gray, you think I am angry with you because you climbed the clock tower. I assure you, I am not. The clock, as you see, has ways of protecting itself.'

'That is what Inge said,' I exclaimed. 'But surely you can't believe—'

'That one of Herr Wachter's mechanisms might defend itself?' he broke in. 'Come, Herr Gray. Do you mean to tell me, after all you have seen, all you have experienced, that you could doubt it?'

I let this pass. Frankly, I did not wish to dwell on the possibility, which I found disturbing. 'If not that, then what?'

'Why, if not the effect, what else but the cause? That is to say, the reason you climbed the tower in the first place. What was it, Herr Gray? Something you saw, perhaps? Something out of the ordinary?'

At this, I had to laugh. '*Out of the ordinary?* Herr Doppler, I have seen little else since I arrived here!' Then, mindful of Corinna's evident desire that I keep secret what we had seen, I asked him, 'Have you not spoken to your daughter?'

He frowned. 'Rather, she has spoken to me. And confessed that it was all her doing – that she tempted you into making the climb with the promise of a kiss. I could well believe her capable of such a wicked promise, the minx, but the fact that she volunteered the information freely makes me suspicious. I know my daughter, sir. She is hiding something. And I think you know what it is.'

I had no intention of revealing what I had seen. I did not understand the significance of it, but I had no doubt that it *was* significant, for not only Herr Doppler but Dr Immelman and even Adolpheus had pressed me on the matter. In any case, it was sufficient that Corinna wished me to say nothing of it.

'I would not have you think badly of your daughter,' I told Herr Doppler. 'She is only trying to protect me, and in her innocence does not understand the injury she does herself. The truth is, it was I who set the terms for that climb, not Corinna.'

'You, sir?'

'I had been pressing her for a kiss all morning. But she had resisted my every advance. At last, as we stood before the clock tower, watching as the automatons crossed the stage above us, I secured her promise – reluctantly given, I assure you, and only out of a desire to put an end to my importuning – of a kiss in exchange for my climbing the tower and planting a kiss of my own upon the cheek of a wooden maiden there.'

'A wooden maiden?' Herr Doppler echoed, his eyes narrowing. 'What maiden is this?'

I wondered if I had said too much and inadvertently revealed what I had hoped to keep secret. I saw no recourse but to press on. 'Just one of the automatons,' I answered with a shrug. 'I hope I do not give offence, Herr Doppler, but to speak frankly, I had expected better. So wondrous are the outsides of Herr Wachter's timepieces that I had thought anything emerging from within them must be equally wondrous. But the figures I saw seemed to have been executed in haste, and otherwise were no different than hundreds of others I have encountered in my travels.'

'Ah, so now you know our darkest secret,' Doppler said with a chuckle, as if relieved. 'The truth is, Herr Wachter had nothing to do with those figures. When it came to such things, he preferred to work on a smaller scale, as with the dragon in Inge's cuckoo clock. There he lavished the full measure of his genius. Do not misunderstand – the clock tower is indeed his masterpiece. But its size and complexity were such that he felt compelled to delegate certain aspects of its fabrication, like the automatons, to others ... or so I was told and do believe. The truth of it seems evident in the craftsmanship, as you say. So,' he added, returning to his subject, 'having secured my daughter's promise, you ascended.'

'The climb was easier than I had expected – the carvings on the façade provided all the hand- and footholds necessary. But I never got the chance to deliver my kiss. My foot became caught in the train almost at once. If not for Adolpheus, I shudder to think what would have happened. I do not think I would have escaped with just a broken ankle.'

'Indeed, you might have lost your leg to the mechanism,' Doppler agreed. 'I hope this will be a lesson to you, Herr Gray.'

'I do not think I am likely to be climbing anything for a while,' I said.

'Oh, it's not as bad as all that,' Doppler said. 'Dr Immelman will have you hobbling about in no time, you'll see. But as to the matter of the kiss ...' He paused and stroked his moustache as if considering how best to proceed. Then, in a grave tone: 'I'm afraid you have disappointed me, Herr Gray. I do not like to be disappointed. I thought we had an agreement. You were to instruct my daughter in horology, all the while subtly discouraging her interest. I did not intend that you instruct her in anything else. But you seem to have mistaken me. My English is lacking, I know, yet I do not believe *horology* begins with a *w*.'

'Come now, Herr Doppler,' I told him. 'That is harsh and unworthy. What blame there is attaches to me, not Corinna. I assure you, I had no designs beyond a chaste kiss, and, indeed, had not really intended for things to go even that far. It won't happen again.'

'See that it does not,' he said, laying a hand upon my bandaged foot. I could feel the pressure of it, the weight, but no pain or other sensation penetrated the numbing effects of Dr Immelman's poultice. Still, I understood the threat that Herr Doppler had left unspoken.

'Then, am I to continue her lessons?' I inquired.

'I see no reason why not,' Doppler said and lifted his hand. 'She has already insisted upon nursing you back to health – though it seems your landlady also has intentions in that regard. Well, we shall let the women battle it out. In the meantime, you may as well continue the lessons. Only, no more talk of kisses, eh? And I would like to see some progress. As of yet, she shows no signs of discouragement. On the contrary, she seems more enthusiastic than ever.'

'The one must precede the other, or else the blow, when it comes, will be insufficient to achieve the result you desire. It is not so easy to kill a dream, Herr Doppler. If the slightest fragment is left, it may take root and grow again – especially when, as is the case here, a genuine talent exists.'

'I leave the details to you,' he said and pushed himself to his feet. 'What matters to me are results. If I do not see some progress by the time you are on your feet again, we shall have another discussion, Herr Gray. A less pleasant one.'

'I understand,' I told him.

'Good,' he said with a satisfied nod. 'I will inform Corinna.

And now I must bid you good night – my dinner is waiting. As, no doubt, is the good doctor, eager to check on his patient. I will send him up directly.'

I was glad to see him go. There was a mercurial aspect to Herr Doppler that disturbed me, especially where Corinna was concerned. Why, he had all but called his own daughter a whore! He seemed almost more like a jealous lover than a father. Yet I reminded myself that he had been both father and mother to the girl, and so had, by necessity, been forced into a relationship outside the normal bounds of fatherhood. How could I, who had no children, presume to criticize? Still, it would have gone better for both of them, I could not help thinking, had he taken another wife.

Alone, my attention was drawn towards my bandaged foot, but the sight of it – combined with the absence of sensation – left me feeling queasy. It was as if the appendage belonged to me and yet was foreign. I had an urge to unwrap the bandages but was afraid to touch them.

To distract myself while waiting for Dr Immelman, I picked up the slim volume that Herr Doppler had been reading and had left behind on the bed, forgotten. The cover was of green-dyed leather and had upon it no writing, just a gold-embossed image of the sun – or what I took for the sun but then realized could just as easily be a stylized representation of a cogwheel. Intrigued, I opened the book.

The page before me was covered in printed symbols I neither knew nor recognized, a sinuous typeface that reminded me of the Arabic writing I had seen in my travels. But I knew it was not Arabic. It was something stranger, more foreign. The shape of the letters – if that was what they were – was such that the lines seemed to move as I studied them, to actually flow across the page. Or, rather, not the lines themselves, but a force within the lines, moving through them like water through an elaborate system of pipes, as if the ink itself were in motion, impelled by some vital power. I seemed to hear the murmur of that activity, and it struck me that the book was whispering to me, telling me its secrets, if only I had the wit to understand them.

As I stared, mesmerized as much by the soft susurrus of sound as by the undulations of the script, I felt a kind of sickness spawn inside me, and I would have flung the book away if I could. Book? Was it a book that I held, or was it instead a living thing, not ink but blood rushing through the exotic markings on the page? I did not know. I only knew that it held me as firmly as I held it, that I could no more tear my hands away than I had been able to wrench my foot free of the train that had caught me and would have carried me into the clock had it not been for the arrival of Adolpheus. Then I had cried for help, but now I could not so much as whisper. I could barely even breathe as the book spilled itself into me, or so it seemed, entering through the skin of my fingers as much as through my eyes and ears, though I still could not have said – nor can I to this day – what was being communicated to me. But I could feel it filling me up, squirming its way inside me, changing me. Perhaps it was teaching me how to read it. Perhaps, on the contrary, I was being read. Maybe both at once.

All I know is that, as time went by – and whether minutes or hours had passed, I could not say – the markings on the page began to seem familiar to me, and I thought I could discern a kind of sense in them. Not the sense of words, inseparable from the sounds we associate with particular shapes, and the meanings thus conjured in our minds, but the sense of machines. Of clocks. Yes, the thought grew in me that I was holding something akin to one of Herr Wachter's timepieces. The shapes on the page, I now perceived, or recognized, were not words at all but parts of an intricate mechanical system; the flowing movement I had detected was the motion of each separate part in harmony with the others. If I looked closely, I could see it all quite clearly, as if through a jeweller's loupe – tiny gears meshing, chains moving, pulleys rising and falling. It was like looking at a sketch for a mechanical device and suddenly realizing that the sketch *was* the device: that the two were one and the same, the representation of the thing, and the thing itself, identical. But to what end did such a machine exist? What work was it performing? I confess that I could not form an answer, or even the beginnings of one. Yet surely if I read further into the book I would discover the answer – or, rather, the answer would make itself known to me.

So deeply was I caught in the coils of the book that I did not register the arrival of Dr Immelman until he wrenched it from my hands. At that, the spell was broken. I fell back against the pillows, bathed in a cold sweat and shivering. The doctor, meanwhile, was gazing at me wide-eyed behind his spectacles, the book – closed now – clasped to his chest. Between his fingers, over his heart, I saw the embossed image of the cogwheel sun. It was turning. Not swiftly, but at a steady rate, as though driving an invisible hand across an invisible clock face. Yet even as I watched, it began to slow. For some reason, this terrified me more than anything.

'What is that book?' I demanded, pointing with a shaking finger.

Immelman did not answer, but turned and crossed the room to the table where he'd left his black bag. His back was to me, so I couldn't see clearly what he was doing there, but when he returned to the bed, the book was gone, and he held a small glass vial in his hands. It was filled with a pearlescent liquid.

'Doctor, the book,' I persisted, groping for the right words but not finding them.

'It belongs to Herr Doppler,' he said. 'I will return it to him. You should not have tried to read it.'

'Read it?' Laughter bubbled between my lips. I felt as if I were going mad. 'There is no reading such a book – if it *is* a book, and not some kind of infernal machine!'

'Every book is a machine, is it not?' the doctor queried as he opened the vial and poured a few drops into a glass on the bedside table. This he filled with water; it clouded and then cleared as he swished the water around the glass. 'Drink this,' he said, holding it out to me.

I looked at him stupidly.

He sighed and spoke as if to a child. 'You are having a reaction to the poultice, Herr Gray. It contains a potent numbing agent which can sometimes induce hallucinations. Do you understand?'

'I know what I saw,' I insisted. 'You know it, too – I can tell. Why are you lying?'

He sighed again. 'Must I call Herr Doppler and Adolpheus to hold you down? Drink, Herr Gray. It's for your own good.'

'I don't believe you,' I said. 'Earlier you were about to warn me of something. What was it?'

The doctor hesitated before replying, as if debating how much to tell me. 'I'm sorry,' he said at last, 'but it is too late. Now, drink up. Don't worry – it's merely a sedative, something to help you sleep. When you wake up, all your questions will be answered, I promise.'

I shook my head, drawing back from the glass he thrust at me. 'No,' I cried. 'Too late for what? Keep it away – I said no!'

'Doctor, let me talk to him.' It was Corinna. I was so glad to see her that I nearly sobbed with relief. She was the only one in this madhouse of a town that I could trust.

Dr Immelman straightened at her words. 'Very well, Fraülein.' He set the glass on the bedside table and stepped back, motioning for her to approach me.

'I should like to speak to Herr Gray alone,' she clarified.

'Why, that's . . .' Whatever he was about to say, he thought better of it. 'Of course.' He crossed the room to retrieve his black bag. Then, bowing to each of us in turn, he left the room. 'I shall be outside if you need me.'

'Please close the door, Herr Doctor.'

He did so without objection.

'What is going on, Corinna?' I asked. I had so many questions, I scarcely knew where to begin. 'Your father's book . . . The automatons . . . All of it. What is happening to me?'

'Shh,' she said as she came forward and sat on the edge of the bed, reaching out to brush back a lock of my hair. The touch of her fingers on my brow accomplished what mere words could not, and I felt at once stirred to my depths and yet soothed in my soul. 'Drink the doctor's potion first, Michael, and I will sit with you and tell you all you wish to know.'

'I'm afraid,' I admitted to her. 'Afraid that I will never wake up.'

'You will wake,' she assured me. 'I swear it. Now, please, for my sake.' And she picked up the glass and held it out to me.

I met her gaze, searching for any hint of deception, but I saw only caring and concern. I took the glass, and it felt to me that I was binding myself to her by the action, or rather the trust behind it, as if we two were plighting our troth in a ceremony that needed no other witnesses but ourselves, a ceremony more significant than anything we had already shared. I saw, or seemed to see, an answering knowledge in her eyes. And so I drank the potion. I tasted nothing but water – though the water of Märchen was anything but ordinary. So swift was the spread of lethargy through my limbs that I would have dropped the glass had she not plucked it from my hand.

'Now ask your questions,' she said.

It was difficult to focus my thoughts, much less speak them aloud. But I persevered. 'The automatons, Corinna. How is that I saw myself there? And why did you not wish to tell anyone what we had seen? Why did you make up that story about a kiss?'

'Why, would you not like a kiss from me?' she answered coyly.

'Of course,' I said, 'but—'

'Then you shall have it,' she said and, before I could say another word, pressed her lips to mine. Despite the lassitude instilled by the doctor's potion, I responded. That her father or Frau Hubner might enter the room at any time and discover us did not cross my mind. But even as I sought to deepen the kiss, opening my lips to coax the same from her, she pulled away.

'That was nice,' she said. 'I could feel your heart beating so fast, like a hummingbird!'

But to me my heartbeat seemed rather like a clock in need of winding, or like the cogwheel slowing on the cover of Herr Doppler's book as whatever energy had powered its turning ebbed away. I felt myself slipping under. I did not think even another kiss from Corinna could keep me awake. I struggled to speak. 'Tell me about the clock, the automatons.'

She frowned but then answered. 'It is some wizardry of Herr Wachter's,' she said. 'The figures are always the same, modelled after the townsfolk. Except today. Today you appeared among them. A stranger. That has never happened before. There is something special about you, Michael. The clock has chosen you.'

I understood her words, but the sense behind them was as far beyond my comprehension as the script in Herr Doppler's book. 'Chosen? How? And for what?'

'For me,' she said, blushing most becomingly. 'We are to be husband and wife.'

I confess I did not follow the logic. Yet there was nothing more I could say; the potion had done its work, and even as she bent to give me another kiss, I felt myself falling away from her as if the mattress had yawned open beneath me. Before her lips reached mine, darkness closed over my eyes.

'I will come back later tonight.' Her voice threaded out of the black. 'When you are awake again. I will show you . . .'

Her words were lost as I slipped completely under.

I was awakened by the sound of a closing door. I sat up, alert in an instant, the effects of Dr Immelman's draught utterly spent. The lamp had gone out, and the only light in the room was a soft glow from the stove, a reddish nimbus like the heart of a dying coal. It illuminated nothing beyond itself, clinging to its source as if for warmth, for the temperature in the room had plunged while I slept. Behind me, I heard the rattle of sleet against the windowpane.

'Who is there?' I whispered. 'Corinna, is it you?'

There came a dry rasping, as of something heavy being dragged across the floor. At that sound, the memory of the dream that had ravished me on my first night in Märchen, when Corinna had crept into my room and stolen my tool kit, flooded over me. I recalled the eldritch glow that had pervaded everything like some radiant property of cold, remembered the inhuman beauty of the woman who had stood before me like some aloof yet hungry goddess made of metal and jewels, demanding a tribute I could not deny. I began to tremble, afraid that the dream was playing itself out in real life . . . yet also half desiring it.

Then the pungent odour of fresh-baked bread rolled over me, as if an oven door had been opened, and I knew who my visitor was.

'Inge,' I said.

And from the darkness, near enough to touch, a whisper: 'Shh.'

As had happened before, her scent proved stimulating, a force of nature beyond my control, and my little soldier had already sprung to attention when I felt her settle onto the bed, which groaned at the weight of her. I reached out, intending to push her away, but my hand sank as if into a mass of dough. She was naked. Her skin did not just envelop my hand but seemed to absorb it. She moaned at my touch as if she had long desired it. When I tried to pull my hand back, she fixed my wrist in a grip of iron and moved my hand over her body in a forceful parody of a caress.

In the darkness, the extent of her was impossible to gauge. She *was* the darkness, darkness incarnate and concentrated, hungry and hot beneath my fingers, as if she were burning with fever. And that fever spread to me. Infected me. Whereas at first it had been a kind of disbelieving horror that stilled my voice, now it was passion that robbed me of speech. I was panting like an animal, straining towards her with mindless need. And she reciprocated. Her hands tore at my clothing, freeing me, and then she – there is no other word for it – engulfed me. I had a moment's anxiety for my injured foot, but I felt no pain as the soft and fragrant immensity of her came down over me, and then all thought was extinguished.

It was as if I had entered a dense and surging sea. I rose and plunged, tumbled and spun, caught in fleshy currents that flexed and slid and oozed around me like the coils of a serpent intent not to squeeze the breath from me but rather to stroke me to heights of pleasure beyond all enduring, pleasure too great for a human body to contain. I had a sense that she was not just ravishing me but also, at the same time, giving birth to me, to a new me, as if I were a lump of dough and she an expert baker whose hands were kneading me, whose embrace was baking me.

All the while, I was spilling without cease. There was no holding back, yet neither did I spend myself. My energies looped back on themselves, feeding on their own expiration. I felt as if every last drop of vitality was being wrung out of me, that, when Inge released me, I would be as desiccated as the victim of a spider, a shrivelled, bloodless husk. But I didn't care. I welcomed that fate. I desired above everything to lay my spark on the altar of her divine corpulence, to light a candle there, even if I had to snuff myself out to do it.

And perhaps I would have done just that had not the door slammed open with a bang that not only penetrated but popped the bubble of our congress. An eerie blue light flooded the room, and Inge drew back with a hiss, releasing me. I lay there, spent and gasping, whatever glamour had gripped me broken. Looking up, I beheld a monster. A creature with the head and torso of a woman but the lower body of a serpent. It was those coils, lying loose around me now, not scaled but fleshy, glistening with the mingled fluids of our exertions, that had embraced me; it was those coils, twined about her torso, that had given Inge the appearance of such fantastic stoutness, for in reality – reality! – she was, from the waist up, as perfect a vision of femininity as any man could desire.

Now her eyes were fixed on the door, and on the figure that stood there: Corinna, returned as she had promised. But it was also the woman from my dream, the frozen succubus that had melted before me into a frightened girl. She was not frightened now. Anger flashed in her quartz-green eyes.

I had thought the room cold already, but now it turned positively frigid. Ice bloomed on every surface. I felt it on my lips, my tongue, deep in my lungs; I watched it precipitate out of the air with every exhalation, a sparkling condensation of fear. I could not move; could not cry out; could only shiver and watch the confrontation playing out before me. Yet even then, struck mute as I was with terror, I felt again an insatiable demand, and my body, though bereft of strength and desire, responded like some collapsed beast of burden lashed erect, so that I was once more as hard as marble and trembling on the edge of climax; it was only the fact that the attention of the two women – if women they were – was on each other and not on me that kept me from tumbling over.

For long seconds they took each other's measure, the temperature meanwhile continuing to plunge, until it had passed the lowest register of my sensibilities and entered into some realm beyond cold, like the very heart of hell. Inge was sheathed in ice; it covered her like a second skin, a skin of glass, a diamond prison. Corinna might have been carved out of stone. Not a word was spoken by either of them.

Then Inge flexed her coils. The prison shattered, and she was free. Free and moving swift as lightning towards Corinna, who shot forward to meet her. They came together in the centre of the room and grappled there like two wrestlers, straining one against the other, wordless and intent, their eyes locked as fiercely as their limbs.

My ears rang from the thunder of their collision, the force of which shook the building like an earthquake. Yet even so I heard the bells in the clock tower begin to chime, as if the shock had reached all the way to the town square. It was no tuneful chorus such as I had heard before but a riotous cater-wauling, strident and clamorous, a noise of panic, of alarm.

The women appeared not to notice, intent on each other. They seemed well matched. Neither could gain the upper hand; their bodies – Inge naked, Corinna clothed – trembled with the choked violence of their efforts, which sent tremors like aftershocks through the room. The floor creaked; the walls cracked; chips of plaster and ice dropped from the ceiling. It felt as if the inn was about to come crashing down around my ears, yet I couldn't stir.

Then not just the room but the whole earth heaved beneath me. The women raised their heads sharply, seeming to listen with every fibre of their beings. And the earth heaved again. And again. If a mountain could walk, I remember thinking, this is what it would feel like.

'You fool,' hissed Inge. 'You've awakened him!'

'It's your fault,' Corinna shot back.

But it was clear that their mutual hatred was dwarfed by their fear of whatever was coming. With an angry cry, Inge pulled free of Corinna's grasp. She could have struck then, yet she did not, and not from mercy – with a flick of her tail, she propelled herself past Corinna and out of the door, leaving the two of us alone.

'Hurry,' Corinna said, turning to me. 'Follow me if you want to live.'

At her words, my paralysis fell away. I fumbled at my

disordered clothing. My heart was pounding, my mouth dry.

'Hurry,' she said again.

'I can't,' I told her, gesturing helplessly. 'My foot.'

With a look of exasperation, she crossed to the bed and, taking hold of my arm, pulled me to my feet. I had an impression of immense strength, as if she could have not just lifted me but thrown me for a hundred yards. Despite everything, her touch, rough as it was, brought me to climax again; there was no pleasure in it, just an involuntary spasm, a reflex that wrung my insides like a cold fist clenching. I groaned, and she glanced down with annoyance, as if I were a favoured pet that had reminded her I was only an animal after all. But perhaps she was equally annoyed at herself, for in the next second I felt a diminution of her presence, a dwindling, as if she had willed herself to become something less than she had been, than she really was. At that, I went as limp as a wet noodle and would have fallen had she not supported me with her arm. This time her touch had no untoward effect. And yet I marvelled, even in the midst of my terror, because I was standing. There was not so much as a twinge of pain from my bandaged foot. It felt as strong, as well, as ever. 'How—'

'This is no time for questions,' she interrupted. 'Or answers. Come – we must flee. Death approaches.'

And indeed, the gargantuan footsteps had not stilled in all this time, nor had the tintinnabulation of the bells. Corinna was pulling me towards the door. I paused only to snatch my tool kit. Then I followed her.

13

The Productions of Time

HAND IN HAND, WE FLED THE HEARTH AND HOME. THOUGH Corinna's touch had lost its uncanny power over me, a chilly blue light continued to radiate from her, a reminder – were any needed! – that she was more than just the simple girl I had known, or thought I had known.

The inn appeared empty, abandoned. There was no sign of Inge, for which I was glad enough, and Hesta was gone from her customary place beside the fire, or what was left of it: glowing embers in a bed of ash. As we hurried through the common room, a flicker of movement behind the bar drew my attention; the door of the cuckoo clock stood open, and the tiny dragon whose appearance had so delighted me on previous occasions was flitting around the clock face in excitement or distress. It came at me without warning, its wings beating about my head and shoulders, its hot breath scalding my neck, burning my hair. I cried out, swatting one-handed at the flames as the infernal creature harried me with the crazed persistence of a mother bird defending its nest.

Then we were outside, in the network of covered passageways that had turned the snow-blanketed town into a maze. The dragon did not follow. I could feel that my scalp and neck had been burned, though how badly I did not know.

'This way,' Corinna said and ran off before I could say a word.

I hurried after her. The lamps of the passageways had all gone out, and the only light came from Corinna; it illuminated our immediate surroundings but no more than that. The result was that I had soon lost my bearings. All the while, the bells of the clock tower rang out in disarray, and the ground shook with the measured tread of whatever enormity was approaching. It seemed that we were rushing straight towards it.

'Corinna,' I gasped, reaching out to grab hold of her shoulder. 'Please, talk to me. I feel as though I've gone mad – or the world has!'

She shrugged me off but slowed enough for me to come alongside her. She addressed me as we loped onwards. 'Haven't you realized that you are no longer in your world?'

I could make no coherent reply to this.

'Märchen,' she continued, 'is like a town that straddles the border between two countries. You crossed from one into the other.'

'Crossed . . . how?' I asked.

'Through the tower clock. It is the gate – one of the last gates.'

'But I never entered the clock,' I protested. 'My foot was caught!'

'You had already passed through,' she told me. 'Adolpheus didn't find you lying unconscious in the snow all those weeks ago. He knocked you out and carried you across the threshold, from your world into this one.'

'But why? Why me? Why . . . everything?'

She shook her head. 'So many questions! There is no time

to explain, and even if there were, you would not understand. But we had need of you, and so you were brought here.'

'Like Dr Immelman?' I asked, remembering the doctor's warnings.

'His name is not Immelman,' she said. 'Nor is he a doctor. He is, or was, the very man you have been searching for – Herr Wachter.'

Now I was more confused than ever.

'You were to be his replacement,' she said. 'But now that can never be.'

'Because of Inge?' I asked.

'No – though she should have left you alone. But she has always been a glutton, unable to control her appetites. And you are so very tempting – all of your kind. You are a drug to us, Michael. You must know that. You are a sickness that we crave; you give us, for a short while, the only thing we lack: a taste of mortality. Of time.'

'Who . . . what are you?'

'We have many names in your world. Some call us the Fair Folk. To others we are djinn, demons, angels. Gods. But these are mere words – human words for something as far beyond human words as beyond humanity itself. As to what we call ourselves, you lack the language to express it. We are old and fierce and forever.'

I was not a religious man, yet I had been raised in the Church of England, and I felt a need of its strong support just then, like the buttress of a cathedral. 'There is but one God,' I said, as much to reassure myself as to contradict what Corinna had told me. 'If you are angels, it can only be the fallen kind.'

'Risen, rather,' she said. 'That is our crime – our original sin, if you will. I repent of it most heartily now, perhaps too late. But I have made my choice at last. I spurn my father and all his works. I will fight him. And you will help me.'

She was right – I understood nothing of what she was telling me. I asked only, 'What is to become of me?'

'Why, I am sending you back across the border,' she said. 'I am sending you home. No more questions now,' she added, for we had come to an exit that I recognized – beyond it lay the town square, and the clock tower. 'Whatever happens, stay close to me, meet no one's eye, say nothing, and follow my every command.'

'It sounds as though you are expecting a fight.'

'A fight?' she echoed, and laughed grimly. 'Michael, I am expecting a war.'

She got one. Or the makings of one, anyway, for when she opened the door and stepped through, taking me by the hand and drawing me along beside her – and a good thing, for I could not have taken a step under my own power – I saw a great armoured host filling the square. The clash of sunlight off their armour and the weapons they held was blinding. But then I realized the light was radiating from the host itself, like Corinna's light only a thousand times brighter because it came from a thousand separate sources. And hotter, too, for the snow was melting all around us with a loud hissing, and steam rose into the air.

Even Corinna seemed taken aback by the sheer numbers confronting us, a bristling silver wall of swords and pikes, shields and helms. Upon those shields, and on banners that fluttered from standards scattered throughout the throng, I saw the same figure of a gearlike sun, or sunlike gear, that I had seen on the cover of Herr Doppler's book. Like that cogwheel sun, these, too, were turning.

Corinna paused as if gathering her resolve, then strode forward, pulling me along with her. No one in that glittering array spoke as we advanced towards them hand in hand. It was only then, in the crashing silence, that I realized the bells had stopped tolling. The ground was still. Whatever had been approaching seemed to have arrived. Yet I saw no giant; perhaps, I thought, it had been the heavy, measured tread of the army arrayed before us, marching into position, that had so shaken the earth. The square as I remembered it could not have contained such a vast throng, yet it did not otherwise appear any different; the buildings looked the same as they always had, as did the hulking shapes of the mountains beyond, their tops lost in a blanket of grey cloud heavy with snow. Of the sun there was not even the palest hint in that gloomy, threatening sky. The resplendent soldiers facing us were the sole source of light. We might almost have been underground.

'Fear not, Michael,' Corinna whispered to me. 'Take courage. They dare not stand against us.'

But she squeezed my hand as she spoke, and I felt she was exhorting herself to courage as much as me. I returned the pressure in the same spirit.

As we drew near, a figure detached itself from the rest and advanced to meet us. Though armoured and wearing a full helm, like some knight of old, its diminutive stature put me in mind of Adolpheus, and my supposition was proved correct when, at a distance of a dozen feet or so, he stopped and lifted his visor. The face thus revealed was both the face I knew and one I did not recognize, as if the Adolpheus I had seen and spoken with had been only a rough sketch for this one, as crude a likeness in its way as the automaton I had seen atop the clock tower. Like Corinna, he had somehow diminished himself in my presence, made himself less than he truly was. But now I was seeing him unveiled, in all his glory, shining like a little sun, his size no indication of his power but rather a necessary component of it, as if he were a god of small things. I felt a familiar stirring in my loins, a lustful quickening. This was no man, I told myself. This was something else, something that only wore the shape of a man, that tugged at me as a lodestone tugs at an iron filing. And then, as fast as that, the pull was gone. I glanced at Corinna and saw that she had resumed her former splendour; she stood once more like a queen of ice and moonlight, and though her cold blue radiance did not outshine his light, it did blunt it, shielding me from his glare.

'Do not do this, Corinna,' he said. 'We do not wish to fight you. Return to the Hearth and Home and all will be forgiven. It is not too late.'

'I have made my choice, Adolpheus,' she replied. 'Join me or stand aside.'

'I will do neither,' he said. 'Your father has given me the power to stop you. I will use it if I must.'

'You are welcome to try. But first there is something you should see.'

'And what is that?' he asked.

Rather than answering him, she whispered to me, though she did not take her eyes from Adolpheus. 'Look away, Michael. Fix your eyes upon the ground, and keep them there on your life. Watch my feet, and when you see me walk, walk with me.'

I dropped my gaze. Thus I cannot tell with certainty what it was that she showed to Adolpheus, though I can guess readily enough. I heard Adolpheus gasp in something like horror, and heard that sound echoed from what seemed ten thousand throats. Meanwhile, shadows stretched and writhed across the ground as if struggling to pull free of what had cast them.

'O, infamous daughter!' cried Adolpheus. 'Traitor and thief!'

The very air seemed to groan.

Corinna began to walk forward. I followed. It was difficult to keep my balance amidst the shifting patterns of shadow and light that danced over the ground. A kind of battle, it seemed to me, was being fought there. A silent and insubstantial battle that was nevertheless as much in earnest as any bloody clash of arms. The sight of it filled me with dread, yet, mindful of Corinna's warning, I forced myself not to look away, though my every instinct screamed to do so. I do not know why I trusted her, but I did; she had said that she was sending me home, and I clung desperately, fervently, to that hope, as a madman clings to a single idea though everything in the world should testify against it.

'Stand aside, Uncle,' Corinna commanded. This time there was no defiance from Adolpheus. Instead, I heard the clanking of armour as he complied. At that, the army behind him followed suit, splitting into two wings that, as they retreated step by noisy step, pivoted towards us with the precision of well-drilled troops on parade, fashioning a narrow corridor that led to the clock tower.

Corinna did not hesitate. Neither did she hurry. With every appearance of calm, as if reviewing troops assembled to do her honour, she walked with regal assurance through the mass of fighters who could have killed us in an instant. They did not strike at us, however, not even with a word, and so motionless were they on either side – though my gaze was lowered, I could see their silver-plated legs, numerous as the trees of a petrified forest – that I could not help but wonder if they were machines, an army of automatons.

Their shadows, meanwhile, stretched and twisted out of all

semblance, continued to make war with each other, or, perhaps, with something else I could not see, and finally, to preserve the crumbling bastions of my sanity – for I could no longer tell my own shadow from the others, and it had begun to seem to me that I was being drawn into their war, or was already a part of it – I shut my eyes and, like a blind man lost in a foreign land, let Corinna lead me where she would.

She stopped walking, and I bumped against her, reflexively opening my eyes. We had passed the army and now stood before the tower clock. Once, in what I had taken for a dream, I had watched a great dragon uncoil itself from the tower. Now that dragon faced us. Its long, scaled body, brown as burnished walnut, and haloed in a soft yellow glow, was looped around the edifice in an intricate knot my eyes could not unravel.

The beast would have towered over us, but it had lowered its flat head to our level to regard us serpentwise, and indeed it seemed more snake than dragon, wingless as it was. One of its eyes was gone, a pitted scar testifying to some ancient injury; the other was a glittering orb bigger than my hand, darker than dark. The warring shadows through which we had walked were gone now, yet I felt as if they had not vanished but only withdrawn into the inky depths of that solitary eye, for the longer I looked, the more I seemed to see movement there, smoky and serpentine. It called to me, that alluring movement, tugged at me with a strength I couldn't resist, and I took a step forward, and then another before Corinna hauled me back.

'I told you not to look,' she hissed, passing her hand before my eyes; it was as if a razor had cut whatever bound me to the dragon's greedy gaze. I gasped and looked away, yet I did not close my eyes as I had before. Instead, I let them roam over the dragon's body, trying to trace the sinuous, scaled, knotted immensity of it, as if it were a riddle I might solve. It was in constant motion, rippling like the surface of a river, which moves and yet stays still. Locked within its looping coils I saw the shadowy figures of men and women writhing as though in torment. The air shimmered with heat; I felt I stood on the very border of hell.

Meanwhile, Corinna addressed the monster. 'I would not fight you, faithful Hesta,' she said, and I started at that, not just because she had called the dragon by the name of the dog but because, when she did so, I perceived that they were one and the same, or, rather, aspects of each other, like two shadows cast by a single object; I could see the shadows, but the object itself remained hidden to me. But that was not the whole of the riddle.

At the sound of its name, the dragon growled low in its throat, and a smell of hot metal and oil gusted over me. It was an automaton. Another of Wachter's incredible, impossible machines, or so I surmised. It opened its jaws, and I cringed, fearing its breath, for I could see a fiery glow deep in its gullet. But instead the creature spoke in a voice as sinuous as its body, as mesmerizing as its eyes. The voice of a woman, I would have said, an empress . . . had I not seen the source of it.

'Go, faithless daughter,' the dragon said. 'I cannot harm you, nor will I impede you. But know this. Leave now and the way back will be for ever barred to you. You will never look upon Märchen again.'

'There are other gates,' Corinna replied. 'I will be back. And I will not be alone.'

'Others have said as much. Where are they now?'

'I shall find them,' Corinna said.

'Then you will die with them,' the dragon said, and there

was sadness in its voice, but also resolution. 'And what of you, human?' it asked then, addressing me. 'Will you share this rebel's fate? You may stay with us if you wish. There is a place for you here. She cannot compel you to go, whatever she may have told you.'

'Do not answer,' Corinna warned.

Too late. 'I did not ask to be brought here,' I said, careful to avoid the dragon's eye. 'I merely wish to go home.'

At which the creature laughed, a low, thunderous rumble. 'You sought us out. You found us. You may leave, but you will never go home again.'

'She lies,' Corinna told me. 'Do not listen to her, Michael. I will bring you home, I swear it.'

'You will be hunted,' the dragon promised. 'Both of you.'

Corinna raised her hand again, displaying what she held clenched in her fist; thin beams of blue-white light streamed between her fingers, and the dragon hissed and shied away as if from a weapon it feared to so much as gaze upon. 'I will be waiting, Hesta,' Corinna said, a promise of her own. Then she took hold of my hand again and stepped forward, advancing towards the dragon. The creature drew back with each step, flattening itself against the façade of the tower. By the time we reached the base, there was only the elaborate wooden carving that had always been there, of a dragon whose coils seemed to encompass hell itself.

Corinna placed her hand against the carving, and a door appeared, summoned by her touch. 'Open it,' she told me. I heard a strain in her voice I hadn't heard before; glancing at her, I saw that she appeared once more as a young woman, her face pale and drawn, as if she were nearing the end of her strength. She had never looked so beautiful to me, and I felt my heart go out to her, wanting to protect her, to sustain her with my own strength, paltry as it might be. I wondered why Hesta, seeing her weakness, did not strike now, or Adolpheus, who stood at our backs with his army. And where, I asked myself, was Herr Doppler? Why wasn't he trying to stop us?

'Hurry,' Corinna hissed.

A wooden hand extended from amidst the dragon's coils like that of a drowning man grasping for salvation; as there seemed to be no other knob or handle, I took hold of it and pulled. The door swung open; beyond was darkness, and a noise like the pumping of a great bellows . . . or a mighty heart. Though my greatest desire since I had arrived in Märchen had been to plumb the insides of the tower, I paused now on the threshold of attaining it. The blackness was absolute, dimensionless, all-engulfing. I feared that it would swallow me up, snuff me out.

Corinna, however, hastened through, pulling me along willy-nilly. The door shut behind us of its own accord. We were in a corridor, a wooden passageway like the ones in town, right down to the oil lamps set at regular intervals along the walls. I hadn't known what to expect upon entering the tower, but it had not been this. I looked around in confusion; really, to all appearances we might have stepped out of the Hearth and Home. The only heartbeat I could hear now was my own.

'What do you see?' Corinna asked.

I told her.

'Good. If you saw it as I do, you would undoubtedly go mad. Come now.' And she set off down the corridor at a hurried pace, pulling me along beside her.

'What do *you* see, then?' I inquired as we went. We passed doors and sidepassages, each identical to the others, but

Corinna ignored them all. I wondered where they led. Into other worlds? Other times?

'Nothing that would make sense to you,' she answered. 'Your language lacks the words to describe it, just as your senses lack the capacity to perceive it.'

'But how is it that we see different things?'

'This is an in-between place. In your language, I suppose you might call it the Otherwhere. It has not had the stamp of reality placed upon it. It can be anything, or many things. Whoever enters gives it shape, whether unconsciously or by an act of will.'

'You mean that I can change what I am seeing?'

At this, she laughed. 'Only our kind has the strength of mind for that. We are creatures of the Otherwhere, you see. It is our home.'

'I thought Märchen was your home.'

'That is a home we have made. This is the home that made us.'

'Made you? You talk as if it were alive.'

She laughed again. 'Everything is alive, Michael. Alive and always. Only, some things have forgotten it and need to be reminded – woken up.'

'What things?'

'All the productions of time. There – I have told you the great secret.'

'I don't understand.'

'That is why I have told you.' She stopped, and I bumped against her. We stood before a door; she turned to me and fixed me with a gaze at once imperious and tender. I felt she loved me then, but it was a love that reached down to me, as it were, from an immense distance, one I could not cross; it was, in short, a love that could not be truly reciprocated, for it was not equal. It could only be accepted and endured. The knowledge of this, too, was in her eyes, and it seemed to sadden her.

'Corinna,' I began, wanting to declare my feelings for her once more, as I had in simpler, happier times, to tell her that I loved her and to place myself at her service in whatever manner she might require. But she interrupted me.

'Here we must part,' she said. 'I deeper into the Otherwhere – you back to your world. Listen, now, Michael. My father will soon awaken and discover what I have stolen from him.'

'Has he not already awakened? Those footsteps . . .'

'The tread of Adolpheus's army. My father, great as he is, sleeps deeply and is slow to wake. But if he should find us here, there can be no escaping, for his will is the strongest of all and can impose itself on everything, including me.'

'Take me with you,' I said. 'I would help, if I can.'

'Then take this,' she said, and thrust what she held into my hand. It was, of course, Herr Doppler's pocket watch. It felt cold as ice, or colder, burning against my palm. Yet I clenched my fingers around it, ignoring the pain – no, revelling in it, for her sake. 'Let no one know of it,' she went on, her gaze holding mine, 'not even your closest friend. Not even your wife.'

'You are my wife,' I told her. 'I shall have no other.'

'Beware of what you say here,' she admonished. 'Words can become reality.'

'If saying you are my wife will make it so, why would I be silent? You are the only woman I desire or ever will desire.'

At that, she smiled but did not otherwise respond to my declaration. Instead, she returned to the subject of the watch. 'Do not attempt to open it; do not seek to learn its secrets.'

'But what is it?'

'Infinity bounded in a nutshell. My father will seek it cease-lessly, but as long as it sleeps, locked in matter, he cannot find it. Without it, he cannot win his war. Keep it secret, Michael. One day I – or, it may be, another – will come to claim it. But be on your guard, for my father has agents mortal and other-wise, and they will fool you if they can, or take it by force if they must.'

'But if it isn't you who comes to claim it, how will I know it is not some emissary of your father's?'

Before she could reply, there came a roar of anger such as I had never heard, like an earthquake wrapped in a tornado and fired from a cannon as big as a ship-of-the-line. At this, Corinna wasted no time, but flung open the door and shoved me through before I could protest or even gather my wits. There was a blinding flash, then the sensation of falling; I screamed, my vision aflame with all the colours of the rainbow, a shimmering display behind whose rippling folds I saw, or seemed to see, geometric shapes floating and tumbling as though suspended in an ocean of light. I could not grasp the size of them – at one instant they seemed huge as mountains; the next, no bigger than motes of dust drifting through a sun-beam. What they were, I knew not – but that they were aware of me, I did not doubt; I felt their attention, their interest. They turned towards me with purpose, coming together like the pieces of a puzzle, or the parts of a machine. Yet their movements were slow and ponderous; or perhaps it was that I was moving so fast, blazing like a comet across their sky. Remembering how Hesta in her dragon aspect had flinched away from the pocket watch, I raised my fist, brandishing the timepiece like a shield or rather a weapon . . . one I had no idea how to use. In Corinna's hand, the watch had shone like a star; in mine it was dead as a stone. But even so, those living geometries drew away and let me pass through their midst, just as Adolpheus and his army had done.

How long I fell, I cannot say. Time had no meaning in that place, that Otherwhere. My vision never cleared; the colours never faded. It came to me after a while that I was the source of them: like a meteor flaring with a fiery peacock's tail, I was shedding colour as some otherwise ineffable part of me was burned away, ablated. This only increased my terror, for it seemed to me that I must be consumed entirely, in hideous ruin and combustion, as the poet says. Yet I never felt so much as a twinge of heat or pain as I fell, faster and faster it seemed.

Then came another flash, as blinding as the first. Only, if that flash had signalled my entrance into a kind of dream, suffused as it was with menace and wonder, this one signalled my emergence from it. What blinded me now was the simple, pure light of the late morning sun peeking over the tops of mountains I had despaired of ever seeing again. Thus did I awaken and find myself stretched on a cold hillside at the foot of Mount Coglians in the Carnic Alps. I was home. Corinna had kept her promise.

I had arrived at Märchen at the turning of the season, autumn giving way to winter, but the chill in the air now was of a different quality, and the frost-rimed grasses and wild-flowers that blanketed the hillside in soft splashes of colour, the lowing of distant cattle and the hollow clanking of cowbells that echoed from the heights – all testified to the burgeoning of spring. I thought of the old tales of Fairyland and how time flowed so capriciously there. Perhaps I had been gone for years, decades, entire lifetimes.

Yet I was not thinking so much of what awaited me in the world to which I had been returned. No, all my thoughts were bent towards the world I had left behind – and Corinna.

I got to my feet – I felt as hale as I ever had in my life – and retraced my steps up the mountain, determined to enter Märchen again despite all that Corinna had told me. I was not thinking clearly. I was not thinking at all. It was the yearning of a broken heart, bereft and disconsolate, that drove me. But when I reached the spot where I had first set eyes on Märchen, there was nothing. I knew I was in the right place, for I could see the icy dagger of the glacier upthrust and glittering in the sun. But of the town not a trace remained, as if it had never been there at all.

PART THREE

14

The Otherwhere

QUARE HAD LONG SINCE PUT UP HIS PIPE, LISTENING TO LONGINUS'S story like a child entranced by a fairy tale. And indeed, as his host sat back and gazed at him, seeming to invite comment by his silence, it struck him that he had been hearing just that. But now, in the comfort of the garden belvedere, with late summer clinging to the afternoon air, the spell of Longinus's words melted away like some fantastic ice sculpture. While it was true that Quare himself had experienced any number of inexplicable occurrences of late, not the least of which being the wound that by rights should have killed him, he found that something in him remained sceptical in the face of what Longinus had related. For what, really, had he been told? He knew no more about the nature of the pocket watch than he ever had; the timepiece remained as mysterious as ever, both in its workings and its purpose. And as to the town of Märchen and its fabulous inhabitants, angels or fairies or what-ever it was they were supposed to be, he had no proof that they were more than figments of an eccentric, if not deranged, imagination. The watch, however uncanny its behaviour, was something he had held in his hands. He had seen it, felt it, witnessed it drinking his blood to provide its motive power. It was unquestionably real. Though he did not understand how it worked, how it achieved the effects he had witnessed, Quare still believed that there must be a scientific explanation for it all. He was not ready to abandon his faith in science for a superstitious credulity in magic. He did not wish to insult the man who, at great personal risk, had rescued him from the dungeons of the guild hall, yet he was not prepared to take Longinus at his word, much less to follow him back into danger.

'Well, Mr Quare?' asked Longinus at last. 'What do you make of my tale?'

'In truth, I hardly know what to think,' he answered. 'The nature of the watch is as clouded to me as ever, and I confess I am utterly at a loss how to account for Corinna and the other townsfolk.'

'I felt the same as I stood upon that empty hillside all those years ago. Yet I knew that something miraculous had happened to me, something that would change the course of my life, even if I did not understand everything about it. After all, I had the watch in my hands. And the memory of all I had witnessed.'

'But I have neither of those things.'

'So, you require more proof, do you?'

'More? Why, sir, you have offered none at all! Only a tale whose airy wonders I might find appealing enough were I still a child, but which, I regret to say, lacks the substance required by an adult apprehension.'

'Then perhaps *this* will be sufficiently substantial.' Without further ado, Longinus bent over his right foot. Quare watched in bafflement as the older man removed his slipper and then pulled off the white hose that covered his leg from ankle to knee. Beneath it, he was wearing a second slipper, white as bone, that came to just above his ankle.

Quare was about to remark on this curious affectation when he realized that the slipper was not a slipper at all. It was, instead, a foot. Or, rather, a prosthetic that resembled, in all but colour, the appendage it had replaced. Carved, no doubt, out of whalebone, and with an exquisite attention to detail that would not have been out of place on a statue by Michelangelo.

Longinus, meanwhile, gazed at him with an expression of amusement. 'Is this proof enough for you, Mr Quare?'

'What . . . I mean, how . . .'

The toes of the prosthetic wiggled.

Quare shot to his feet with a cry.

At which Longinus laughed heartily. 'Forgive me,' he said, his eyes flashing with mirth. 'But you cannot imagine how often I have wished to do that.'

Quare could make no rational reply.

'Extraordinary, isn't it? However, I confess that my first reaction upon encountering this object at the end of my leg was not one of fascination but horror. It was that same night, after I had hiked back down the mountainside and retraced my steps to the town I had last visited, what appeared to have been many months ago. There I obtained a room, and a hot bath . . . and it was then, when I stripped away the bandages that still swathed my foot, that I made the awful discovery. After I had calmed somewhat, and regained a modicum of reason, and pacified the alarmed proprietors who, summoned by my screams, had first threatened to break down my door, and then to evict me from the premises, what must have happened became clear to me. As I had lain unconscious in the Hearth and Home, Dr Immelman – or, as I now had reason to believe him to be, Herr Wachter himself – had amputated my mangled foot and replaced it with a prosthetic . . . a prosthetic that in all respects functioned as well as – and in some respects, as I was to discover, a good deal better than – the flesh-and-blood original.'

Quare had by now taken his seat once more. Not because he had regained possession of himself, but because he did not trust his legs to support him.

Longinus crossed his ankle over the opposing knee, bringing the prosthetic near enough to Quare that he could perceive where the white bone – if it were bone – met pale flesh. There was no scar, only a seamless joining. As he marvelled at this, senses reeling, Longinus removed a small tool kit from his coat pocket, calmly opened it, and, holding it in one hand, selected an instrument from within – a slender pick-like tool useful for prising open watches and probing their insides. Quare carried just such a tool in his own kit. But the sight of this familiar object did not soothe him. On the contrary, it underscored the perceptual clash he was experiencing, of two things fundamentally antithetical to each other brought into an impossible proximity.

Setting the open tool kit upon his thigh, Longinus tapped the probe against the side of the prosthetic. It made a sharp clicking sound, as if it had struck marble. Then, though to Quare's discerning eye the appendage appeared smooth as an eggshell, he somehow found an opening, and with a flick of the wrist caused a narrow panel in the side of the foot to swing open. Beneath, exposed to Quare's all but stupefied gaze, was a system of gears and fine chains that resembled nothing so much as the insides of a clock – or, rather, a watch. And not just any watch, but one in particular: the hunter he had examined in the work room of Master Magnus.

The bone-white gears turned smoothly, soundlessly, meshing as if they were not pieces fitted together by hand but instead organic parts of a single whole; the chains slid past the narrow opening at varying rates of speed, here a silvery blur, there a measured inching. Behind them, deeper in the recesses of the prosthetic, Quare could make out other gears, other chains; the impression was of constant, complex motion. It dizzied him to look at it. Yet he could not tear his eyes away. Twined through the cluttered insides, as out of place as worms in a watch, were thin red threads that shone against their pale surroundings, seeming to pulse with vitality: veins, Quare registered with some distant part of his mind, or something analogous to them. Then a nearer, more visceral part of him rebelled against what he was seeing, against the wrongness of it, and he lurched to his feet and out of the belvedere, where he spewed the contents of his stomach upon the green lawn of Lord Wichcote's garden.

By the time he returned to the belvedere, Longinus was once again wearing his hose and slipper. The tool kit was tucked away. He stood gazing at Quare with a look of concern. 'Are you quite all right, Mr Quare?'

Quare managed a nod. 'I-I'm sorry, my lord,' he stammered.

'Nonsense,' his host replied, waving away both the apology and, it seemed, the offence that had prompted it. 'You have seen something I have shown no one else, not even Magnus. Something that by all rights and reason should not exist. It would be a wonder if you did not have a violent reaction to it.'

'But . . .'

Longinus raised a forestalling hand. 'And none of this "my lord" business, if you please, sir. We have been over this already. You must get into the habit of calling me Longinus, for it is imperative that my true identity remain unknown to our enemies – whom we shall soon enough be facing.'

Everything was happening too quickly for Quare to process. 'I . . .'

'Come, Mr Quare,' Longinus said, gesturing towards the house. 'Let us go inside. I shall have this mess attended to. But there is more I must tell you. Much more.'

Quare allowed Longinus to shepherd him back into the house. They entered by the same door through which they had gone out some hours ago. The room where they had breakfasted was now arranged for dinner, but the sight and smells of the rich food that had been laid out upon a sideboard left Quare feeling as if he might become ill again.

Alert to his discomfort, Longinus led him through a side door and into a sitting room plainly used by Lord Wichcote and his male guests for card-playing, pipe-smoking and drinking. As with all the rooms in the house, and the belvedere as well, a variety of clocks were in evidence, none showing the same time, the soft, hollow clatter of their ticking like a gentle rain falling against the roof of an empty house.

Quare took the seat that Longinus indicated, watching as his host crossed the room and poured out a glass of brandy. This he brought back to Quare. 'Drink it down, sir. You will feel better for it, I assure you.'

The warm burn of the brandy settled his stomach and rallied his reason. Longinus, meanwhile, went to the door, where a velvet bell pull hung; this he tugged, then opened the door to speak to someone Quare could not see: a servant, presumably. When he was done, he returned and seated himself in an adjoining chair. Quare observed closely as Longinus walked but could see no evidence that he favoured his false foot over the other; had he not witnessed it with his own eyes, he would never have guessed that the man was crippled in any way. It was extraordinary. He said as much to

Longinus, who seemed to take his words as a compliment. 'Whatever else, Wachter was a craftsman of the very first order. Not once in all the years I have worn this appendage has the mechanism failed or even faltered. In that time, it has caused me pain but twice. The first time was the same night I discovered it, when in my revulsion I thought to have the thing removed. Amputated. Repelled, I swore to myself that I would have it cut off as soon as I returned to London. I felt I should prefer a block of dead wood to such a monstrosity! But the mere idea of it so racked my body with agony that I never again considered it. And the same thing happened again some time later, back in London, when I made an attempt to probe the workings of the mechanism, to learn its secrets. In both cases, the prosthetic defended itself, you see. Just as the great clock in Märchen had done. Like that clock, Mr Quare, my appendage is not simply alive in some sense: it is *aware*.'

Quare could not suppress a shudder.

Longinus chuckled. 'Oh, it does not speak to me, sir. I should be a fine figure of a man were I to engage in conversation with my foot. No, speaking with my footman is as far down that road as I care to go. And yet it does communicate after a fashion. It connects me to the realm Corinna spoke of: the Otherwhere. Some men sense changes in the weather by the ache in their bunions. I sense perturbations in that dream-like dimension, which lies, I am convinced, just alongside our own, separated by a barrier thinner than the thinnest veil yet impossible for humans to cross unaided. That barrier, Mr Quare, is time.'

'Time?'

Longinus gestured, indicating the gossipy assemblage of clocks. 'What I have deduced over the years, through trial and error, and from my memories of Märchen, is that time is as much an artifice as the clocks that purport to measure it. It is not some intrinsic property of the universe, an extension of the mind of God or a manifestation of the natural order. It has been imposed upon the world – upon us. Indeed, we have been infected with it, like a plague. Or, rather, we *are* the plague, for we are not separate from time, Mr Quare. We are its very embodiment.'

'I don't understand,' Quare confessed.

'Time is foreign to Corinna and her kind. So she told me, and so I have come to believe. It is something strange and terrifying to them. Unnatural, as it were. Yet beautiful, too. It attracts them. Draws them like moths to a flame. And then burns them. Being immortal, they do not die of it. They do not age, as we do – for what else is aging but a slow burning, a fire that consumes itself in the end? Mortality is the fire in our veins. It feeds on us, swells and gutters over the course of our lives, leaving naught but ashes. But it spreads, too, does it not, that fire? Through procreation, we pass it on to our progeny, who do the same in turn, ad infinitum. Do you not see that we are mere vehicles for its expression? We are like lumps of coal endowed with mobility and reason, yet ignorant of our true nature. But not Corinna and her kind. They know what we are, what we carry. And do we not make tribute of it for their sake? Recall the effect that the townsfolk of Märchen had upon me. I was helpless to resist the demands of their desire, whether openly expressed or not. I spilled my seed at their whim. I employed the metaphor of fire, yet you might also think of us as bottles of wine, Mr Quare. We must age a bit to achieve our full potency. But then we must be drunk. And a true connoisseur of wine does not drain his bottles at a gulp. No, he sips them. Savours them. So it is with these connoisseurs of time. They sip at our mortality, at the wine of time that has matured within us. And they do not perish of it, as we do. No doubt that is why the taste of us is so sweet to them, Mr Quare – sweeter than we can imagine. That is why they are fascinated by us. Why they long for us . . . yet hate us, too. We are their laudanum. Their weakness. They are addicted to us. Addicted to time.'

Quare made an effort to marshal his thoughts. 'You said imposed. Imposed by whom? And for what purpose?'

'As to whom, why, Doppler, of course – that is, Corinna's father, whatever his true name may be. It was plain to me, as I thought back over the circumstances of my escape from Märchen, that Herr Doppler, not Wachter, was the real power in that place. Corinna had told me, you will recall, that the Otherwhere was shaped by strength of will, and that her father's will was the strongest of all. Wachter, or Immelman, rather, seemed a pathetic creature, frightened, his spirit broken. He claimed to be as human as I. No doubt he had been brought across the border much as I had. They had need of him, just as they had need of me. Indeed, Corinna said that I was meant to replace him. But for what purpose, to what end, I do not know. Only that it must have had something to do with time. With clocks and time, Mr Quare.'

'What, then, of the watch that Corinna gave to you? What is *its* purpose?'

'I cannot say for certain. But I have some ideas. It is plain that Doppler does not rule over his realm unopposed. Clearly, there are factions among his kind. Some, like Adolpheus, are loyal, while others are engaged in a rebellion of sorts. Corinna went in search of the rebels at the end, to join their fight. Why, if the hunter were some powerful talisman, would she entrust it to me, rather than take it with her? The answer must be that it is too dangerous for them to employ, or even to possess. Thus I deduce that it is a weapon of awesome destructive power. And what is it that these creatures seem most to fear . . . and most to desire? Why, time, of course. The watch, then, must be a kind of bomb, Mr Quare. A time bomb, if you will. Now, let us consider what the effects of such a bomb might be, were it ever to be triggered.'

'But it *has* been triggered,' Quare interjected. 'In Master Magnus's study, when it killed his cats in the blink of an eye. And again, when it took Magnus's life, and somehow spared my own.'

Longinus nodded. 'Unquestionably, the watch – how shall I put it? – intervened at those moments. I say *intervened* because it seems obvious to me that the hunter, like other, similar artefacts attributed to Wachter – and for all I know, they were in fact crafted by him, but, if so, at Doppler's direction – at any rate, the hunter, too, is in some sense alive. Aware. It can choose how and when to act. Perhaps it can even decide the moment of its own detonation. But neither of the instances you have mentioned rises to that level. The proof of it is that the watch still exists . . . as do we, and everything around us. The world goes on, Mr Quare. Time passes as it always has. But in those effects, can we not see, in miniature, clues to the ultimate purpose and greater effect of the bomb? For what else could be the purpose of such an infernal device but the obliteration of every living thing in a sudden and catastrophic release of time? And yet that cannot be all, for it did, as you point out, spare your life. Therefore that, too, must be part of its design. The hunter is both a destroyer and a preserver of life. But which life will it destroy? And which preserve? I find it unlikely in the extreme that Doppler, whose will is supreme in a place where that is the measure of ultimate power, would create, or cause to be created, a device capable of causing his own death. No, it is far more likely, is it not, that he would instead create a weapon to cow his enemies – his allies, too, no doubt – and maintain his own pre-eminence. That, if my suppositions are correct, is the true purpose of the hunter. To destroy all life – not just mortal life, but immortal, too, for why else would Corinna and the others so fear it? – while preserving Doppler's life. To return every living thing – save himself – to the primordial state from which it was born. Perhaps, after such an apocalypse, he might, as the sole survivor, begin again, crafting new worlds, new lives, out of the malleable stuff of the Otherwhere.'

'You speak of him as if he were a god.'

'What better word is there to describe him, or any of them? There was something that Corinna said to me as we were fleeing – a remark I little noted at the time but have had years to reflect upon. I confess it is behind all that I have told you.'

'What remark?'

'I referred to Corinna and her kind as fallen angels. She was quick to correct me, Mr Quare. "Not fallen," she said. "Risen, rather." She called it their crime, their original sin. Imagine, Mr Quare, that spontaneously, as it were, out of the primal stuff of the Otherwhere, creatures arose that possessed self-awareness, intelligence, and, most of all, will – that is, the ability to shape the Otherwhere to their own purposes. Now imagine that after untold eons of existence, in which each of these creatures was effectively equal to the rest, one of them, filled with ambition and desiring to rule over the others, to set himself above them and impose his will upon them, created something never before seen or even imagined: time. Thus, I believe, was our world brought into being, and every living thing in it, ourselves included. We exist to serve as receptacles for time.'

'But what advantage would that give to Doppler?'

'Why, the same advantage that accrues to any man in control of a substance prized or, indeed, required by others. Do you not see? I have told you that time is a drug, Mr Quare. I meant it as no mere metaphor! Doppler created time, and then addicted his fellow gods – to use your word, if I may – to that drug. No doubt it began with worship, with prayers and sacrifices. It must have seemed harmless enough! A new diversion amidst the stale pleasures of eternity. But now they are in thrall to it, to him. And, in a sense, to us as well, for we humans are, after all, the ultimate source of the drug. In us, it reaches its greatest potency, perhaps because we, of all mortal beings, possess self-awareness, the knowledge of our own inevitable death. Certainly that must confer an exquisite piquancy to the drug!'

'But this is sheer speculation,' Quare protested. 'Pure fantasy . . . if not madness!'

'If you can supply a more cogent explanation for the facts at hand, I should be glad to hear it,' Longinus answered. 'You have seen my prosthetic. You have seen the hunter – and experienced for yourself its uncanny power.'

'I do not dispute any of that,' Quare said. 'But you go too far, surely, in your suppositions! What place is there for the Christian God in your system? Indeed, sir, you have turned Christianity upon its head, and made the Almighty into a very devil! I am no Bible-thumper, yet neither do I subscribe to rank atheism . . . or worse.'

'Perhaps it is Christianity that has turned things topsy-turvy, not I. Yet some shred of the truth, however distorted, can be discerned in the gilded trappings of that religion, and of other faiths, or so it seems to me. But that is beside the point.'

'And what *is* the point, if I may ask?'

Longinus shook his head, a superior smile upon his face. 'You have a long way to go, Mr Quare. You cling to your illusions.'

'To my sanity, rather.'

'That is merely another illusion.'

'For a man who claims to require my help, you have a strange way of going about it.'

Here Longinus seemed to come to an abrupt conclusion. 'You asked for proof, Mr Quare. Very well. You shall have it, or as much as lies within my power to give. I had not intended a demonstration. I had hoped to convince you with words, with reason. But now I see that I lack the eloquence to persuade, and you the broad-mindedness to be persuaded, by words alone. I must warn you, however. There is some risk involved.' He gestured about the room. 'All these clocks, ticking at their various rates, weave a tangle of time that shields this place and those within it from the attention of Doppler and his kind. That is why I carry so many misaligned watches upon my person – so that I may safely leave this sanctuary, enclosed in a cloud of conflicting time that deflects their scrutiny like the magic ring in Plato's myth, which cloaked its wearer in invisibility. Make no mistake – Doppler has been searching for me tirelessly in the years since my escape. He has bent every particle of his iron will towards finding me . . . and taking back the watch that Corinna stole from him and placed into my safekeeping. Now, in order to afford you visible proof that what I say is true, in order, as it were, to speak with actions rather than words, I must weaken the barrier, unlock it, for, just as it keeps Doppler out, so, too, does it trap me within.'

'I require no more proof,' Quare protested. 'I have had too much already.'

'Proof of my madness, you mean.' Longinus gave him a wolfish smile. And proceeded to divest himself of the watches he carried upon his person, stopping each one before placing it atop the table that held the decanter of brandy.

Soon quite a pile had accrued there; it would have been comical, thought Quare, were it not so bizarre. It almost seemed to him that he could feel a curious lightening of the room's atmosphere as Longinus progressed. 'Er, what did you say would happen if Doppler were to find us?'

'I didn't.' Longinus moved about the room as he answered, stopping each of the clocks in turn. 'No doubt it would be quite unpleasant. But if we are quick, and quiet, we should not draw his attention. Especially since the watch he seeks has been removed from my protection. The guild hall, with its cacophony of clocks, provides protection of a sort – I have made certain of that – but it is less complete, for I do not have total control over that establishment, as I do this one. You have been in the Old Wolf's den. There the timepieces march in strict conformity to each other, like soldiers on parade. The temporal emanations arising thereby are not chaotic but regular. They do not result in an obscuring cloud, but instead an open window, a doorway – an opening through which Doppler can enter our world . . . or, rather, through which his influence may enter, for I have reason to believe that Doppler himself cannot cross whatever boundary divides the worlds, or at any rate chooses not to, perhaps to spare himself the addiction he inflicted upon his fellows. Or it may be that none of them has the power to visit our world in the flesh any more, as, to judge by myths and legends, they, or some of them, must once have done. Perhaps something prevents them, bars them from direct access to us. I have my theories about that, but I will leave them for another time. Whatever the truth, their agents are active here – men like Aylesford, corrupted to their influence, who may not even be aware of whom or rather what they truly serve. But no matter. I have strayed from my subject. My point is that the watch is no longer here, under my roof. The Old Wolf has it now, and thus it is no longer veiled from Doppler's view. No doubt he has already located it. And all his attention is fixed upon it – upon retrieving it. He will not notice us.'

'Why, if you know all this – or, I should say, are convinced of it, as it is plain to me that you are – would you give up the watch so easily to Grimalkin? And having done so, why would you not take it back from Master Magnus when it came into his possession?'

'Good questions all.' Longinus nodded approvingly. 'I am glad to see you still have your wits about you, Mr Quare. You shall need them. As for Grimalkin, you were in no position to judge what took place in the attic that night, perched as you were upon the rooftop. The fact is, I did not give up the watch easily. The defence of it cost good men their lives. That I did not care to throw my own life away into the bargain cannot be counted against me. As it is, I am fortunate to have escaped alive; why, the brigand held a blade to my throat! You may see the scab, if it please you. As to your second question, the answer is simple. Once Master Magnus had his hands on a timepiece that interested him, there was no getting it away from him – I had ample experience of that, believe me. And so I could only watch helplessly as he turned his prodigious intellect upon the mystery of the hunter. Helplessly, yes ... but also with hope, for surely if there were any mortal man equipped to solve its secrets, that man

425

would be my old friend and master. Alas, it was not to be.'

'So Grimalkin told me, when I took the watch from her.'

Longinus's eyebrows shot up. '*Her?*'

'Yes. Grimalkin is a woman.'

At this, Longinus burst into laughter.

'You don't believe me?'

'Oh, I believe you, Mr Quare, as far as it goes. Which isn't very far. That woman was not Grimalkin.'

'Master Magnus was of the same opinion. He did not believe it possible that a mere woman could be such a dangerous and successful thief.'

'A regrettable prejudice,' Longinus said. 'There is nothing a woman cannot do, as I know very well from personal experience.'

'Then how can you be so certain that this woman was not Grimalkin?'

'Why, because *I* am Grimalkin, of course.'

Once more, Quare found himself shocked into silence. Lord Wichcote, Longinus, Michael Gray, now Grimalkin – was there anyone in the world whom his host had not been at one time or another?

'I had not intended to reveal myself just yet,' Longinus continued blithely, 'but as you have raised the issue . . .'

Quare shook his head. 'No. This is entirely too much, sir.'

'How better to pursue my researches into time than as a thief? How better to gain access to timepieces that would otherwise be beyond my grasp? After my return from Märchen, as I resumed my work with Magnus, I resumed as well my solitary search for other examples of Wachter's work, creating the persona of Grimalkin to hide my efforts from Magnus. He never did learn or, as far as I know, suspect that Grimalkin was yet another of my aliases.'

'I do not know what to think, what to believe,' Quare said.

'I dared not turn my attentions to the hunter Corinna had stolen from her father, for my speculations as to its nature and purpose had convinced me that it was best left alone, untouched, all but forgotten. Still less did I trust Magnus to respect its dangers. So I hid it away and looked elsewhere for enlightenment, using the skills of a regulator and, as Grimalkin, the abilities my new appendage had bestowed upon me. Abilities you are about to experience for yourself.' He stepped towards Quare, extending his hand. 'Your watch, Mr Quare, if you please.'

'I beg your pardon?'

'You have seen me divest myself of my own personal time-pieces. I must ask you to do the same. Even if it is only the one. It may still misdirect us. Unlikely, but under the circumstances, it is better not to take the chance.'

With misgivings, Quare handed over his watch. Longinus stopped it and placed it in the same pile with his own. Then he turned back to Quare and extended his hand once more. 'Now, Mr Quare. Take my hand, sir. Come and walk with me.'

Quare rose from his seat. But he did not take the proffered hand. 'Lead on,' he said cautiously, 'and I will follow.'

'You cannot follow where I would lead,' Longinus answered. 'To go where I go, you must place your hand in mine. Then, in a manner of speaking, I will carry you along with me.' And he stretched his hand nearer to Quare, as if in emphasis.

Quare felt giddy with confusion. Part of him wanted to leave the room, leave the house, deny all that he had heard and seen. But he knew too well what awaited him outside this sanctuary. Besides, for all his eccentricities, which verged on, if not crossed entirely over into, madness, Longinus – or whoever he truly was – had not harmed him, though it had lain within his power to do so at any time had he wished. It was this reflection, combined with a sense of rebelliousness that seemed to have no other outlet, that prompted him to grab hold of the older man's hand.

'Brave lad,' said Longinus with a nod. He stared into Quare's eyes. 'Whatever you do, whatever you see, do not let go of my hand, or you shall be irretrievably lost. Say nothing, lest you alert Doppler or his allies. Save your questions until we are safe again. Do you understand?'

Quare nodded, his mouth dry.

'Very well,' said Longinus with a smile. 'It has been years since I travelled thus. I find that I have missed it more than I realized. They say that the longest journey begins with a single step, Mr Quare. Let us begin our journey.'

15

Tiamat

BUT THOUGH QUARE STOOD READY TO FOLLOW LONGINUS, THE man did not move. Instead, regarding Quare with a sceptical expression, he asked hesitantly: 'This woman calling herself Grimalkin . . . What did she look like?'

'You think it might have been Corinna?' Quare asked. 'But surely she would be an old woman by now. The woman I encountered did not appear to be much older than myself.'

Longinus pulled his hand from Quare's and made a dismissive gesture, as if to push him away. 'They are immortal beings and do not age as we do. Besides, I have reason to believe they can alter their shape to appear however they desire. But you're right – how could it have been her? Why would she not have revealed herself to me?' He seemed to be addressing himself as much as Quare. 'No – it is impossible. The woman could not have been Corinna.'

'You do not seem entirely convinced of it.'

Longinus sighed. 'I wanted it to be her. I have missed her so much, you see. But as I told you a moment ago, their kind cannot cross over to our world as easily as they once did. No, it was not Corinna.' He spoke with confidence now. 'Nor was this woman sent by Corinna, for then she would have said as much, and I would have given her the watch freely. There would have been no need for her to fight, to kill those men. She could only have been sent by Doppler. There is no other possibility.'

'It seems your wards were not as impenetrable as you thought,' Quare observed.

Longinus made the same dismissive gesture. 'I had heard rumours that Grimalkin had come out of retirement, as it were. So I spread rumours of my own, to entice him – for the idea that the imposter might be a woman had not occurred to me, any more than the possibility he was working for Doppler – to my house, where I hoped to expose him and learn his history. Instead, I was the one surprised, both by his – or, rather, her – fighting skill . . . and her knowledge of the watch. Though I had hidden it away inside a clock that was altogether unremarkable, she nevertheless saw through the disguise and snatched it without hesitation. Then, before I could react, she smashed a glass vial upon the floor, just such a vial as I had once used in my thieving days, containing chemicals that give birth to a dense, obscuring cloud, and, behind that screen, she fled, taking the clock with her. A most formidable adversary! Tell me, Mr Quare, was there anything distinctive about her? Any peculiarities that impressed themselves upon you?'

Quare did not have to consider long. 'I saw her in moonlight, and she seemed to me like some maiden descended from that orb, her hair spun of moonbeams and shadows, her skin pale and luminous, without blemish. Her features were exotic, as if she were a blend of races unknown to me. She was the most beautiful woman I have ever seen. And, at the same time, the strangest.'

'Why, I believe you fell a bit in love with her, Mr Quare!'

'Love? I desired her, true enough. There was a kind of raw

sensuality about her, and the effect she had on me was, I confess, not entirely unlike what you told me of your experiences in Märchen, though, as it were, in a minor key. But despite her allure, and the longing she inspired in me, I feared her, too. I had a sense that we were playing a kind of game . . . a deadly game in which only she knew the rules.'

'A game?'

Quare nodded. 'She told me that she would answer three questions truthfully – why, I felt as if I had stumbled into a fairy tale! But a dark one, for I believe she would have killed me in a second. Though I had the advantage of her, I suspect she could have done so with ease. I have never seen anyone move as swiftly as she did. But something prevented her. Bound her, as it were, against her will. She mentioned an ancient compact, but explained nothing more. It was most curious.'

'And did you ask your three questions, Mr Quare?'

'Two I asked, but not the third, for some intuition or instinct warned me that once she had answered, my life would be forfeit. It sounds ridiculous, I know. But at the time it was not ridiculous.'

'And what did you ask her? Tell me everything.'

Quare blushed. 'I'm afraid I wasted my first two questions. I didn't understand the rules of our game and so did not take time to properly formulate my inquiries. Then, once I realized what was at stake, I took care to avoid anything that might be construed, however remotely, as a query.'

'Most wise. So you left her there, did you, and returned to the guild hall with the watch, as you told Master Magnus?'

'That is not quite true,' Quare admitted. He decided that he would tell Longinus everything. There seemed no reason to keep his secrets any longer. This resolve brought a sense of relief that further encouraged him to honesty. 'I had subdued her, more by luck than skill, yet though I had bound her hands securely behind her back, she freed herself – or, rather, was freed by an accomplice.'

'An accomplice! You might have mentioned that detail sooner!'

'Listen, and you will understand why I did not. The accomplice was a mouse, sir. No doubt you find that hard to credit. But so it was, as I saw to my astonishment. A trained mouse that nibbled through her bindings and then, quick as a wink, vanished into her clothing.'

Longinus gave a start. 'A mouse, you say? Why, Corinna kept a mechanical mouse upon her person – I believe I mentioned it.'

'Yes, but this was no machine, no automaton.'

'You would have said the same had you seen the little dragon that lived in Frau Hubner's cuckoo clock.'

'So . . . you believe it was Corinna after all?'

Longinus considered, then shook his head. 'No . . . for all the reasons I have said. But the mouse is meaningful. I am sure of it. It bespeaks some connection to her.' He sighed again. 'It is a riddle I cannot solve. Unless . . .'

Quare spoke into the hush. 'Unless what?'

'Nothing,' Longinus said with a shrug. 'An idle thought. Only, I regret not having had the opportunity to question this young woman.'

'That would have been a most dangerous undertaking,' Quare said. 'I do not believe she would have spared you as she did me.'

'Spared you? But she was at your mercy, was she not?'

'I had my pistol pointed at her, but even so, I was not confident I could pull the trigger before she was upon me. She was that fast. But though free, she did not attack. The fight had gone out of her. Indeed, she seemed resigned to the loss of the watch. It was as if she'd had her chance and must abide by the result, however little she liked it. She was much struck by the fact that, in subduing her, I had spilled her blood – and she mine. That seemed, in her mind, to create a bond between us, to join us in some way I did not understand then and still do not, even now. Yet I cannot but recall the effect that my blood had upon the watch in Master Magnus's study. I had thought that was the first time the watch had drunk my blood, but perhaps it had already tasted it, upon the rooftop. Perhaps, after all, it was not Magnus who awoke the watch with his probings, but I – or, rather, the girl and I. At any rate, she warned me of its dangers – called the watch a weapon – but made no attempt to take it back. Instead, she flung another of those glass vials to the rooftop and vanished into the cloud thus conjured. When the smoke lifted enough for me to see, she was gone. Nor did it seem that she had used the diversion to make her escape across the rooftops. There was not time enough for that. No, she disappeared, sir. Like a phantom, into thin air. And that is not the only time she did so.'

'What? You have seen her again?'

'Rather, it is she who has seen me. The other night, as I sat at the Pig and Rooster, she accosted me. Asked for my help in stealing back the watch, if you can believe it! But vanished as suddenly and completely as she had upon the rooftop, without shedding any more light on these mysteries. I confess, I have half expected to meet with her at any moment since. Indeed, there have been times I could have used her help! But I have had no further contact with her.'

'Most intriguing,' said Longinus. 'You have given me much to consider, Mr Quare. But for now, I think it best that we resume our journey.' He extended his hand again, and Quare clasped it. 'Recall my warnings of a moment ago,' he added. 'Keep hold of my hand, no matter what, say nothing unless or until I indicate it is safe to do so, and shut your eyes until I give you leave to open them.'

'Very well, but where—'

'Humour me, Mr Quare. All will become clear.'

So saying, he took a step forward. Drawing a breath, and closing his eyes, Quare followed.

He had an impression of swift movement, almost as if he were falling, similar to but more pronounced than what he had experienced in the stair-master. Despite his intention to comply with Longinus's instructions, he could not control an involuntary reaction – he opened his eyes. Madness confronted him. There was no fixed point of reference upon which to hang his understanding. Up, down, sideways: none of those terms described what he was seeing, or his position in it. The room in which he had been standing seemed to have stretched out to an infinite length, as though it had become a corridor leading to the very end of the universe. In the process its walls and floor and ceiling had faded to insubstantiality. Through them he could see other corridors, more than he could count, cutting through this one at every angle imagin-able . . . and some he could not have imagined. Amidst this dizzying display he saw that Longinus was still taking the step which had begun the journey; his foot had not come down. Yet the sensation of movement grew more intense by the second, and the strange elongation of the room and every-thing in it – including Longinus and himself – accelerated. It was as if they were standing still, frozen in place, while around them the world was being pulled away in all directions at a speed greater than time could measure or human senses perceive, so that each object was, or seemed to be, in multiple locations at once. Longinus's leg stretched farther and farther ahead, becoming increasingly attenuated. It no longer resembled a human limb but rather a black line . . . and the same was true of his own leg: two black lines extending in parallel into an immeasurable distance. But not straight. The lines, which were yet somehow themselves, traced a route that was full of sharp and sudden turns, abrupt cornerings that should have shattered bone but did not; instead, their legs bent as easily as copper wire being threaded through the labyrinth of a watch's insides. Quare would have cried out, screamed in terror, but even that would have required more presence of mind than he possessed just then.

'Close your eyes,' hissed Longinus beside him.

But it was too late for that. Quare felt as if he had become a single all-seeing eye, open to everything, mute witness to a reality he could not comprehend. He clung to Longinus's hand with every bit of strength and intention in him; how easy it would be to forget that he had a hand, that he was a body, that he had some stable, enduring centre which could not be dissipated in this place, swallowed up in its crazed immensity.

'This may,' gasped Longinus, 'have been a mistake. Something is tugging at me, pulling me towards it, too strong to resist. I am sorry.'

And with that, the world returned to normal. Limbs and everything else shrank to their customary proportions. Quare stumbled, wrenching his hand from Longinus's grasp. He looked around in wonder; they stood upon a London rooftop. He sank to his knees, dumbfounded.

'I don't understand,' said Longinus. 'That has never happened before. I had thought Doppler must have caught us and was reeling us in, like an angler his prey. But we are quite alone here – wherever we are.'

'I know where we are,' Quare managed to gasp out at last. He clutched his arms about his chest, shivering as if with cold.

'Do you? Pray enlighten me, Mr Quare.'

Quare breathed deeply. He felt as if he might be sick again. But finally the nausea receded enough for him to go on. 'This is where I caught up with Grimalkin. Why did you bring us here? And how?'

'I did not bring us to this place,' Longinus said. 'My intended destination was quite other. I had thought to show you the peak of Mount Coglians. As to how . . .' He shrugged. 'I have the ability to walk between worlds, to cover vast distances in the blink of an eye.' He spoke matter-of-factly. 'I have no idea how it works, but it is as if I were wearing a pair of seven-league boots, like Jack in the fairy tale. Only in my case it is not magical footwear but instead the wondrous foot with which I was fitted in Märchen. With this appendage, there is no earthly room I cannot enter, no door that can lock me out, no distance I cannot travel. I need merely think of the place, take a step, and I am there. It is the secret of my success as a thief . . . or was, until, over time, I began to sense that I was not alone in my journeying, that others were present in that in-between realm of which you, too, have now caught a glimpse: vague shapes and shadows, or things even less substantial than that . . . yet which nevertheless filled me with unease, as though their insubstantiality did not make them harmless but, rather, more dangerous than I knew. Creatures of the Otherwhere, perhaps. Or agents dispatched by Doppler. Perhaps both. In any case, I became convinced that I was being hunted. I did not care to discover by whom . . . or what. Some years ago, after a particularly narrow escape, I stopped travelling in this way altogether. I had no wish to push my luck.'

'But if you did not bring us here, who did?'

'Why, I can only assume it was you, Mr Quare.'

'I assure you I did no such thing.'

'Not consciously, perhaps. Yet do you not find it telling that we were discussing this very place before we set out? In the past, the mechanism – or some lively spirit bound within it – fastened upon my intent and translated it into action. And indeed, it was that demonstration I hoped would convince you of the truth of my words. But this time I believe it was *your* intent that was translated, that overpowered my own. For some reason, Mr Quare, it is you who are the master of this magic – or, if you prefer, this science indistinguishable therefrom. Whatever it is, it answers to your whim above my will.'

'B-but why?' Quare stammered. 'How?'

'No doubt the answer lies in your connection to the hunter. Both artefacts had their origin in Märchen, after all, and both, or so it seems, were crafted by the same hand. Your blood brought the watch to life, whether here on this rooftop or later, in Magnus's laboratory: provided it with a motive power it had lacked until that moment, and through that shedding of blood you gained a second life, for the watch stepped in when you were mortally wounded and miraculously preserved you. Perhaps even now, for all we know, it is the only thing keeping you alive.'

Quare shuddered, still on his knees. The afternoon was drawing on towards evening, the sun dipping low in a hazy, coal-smudged sky. His shadow, and that of Longinus, stretched across the dirty rooftop, a stark reminder of what he had seen as they travelled here. Longinus had called him the master of the magic, yet he did not feel himself to be the master of anything, least of all himself. He wanted to run . . . but run where? To lash out . . . but against whom? There was no place of refuge, no enemy to strike.

'Come,' said Longinus gently, as if pitying his distress, and once again extended a hand to him. 'The hour grows late. We must ready ourselves for what lies ahead. Let us return to my house.'

Quare drew back. 'Do you mean to take us back by the same route that brought us here?'

'There is no other way,' Longinus said. 'For all its risks, it is safer than trying to navigate the streets of London, where we may be recognized and apprehended at any moment.'

'And once we are safely returned, what then? Will we step from your house to the guild hall in the blink of an eye?'

'Alas, that is beyond my power. The presence of so many ticking timepieces fences me out, even were I to try and step directly into the Old Wolf's den. His clocks may keep a common time, yet though that regularity does not, as it were, throw up an impenetrable wall, like the one protecting my own house and its environs, it does engender obstacles, like the bars of a cell that are too narrow to squeeze through from either side. But never fear – I have another way to get us into the guild hall.'

'You mean for us to return as we escaped – through the air? I tell you truly, sir, I am sick to death of such unorthodox means of transportation as you seem so readily to employ.'

Longinus smiled. 'I assure you, Mr Quare, I have in mind a more mundane means of entry.'

Quare grunted. He took Longinus's hand and allowed the other man to pull him to his feet. 'Somehow, I do not find that comforting.'

'But you believe me, don't you?' Longinus asked rather anxiously. 'Surely, after all this, you must believe!'

'I don't know what I believe any more,' Quare said. 'I cannot explain how we came here; I cannot even explain what I saw along the way.'

'What did you see?' Longinus asked, peering at him with genuine curiosity. 'All those years ago, when I escaped from Märchen, Corinna told me that the Otherwhere revealed itself differently to everyone who passed through it. That is why I warned you to close your eyes, as she had warned me, once upon a time. And to as little effect. To me, it has always seemed as it did then: a maze of corridors, with doorways leading to various destinations. Somehow – until this evening – I have always moved unerringly to the correct door; the rightness of it has always been apparent to me. But this time, I could sense immediately that the door was wrong – it was not the door that would lead to Mount Coglians. But I could not hold back from entering it.'

'I did not see anything like that,' Quare said. 'I saw . . . But I do not have the words for it.' A shiver ran through him. 'Madness. That is what I saw. Madness.'

'Yet even that may be proof of a kind,' Longinus said.

Quare gave a sickly laugh. 'Proof that the universe is mad?'

'Or that we humans, for all our vaunted intellect and powers of reason, are helpless when confronted by the true mystery of existence.'

'That is no comfort,' Quare said.

'Why, the truth seldom is,' Longinus answered, raising his eyebrows. 'At least, not at first. It is always painful to have one's illusions dispelled. But salutary. Would you not rather know the truth than continue in ignorance?'

'But what good is that knowledge if it merely reveals the extent of our helplessness, our ignorance?'

'Every increase in knowledge is beneficial in and of itself,' Longinus answered. 'And perhaps we are not so helpless after all, Mr Quare. What seems like magic or miracle – or, indeed, madness – may be nothing more than a mechanism we do not yet understand. But that does not mean it lies forever beyond our understanding. Or our mastery.'

'It sounds as though you would make yourself one of them,' Quare said. 'Raise yourself above the human and become a god.'

Longinus's eyes flashed; suddenly Quare was reminded that the man, for all his eccentricity and fondness for disguise, was an aristocrat, a peer of the realm. 'We are beings of reason and self-awareness. Our birthright is one of dignity and freedom. No one has a right to be our masters. If I would raise myself to their level, what of it? How better to pull them down?'

'Why? To take their place? Exchange one pantheon for another, make yourself the Zeus to Doppler's Cronos?'

'I am an Englishman, sir,' Longinus responded with heat. 'I am no advocate of absolute monarchy, not in this world or any other. I have not forgotten Corinna's words: that Doppler and the rest are not fallen but risen angels, and how their sin lay not in rebellion but rather in the act of setting themselves above others. And yet, is it right that we humans, through no fault of our own, find ourselves locked out of the Otherwhere and whatever lies beyond it?'

'I do not know,' Quare said. 'I wish I had not learned of it, or seen it with my own eyes. I wish I could forget it now – all of it.'

'Yes, but not even Doppler's watch can turn back time and

erase the past. What's done is done and cannot be undone. I am afraid there is no forgetting, Mr Quare – for either of us. Fate, or some other power, has touched us, changed us. We are no longer what we were. For us, there can be no going back. Only forward.'

Quare nodded grimly. 'Then let us go forward, by all means.'

Together, side by side, they returned to the Otherwhere. And this time, Quare did not flinch or close his eyes, but faced as squarely as he could the madness that he saw there. He did not try to make sense of it, to squeeze its disparate dimensions into the Procrustean bed of his reason; instead, he let it wash over and through him. And to his surprise, he did not go mad. He did not become so attenuated, so stretched out, that nothing remained of him, as he had feared might happen. He was not swallowed up. He felt it now: this place, for all its terrible strangeness, was not foreign to him . . . at least, not any longer. Longinus was right. He had been changed. He was no intruder here, no trespasser. He belonged. It was as if something that had been within him all his life, but so deeply asleep he had not known of its existence, or even suspected it, had awakened at last, and was now sitting up in bed and rubbing the last grains of sleep from its eyes, looking out with wonder and eager anticipation upon the home it had been dreaming of. That part of himself did not see madness here. Instead, it grasped the order within the chaos. How could he have failed to see it before? Why, the path back to Wichcote House was so clear a child could not miss it! Laughing now, he brought his foot down and finished the step he had begun on a rooftop miles away.

'That was . . . most interesting,' said Longinus, standing beside him in the same room from which they had departed.

'Not since Corinna brought me out of Märchen have I felt so
. . . superfluous on a journey through the Otherwhere.' As he
spoke, he methodically set into motion all the timepieces
he had stopped in the room, beginning with the larger clocks
and then moving on to the pile of watches on the table, each
of which he returned to its place upon his person.

'I saw the way,' Quare said. 'The path was plain – I merely
followed it.'

'And now?' Longinus asked, turning to study him. 'Can you
still see the path? Could you follow it if you liked?'

Quare shook his head. 'The path is gone. Everything is as it
was. Why do you ask?'

'You brought us here so easily that I wondered if you might
be able to travel through the Otherwhere entirely on your
own – whether you needed me at all. Corinna required no
talisman to enter that maze or navigate its twists and turns; it
was her birthright.'

'You think I am like her?'

'I do not know what to think about you, Mr Quare. You are
a mystery. A paradox. My time in Märchen changed me
greatly from what I had been, but you have been changed
more greatly still without ever setting foot there. Look at
yourself, sir. You stand before me, a living and breathing man
who yet bears a mortal wound. By all rights, you should be
stretched out in a coffin. And that is not all. You have taken to
the Otherwhere like a fish to water. I led you from this room,
but it was you who brought me back. Do I think you are like
Corinna, like Doppler and his kind?' He shrugged. 'Perhaps
you are something new. Human, yet also more than
human. You warned me of the dangers in seeking to raise
myself above my natural station. But haven't you been
raised in just that way?'

Quare shook his head again, more vehemently now. 'You would make me into something I am not – something I have no wish to be.'

'It is not I who have done the making,' Longinus answered.

'I am as I always was,' Quare insisted.

'Are you indeed?'

Quare found himself growing angry. 'I do not wish to discuss this any further,' he said. 'And if you want my help, you will not press me.'

Longinus sketched a bow. 'I meant no offence. And I am gratified that you have decided to help – or so I judge by your words.'

'Yes, I'll help,' Quare growled. 'I do not think I have a choice. Not if I wish to learn what has happened to me. It is all bound up with that cursed watch. Perhaps, if I can examine it again, or even hold it in my hands, much will become clear.'

'For your sake, I pray it is so,' Longinus said. 'Yet we must not count our chickens before they are hatched. A difficult and dangerous task lies before us, Mr Quare, with no guarantee of success. Indeed, I should judge the odds very much against us.'

'You have a strange way of inspiring confidence,' Quare observed.

'It is to avoid overconfidence that I speak so plainly. But we shall have a few tricks up our sleeve, never fear. With a bit of luck, we will prevail.'

'What, then, is your plan?'

'There will be time enough for that later,' Longinus said. 'We must wait until the very witching hour of the night before we make our move. I suggest, until then, that you get some rest. That is certainly my intention. We must be at the top of our game tonight, Mr Quare. There will be no room for hesitation or error.'

'I don't believe I could sleep now even if I wanted to,' Quare said.

'Nevertheless, I advise you to try. Before my retirement, I went on many such missions as this, some on behalf of Master Magnus, others for reasons of my own, and I learned the value of this approach. Sleep if you can; and if you cannot, why, then do whatever it is that relaxes you. Have a hot bath—'

'So that you can drug me again?' Quare demanded.

'I apologize for having done so last night. You need not fear a repetition. I am a great believer in the benefits of daily bathing; it is a habit I learned on my travels to the east. But if a bath will not relax you, try a book. Tinker with one of my timepieces if you like. I will send a man to wake you, or simply fetch you, as the case may be, shortly before midnight. Then we will fortify ourselves with a brief repast, and I will explain how we are going to gain entry to the guild hall, and how we shall proceed once we are there. In the meantime, should you require anything, the bell pull in your room will summon a servant. Oh, and one more thing, Mr Quare. Your pocket watch.' Longinus passed it to him. 'Wind it,' he added after Quare had taken the watch and made to tuck it into his waistcoat pocket. 'It may be that in moving through the Otherwhere, you have revealed yourself to Doppler or one of his minions. If so, they will be seeking you now. The defences of the house are likely sufficient to protect you, but it cannot hurt to get into the habit of shielding yourself as I do. In any case, I will be providing you with a number of watches to distribute about your person before we depart tonight.'

Such was the intensity of Longinus's gaze that Quare felt obliged to follow his suggestion. Yet as he wound the watch, he couldn't help feeling a deep-seated wrongness. It disturbed him to use the watch in a way that was contrary to its intended purpose: not to tell the correct time, but instead to employ a false time in order to confuse and misdirect . . . Of course, if what Longinus had told him was true, then everything he had ever known – or thought he had known – about time was wrong. But despite all he had heard and experienced, he was far from ready to accept his host's assertions on that subject. He was far from even understanding them.

Back in his room – to which he had been led by a servant – Quare divested himself of coat and sword. A hot bath had been drawn in his absence, and so tempting were the steaming waters that he decided to risk them. He thought it unlikely that Longinus would drug him again, not if he required Quare's assistance in retrieving the hunter from the Old Wolf in a matter of hours.

The water was hot enough to make him catch his breath, but he released it in a long, luxurious sigh as he settled down. The tub resembled a giant tin boot; there was ample room to stretch his legs out in front of him, while his back was firmly supported. The water smelled of fresh limes.

He could feel tension seeping from his body, but his mind was not so readily soothed. The details of Longinus's adventures in Märchen, added to his own experiences of the past few days, left him feeling as though he had stumbled into a fairy tale. A nightmare, rather. And at the centre of it all, the uncanny pocket watch that, so it seemed, had belonged to Herr Doppler, a creature of the Otherwhere so powerful he was indistinguishable from a god.

Or, if Longinus were to be believed, not a watch at all, but a weapon, a time bomb whose purpose was to destroy everything that existed, to scour the universe free of life and order like some great cosmic Flood, returning things to a primal soup of limitless potential, so that a single survivor, Doppler, not a fallen but a risen angel, might begin again. Where, in this insane cosmology, was there room for the Christian God, the loving God who had created all things, visible and invisible, had wound them up like a watch and set them in motion, then stepped back into his heaven to watch the flawless operation of his benign universal machine? Quare had never considered himself to be religious; on the contrary, he had prided himself on his rational approach to the mysteries of life. Yet he had always, he realized now, kept a childish faith in the God of his boyhood tucked away in a corner of his heart, all but forgotten. Only now, that faith was being tested for the first time. More than tested: it was being overwhelmed. Routed. There was no room for such pretty delusions in the real world, the world in which a pocket watch might run on blood, a deadly stabbing have no more effect than a pinprick, a mechanical foot enable a leagues-spanning stride. A world of dragons, dwarfs and succubi, as if all the old myths and legends were true. A world that floated, like a bubble of time, on a vast sea of unbeing: the Otherwhere. And in which time itself was . . . what? A disease? A drug? An imperfection introduced into a perfect creation, a flaw in that glittering jewel, the original original sin? It seemed to be all of those things and more – for it also protected this place from Doppler, all the mismatched timepieces throwing up a snarl of thorny time, like the forest of briars surrounding the castle of Sleeping Beauty.

And what of his role? Why had he of all people been chosen . . . for it seemed to Quare that he *had* been chosen, that there was more to his involvement than just bad luck, being in the wrong place at the wrong time. No, the conviction had been growing in him for some time, and by now it was so strong that he could not doubt it any longer: everything that had happened to him had happened for a reason, in response to a greater intention than his own, a sovereign will that could not be denied, that had pulled and pushed and prodded him towards the fulfilment of its ends just as he, however unknowingly, had forced Longinus from his chosen path in the Otherwhere.

But what reason? And whose will?

He didn't want any of it. Didn't want to play whatever part had been prepared for him. There were wars within wars, it seemed. A war in heaven, so to speak, between Doppler and his followers and those, like Corinna, who opposed him. A war that centred upon the hunter, which Grimalkin had been sent to acquire on behalf of one side or the other – he wasn't sure where her allegiance lay. And, mirroring it, a war on earth, between England and her enemies, chief among them France: a war that could very well determine not just the fate of his country but that of the hard-won liberties which were the birthright of all Englishmen. And that war, too, centred upon the watch, for Aylesford had been sent in quest of it, and the Old Wolf, who now possessed it, yearned to unlock its deadly secrets and use them in defence of king and country. But in doing so, Quare now understood, he would only be serving the interests of Doppler. And the same would be true if it were Aylesford who possessed the watch and brought it to his French masters to further the cause of Scottish liberty.

He saw now that the watch could not safely be used by any human being. Whoever did so risked acting on Doppler's behalf. Yet neither could it be hidden away. Recent events had proved that. Doppler and his fellow creatures were immortal, after all. A human lifetime was nothing to them. They could be patient in their pursuit of the hunter. Sooner or later, it must come to light.

No, he realized, the watch had to be destroyed. That was the only way. But was it even possible? And if it was, could the hunter be destroyed without unleashing whatever terrible forces it contained? If the watch were destroyed, would it take the world with it? He remembered what it had felt like in the aftermath of the watch's brief awakening, when the world had seemed to blink in and out of existence, and Master Magnus's beloved cats had died: all of them, in an instant. He remembered the sight of their limp corpses lying like so many scattered leaves strewn by a whirlwind. Then he imagined London filled with such corpses: human corpses: the bodies of men, women and children felled as they went about their daily business, like victims of a plague far swifter and less merciful than the Black Death. Some, at least, had survived that calamity. But he did not think there would be even a single survivor of this one. Apart from Doppler, anyway.

Despite the warmth of the bathwater, a shiver rippled through him. He felt more alone than he could remember ever having felt since his orphan days in the workhouse. In that moment, the image of Grimalkin came to him, the memory of her moonlit face on the rooftop, and, later, that same face smeared with paint yet still lovely, exotic in its beauty. Who was she? Where had she gone? He could not help but feel that she knew the answers to his questions, if she would but speak plainly. He recalled how she had vanished from the rooftop, and disappeared in the blink of an eye from the Pig and Rooster, and he wondered if she, like Longinus, had access to the Otherwhere. Was she a traveller in that strange country ... or a denizen of it? And what of the connection she claimed, the bonds of blood that linked them? Those bonds, if they existed, had not pulled her to him, or he to her, for that matter, when he navigated the Otherwhere or at any other time.

Quare's ruminative gaze settled upon the Chinese screen that stood at the foot of the bath. The scene depicted there, of a peaceful, mist-wreathed mountain landscape, seemed to call to him as it had before. What would it be like to step from this world into that one? Longinus had asked if he could still see the path he had followed back from the rooftop, wondering if Quare possessed the same ability he did to traverse the Otherwhere, but whatever ability or instinct had guided Quare on the return journey seemed to have deserted him now. He saw no path, no doorway . . . unless the screen were itself a door. Yet he did not see a means of passing through it and into the remote but restful scene beyond, which, as he studied it with weary, unfocused longing, seemed to grow more real, though without becoming more immediate, as if he were gazing through a window that could neither be opened nor broken.

And then, as though it had been there all along, just waiting for the opportunity to show itself, a wingless dragon drifted into view, its long body eeling through the air, seeming to swim there: blue-scaled, wide-eyed, open jaws revealing teeth that looked sharp enough to shear through iron as easily as they might rend flesh and bone.

It hovered before him, within or behind the screen, the undulations of its body, like the gentle flexions of a water snake, holding it fixed in mid-air . . . and holding Quare's attention, too, the movements deeply entrancing, as was the thing's gaze, its eyes as big as plates yet placid as the eyes of a hare, sky-blue irises with centres of inky night.

Those eyes regarded him with shrewd intelligence ... if *intelligence* was even the right word for what he saw there, and the longer he looked in mute fascination, the more certain Quare was that it was not, at least not by any human standard ... though he had no better word, either. He felt a breeze caress his skin, and the tangy smell of limes grew stronger, more concentrated, seeming to emanate from the dragon itself. The scent had a stimulating aphrodisiacal effect; he felt himself grow hard, his erection pointing towards the dragon like the needle of a compass fixed at true north. He felt no shame – nor even excitement; the effect seemed to be independent of his will or desire, a reflex over which he had no control, exactly like what Longinus had reported of his erotic encounters in Märchen.

'You may call me Tiamat,' the dragon said without preface, and he felt neither surprise nor fear at hearing it speak. 'But do not imagine that is my real name and think to use it against me. Three questions will I answer freely. Think well before you ask.'

Quare felt as if he had entered into a dream. 'Three nights ago, I had a thief at my mercy. Grimalkin was her name. She, too, invited me to ask three questions, as in a fairy tale of old. She spoke of an ancient compact ...'

'The Law of Threes,' the dragon said, its jaws spreading wide as if in silent laughter. Its teeth were the size and shape of scimitars. From its throat came a rumble of thunder. Then: 'Do you think *I* am at your mercy?'

'No,' he said. And the knowledge was upon him from he knew not where: 'Neither am I at yours.'

The dragon lashed its tail. 'Not here,' it admitted. 'Not now. But know that things will go differently between us if we meet outside this screen and you do not please me.'

By *screen*, Quare understood the dragon – Tiamat, it had named itself – to mean not just the ornamental partition with its delicate Chinese brushwork but the barrier of time erected by so many clocks and watches ticking away in riotous disharmony. A distant part of him was amazed at his calmness, his ability to face the dragon without fear, naked and erect as he was, all but imprisoned within the narrow confines of the bath. Was he dreaming? Had he been drugged again? Or was the dragon casting some kind of spell over him? He did not know, and, strangely, it did not seem important. What *did* seem important was what questions he should put to the beast. He had wasted the three questions Grimalkin had offered him; he would not make that mistake again. 'Two nights ago,' he said at last, choosing his words with care, 'I received a wound that should have killed me. Yet I did not die. How is that possible?'

'All men die,' Tiamat answered. 'That is their nature, and the nature of all time-bound things.'

This was not illuminating. The dragon seemed to be suggesting that he had died after all. For the first time, Quare felt a frisson of real fear. It warned him to pursue the matter no further, lest he learn things he could not unlearn, truths that would destroy him.

'Tell me about the watch,' he said instead. 'The hunter. What is its secret?'

Tiamat grinned, baring its formidable teeth again. 'It is just what you have called it: a hunter. It hunts. That is its secret, or one of them. It has drunk your blood and left its mark upon you. That is how I sensed you. It will answer to you now, protect you . . . but do not imagine yourself its master. It is a weapon, a very great weapon – too great to be left in the hands of men.'

Too great to be left in anyone's hands, Quare thought to himself. 'If you've come to get it back, you're out of luck,' he said. 'I don't have it any more.'

'But you know where to find it,' the dragon said. 'You will bring it to me.'

'Why should I – so that you can give it to Doppler?'

'No . . . but what do you know of Doppler?' the creature asked in turn.

'Longinus has told me of his experiences in Märchen and the Otherwhere. He met a dragon there – Hesta was her name. Her master was a man called Doppler. Or, rather, a thing that wore the shape of a man.'

'Longinus understands less than he imagines. But you are right that Doppler only wore the shape of a man. Just as I wear the shape of a dragon. Why? Because it is fitting – that is to say, it suits me. We are born of what you called the Otherwhere, and our true forms are beyond physical representation. To take on any form diminishes us – but some forms diminish us more than others, as they are in some sense further from our origins and what we truly are. But to answer your question – I do not serve Doppler. He is as much my enemy as he is yours. You must give me the hunter because I am the only one who can keep it from him. There is war among the immortals, a war in which the fate of all that lives hangs in the balance. Whoever holds the hunter holds the key to victory. If Doppler should win, he will use it.'

'And you won't?'

'That is your fourth question. I could answer and put you in my debt. But to show my good faith, I will answer freely one last time. I have no intention of using the hunter. On the contrary, I mean to destroy it.'

'I don't believe you,' Quare said.

'It is too dangerous to use. Too dangerous to keep. It was a mistake to make it. It must be unmade. That is why I have come to you, Daniel Quare.'

'Why me? Why not Longinus?'

'Because you understand that it must be destroyed, while he does not. And *that* answer I do not give freely. You have incurred a debt.'

'No,' Quare said. Truly, he had not meant to ask another question. It had just slipped out. Unless the dragon had coerced him somehow . . .

'You should have kept better count,' Tiamat said, and its grin grew wider still, as though to devour him. 'By ancient compact, I have the right to lay a geis – a fateful compulsion – upon you. And this right I do hereby invoke. Seek out the hunter. It has tasted your blood and will tug at you no matter where it may be. Once you have it, call to me and I will come.'

'I won't.'

'You will,' the dragon said. 'Whether you fight it or not, whether you believe it or not, you answer to *me* now.'

Before Quare could reply, the dragon flexed its muscular coils, and there was something irresistible in the movement, a sovereign directive that sank deeper than reason, right into the animal heart of him. Suddenly he was ejaculating with a force that nearly bent him over in the bath, wringing him like a sponge. There was nothing remotely sensual about it; it seemed more like an act of rape.

The next instant, Quare jerked upright, shivering in water that had grown ice cold. The Chinese screen stood where it had always stood; of Tiamat, there was no sign. Someone was knocking at the door to his room.

16

A Whole Different Order of Drowning

QUARE LOST NO TIME IN RISING FROM THE BATH. HE WRAPPED himself in a towel and called to whoever was knocking at the door. A liveried servant entered the room.

'His lordship requests that you join him downstairs,' the man said.

'I'll not be long,' Quare said.

'If I may assist,' the man began.

But Quare interrupted. 'I'm capable of dressing myself. If you wait in the hall, I'll be out directly.'

'Very good, sir,' said the man, and left a bow.

Quare rubbed himself dry, his thoughts racing. If anyone had told him that he would one day converse with a dragon, he would have called that person a lunatic, yet he did not for a second doubt what had just occurred. The experience had left him drained in every way. His hands trembled, and his legs felt boneless as he stumbled to a nearby chair and collapsed into it. The only illumination in the room was from burning candles; the windows had gone dark behind their curtains; it appeared that he had been in the bath for some hours, though it had not seemed longer than a few minutes.

The dragon – Tiamat – had said that the hunter had marked him. There was a small cut on his finger, where Master Magnus had jabbed him, spilling his blood, but he did not think that was the mark Tiamat had been referring to. No, the dragon had been speaking of a deeper marking, a connection binding him to the watch, and the watch to him.

It has tasted your blood and will tug at you no matter where it may be, the dragon had said. *It will answer to you now, protect you . . . but do not imagine yourself its master.*

He closed his eyes and tried to feel that connection. But, as with the link that Grimalkin had mentioned, he detected no tug, no hint of a presence pulling at him the way a lodestone might pull at a nail, or as the house had pulled at him when he'd stepped from the rooftop back into the Otherwhere. No, what he felt was weak. Empty. And afraid.

Whether you fight it or not, whether you believe it or not, you answer to me now.

And as if to prove that claim, Tiamat had demonstrated just how little Quare controlled his own body. What if, when the moment came – if it came – and he held the hunter in his hand, a similarly irresistible compulsion took hold of him, and, despite his intent, he called out to Tiamat, summoned the dragon to him and gave up the watch? He did not believe that the dragon intended to destroy so powerful a weapon. Nor was he at all convinced that the creature was not one of Doppler's minions.

He was in over his head. That much was plain. Had been for some time now. But this was a whole different order of drowning. He was used to the idea that he could not trust anyone else. But now it seemed he could no longer trust himself. He had to tell Longinus. Explain that he could not accompany him back to the guild hall. It was too dangerous. Too risky. They could recover the watch only to lose it again, and everything with it.

He dressed and belted on his sword. The servant led him down to the same room in which he and Longinus had breakfasted that morning. As before, enough food for a feast had been laid out. There, too, his host was waiting.

'Ah, Mr Quare,' Longinus said as he was ushered into the room, which was ablaze with light from a chandelier that bristled with creamy white candles. 'I trust you had a good rest?'

It certainly appeared that Longinus had. The man – who had been sitting at the table, a plate of roasted chicken and a glass of red wine before him – rose to greet Quare energetically. He was wearing a bright green *robe de chambre* with a red cap that stood up like the crest of a bird, and beneath the gown a ruffled white shirt, forest green breeches, and white stockings. The beauty mark that had been on his left cheek earlier in the day had migrated to the other side of his face.

'Actually,' Quare began . . . but got no further.

'Capital,' Longinus said. 'Capital.' He dismissed the servant with a gesture as he advanced to take Quare by the arm and guide him to a sideboard loaded with dishes of food: there were meats and pies, cheeses, soups, and pastries. 'Refresh yourself, sir.'

'I-I'm not hungry,' Quare said.

'Nevertheless, eat,' Longinus directed. 'You will be glad of it later, I assure you. We shall need all our strength.' As he spoke, he prepared a plate of roast chicken for Quare.

Quare had no appetite; indeed, the sight of so much food, along with its attendant odours, was making him queasy. Yet even more unsettling was the fact that he had not succeeded in broaching the subject of the dragon. And not for lack of try-ing. From the point Longinus had dismissed the servant, leaving the two of them alone in the room, Quare had been attempting to tell his host about his monstrous visitor and what had passed between them. At first it had seemed that what prevented him was the difficulty of framing the event intelligibly, of finding the right words. But it soon became obvious that he could not speak of it at all. His will was not his own.

You answer to me *now . . .*

He clenched his fists at his sides, struggling to break free of the dragon's influence, the geis laid upon him.

'Are you well, Mr Quare?' his host inquired with curiosity and concern.

I have just been visited by a dragon called Tiamat, he said . . . but only in his mind.

I am ill; I fear I cannot accompany you tonight, he tried to say . . . but again, the words remained unspoken.

'I . . . did not get much rest,' he forced out at last.

Longinus nodded and steered him back towards the table. 'I was the same when I first began my career as a regulator. Too anxious to eat or sleep before a mission. But I learned better, and so will you.' He set the plate upon the table and guided Quare to a seat, then returned to his own place, where he tucked into his meal with relish.

Quare watched glumly.

'Wine?' Longinus inquired, his mouth full.

Quare shook his head. If he could not speak openly about the dragon, or refuse the mission outright, perhaps he could accomplish both aims in a more oblique fashion. 'Ever since I spoke with Grimalkin,' he said, trying to hurry the words past whatever internal censor the dragon had set up in his mind;

and, indeed, the strategy seemed to work, for nothing impeded him now, 'or, rather, the woman who went by that name, I have wondered about the business of three questions. Is that something you encountered in Märchen?'

'I had remarked on that aspect of your tale as well,' Longinus said and took a thoughtful sip of wine. 'I confess I did not experience any such thing in my time there. It is most curious. She mentioned an ancient compact, did she not?'

'Yes,' Quare affirmed. And attempted again to evade the censor – again with success. 'The Law of Threes.'

'I have heard of no such law,' Longinus said. He paused, then continued: 'Yet it strikes me that the number three is ubiquitous in the world. In religion, we have the trinity of Father, Son, and Holy Ghost; and this threefold divinity is repeated in pagan systems as well: the three Fates, for instance. In natural science, Newton's three laws of motion are paramount, and there are as well the three states of matter: gas, liquid, and solid. In alchemy, the *Emerald Tablets of Toth* at once elucidate and obfuscate the esoteric mysteries of that number. And in fairy tales there are three wishes – indeed, there is something very like a fairy tale about your encounter with this imposter. It may be that such old tales, passed on by word of mouth, preserve an ancient wisdom civilized man has long forgotten. They are ripe, I have often thought, for systematic scientific study, as opposed to the purely literary approach of Monsieur Perrault, Madame d'Aulnoy, and their imitators. Much might thereby be revealed. But as to the compact of which the imposter spoke, I must confess ignorance. Only, I do wonder at one thing.'

'What is that?'

'With whom was this compact entered into?'

'Why, surely with us – that is, with human beings.'

'Perhaps. Yet why should creatures of the Otherwhere deign to bargain with us? What could compel them to lower themselves so? Surely nothing in *our* power. Is it not more likely that the compact, though it may include us in its terms, is not really about us at all – that we are, as it were, incidental to it?'

'But if not us, who is the other party?'

'You have put your finger on it, Mr Quare. Until now, I have conceived of the struggle in binary terms, with Doppler and his risen angels on one side and the rebels whom Corinna sought to join on the other. But what if there is a third party in this war? Indeed, the Law of Threes, whatever it may be, would at least seem to imply the involvement of another power. And is that not the case in our earthly war, which, as we have both been told, mirrors the war in heaven? England and her allies fight against France and her proxies, but on the outside, waiting its opportunity, sits Russia.'

'But who, then, would this third power be?'

'That I do not know. But if my experiences in Märchen are any indication, Doppler, if he was ever a party to this compact, feels no need to comply with it now. That the false Grimalkin behaved otherwise with you suggests that the unknown third power remains a factor – that she, or, rather, whoever it is she represents, either the rebels or this third party itself, still consider themselves bound by the compact. More than that, I do not think we can infer. And even this much, frankly, seems speculative. Yet it would explain much.'

On this point, Quare could not agree. Rather than simplifying matters, it seemed to complicate them. Who – or what – was this mysterious third power? Had Tiamat been its representative? Grimalkin? Even more disturbing was the idea that now came to him: namely, that he had not, after all, managed to sneak his question past Tiamat's internal guard or geis but, rather, had been compelled, not so much against his will as beneath his very notice, to ask it. If that were true, then Tiamat had encouraged these speculations – if speculations they were. For what if Longinus, whether he knew it or not, was also subject to a geis and was acting as Tiamat's agent – or even Doppler's? Perhaps in grafting the unnatural foot upon him, Immelman – Wachter, rather – had also grafted something less visible, a mechanism purely interior, which Longinus remained unaware of . . . even as he conformed in word and action, in thought itself, to whatever strictures that interior grafting imposed. Indeed, for all he knew, appearances to the contrary notwithstanding, Longinus could be as artificial in his whole person as he was in the matter of his foot. Yet if that were the case, and the man sitting opposite him at the table, eating with every appearance of an appetite, and seeming to savour every sip of wine, was not a being of flesh and blood but rather some kind of automaton – which seemed ridiculous, but not quite as ridiculous as he would have thought a few days or even hours ago – then how could he be sure of anyone else? The servants, for instance. Or Master Magnus, whose dead body he had never seen.

Or, for that matter, himself. For was he not still alive – at any rate, continuing to function – despite a wound that would have proved fatal to any living person? And now Quare recalled something else the dragon had told him. When he had asked how he could have survived such a mortal injury, Tiamat had replied, *All men die. That is their nature, and the nature of all time-bound things.*

He had interpreted this as a confirmation of his death – an indication that, as Longinus had suggested, it was only the mysterious blood-engendered power of the hunter that was keeping him alive. Yet now Quare realized that there was another interpretation. *All men die* – did that not imply, since he had *not* died, that he was not a man? That he was not, in the dragon's suggestive phrase, 'a time-bound thing'?

The notion shook Quare to his very core. A ball rolling down a slope was subject to absolute laws whose operation continued in effect regardless of whether or not the ball had a destination in mind, knew that it was rolling, or even conceived of itself as a ball: Newton's law of threes! Wasn't he, too, in motion, subject to the same or similar laws? He could no more halt his descent than could the ball, of its own accord, decide to stop rolling downhill or reverse its course and roll back up the slope.

This was a disheartening realization, to be sure, as if he were a pendulum in a clock. Yet it was also liberating. Quare felt a kind of peace settle over him, a despairing yet nonetheless welcome numbness as soothing to his distressed mind as it was to his weary body and anguished heart. He need not fight, need not worry, need do nothing at all. Far from shameful, this surrender seemed like the beginning of a hard-earned wisdom. It was, he realized, an embrace of a sort of faith . . . though one that rejected reason as much as it did religion. This was a new faith, a faith without hope of redemption or resurrection, yet without fear of damnation, too. It was a clockwork kind of faith.

Longinus, meanwhile, glanced at one of his assortment of pocket watches and declared that it was time to get started.

'So, at least one of your timepieces keeps the correct hour,' Quare observed.

'Only one,' Longinus answered with the ghost of a smile as

he pushed his chair back from the table and stood. 'And of course no hour can be in and of itself correct, but merely in greater or lesser accord with a measurement arbitrarily fixed and agreed to by others. As the Bard wrote, "If it be now, 'tis not to come; if it be not to come, it will be now; if it be not now, yet it will come – the readiness is all."'

Longinus did not lead him out of the room but instead to a wall where, with a touch to the moulding, he caused a hidden door to spring open, revealing a small candlelit chamber that Quare recognized at once as a stair-master.

He entered at Longinus's invitation. 'Will this take us back to the guild hall?'

Longinus stepped in behind him, closed the door, and tugged at the bell pull. The chamber gave a shudder and began to glide sideways. 'The mechanism does not extend so far as that,' Longinus said. 'Though Magnus spoke of one day establishing a network of stair-masters linking disparate parts of the city. Imagine the ease and comfort of travelling from one end of London to the other without ever setting foot upon a crowded, filthy street!'

'But where would this network run?'

'Why, below the streets, of course, in rooms much larger than this one – big enough to accommodate dozens or even hundreds of people. Magnus even had a name for this interior network of his: the internet.' As Longinus spoke, the stair-master shifted course from the horizontal to the vertical, dropping smoothly but with a speed that left Quare's stomach aflutter. 'Alas,' his host continued without missing a beat, 'I doubt we shall see the internet implemented now – not without the force of Magnus's genius and personality behind it. Such a project could only be brought to fruition by the government – no private fortune, even one so large as mine, could accomplish it. I covered the costs of installing the system in the guild hall, and here, in my own home, but nowhere else. Perhaps some day Magnus's dream will be realized, but I dare say not for many years yet, until another such outsized intellect emerges.'

Quare's grieving was twofold. First, for the death of the man who had been friend and mentor, albeit distant and stern, and second for loss of a mind whose quicksilver workings he had observed with awe and envy. Though he had, on occasion, mocked to himself the impracticality or sheer eccentricity of Magnus's ideas, he had far more often found himself inspired by their example to greater efforts of his own. It was Magnus who had first recognized his potential and encouraged it, Magnus who had pulled him from obscurity and brought him to London, providing him with the opportunity to better himself and advance his position in the guild and the wider world. Yet it was also Magnus who had set him in pursuit of the hunter, who had pricked his finger and used his blood to bring the watch to life, or a semblance of life, who had, in short, embarked him down the perilous road whose twists and turns had brought him to this place, this moment. Could he not thereby infer that Magnus, too, had been either an active agent of some greater power or, like himself, its helpless tool? He shrugged the question aside. What did it matter now?

The stair-master came to a halt. The door slid open, revealing a corridor lit by candles burning in bronze sconces upon the wall. Longinus gestured for Quare to step out. He did so, and his host came out behind him.

'Follow me, Mr Quare,' he said. 'I am about to show you something no one else has ever seen.' The corridor was lined with doors on both sides; a hotchpotch of timepieces cluttered the walls, gleaming in the candlelight. The corridor ended in another door, which Longinus opened with a key produced from a pocket in his robe. Quare, looking over Longinus's shoulder, saw the vague outlines of a room but could make out nothing of its dimensions or contents in the wavering light from behind. Then, plucking a candle from one of the sconces, Longinus entered the room, where he lit other candles, revealing all.

'Behold Grimalkin's lair,' he said with a theatrical flourish.

The room was smaller than his room at Mrs Puddinge's establishment but far more luxurious in its appointments. Yet it was not the furnishings that left him most amazed. A veritable armoury covered one wall: swords and daggers, crossbows, pistols, and other, less ordinary weapons: a pair of sticks joined by a chain; a sharply hooked, flat but wide wooden blade something like the hands of a clock frozen at the hour of three; a flute-like instrument with tiny feathered darts alongside; small, thin silver discs like gears with teeth as cruel as a shark's. Everything was immaculate: the metal shone, the wood gleamed. On the adjoining wall, to Quare's right, hung items of clothing – breeches, shirts, boots, cloaks, hoods, kerchiefs . . . all in the same shade of ash grey. A long table of dark wood against the wall to his left displayed as many glass vials and clay pots as an apothecary's shop or an alchemist's laboratory. Interspersed with everything on the walls were still more clocks, all of them ticking busily, none of them showing the same time.

'Come, sir,' said Longinus. 'Let us dress and arm ourselves. Then we shall be off!'

Quare stepped into the room. 'So it's true,' he said. 'You really are Grimalkin.' He had not entirely believed it until now.

'Was,' Longinus corrected. 'And will be again, for tonight,

at least. As will you; we shall both be garbed as Grimalkin, the better to— Why, what is so amusing?'

For Quare had begun to chuckle. 'How strange!' he said. 'When I told Master Magnus of my rooftop encounter, and revealed that the great Grimalkin, as I thought then, was a woman, he advanced a hypothesis I considered most unlikely – so unlikely that I argued against it . . . with as little success as, knowing him, you may imagine.'

'What was this hypothesis?' inquired Longinus with an expression of interest.

'Magnus believed you had been confronted by not one but two Grimalkins. The real one and a disguised confederate, the object being to sow confusion and apprehension in their target – that is, in you. And now here we are, adopting the very strategy ourselves!'

Longinus did not appear to share Quare's amusement. 'A coincidence, no more. Or less even than that, for two generals, after all, may employ the same means to achieve an objective; it is the circumstances that dictate a particular tactical approach. Magnus may have been wrong in his hypothesis – though strictly speaking he was not, for there *were* two Grimalkins in the attic that night: myself and the imposter! – but the logic behind his reasoning was sound. Grimalkin has a fearsome reputation, as you know. He is rumoured to be a ghost, a devil. No walls can keep him out; no weapons, it is said, can harm him. That reputation will aid us, giving us an advantage over our adversaries, even if it is only a matter of seconds. In such situations as we are about to enter, Mr Quare, life or death, success or failure, hinges upon seconds. The one who best exploits them will almost invariably win.'

'You speak as if it were a game.'

'Why, and so it is – like a game of chess, which can be won

in an instant, through checkmate, or the sudden capture of a queen, or more slowly, by the accumulation of lesser pieces, even lowly pawns. Gain enough pawns, or seconds, as the case may be, and victory becomes that much more likely.'

'A game of time,' Quare said; then added bitterly: 'Only, we are not the players. We are the pawns.'

'That is so,' Longinus agreed. 'But do not forget that pawns may be promoted.'

'To other pieces,' said Quare. 'They cannot become players themselves.'

'In chess. But this is not chess, Mr Quare. In this game, as you have seen, we can rise up from the board and move into the world beyond it, the world of the true players: the Otherwhere. Once there, why should we not become players? It is our right, as thinking beings and as Englishmen, to determine our own destiny, or at least to have a say in it, just as our representatives in Parliament act as a check on the powers of the king. Tonight we take the first, indispensable step towards that goal.'

Quare was unimpressed. 'You think that gaining possession of the hunter will make us the equal of Doppler and the others?'

'Obviously not,' Longinus granted. 'But it will, at the very least, improve our position.'

'Or simply make us more of a target than we are already.'

'Faint heart never won fair lady, Mr Quare! To do much, one must dare much. When Corinna held the hunter in her hand, neither Adolpheus nor the dragon Hesta dared to strike us down: the one with an army at his back, the other mightier still. There is power in that watch, a power feared even by those we must regard as nearer to gods than to men. Should we, for that reason, bow our heads meekly and offer up our surrender? No, sir. That I will never do! Not while I have the strength and wit to seek a better outcome.'

Quare felt ashamed. 'I am merely trying to be realistic.'

'It is our plain duty to deny this infernal device to anyone who might trigger it, whether purposely or by accident. Doppler seeks it still. The Old Wolf possesses it – who can say what mischief he is up to even now? Nor is it likely that the French have given up their pursuit; the villain who stabbed you and murdered eight people in cold blood is still at large. Doppler I fear because of his knowledge; the others because of their ignorance. No, Mr Quare. I mean to have that watch – with your help, if you will give it, but alone if I must.'

'And once you have it – what then? Anything we attempt with the hunter is as likely to have a catastrophic as a beneficial result. We do not know how to use it safely, or, indeed, how to use it at all, beyond the fact that it has a taste for human blood. I, for one, do not care to give it any more of mine than it has drunk already.'

'We do not need to do anything with it,' Longinus persisted. 'Possession alone will give us a seat at the game . . . and guarantee our safety as well.'

'How so?'

'We know that there are at least three factions vying for the hunter: Doppler and his risen angels; another group of angels – let us call them rebels – who oppose him; and a third party, whose identity and interests we do not precisely know but whose existence we have inferred from certain hints dropped by the false Grimalkin, who may or may not have been sent by them. If we possess the hunter, and any one of those parties should seek to move against us, the self-interest of the others must compel them to intercede on our behalf, so as to maintain the status quo. The logic is impeccable, Mr Quare.'

'Is it? Men are not logical creatures, Longinus. We do not act according to the cold dictates of reason, nor out of enlightened self-interest – not in the small events of our everyday lives, and still less in the pursuit of such power as this. It has always been thus. And, from what you have told me, and my own small experience, I judge that things are no different among the angels, risen or rebel.'

'I would be a fool to deny it,' Longinus said. 'Still, I will go regardless. Are you with me, Mr Quare? You have misgivings, it is plain. That is understandable. But if you mean to withdraw, do it now. If that is your decision, I will respect it – though I confess I would think less of you.'

'I will go,' he answered, feeling again the iron compulsion laid upon him by Tiamat. 'I have no choice.'

'Good man.' Longinus grinned. 'Master Magnus would be proud.'

Quare knew better, but could say nothing.

After they had dressed – Longinus transferring from his old clothes to his new ones the array of timepieces he always carried, and supplying Quare with ten watches he had brought for that specific purpose; shirt, breeches and boots all had pockets sewn to hold them – the two men regarded themselves in a full-length mirror.

'Why, we are as alike as two peas in a pod,' Longinus exclaimed, delighted.

Indeed, with hoods raised and masking kerchiefs in place, the two Grimalkins reflected in the glass were indistinguishable. In height, there was not an inch of difference between them; in build, both were slender as whippets; the eyes that peered out beneath the hoods were the same ghostly greyish blue. Longinus had divested himself of his powder and beauty mark, so even the exposed skin of their faces was the same pale hue.

Faced with this resemblance, Quare experienced a sudden and shocking surmise. 'Longinus,' he said, then paused and removed his mask. He took a breath and began again. 'Lord Wichcote . . . forgive me, but there is no discreet way to ask, and I must know. Are you my father?'

At this, Longinus removed his own mask. 'I beg your pardon?'

'You said yourself we are alike as two peas in a pod,' Quare said.

'But why should that make you think I might be your father?' Longinus seemed baffled. 'Many men resemble each other without there being a drop of blood between them.'

Quare could not keep a tremor of emotion from his voice. 'Surely you must know that I am a bastard – it is no secret. All the guild knows. But Master Magnus once told me that my father was still alive. Indeed, he promised to help me find him if I agreed to become a regulator. Now I cannot help but wonder if that is why he sent me here, to you, for my first assignment. Why, before his death, he had planned to bring us together – you told me so yourself!'

'That is true. But I am sorry, Mr Quare . . . Daniel. I would be proud to have such a son as you. And if somehow you were my son, and I had been in ignorance of your existence, I would make up for it by acknowledging you before the world, gladly and without hesitation. Yet the fact remains that I am not.'

'How can you be certain?'

'Do you recall what Corinna told me as we were making our escape from Märchen? She warned me to be careful of what I said, because words spoken in the Otherwhere had a way of coming true. And so it has proved. I swore to her that I would desire no other woman, and that is exactly what has come to pass. I am not your father, sir. I am no one's father and shall never be. I am impotent, you see – and have been ever since my return from Märchen.'

Quare studied the man's face, but there was no hint of anything there but sincerity. He swallowed his disappointment. 'I am sorry, sir.'

'I am sorry as well,' Longinus said, still holding his gaze. He laid a gentle hand on Quare's shoulder. 'I meant what I said about being proud to have you as a son. Any man would be.'

'Save for my father, apparently.'

'In fairness, he may not know. I have no doubt that Magnus would have uncovered the truth, had he lived. But I am not without resources of my own. I will look into the matter, sir. I give you my word.'

Quare, unable to speak, nodded.

Longinus returned an encouraging smile and clapped him upon the shoulder. 'Now, sir, let us arm ourselves.'

Longinus took a sword, a dagger and a crossbow, strapping the latter, with a brace of bolts, across his back. He took a handful of the silver stars, which he explained were for throwing, and the flute-like instrument with its collection of small, feathered darts; this, he said, was a blowpipe, a weapon he had come across in his travels. The darts were tipped with a poison that would swiftly paralyse their target. The throwing stars, blowpipe and darts he tucked into the underside of his cloak. Finally he took down a pair of pistols and slid them into holsters strapped to his thighs. These trim guns were unlike any Quare had seen before.

'Another of Magnus's inventions,' Longinus said. 'They

require no priming and are always ready to fire, even in the most inclement weather.'

'No primer? How, then, does the pistol discharge?'

'The primer is already added, part of the projectile itself. What's more, each pistol can fire four shots without reloading.'

'Why aren't His Majesty's troops equipped with these weapons?' Quare wondered. 'They could turn the tide in the war.'

'As to that, you must ask Mr Pitt. But I can hazard a guess. The problem with such innovations as this is that they represent a kind of Pandora's box. If we were to make thousands of these guns, and equip our soldiers with them, it would not be long – perhaps even before the first shot was fired on a battlefield, for England is riddled with spies – before the enemy had learned of it, analysed the mechanism, and introduced an equivalent or even superior weapon. I believe, then – though I have no first-hand knowledge of it – that we are holding this and other, similar inventions in reserve, in case the French cross the Channel in force. I certainly hope that is the case. For if that should ever come to pass, we would be in desperate straits indeed.'

Turning to the table, Longinus filled a number of glass or clay containers with an assortment of powders and liquids, which he then slipped into small grey pouches and attached to his belt; here were smokescreens, bomblets, gases to burn the eyes and the lungs.

'You seem prepared for any eventuality,' Quare said, impressed.

'One endeavours to anticipate,' Longinus said. 'But one invariably encounters the unexpected. No doubt that will be as true tonight as any other night, if not more so. I dare not supply you with any of my potions or powders, Mr Quare; you would be as likely to use them accidentally against us as against any enemy we may encounter. The same goes for my more exotic weapons. When we have sufficient time, I will train you in their use. But for tonight, you will carry only your sword, a dagger and a crossbow. And, if you like, one of Magnus's pistols.'

'I should like that very much. Only, I hope I shall have no cause to fire it.'

'As do I. But if the need arises, do not hesitate. You will find the recoil somewhat more than you are used to, but the accuracy substantially improved.'

Once Quare was fitted out – this included pouches attached to his belt, each filled with another pocket watch, so that his appearance matched that of Longinus in every outward detail, at least upon casual examination – Longinus drew a close-fitting pair of grey silk gloves onto his hands, completing his transformation into Grimalkin, then presented another pair of gloves to Quare, who found them a tight squeeze but no impediment to his manual dexterity.

'Now let us pay the Old Wolf a visit,' Longinus said with a grin.

Quare nodded, his mouth dry.

Longinus returned to the full-length mirror, as if to inspect himself once more. He touched a corner of the frame, and the mirror swung open, revealing the small candlelit chamber of another stair-master.

'Why, is there a room in your house that does *not* contain one of these devices?' asked Quare.

Longinus said nothing. He gestured Quare into the chamber, then followed him inside. He closed the door, tugged the pull, and the stair-master began to descend.

Quare counted the seconds to himself. When he reached twenty-two, the stair-master slowed; at twenty-eight it stopped. The door slid open, revealing what appeared to be, at least as far as Quare could judge in the weak light, a fissure carved out of solid rock, scarce wide enough for two men to stand side by side. He could not see very far before a curtain of darkness descended, but he felt a whisper of cold, damp air that suggested the fissure extended a good distance ahead.

'What is this place?' he whispered, as if standing on the hushed threshold of a cathedral.

'You shall see,' Longinus answered in a whisper of his own. He gestured for Quare to step out and then followed him out of the chamber, lifting two candles from their sconces. One of these he passed to Quare.

As the door closed behind them, Longinus led Quare into the depths of the fissure, which narrowed as they advanced, until they were walking single file. The path zigged and zagged, following a gentle but steady decline. The chill in the air grew more pronounced, and Quare smelled a damp mineral tang. The words *walls*, *floor* and *ceiling* were too suggestive of civilization to describe what surrounded him; this passage, he realized, had not been carved or even extended by the hand of man but instead had been cut into the bedrock of the earth by Nature herself in some ancient paroxysm of violence that had sundered stone from stone. The rock was slick with moisture, and there was a sound of dripping, eerily magnified, that wove in and out of the sounds of their own footsteps and breathing: a sound very much like the ticking of the clocks in the rooms above, as if Longinus's temporal shield extended even below the surface.

'How deep are we?' he asked, still whispering.

473

'A quarter of a mile,' said Longinus.

'Does this passage lead to the guild hall?'

'Not this passage, no,' Longinus said. 'We must go deeper for that.'

'Deeper? How far does this fissure descend?'

'Why, we have barely scratched the surface,' Longinus said, sounding amused. 'Did you not know that the netherworld of London is honeycombed with such spaces as this? Here one might see Nature's rough draft of Magnus's internet.'

As he spoke, the fissure widened. Longinus used his candle to light a torch that lay, along with a supply of others, against the rock face to their right. The flame sprang up, and the darkness fell back, revealing a vast chamber whose full extent was impossible to judge. Quare lit a torch of his own and raised it, gazing about in awe. 'Incredible – we might almost be standing beneath the dome of St Paul's!'

'There are larger caverns by far to be met with below the ground. Indeed, I have often thought that another city exists here, a kind of anti-London . . . or, since these spaces long pre-date the first rude building raised above them, it is London that is the obverse reflection of this place.'

'A city below a city . . . Do people live here, then?'

'Some,' said Longinus. 'It was through one of the branching tunnels of this London underground, if I may term it such, that Guy Fawkes and his fellow conspirators gained access to the cellars of Parliament. Others have found their way here for more benign purposes, compelled by curiosity or misfortune. I learned of the tunnels from my father, and he from his, and part of my inheritance was a collection of maps, to which I have added substantially over the years, for, as you can imagine, a working knowledge of this maze might well benefit anyone desirous of moving about the city in secrecy.

Yet I do not believe I have discovered more than a fraction of what exists. There are routes I have not explored, passages too dangerous to traverse unaided, if at all. Many who come here, for whatever reason, do not find their way out again – I have come upon their bodies, or what is left of them, often enough in my explorations. Others do not wish to leave, and dwell here like the kobolds of legend, furtive and sly, inured to the dark and suspicious of surface dwellers; I have done much over the years to gain their trust, for they do not take kindly to intruders. But tonight we shall not stray from the familiar paths – familiar to me, at least. They will take us back to the guild hall, with no one the wiser.'

'How can you be certain the Old Wolf doesn't know of these paths? Perhaps there will be guards waiting to take us as we emerge.'

'There is always a risk,' Longinus said with a shrug. 'But I think it unlikely. I have shared my knowledge of the under-ground with no one – not even Master Magnus himself. Do not forget that I have spent many hours in the guild hall, dis-guised as a servant. If the Old Wolf or anyone else there knew of these spaces, I would have discovered it before now. No, their knowledge of the underground extends no further than the dungeon in which you were imprisoned. They have no notion of what lies below those cells. No doubt they did once, long ago, for some of the old entrances have been bricked up ... though even those barriers are crumbling now, and useless.'

'And when we gain entrance to the guild hall – what then?'

'That will depend on what we find there. Planning can only take one so far, Mr Quare; we regulators live or die by im-provisation. But let us "suit the action to the word, the word to the action", as the Bard has it. Come.' He advanced into the cavern, leaving Quare to follow.

This he did, albeit slowly, gazing about with a mix of trepidation and wonder. The ceiling was so high overhead that he could not see it, only long fingers of rock that depended out of the dark like icicles . . . melting icicles, for they dripped with water whose mineral content – the rich tang of iron and limestone freighted the cold air – had accreted into slick stone fingers on the cavern floor that reached up to clasp what had given them birth, a many-handed infant grasping for its many-handed mother, as if this were the pits of Tartarus into which Zeus had cast the Titans. Or as if these two sundered halves strove to pull themselves back together, repairing the ancient breach that had separated them. Despite the spaciousness of the cavern, Quare was very aware of the weight pressing down, all the streets and buildings of the London he knew resting on the shoulders of this secret sister city, which seemed at once as solid as a fortress and as fragile as a bubble.

'No dawdling, Mr Quare,' came Longinus's impatient voice.

Quare hurried to catch up.

His guide stood waiting at the far side of the cavern, beside a fissure angling sharply into the rock – one of many such passages converging here, Quare thought, like streets and alleys leading to a central square in the world above.

'It is impressive, I know,' Longinus said. 'Like something out of Dante. Later, when we are not so pressed for time, I will take you on a tour. But for now you must not let yourself be distracted. Follow as closely as you can, as lightly as you can, and speak only as necessary, for sound travels in peculiar ways in these convoluted spaces.'

Quare nodded. His mouth was dry, his skin covered in

clammy sweat beneath the loose grey costume of Grimalkin. Once again, he tried to discern some connection to the hunter, straining not just with his ears but with every fibre of his being to hear the timepiece calling to him as Tiamat had said it would. To feel its tug. But all he felt was a diffuse tingling, as if his garments were imbued with a faint electrostatic charge.

This sensation he associated, after a moment's reflection, not with the hunter but with the various timepieces secreted about his person, whose ticking constituted a steady background noise that merged into the echoes of dripping water until – as he had often felt in the guild hall – it was easy to fancy himself within the workings of a gigantic clock. Only this was a clock far older and greater than any built by human hands.

He had a sudden glimpse then, in his mind's eye, of a clock greater still: the moon and the planets, the sun itself and all the far-flung stars, pieces of a vast and intricate orrery marking the minutes and hours until time and the universe ran down. And then? Would it be the Last Judgement, life or torment everlasting meted out by the stern justice of the Almighty, as he had been taught from childhood and, with a child's credulity, had always believed? Or, on the contrary, was oblivion the common fate of men and the universe?

Or was there yet another alternative – again, the Law of Threes! – bound up with the watch and the Otherwhere, an alternative that lay coiled in the secret heart of the hunter like a charge of gunpowder awaiting a spark?

At that moment, as if in answer, and without a glimmer of warning, what might have been a ghostly hand reached inside his chest. It slid past whatever shield the timepieces had knit around him, wrapped icy fingers about his heart, and yanked, as though to pull it out of his body. He gasped, more from shock than pain. Every inch of his skin erupted in a fierce buzzing. Then, in the blink of an eye, the hand was gone – whether of its own volition or banished by the effect of the watches, he did not know.

Stumbling forward with a groan, Quare put out a hand to steady himself against the cavern's rocky side. Dark spots flashed before his eyes; a mass of bees seemed to have chosen his head for a hive. He gulped air, afraid he would be sick. At some point, he had dropped his torch; it lay guttering on the ground.

Longinus's voice reached him through the buzzing. 'What is it, Mr Quare? Are you all right?'

He nodded, speech beyond him. Nor, he found a moment later, when the buzzing had receded and he could speak again, was he able to relate what had happened. The dragon's geis prevented him . . . another ghostly hand, or rather claw, this one squeezing his throat. But he did not doubt that the hunter had made its presence felt at last. One more power seeking to pull his strings.

'I have seen this before,' Longinus said meanwhile. 'There are those who cannot bear to abide beneath the ground for any length of time. It is not a question of cowardice; here, the stoutest heart may quail without shame. If you cannot go on—'

'I can,' Quare interrupted, his voice echoing hollowly. He stooped to retrieve the torch, which blazed up again once clear of the ground. His arm, his whole body trembled, though the buzzing had subsided, dwindling to a kind of background hum. His heart felt bruised. Helpless he might be, but that did not make him any less angry; on the contrary. He was seething with rage. He lacked only the means to express it, and a target on which to focus it. Both, he felt sure, lay ahead. 'By all means, let us continue.'

Longinus held his gaze with his own, then nodded and slid into the passage.

Thus began a journey that Quare would always remember as a kind of dream. With his vision curtailed by the narrow fissures they squeezed through and the caverns into which those fissures opened, only to contract again, it was easy to imagine that they were not moving at all, but instead walking in place while the subterranean world moved around them, changing its shape and even its substance from moment to moment under a torch-spun magician's cloak of shadow and darkness, as if Longinus had brought him back into the Otherwhere. And it occurred to Quare that perhaps this was as close to the Otherwhere as could exist in what he had always thought of as reality but which now seemed to him merely, as it were, a special (and necessarily lesser) case of a *realer real*, like Plato's shadows cast upon the cave wall. Here was the primordial stuff of the planet, out of which the world above and its myriad wonders, living and unliving, had arisen . . . and into which they would all return, earth to earth, ashes to ashes, dust to dust, just as this reality itself would one day be enfolded back into the Otherwhere if Doppler – or, he suspected, Tiamat – gained possession of the hunter.

Yet how could he deny Tiamat the hunter, assuming they were able to retrieve it from the Old Wolf? He had seen how fruitless it was to fight the geis Tiamat had laid upon him. Every detail of their encounter was engraved upon his memory, so much so that he felt the creature's reptilian presence still, as if it were lurking somewhere near by, for if there was ever a place that a dragon might find hospitable, this was surely it. He half expected, each time they entered a cavern, to see a pile of bones and treasure with a scaly form coiled on top of it like a sovereign seated on a throne.

Longinus set a fast pace, and Quare had to hurry to keep up. There was no time to study his surroundings or even to mark the path. If he were separated from Longinus, or if the other man were captured or killed at the guild hall, he would not be able to find his way back through this underground maze. He thought to mention this to Longinus but then decided to hold his tongue, afraid that anything he said, however softly, would find its way to their enemies, mortal or otherwise. In any case, he felt that as long as Tiamat had need of him, it would not abandon him here; if he called to it, it would come: it had promised – or threatened – as much. And however little he liked it, he knew that he *would* call upon the dragon if it were a question of dying down here, alone in the cold dark.

Longinus had spoken of men and women driven to seek shelter underground, and as they progressed farther into the journey, their course continuing ever downward, Quare began to see occasional evidence of it: rubbish left behind, scraps of old clothing and rags, the bones of small animals, the remains of fires. Markings on the walls made with charcoal or simply scratched into the stone: crude drawings of human and animal figures, simple declarations, names, initials, dates . . . and symbols he did not recognize, like letters in an unknown language. But he did not see a living soul.

After some time – how long, Quare could not have guessed – Longinus drew to a halt at the entrance to yet another cavern. Looking back at Quare, he raised a finger to his lips for silence, then motioned for him to approach.

'We are not alone,' he whispered as Quare came up.

Quare glanced behind him, but saw only the shadows thrown by their torches.

'You must let me do the talking,' Longinus continued. 'Say nothing unless you are spoken to, and then be brief and respectful in your replies. Comply at once with whatever is asked of you. Under no circumstances draw your sword or any other weapon, unless I draw first. Is that clear?'

'Yes. But should we not don our masks?'

'No. My face is known here, though not my true identity.'

'But—'

'Shh,' he hissed. 'This is not the time for questions or arguments. I have broken no laws in bringing you here, but I have stretched certain . . . understandings. I had hoped to avoid discovery, but like so many hopes, it appears to have been futile. So be it. In a way, Mr Quare, you are fortunate indeed. First, to see what few surface-dwellers have ever seen. And second, to do so in my presence, for otherwise you would almost certainly be dead.'

'If this is fortune,' Quare replied, 'I could do with less of it.'

''At could be arranged,' came a voice from out of the darkness ahead, speaking in the thickest Cockney that Quare had ever heard, so that it seemed almost a foreign language even to his London-trained ear.

Quare put a hand to his sword, but Longinus grasped his wrist, preventing him from drawing. 'Be still, sir!'

Now a second voice spoke, this one from behind. ''At's right. Ain't no cause ter be all berligerent like. We don't mean no 'arm to them what means us no 'arm. We Morecockneyans is a peaceful folk.'

'More . . . what?' Quare asked, pulling free of Longinus's grasp.

'Cockneyans,' came the first voice. 'Morecockneyans, on

account of 'ow we're more cockney than the blasted Cockney.'

The second voice laughed. 'We're the original article, yer might say – been down 'ere since before the Great Fire, we 'ave. This is our kingdom, your lordships, and you may pass 'ere by our leave or not at all. Now, put out them torches and let's 'ave a look at yer.'

'Put out—'

'Do as he says,' Longinus interrupted. 'They have become so habituated to dark that even the poor light of these torches blinds them.' So saying, he let his torch fall to the ground and stamped it out. 'Go on, Mr Quare. We're perfectly safe, I assure you, as long as we behave in a manner befitting guests.'

'If you think I'm going to— ow!' Quare dropped his torch as what felt like a hornet's sting pierced the back of his hand. In the seconds before Longinus stamped out the torch, he saw an angry red welt rising there. Then a darkness fell that was beyond any darkness he had ever experienced; it seemed to require another word entirely. He fumbled for his weapons, then froze as the tip of a blade pricked his throat.

'Quare, is it?' queried the voice that had laughed. It was not laughing now. 'You'd best listen to your mate, Mr Quare.'

'Gorblimey, if it ain't the Grey Ghost, old Grimalkin 'isself!' exclaimed the first voice meanwhile. 'It's been an age. I 'eard tell you'd retired.'

'I had.'

'A bit old ter be gallervantin' about down 'ere, ain't yer?'

'No older than you, Cornelius.'

The voice chuckled. 'Sharp ears for an old man.'

'My blade's grown no duller, either. Hello, Starkey.'

482

Quare felt the blade at his throat withdraw.

'Grimalkin,' came the reply. 'Up ter yer old tricks again, are yer?'

'You could say that,' he answered. 'Mr Quare and I are in pursuit of a certain timepiece.'

'And who is Mr Quare at 'ome, eh?' asked the voice of Cornelius. 'Took on a 'prentice, 'ave yer? Never thought I'd see the day. You was always solitary as a cat.'

'Mr Quare is a journeyman of the Worshipful Company of Clockmakers,' Longinus said.

'Oho,' said Starkey with a laugh. 'A regulator, you mean. One of the Old Wolf's whelps, is 'e? Or does 'e answer to Master Mephistopheles?'

'Master Magnus is dead,' Longinus said.

Silence greeted this news. Quare, meanwhile, had begun to notice that all was not as dark as it had first appeared. A diffuse, pale glow, fainter than the first pale smudge of dawn, hung like a sourceless fog in the air, and though it did not exactly illuminate anything, it did place objects into a kind of relief, so that he was able to discern, though none too clearly, the silhouettes of the two Morecockneyans. Cornelius, it appeared, was a large, stout man, nearly as big as the Old Wolf himself, while Starkey was thin as a greyhound.

'Dead 'ow?' asked Cornelius at last. 'Was it murder?'

'Did the Old Wolf do 'im?' Starkey chimed in eagerly.

'I cannot say,' Longinus replied.

'Cannot . . . or will not?' Cornelius demanded.

'In truth, I do not know for certain how he died. I cannot explain it. All I know is that it involves the timepiece I spoke of.'

'Worf a lot, is it?'

'It does not even tell the time,' Longinus demurred.

'Then why are you and Mr Quare 'ere so innerested in it?' asked Starkey in a sceptical tone.

'For two reasons. First, it belonged to me once, and was stolen by—'

At this, Starkey guffawed. 'What, the great Grimalkin robbed? There's a larf!'

Longinus continued testily. 'You can see why I wish it back. No self-respecting thief enjoys having the tables turned. And to add insult to injury, the churl who stole it did so in the guise of none other than' – and here he sketched a self-mocking bow – 'the great Grimalkin.'

'The cheek of it!' Starkey sounded delighted. 'The rogue!'

'Second,' Longinus resumed, 'the timepiece is of considerable scientific interest.'

'Pull the other one,' Cornelius objected. 'You said it don't tell the time.'

'Neither does a cannon or a musket.'

'What, is it some kind of weapon, then?'

'In a manner of speaking,' Longinus said. 'Its mechanism is unique, to put it mildly. It is no exaggeration to say that whoever can uncover its secrets will gain considerable power thereby – perhaps even enough to decide the outcome of the war.'

'What war?'

'Come now, sir,' said Longinus. 'You cannot expect me to believe that you are ignorant of the fact that our country is fighting for its very life against the French and their allies!'

'You surface dwellers are always fightin' over somefin' or other. It don't make us no nevermind down 'ere,' said Starkey with a shrug of his narrow shoulders.

Quare's vision had continued to improve, and he saw now that the faint glow he had discerned earlier had its source in

Starkey and Cornelius; or, rather, in a kind of pale powder that covered their faces and clothes. It radiated a sickly greenish light, giving them the aspect of mouldering ghosts. Cornelius had a nose like a warty potato above a beard like a tangle of moss, while Starkey's face was gaunt, his nose sharp as a knife's edge, his eyes sunk so deep in their sockets that their existence could only be inferred. And though Cornelius was fully as large as the Old Wolf, his bulk, unlike that of the corpulent clockman, was made up of muscle.

'Whether you live above the ground or beneath it, you're still Englishmen,' Longinus said meanwhile.

'We're Morecockneyans first,' Cornelius replied matter-of-factly. 'We 'ave our own king, our own country.'

'Maybe we orter 'ave a look at this timepiece, Corny,' put in Starkey. 'Might be we should take it to 'is Majesty.'

'A capital idea, Starks.'

'Gentlemen, the timepiece has already been stolen from me once,' Longinus interjected. 'I do not mean to put myself to the trouble and risk of retrieving it only to have it stolen again. Nor is it to be idly handled – poked and prodded like some common chronometer. That is what killed Master Magnus, or so I do believe. And if he could not handle the timepiece safely – he, the foremost horologist of the age – I do not think you, or any Morecockneyan, would be advised to try.'

'What about you, then, eh? You fink you're better than Magnus?'

'On the contrary, I know my limits.'

'Then 'ow—' began Starkey, but Cornelius interrupted:

'Mr Quare.'

Quare started; he had begun to think himself forgotten. 'Yes?'

'That's why you brung 'im along,' Cornelius continued, ignoring Quare completely. 'You fink 'e can do what Magnus couldn't and what you dare not even try. That's right, ain't it?'

'Hardly. There may be one other in all of England who can discern the secrets of this timepiece, but that person is not Mr Quare. However, it's true enough that my young friend has a certain . . . affinity with it,' Longinus said. 'I do not think it will kill him.'

''Ear that, Mr Quare?' asked Starkey, more amused than ever. ''E don't *fink* it'll kill yer. 'Ow's that for a vote o' confidence?'

'It's not the watch I'm worried about,' Quare answered.

'So it's a watch, is it?' Starkey rejoined.

'Of course it's a watch,' Longinus replied before Quare could add anything. 'Did I not say so already?'

'No, you did not,' said Cornelius, measuring out his words. 'What else 'ave you omitted to mention, I wonder? I thought we 'ad an understandin', Grimalkin. An agreement. We give you the right o' passage through our dark domain, and you give us bits o' information and a cut o' the swag from up top. Ain't that always been the way of it?'

'Might be it's time to renegotiate our agreement, Corny,' put in Starkey.

'I was thinkin' the very same, Starks.'

'We don't have time for this,' Longinus said, exasperated. 'Gentlemen, I assure you, our need is urgent. More urgent than you can imagine. As for the agreement to which you refer, neither you, Mr Cornelius, nor you, Mr Starkey, has the right to renegotiate so much as a syllable. Do not forget that I saved your king's life once. I dare say *he* has not forgotten.'

'There you would be wrong,' Starkey said. 'King Jeremiah 'as grown rather forgetful of late, I regret ter say.'

Cornelius added, in a voice edged with mockery, 'Come now, sir. You cannot expect me to believe that you are ignorant o' the fact that King Jeremiah is no longer among the livin'.'

Longinus drew in a sharp breath. 'Jerry dead? When? How?'

'That don't concern you,' said Cornelius. 'But there's a new king on the mushroom throne. And 'e might not feel 'isself bound by any agreements entered into by 'is predecessor – kings is peculiar that way, I find.'

'You know what I fink, Corny?' piped up Starkey.

'What's that, Starks?'

'I fink we should bring our guests to meet 'is Majesty.'

By now the conversation had undergone so many twists and turns that Quare was positively dizzy. Whether the 'Morecockneyans' were friends or enemies or something in between, he didn't know, but he did know that he had no desire whatsoever to meet their so-called king. And the same, it was apparent, was true of Longinus.

'Gentlemen,' he said, as if speaking to guests in his own drawing room, 'you know me. You know what I can do. That I have not thus far drawn my sword is a measure of my friendship with your late king, and my belief that the agreement between us was still in effect even after so many years. If that is not the case, I shall feel justified in defending myself.' And here he did in fact make to draw his sword; seeing which, however indistinctly, Quare did likewise.

The effect was electric. 'No need ter be so 'asty,' said Starkey, backing off a step.

'Indeed not,' Cornelius said. 'We was only tryin' ter be 'ospitable like. But I can see yer in a 'urry. Yer can always meet 'is Majesty some uvver time.'

'Then our agreement is still in effect?'

''Course it is,' said Cornelius. 'Now, if you'll excuse us, we'll just—'

'Very well,' Longinus interrupted with a satisfied nod. 'Then by the terms of that agreement, I require your assistance, gentlemen.'

'But—' began Starkey.

Faster than Quare could follow, Longinus's sword was out of its scabbard. 'You will accompany us to the guild hall of the Worshipful Company of Clockmakers,' he said. 'That way we can travel without the need for torches. Your vision, after all, is considerably better than our own down here. Though never fear: I can see well enough to employ this' – he flourished the blade – 'if we should run into any trouble along the way.'

'That's ... comfortin' ter know,' Cornelius said after a glance at Starkey.

'Mr Starkey, you will oblige me by joining Mr Cornelius at the head of our little group. Sword sheathed, if you don't mind.'

'Wiv pleasure,' he grumbled, sliding his sword back into its scabbard as he pushed past Quare, who only now drew his own blade, feeling slow and clumsy.

'Now,' Longinus said, 'let us resume our journey in silence, for we would not wish to alert our enemies above – or, for that matter, our friends here below, who might misconstrue the situation. I trust we would all prefer to avoid such misunderstandings, eh, gentlemen?'

'Assuredly,' said Cornelius.

'By all means,' Starkey agreed.

'You would do well to remember that I know the route as well as you, if not better. So you will oblige me by avoiding any short cuts or other unpleasant surprises along the way.'

'Wouldn't dream of it,' Starkey said.

'Do you really mean to proceed without torches?' Quare asked, not quite believing what he had heard.

'The Morecockneyans, as you have surely noticed, employ a fine powder made of the crushed spores of phosphorescent fungi specially grown for the purpose,' Longinus said. 'You'll find the light sufficient to travel by . . . or fight by, if it should come to that.'

'It won't,' Cornelius said with assurance. 'No surface dweller can move as quiet as a Morecockneyan, or 'ear us if we don't wish to be 'eard. Present company excepted. Everyone knows the Grey Ghost ain't no ordinary surface dweller.'

'Ain't no ordinary 'uman bein', yer ask me,' Starkey opined.

'Nobody did ask, so shut yer 'ole,' Cornelius responded with a snarl. 'What I mean to say, Grimalkin, is that we'll get the two of yer safely up to the guild 'all, never fear. But that's as far as me and Starks is prepared ter go, agreement or no.'

'I had not thought to presume upon you one step farther,' Longinus said. 'Now, pray, lead on. And remember: not a word, not a sound.'

The two Morecockneyans set off, followed by Longinus and Quare. At first their pace was brisk, but Longinus soon called them to heel. The light emanating from the Morecockneyans, while sufficient to illuminate the way, if only just, gave the already dreamlike surroundings an even stranger aspect, so that Quare felt more than ever that he had slipped back into the Otherwhere. Everything seemed created out of nothing an instant before they came to it, and then, as soon as they were past, to dissolve again into the primordial soup that had spawned it. Quare, after some moments, had sheathed his sword, concentrating on avoiding the obstacles that emerged as if out of thin air; at the same time, he was intent upon any hint, however faint, of the hunter's ethereal touch. His heart pulsed; his skin tingled; his every nerve was pulled taut, vibrating like a violin string. The discordant ticking of the timepieces he carried in his clothing, a constant soft patter of sound, set him further on edge.

But as Cornelius had promised, they encountered no one, and soon enough they stood at the entrance to a passage that, according to Longinus, led into the lowest levels of the guild hall. Quare had no idea how much time had passed since he and his mentor had begun their subterranean journey, but it seemed impossible that it should still be night. Nevertheless, Longinus appeared unconcerned.

'Gentlemen, thank you for the guidance,' he said. 'We are in your debt.'

'Quite all right,' whispered Cornelius. 'I reckon you can find yer own way from 'ere.'

'I should hope so,' he said.

'I guess we'll be 'eadin' 'ome, then,' Starkey said. 'Best o' luck to yer both.'

'I'm afraid I can't allow that,' Longinus said, already moving as he spoke, a shadowy blur.

Quare heard two surprised exhalations, so close in time as to be almost a single sigh. Cornelius and Starkey sank to the ground. He gaped like a schoolboy.

'Don't just stand there,' Longinus hissed. 'Help me move them.'

'Are they . . . dead?'

'Do you take me for a cold-blooded murderer?'

'No – a regulator.'

This drew an appreciative chuckle. 'Touché, Mr Quare. But they are not dead, merely rendered insensible by a salve on my dagger point. They will regain consciousness in a few hours, none the worse for wear. By which time we shall either be long gone . . . or it will no longer matter.'

'But why . . .?'

'Surely you could see that they were not to be trusted. Things are different down here. I have been absent too long. Jerry – that is, King Jeremiah – is dead. I confess, I hadn't expected that. From the sound of it, I do not think my old friend died peaceably in his sleep. He had no heir, only a gaggle of bastards – no offence, Mr Quare. But it seems plain that Cornelius and Starkey serve whoever it is that now sits upon the mushroom throne. Had I allowed them to depart, they would have reported back to him and then returned here with others to wait for our exit. They would have set upon us, stolen the timepiece, and left us for dead. There is no doubt whatsoever in my mind.'

'Well, you have made an enemy of them now . . . and of their new king, whoever he may be.'

'Regrettable but necessary. With luck, I shall have time to make amends, if warranted, though in truth I have shown our friends here more mercy than they would have given us, had they not been too intimidated by the reputation of the Grey Ghost.'

'Another of your aliases?'

'A nickname bestowed by King Jeremiah. I am most sorry to learn of his death. He was a giant in stature and in heart – every inch a king. When we have finished here, I shall look into the manner of his death. If it be murder, I will see that justice is done, one way or another. I swear it. But that is for later. The hunter awaits us, and time is short. Come, sir – let us be about our business.'

With that, he laid hold of Cornelius's bulky form and, again evidencing his surprising strength, dragged the man into the passage; Quare did likewise with Starkey, who was as light as a bird. Beyond the narrow opening, the passage widened considerably, and they were able to deposit the bodies off to one side, leaning the two men against the rock wall, their legs stretched out before them, heads lolling, so that they resembled two sentries napping on the job.

'Should we not bind them?' Quare asked.

'No need,' Longinus assured him. 'One way or another, this will be over by the time they regain their senses.'

'Still, I should rather be safe than sorry.' Quare cut strips of cloth from the Morecockneyans' clothing and secured their hands behind their backs. 'That will slow them down at least, if they awaken sooner than you expect. I would not like to find them waiting for us when we return. Perhaps we should take their weapons as well . . .'

'And dispose of them where, precisely? Caution is commendable, but what is required now, Mr Quare, is speed and stealth. From this point on, not a word unless absolutely necessary. We shall endeavour to escape detection and to avoid violence for as long as possible; with luck, we shall be in and out without any bloodshed. But if we are not so lucky, do not hesitate – strike to kill. Do you understand?'

Quare, however, did not reply.

'Mr Quare, do you understand? What has come over you, sir?'

And indeed, Quare had not heard a word Longinus had spoken. Instead, he was listening to another voice: faint but insistent. It called to him like a siren's song. Not at all the brutal invasion he had experienced earlier, as of invisible talons clawing at his heart. This was a gentle suasion, an invitation, a seduction. If this was the hunter, then what had assailed him before?

'Mr Quare!'

He blinked, recalled to himself. 'The hunter is here,' he said. 'It calls to me.'

'I hear nothing,' Longinus returned.

'As you said, I have an affinity with the timepiece.'

'Can you discern its location?'

Quare pointed upwards.

17

The Song of the Hunter

LONGINUS ASKED NO MORE QUESTIONS BUT DREW HIS GREY SCARF over his mouth and nose. It was astonishing how the man vanished behind the mask; Quare could not have guessed, had he not already known, the age or even the sex of the person who stood before him. Longinus was gone: there was only Grimalkin, a lithe, shadowy figure exuding quietly coiled menace. As Quare drew his own mask into place, he wondered if he presented a similarly forbidding aspect.

Now, from one of the pouches at his belt, Longinus produced a glass vial whose contents were aglow with the same greenish light that emanated from the powder coating the unconscious Morecockneyans cap-à-pie. He gave this a shake, at which the light brightened; holding it upraised before him, he set off down the passage. From Quare's perspective, trailing close behind, it was as if they were being led by a flitting firefly, or perhaps a fairy.

The latter association seemed all the more fitting in that the call of the hunter continued to beckon him onwards, or rather upwards, growing clearer and more enticing with every step, so that he had to keep himself from rushing ahead. The song was like no music he had ever heard; it was closer to birdsong, he decided, in that it seemed the spontaneous expression of a nature shaped to give voice to just that sound and no other; there was joy in it, a wild and carefree delight in being that lifted his heart on echoing swells, but there was also urgency, as if the watch were calling out for something needful, whose lack left it incomplete.

He recalled the words of Tiamat: *It is just what you have called it: a hunter. It hunts.* Was it hunting him? And, if so, for what purpose? *It will answer to you now*, the dragon had said, *protect you . . . but do not imagine yourself its master. It is a weapon, a very great weapon – too great to be left in the hands of men.* But was there ever a weapon that sang so sweetly?

He would not have stopped or turned back now even if it had been possible, impelled as much by his own curiosity as by any geis laid upon him by Tiamat or the hunter. Anticipation grew in him with every step. He felt that he was advancing to meet his destiny. *I am coming*, he thought, wondering if the hunter could hear him or sense his approach somehow. Perhaps his thoughts, too, made a kind of music.

At last, after a steady but not precipitous upwards climb, they reached a solid wall of packed stones. Longinus put his ear to the wall and listened. Then, satisfied, he set the glowing vial upon the ground to one side and began to prise out certain of the stones. Though they had appeared to be tightly wedged together, the stones slid out with ease, and soon there was room enough for the two men to crawl through, which they wasted no time in doing, Longinus still leading the way, the vial once again held before him.

The passage on the far side of the barrier looked no different than it had before, yet Quare sensed they had entered the precincts of the guild hall. The oppressive atmosphere lifted; it was as if they'd left a dense and gloom-ridden forest behind and, though still among the trees, had reached the out-skirts of civilization. Perhaps, he thought, it was a subtle change in the hunter's song that communicated this knowl-edge to him; he could not say for certain, but he did feel that the song, though wordless, had meaning . . . just as birdsong had its own meaning, hidden as it might be to human ears.

Longinus set a faster pace now, though he continued to move with the stealth and silence of his feline namesake. Quare, try as he might, could not match him in either respect, and he winced more than once as an errant footfall broadcast his presence. But no voices were raised in challenge, and he saw no glimmer of torchlight from ahead, just the lambent glow from the vial, preceding them like a will-o'-the-wisp.

The rough stone of the passage gave way to cut stone, and then to the long corridor of cells he'd last visited little more than a day ago – it seemed another lifetime! The corridor, too, was lightless, nor was there any hint of illumination behind any of the cell doors. He wondered if Longinus meant to make use of the same stair-master by which the two of them had escaped to the rooftop, but it appeared not, as the man passed cell after cell and made straight for the doorway at the end of the corridor.

'Hsst! Who goes there?' came a quavering voice from the last cell on the left.

Quare froze, as did Longinus; the green light winked out in an instant.

'Who's there?' the shaky voice repeated from out of the dark. It was a voice Quare recognized but had not thought ever to hear again.

Receiving no reply, the voice grew louder, edged with panic. 'For God's sake, say something! Stop this damned torture and show yourself!'

Quare kept silent, following Longinus's lead. But questions were swirling through his brain, clamouring to be asked.

'Answer me, damn you!' the voice cried angrily. 'If you mean to kill me, come and try, you damned cowardly curs!'

At this, Longinus spoke at last. 'Hsst! Quiet, man. I have no interest in killing you. I have no interest in you at all.'

Quare did not recognize this voice: a deep, intimidating growl. The voice of Grimalkin.

It did not intimidate the prisoner, however. 'You're not one of the Old Wolf's gang, are you? Listen, if you get me out of here, I swear I won't betray you!'

'I could be a French assassin for all you know, come to murder your grandmaster.'

'I don't give a fig if you are! The bloody bastard means to murder me!'

'You say you would not betray me, yet already you have offered to betray your country.'

'This is not my country! I wasn't born here, and I have no desire to die here. Let me out, damn you, or I'll bring the whole nest down on your heads, I swear it!'

'These walls are thick. No one will hear your cries.'

'Let us put it to the test, shall we?' And he began to scream: 'Help! Murder! Help! Treason!'

'Quiet!' Longinus said. 'Very well, I will see what I can do. Step away from the door.'

'Gladly,' said the voice.

The green light rekindled; by its glow, Quare saw Longinus approach the door of the cell. He hurried towards him. Longinus glanced at him and motioned for him to stay put. But he stepped close and laid a restraining hand on Longinus's arm.

'I know this man,' he whispered. 'It's—'

'Yes, there is no mistaking that uncouth accent,' Longinus whispered back.

'What do you mean to do to him?'

'I'll put him to sleep, as I did the Morecockneyans.'

'We must question him first,' Quare said.

'There is no time.'

'What's going on out there?' the voice demanded. 'How many of you are there?'

'I told you to step away,' Longinus replied in the stentorian tones of Grimalkin. Reaching into another of the pouches at his waist, he produced an iron key and fitted it to the lock. There was a dull clank of tumblers turning. Then, after replacing the key, he drew his dagger. Quare drew his own. Stepping back, Longinus gestured for Quare to open the door.

The heavy door swung inwards; both men tensed, as if expecting the prisoner to hurl himself upon them, but no one emerged. Cautiously, the glowing vial held before him like a shield, dagger at the ready, Longinus stepped into the room; Quare followed, swinging the door shut behind him.

There, blinking in the weak light, stood Gerald Pickens.

Though Quare had recognized the voice and its bland American accent, seeing the man in the flesh was a shock. He had thought Pickens dead, murdered by Aylesford along with Mansfield and Farthingale that horrible night at the Pig and Rooster. But here he stood, very much alive – though the worse for wear. His once-fine clothes were torn and stained with what looked to be blood, and his once-handsome face bore the marks of a thorough beating. His left arm hung useless in a sling; the other was upraised as if to fend off a killing blow.

'Who are you people?' he asked now. 'Why are you wearing those masks?'

'You wound me, sir,' growled Longinus. 'Have you not heard of Grimalkin?'

'I have . . . But I had not heard there were two of him!'

'Who is to say there are not three, four, a hundred Grimalkins? But we mean you no harm,' Longinus continued. 'Who are you, and how did you come to be here?'

'I'm Gerald Pickens, a journeyman of this company. As to how I came to be here, why, I scarcely know myself! But it seems I am a pawn in a larger game – a pawn about to be sacrificed.'

'What do you mean? Quickly, now!'

'Have you not heard of the foul murders that have set the whole city on edge? You called me traitor, but the real traitor is still at large somewhere in London!'

'You mean Aylesford,' said Longinus.

'Aylesford?' Pickens shook his head. 'He is dead, another victim of the traitor, or so I am told.'

'What traitor?'

'Why, the infamous Quare, of course.'

'What?' The word burst from Quare before he could help himself.

'Another journeyman of this company,' Pickens explained. 'A friend – or so I thought. But would you believe it, in the pay of the French all along. It was he who murdered Aylesford and the rest – including poor Master Magnus, God rest his soul. Only, don't you see, the man has fled. To where, who can say? Back to his masters, no doubt. But now, with the city in an uproar, the powers that be require a scapegoat. You are looking at that unfortunate man. Quare attacked me at the Pig and Rooster – from behind, the blackguard! – and left me for dead, but I was only stunned. I survived. And this is my reward! I am to hang for the crimes of another man. My name is to be blackened, my family dishonoured. So much for the king's justice!'

'This is intolerable,' Quare said.

'There is naught to be done about it now,' Longinus said.

'Take me with you!' Pickens cried. 'I won't give you away – I swear it! And I can help you navigate the twists and turns of this infernal labyrinth of a guild hall! I must be free to clear my name – to find Quare and bring him to justice.'

'You have found him,' said Quare, and pulled down his mask even as Longinus called out 'No!'

Pickens sagged back as though struck a blow. Then, gathering his courage, he said, 'So, traitor, have you come to finish the job?'

'I am as innocent as you are,' Quare said. 'I, too, was meant to be a scapegoat for these heinous crimes, but I escaped . . . with the help of Grimalkin here – the real Grimalkin.'

'Why would a thief help you escape?'

'He is no thief, any more than I am a murderer.'

'Then who . . . ?'

'Aylesford,' Quare said. 'He confessed as much to me across swords, but I was unable to dispatch him. He is the traitor – a Scottish loyalist in the pay of the French.'

'Can you prove this?' Pickens demanded.

'Alas, no,' Quare said. 'I cannot yet clear my name – or yours, for that matter. The conspiracy against us goes beyond the Old Wolf, all the way to Mr Pitt . . . or so I am reliably informed.'

'It is true,' Longinus said. 'It may well be that His Majesty himself, misled by others, has ordered your sacrifice, Mr Pickens.'

'Then why have you come here,' Pickens asked, 'if not to clear your name? Do you mean to kill the Old Wolf after all?'

'To answer that would be to unfold a story we do not have the time to tell – nor would you be likely to believe it in any case,' Quare said.

'The question is, rather, what shall we do with you, Mr Pickens?' asked Longinus. 'We cannot simply render you unconscious, as I had planned, since Mr Quare has revealed himself to you, and you would surely, whether willingly or not, reveal this in turn to the Old Wolf under questioning.'

'You cannot mean . . .'

'I should hate to murder a man in cold blood, especially an innocent man. But I will do so if there is no alternative.'

'Take me with you,' Pickens implored. 'I may be injured, but I can still be of help. I dare say I know the guild hall as well if not better than Quare does, and if it comes to a fight, why, I am right-handed and not unskilled with a blade. I am – or, rather, was, as I have now been expelled from the Most Secret and Exalted Order – a regulator. I suppose it can do me no harm to confess that now.'

'I, too, was a member of that order!' Quare said. 'Master Magnus, God rest his soul, recruited me.'

'As he did me,' Pickens said with a grin rendered ghastly by the green light and the bruises covering his face. 'I know I used to tease you about being a regulator, Quare, but I swear it was only as a joke, to deflect any suspicion from myself! I had no inkling that you might really be one!'

'Nor I you,' said Quare, grinning himself.

'Enough,' Longinus interjected in Grimalkin's growl. 'There may be a way. But know this, Mr Pickens: if you betray us by word or deed – or even by thought – I shall know it, and I shall know how to repay it. In that case, you will be the first to die.'

'I shall give you no cause to doubt me, I swear it,' said Pickens.

'We are about the business of the kingdom this night, Mr Quare and I, and the fate of crown and country may well hinge upon our success,' Longinus said. 'If you would aid us, then you must swear to obey me without question or hesitation, on your honour as a journeyman of this company, by the oath you swore to be true to His Majesty, so help you God.'

'I swear it. So help me God.'

'Very well.' Longinus put up his dagger and made his way to the back of the cell. There he paused, examining the wall, though Quare could see nothing of note there, just blocks of heavy stone mortared into place. This cell was both smaller and less well appointed than the one in which he had been held: there was no desk, no pallet, no fireplace. Clearly, after his escape, the Old Wolf had intended to take no chances with Pickens.

'I say, Quare, is it really the fabled Grimalkin?' Pickens asked him meanwhile in a whisper.

'None other,' Quare said.

'Who is he behind that mask?'

'I cannot say,' Quare replied. 'He is a man of unexpected talents. A regulator, in fact, if you can believe it.'

'I . . . scarcely know what to believe any more.'

'I know the feeling.'

'Ah, here it is.' Longinus's gloved fingers moved over the wall; with a sudden grinding sound that made Quare start, a single block of stone, at chest height, slid into the wall, leaving a hollow space. 'Mr Quare, Mr Pickens, if you please, gentlemen.'

The two men glanced at each other and then approached Longinus.

'I am no stranger to this place,' he said, addressing Pickens. 'As Mr Quare has told you, I, too, have been a regulator in my time, recruited, like yourself, by Master Magnus.' As he spoke, he reached into the hollow, then withdrew his hand.

Pickens stepped back with a cry as a narrow section of wall, extending from floor to ceiling, pivoted in silence, like a door swinging on oiled hinges, to produce an opening where none had been before. Quare, who had by now almost come to expect such surprises where Longinus was concerned, looked on with curiosity. Was this another stair-master?

'Every cell has its secrets,' said Longinus. 'The guild hall is riddled with hidden rooms and passages added piecemeal over the centuries by men whose names have been as thoroughly forgotten as their constructs – but not by me. Thus I have prepared these cells against the eventuality of my ever being imprisoned here.' He stepped into the opening, taking the wan light with him, which dwindled and then winked out altogether.

Pickens's voice wavered out of the dark. 'Where has he gone, Quare? What the devil is he up to? Does he mean to abandon us?'

Grimalkin's gruff voice replied from within the wall before Quare could answer. 'Quiet, Mr Pickens. From this moment, you will say nothing unless it is in reply to a question I have asked you.'

The light reappeared, a distant, solitary star whose shine increased until Longinus emerged back into the cell. In his arms he carried a dark bundle. 'Mr Quare, you will help Mr Pickens into these clothes.'

Pickens looked somewhat sceptical at this but did not protest or speak a word as, with Quare's help, he dressed himself in the clothing provided. His torn and bloodstained clothes he handed to Longinus, who, pinching them between his fingers with evident distaste, flung them into the opening, where they vanished as if into an abyss.

'Gentlemen,' said Longinus when at last Pickens was fully dressed, 'your masks, if you please.'

Quare tugged his mask into place; Pickens did likewise; and suddenly three Grimalkins stood in the cell where only two had entered.

Longinus studied Pickens thoughtfully. 'You'll do, Mr Pickens. I do not trust you sufficiently to provide you with a weapon, but if all goes well you shall not need one, and if things go badly the lack is not likely to matter much. Now, sir, have you heard or seen aught of an unusual watch in the possession of the Old Wolf – a hunter, in point of fact?'

'N-no,' stammered Pickens.

'That watch is our objective,' Longinus said. 'It will likely be hidden, in which case an extra pair of eyes will not go amiss.'

'What does it look like?'

'Mr Quare?' Longinus invited.

'It appears at first to be an ordinary pocket watch,' Quare said. 'Its casing is of silver, but without outward embellishment or ornamentation. Yet two peculiarities are evident upon closer inspection. First, the watch is unusually thin. Second, it lacks any winding mechanism. Should you find it, do not open it for anything.'

'If you find it, Mr Pickens, you are to alert Mr Quare or me at once,' Longinus added. 'Is that clear?'

'Absolutely . . . and yet not at all. What is the significance of this watch? Does it hold some secret message?'

'Perhaps we shall take you more deeply into our confidence once you have proved yourself worthy of it. But that is all you need to know at present. And now, gentlemen, let us return to the matter at hand. I will take the lead; Mr Pickens, you will follow; Mr Quare, you will bring up the rear. Remember: not a word, not a sound. You will keep your dagger to hand, Mr Quare, and if it seems to you that Mr Pickens is about to betray us in any way, you will use it at once, without ·hesitation.'

'I won't,' Pickens said.

Quare nodded, his mouth dry.

Longinus stepped past them, to the door of the cell, where he listened for a moment before opening it and slipping out into the hallway. Pickens followed, then Quare, who closed the door behind him. Regarding the grey shape before him, Quare drew his dagger, wondering if he could really stab the man in the back should it prove necessary. He hoped he would not have to find out.

Longinus led them to the end of the corridor, where a large, heavy door blocked their passage. He put his ear to it, and, after a moment, satisfied, produced the key that had opened the door to Pickens's cell; it proved effective here as well. They passed through in single file, Quare again bringing up the rear and closing the door behind him.

In the excitement of finding Pickens, the song of the hunter had faded to the back of Quare's mind. Now it surged forward again, louder and more insistent, as if some fresh urgency had arisen. He did not know how to communicate this to Longinus without speaking, and yet he did not dare say a word; they had entered a more frequently travelled area of the guild hall, one lit by candles burning in sconces, though this passage was deserted now. Ancient oil paintings and tapestries decorated the walls, their subjects faded to mere suggestions of shape and colour.

Longinus glided like a fog across the floor. Pickens could not match him but acquitted himself well enough, as did Quare, whose attention was divided between the summons only he could hear and the back of the man he might at any moment be called upon to murder.

They traversed one corridor, then another, then climbed a flight of stairs, all without encountering a soul. But just as they reached the top of the stairs and entered another candlelit hallway, this one lined with doors, a man came around the far corner, short and rotund, waddling with haste. It was Master Malrubius, the Old Wolf's sycophant and shadow.

Malrubius stopped short at the sight of them, as did the armed servant who stepped into view beside him an instant later. Quare and Pickens also froze, but Longinus accelerated.

Quick as lightning, two blurs shot down the corridor; each found its mark, and the two men stiffened and collapsed before they could cry out a warning or indeed make any sound at all. By the time they hit the floor, Longinus was kneeling beside them to retrieve what he had thrown. He glanced up as Quare and Pickens arrived at a run, putting a finger to his mask for silence.

'Have you killed them?' Pickens demanded in a breathless whisper.

'They are merely unconscious,' said Longinus.

'Good.' With no more warning than that, Pickens drew back his boot and delivered a vicious kick to the unprotected face of Master Malrubius. And then another. Quare heard the crack of the man's nose breaking. By which time he had resheathed his blade and locked his arms about Pickens from behind, pinning his arms to his chest and hauling him back.

'Let me go!' Pickens said, still whispering, though he did not struggle to free himself. 'My arm—'

He fell silent as Longinus, who had risen to his feet, stepped up and laid the edge of a dagger against his throat.

'You are making me regret my decision, Mr Pickens,' he said.

'You saw what that swine did to me,' Pickens gasped out in reply. 'He doesn't deserve to live. Give me a dagger and I'll finish the job.'

'We have not come here to murder anyone if we can help it,' Longinus said. 'Personal vendettas have no place in our mission. If you cannot restrain your temper, I shall have no choice but to give you the same treatment I have already administered to these gentlemen.'

It was a moment before Pickens replied. He sighed, and Quare felt the tension drain from his body. 'Very well, Grimalkin. I'll put vengeance aside . . . for now.'

'Let him go, Mr Quare,' Longinus said. Quare did so. Yet Longinus had not removed his dagger, and thus Pickens did not dare to so much as twitch.

'This is the last interruption I will countenance,' Longinus said, gazing into the other man's eyes. 'You will follow my commands with alacrity, keep silent, and otherwise give me no cause to employ this dagger, for I assure you, Mr Pickens, I will not hesitate to use it, and you will not receive another warning before I do. The substance coating this blade will put you to sleep in an instant, and we will leave you behind, to the tender mercies of Master Malrubius, which you are already so well acquainted with. Is that clear?'

'Quite.'

Longinus put up his dagger. 'Very well. I think it time that we take a less public route. Mr Pickens, you will keep watch. Mr Quare, if you would assist me ... .'

Longinus unlocked one of the doors off the hall and pushed it open; then he and Quare, with some difficulty in the case of Malrubius, dragged the two bodies into what, it became evident, by the greenish light of Longinus's vial, was an old and disused storeroom containing oak barrels caked with dust and rat droppings. Malrubius left a trail of blood across the stones of the floor, but there was nothing to be done about it now, Quare supposed. Pickens, meanwhile, looked on from behind his mask, dividing his attention between them and the empty hallway.

'Come along, Mr Pickens,' Longinus said at last from inside the room.

Pickens stepped forward but baulked at entering the store-room, as if afraid that Longinus meant to leave him there after all, slumbering alongside Malrubius and the guardsman. Nor, Quare reflected, was that fear unfounded, for the room had no other visible exit. But he had experienced enough of Longinus's surprises to feel confident another was imminent.

'It's all right, Pickens,' Quare said. 'One thing I've learned about Grimalkin: he always leaves himself a way out.'

'Mr Pickens, if you please,' Longinus said.

Pickens entered the room. Longinus nodded to Quare, who closed the door behind him. They stood uncomfortably close in the small, ill-lit space, the two unconscious men sprawled at their feet.

The guardsman was quiet as a corpse, but Malrubius was making small sounds of distress, rather like a piglet rooting in the ground; Quare thought his breathing must be impeded by his broken nose, or perhaps by blood draining into his throat. He had no more love for Malrubius than Pickens did, but neither did he care to stand by while the man choked to death.

Kneeling, he repositioned the head so as to improve the man's air flow.

Longinus, meanwhile, had turned to rummage behind a stack of barrels that reached from floor to ceiling. A sharp clicking sound, and the front of the stack slid into the back, exposing a half tube, like a chimney, that rose into darkness. 'Now we ascend,' Longinus said. 'I will go first. Then Mr Pickens. Mr Quare, you will bring up the rear.'

Quare glanced up at this. 'Shall we not first bind and gag your latest victims?'

'No need,' Longinus said with a shake of his head. 'They will not wake for hours, and our own time grows most pressing; the bulk of the night is already behind us. Take this, Mr Quare.' He passed over the glowing vial, which Quare, standing, accepted. 'Gentlemen, I will await you above.' With that, Longinus stepped into the half tube and turned to face them, arms at his sides. There was another clicking sound, and suddenly, to the accompaniment of rattling gears, he was rising, borne swiftly out of sight.

'What wizardry is this!' exclaimed Pickens.

'No wizardry,' Quare replied with a chuckle. 'Merely common horological principles applied on a grander scale.' Though saying that did not diminish the wonder he too felt.

'Who built this mechanism?' Pickens demanded. 'And how is it that Grimalkin should know of it?'

Quare shrugged. 'I cannot say.'

'I thought I knew the guild hall as well as anyone,' Pickens said. 'I see now that I was mistaken. About that . . . and other things.'

As he spoke, the rattling sound returned, bringing with it the platform, empty now.

'You next,' Quare told him.

'Is it quite safe?'

'Grimalkin did not hesitate.'

'That is far from reassuring. The man is rash and impulsive.'

'He is also our only chance to get through this in one piece.'

'Good point.' Pickens stepped into the half tube just as Longinus had done. And was carried as quickly aloft.

As he waited for the platform to return, Quare focused again on the song of the hunter. Its urgency was unabated, as was its beauty. How the music was made, how it reached him, and him alone, were mysteries he could not unravel; he knew only that the watch was a mechanism that made Magnus's marvels seem crude by comparison. He had examined it, seen its workings stir inexplicably to life, experienced, for the briefest instant, the release of its uncanny destructive power – which, despite everything, he could not help thinking had been merely a fraction of what it was capable of, under the right conditions . . . whatever they might be. He imagined whole armies laid to waste in the blink of an eye, proud cities reduced to rubble. And here he was now, closer than ever to claiming it for himself . . . or, rather, he reminded himself with a sinking heart, for a creature of the Otherwhere, whose unwilling agent he had become. Like it or not, when he finally held the hunter in his hands, he would call for Tiamat . . . and he had no doubt that the dragon would come to claim its prize.

The rattle of the returning platform roused him. He stepped in, then turned to face outwards, arms at his sides. He heard a click, followed by the ratcheting of gears, and felt the gathering force of the mechanism an instant before it engaged and lifted him more smoothly than he would have thought possible. The pallid green light of the vial he clutched in one hand slid upwards along with him like sap rising in the trunk of a tree.

Then the platform slowed and halted, and there was Longinus, pulling him into a storeroom the twin of the one he had left behind, save that this one was lit by a solitary candle set in an iron brace upon one wall. Quare, standing beside Pickens, watched as Longinus reached behind the stack of barrels from whose hollow insides he had just emerged; another click, and the missing front of the stack swivelled around and back into place.

Longinus turned to them, his eyes hard and glittering as chips of flint. 'Here is where it gets interesting, gentlemen,' he whispered. 'I regret to say that there is no secret entrance to the Old Wolf's den. Or, if there is, even I do not know of it. Nor will my key unlock that door. I must pick the lock. While I am doing so, we will be at our most vulnerable. If we are discovered, and an alarm is raised, we shall have no recourse but to fight our way back out. I do not rate our chances highly in that regard. Thus, it is essential that anyone who stumbles upon us be silenced before they can give warning. As I will be otherwise occupied, and Mr Pickens is unarmed, that duty falls to you, Mr Quare.'

He nodded.

Longinus produced a watch from within the folds of his cloak. 'It is almost three o'clock. I do not think we can safely tarry more than an hour.'

'But what if the hunter we seek is not here?' Pickens asked. 'What if the Old Wolf has taken it to his chambers for the night?'

'It is here,' Quare said before Longinus could reply.

Pickens threw him a sharp glance. 'How can you know that?'

'Let's just say I have a feeling. A very strong feeling.'

'But—'

'Enough,' interjected Longinus. 'Let us be about our business, gentlemen.'

He listened for a moment at the door of the storeroom before cracking it open and slipping out. Pickens followed, and Quare came after, emerging into an empty hallway. The candles in their sconces had been extinguished for the night, and the greenish light of the vial in his hand gave everything a murky, underwater glow. Pickens and Longinus held vials of their own. Longinus was already halfway down the corridor, heading for the door of the Old Wolf's den, Pickens as close behind him as a shadow. Quare made to draw his blade, then, reconsidering, unslung his crossbow instead, armed it, and hastened after them, his heart keeping time with the song of the hunter, which had, once again, ratcheted up its intensity, as if sensing his approach.

Longinus reached the door and knelt before it. Pickens stood at his back, holding his vial up to illuminate the lock while glancing up and down the corridor, though little was visible beyond the nimbus of their chemically generated lights.

Quare's skin prickled with the sense of unseen eyes upon him. He had always felt this way in the guild hall – and not without reason. But there was no obvious sign of observation now. The doors on either side of the corridor, as far as he could tell, remained closed, and no sound intruded on the hush of the great house or the music of the hunter that only he seemed able to hear. Luck, it appeared, was with them.

A faint click from the door announced Longinus's success. He stood, tucking his lockpick away and then drawing his sword. He locked eyes with Quare and Pickens in turn. Then, with a nod, he cracked the Old Wolf's door open just wide enough to slip through. Pickens pushed in after him, and Quare followed, once again shutting the door behind him.

The instant he did so, sparks flared out of the darkness. Suddenly torches were ablaze, revealing perhaps a dozen guardsmen with pikes – and, in some cases, pistols – pointed in their direction. Revealed as well was the Old Wolf, who regarded them from behind his desk with a smile of predatory satisfaction on his fleshy, florid face.

Quare took this in through senses dulled by the wild din of the hunter; its song had skidded into a shrill caterwauling that had him pressing the hand that held the vial to the side of his head as if its light might somehow penetrate and soothe his skull. It occurred to him that perhaps the hunter hadn't been calling to him at all. Perhaps it had been warning him away.

Pickens cursed, at which the Old Wolf heaved himself erect.

'Drop your weapons, gentlemen. I shall not ask twice.'

Longinus seemed to consider his chances for a moment, then complied with the command. Quare followed his lead, lowering the crossbow to the floor.

Grandmaster Wolfe's smile widened, and he leaned forward over the wooden desk, his large hands, with their glittering rings, laid flat on its surface. 'I had hoped my little trap might snare the great Grimalkin, but I did not think to catch three. How positively profligate! Is this all of you, or should I be expecting more?'

No one answered.

'Remove your masks,' the Old Wolf said. 'I would see your faces.' After a moment, he added: 'Do it, or I will have it done, and none too gently.'

'You mean to kill us in any case,' said Longinus in the gruff voice of Grimalkin.

'Of course. But not before you are put to the question. A good deal of unpleasantness lies ahead for you, I'm afraid. A good deal of pain and suffering. But it need not begin now.'

Longinus pulled off his mask and flung it defiantly to the floor.

'Lord Wichcote,' said the Old Wolf without batting an eyelid. 'I cannot say I am surprised. Your involvement in this affair has been most suspicious from the start. You should have stayed ensconced behind the walls of your estate, my lord. Your title will not protect you here, nor will His Majesty intervene.'

It struck Quare that the grandmaster had not recognized Longinus, the servant, but saw only the lord. Class, it seemed, could be a more effective disguise than any mask.

When Longinus did not reply, the Old Wolf shifted his gaze to Quare and Pickens. 'And what of these two? Who else have we caught in our web? Shall I guess? Nay, it is no guess. If Wichcote is here, Quare cannot be far behind.'

Quare tugged his own mask down.

'The prodigal returns. Alas, I'm afraid I cannot welcome you with open arms, Mr Quare. No fatted calf for you. But never fear: you shall receive the welcome you deserve.' He looked to Pickens. 'And you, sir? I confess, I cannot imagine who you might be. The servant who spirited Mr Quare away? Or the real Grimalkin, perhaps?'

The mask came off.

'Mr Pickens,' said the Old Wolf, straightening up and seeming surprised for once. 'I am disappointed to find you in such disreputable company. For all your protestations of innocence, it would seem you are a traitor after all.'

'It is you who are the traitor,' Pickens shot back.

'Keep a civil tongue in your head, sir,' the grandmaster growled, 'or I shall keep it for you – in a jar.' He addressed Longinus. 'What game are you playing, my lord? Coming here dressed as Grimalkin like some urchin on Gunpowder Night! I suppose Mr Quare must have brought you.'

'I am playing no game, I assure you.'

The Old Wolf chuckled, a phlegmy rumble. 'Why, am I to believe that *you* are Grimalkin? A man of sixty or more? It is absurd on its face, quite apart from the fact that Grimalkin – the real Grimalkin – stole the very watch from you that you have come here to reclaim. Or was that theft a charade? Are you, perhaps, in league with Grimalkin? Is he likely to join us after all?'

Longinus shrugged but said nothing.

'I have set guards outside this door, my lord. No one will be getting in – or out – unless I give the word.' As he spoke, he gestured to one of the guardsmen, who began to move about the room, lighting candles from his torch; when he had finished, he extinguished that torch, as well as the others, so that the garish illumination was replaced by a more mellow flickering of light and shadow.

'You will answer my questions truthfully,' the Old Wolf said meanwhile. 'If not here and now, then later, in circumstances much less pleasant . . . for you.'

'Your threats do not frighten me,' Longinus rejoined. 'I have faced far worse in my time. It is you, Sir Thaddeus, who should be afraid.'

This elicited another chuckle. 'What, of a toothpick like you? Why, I could snap you in half with my bare hands! As for your associates' – he gestured to the guards – 'I think I may rely on these gentlemen to protect me.'

'I am speaking of the watch,' Longinus answered. 'The hunter.'

'Yes, the watch. A most intriguing timepiece. I confess I have been unable to unlock its secrets.'

'Then you should count yourself most fortunate,' said Longinus. 'Be wise as well, Sir Thaddeus, and return the watch to me. It is my property, after all. No real harm has yet been done. Let me take it back and keep it safe.'

'I think not,' the Old Wolf said. 'If the watch is a weapon, as Mr Quare avers, and as I do believe, then it belongs to England, especially now, in her hour of need. If you were a patriot, my lord, you would see that and help me discover how to use it.'

'It is because I am a patriot that I do not.'

'Bah. I do not think you know the first thing about this watch, despite having had it in your possession. I think it defeated you as much as it does me. But it did not defeat Magnus, did it?'

'No.' Quare spoke up now, ignoring the clamour in his head. 'It killed him.'

'But not, I suspect, before he communicated the secret of its operation to you.' He nodded, and six guardsmen stepped forward as one to take hold of Quare, Longinus and Pickens while the remainder of their brethren kept pistols aimed at them. Pickens struggled, to no avail, as did Quare, though Longinus offered no resistance. Grandmaster Wolfe, meanwhile, opened a drawer of his desk and produced a small leather-bound tool kit. He laid this out on the surface of the desk and then stepped to one side, nodding again to the guardsmen. 'Bring him,' he said.

The pair of guardsmen who had taken charge of Quare frogmarched him around the desk and pushed him down into the Old Wolf's voluminous chair. They remained standing to either side of him. Longinus and Pickens were similarly flanked.

'Now, Mr Quare,' the grandmaster said, stepping forward again. 'I find I have been too lenient with you in the past. I shall be taking a firmer hand now.' As he spoke, he took a pocket watch – *the* pocket watch, as Quare saw at once – from his waistcoat and turned it in his pudgy fingers, the silver casing winking like a coin. 'Strange to think that such a small thing could possess power enough to win a war. I have examined this watch most thoroughly, and a more curious and confounding timepiece I have never encountered. It appears to be nothing more than a child's toy. It lacks a winding mechanism. It has no recognizable numbers painted upon its face, only sigils of arcane significance. My finest tools could not prise open its casing – yet behold how that same casing springs open of itself when the hour and minute hands are properly aligned.'

Quare looked on with a sense of mounting dismay as the Old Wolf manipulated the hands of the watch just as he himself had done in Master Magnus's study . . . and with the same result. The fact that those hands were carved in the semblance of a wingless dragon had taken on a new and decidedly sinister significance, reminding him – were any reminder necessary – of Tiamat.

Another nod from the grandmaster, and each of the two guards flanking him grabbed one of Quare's arms, lifted it over the top of the desk and slammed it down, then held it there in a grip of iron. The Old Wolf set the opened watch face-down on the table before him, between his arms. 'Let us begin with the workings. Of what are they made, sir? Wood? Bone? Some new substance heretofore unknown to science? I confess I cannot say.'

'No more can I,' Quare answered, shuddering at the sight of the gears, wheels and pinions packed so elegantly into the tight interior of the hunter, all of a silver so pale as to be almost translucent. He recalled all too well how his blood had made the inert workings bloom with fiery incandescence and take on for a brief moment a sickening semblance of life. Yet at the same time, he felt the sovereign pull of the timepiece, and he knew that if his hands had not been immobilized, he would have snatched it up. The roaring in his head grew louder.

'Thus far I have come, but no further,' the Old Wolf said. 'I have searched Master Magnus's notes in vain for the means of powering the watch. Yet I know – we both know, Mr Quare, do we not? – that such a means exists. What is it? Tell me.'

'No.'

Grandmaster Wolfe nodded, as if he had expected no other reply. He leaned forward and calmly opened the tool kit he had placed upon the table. Within were not implements of the horologist's art, as Quare had expected, but the shining, sharp-edged tools of a surgeon. Quare's eyes widened; he felt his heart quail.

'I am going to ask you again, Mr Quare,' the Old Wolf said as he removed a scalpel from the kit. 'Each time you refuse to answer, or respond with a lie, I will remove one of your fingers.'

Quare struggled to rise from the chair, but the grip of the guards was unbreakable. Now a third guard came over and forced his left hand open, until his fingers were splayed upon the table, his palm pressed down against the wood.

'You call yourself a man of science?' interjected Longinus from across the room. 'You're nothing but a butcher! Courage, Mr Quare. Tell him nothing. Remember what is at stake! Re—' He broke off as one of the guards punched him in the face.

'Yes, remember, Mr Quare,' said the Old Wolf. 'Remember that you are an Englishman, a journeyman of the Worshipful Company of Clockmakers who has sworn a solemn oath to our Sovereign Lord the King's Majesty. Why would any loyal Englishman, having the means to spare king and country the grievous losses of a war whose outcome is, to say the least, uncertain, withhold it? He would not. If you would show yourself loyal, speak now. Share your knowledge of this watch – or weapon, rather.'

Quare could not concentrate for the roaring between his ears. His skull rang with it. How was it the others could not hear? He shook his head to clear it, but the noise intensified, bringing tears to his eyes.

'What, do you weep already?' demanded the Old Wolf in a scornful voice. 'I will give you something to weep about!' And without hesitation, as if this were not the first time he had performed such an action, he sliced through the little finger of Quare's left hand.

The blade passed cleanly through the middle joint of his finger. It happened so fast that he felt no pain at first, just the scalpel gliding through his skin and an unpleasant popping sensation as the ligaments holding the phalanges together were severed. Then the top of his finger lay upon the table like a white grub. Blood welled from the stump, shockingly red in the candlelight.

'Ready to answer, Mr Quare?' the Old Wolf inquired.

Quare moaned as pain throbbed into his awareness, carried along on the beating of his heart. Feeling his gorge rise, he glanced away from the ruin of his hand. Pickens looked pale as a ghost, slumping in the grasp of his captors as if about to faint, while Longinus, a bruise already blooming below his right eye, was staring at the table with an expression of horror that seemed to transcend any physical cause. Horror . . . but also a hunger terrible to see.

It was that which recalled Quare to his senses. That and the gasp of surprise from Grandmaster Wolfe. Looking down, he saw that the flow of blood from his hand was streaming to the hunter as if following a groove cut into the table. As he had witnessed before, the watch drank the liquid, absorbing it. It began to glow like a hot coal. At the same time, the works leapt into motion, gears whirring in a silent crimson blur.

'What in God's name . . .' The scalpel dropped from the Old Wolf's fingers to clatter upon the desktop, and he took a step back.

At the same time, the three guards attending to Quare recoiled as one, releasing him in their instinctive retreat from the engorged timepiece.

Quare's maimed hand moved of its own accord to claim the watch. The instant he touched it, a powerful shock reverberated through his body and across his whole awareness. A black wave rolled in from one side and swept him along with it. It seemed to carry him not just out of the room but out of himself.

All was darkness. He floated in it, suspended. The words of Genesis flashed into his mind: *And the earth was without form, and void; and darkness was upon the face of the deep* . . .

He felt that he had come to such a place. Nothing existed here: all was potential, emptiness fraught with what could be, lacking only the spark of creation to make the immanent real. Yet he also felt, with a certainty he did not question, that something needful was lacking for that spark to be struck.

This was not the Otherwhere, of that he had no doubt. It was something else, something more primal still.

He realized then that he was no longer hearing the song of the hunter. There was no sound at all. Or, rather, only a silence so deep it was itself a kind of sound – a sound that passed beyond the audible and into the realm of the tangible. He felt it all around him, this pregnant silence; it was the darkness in which he floated; it coursed about him like a playful ocean; its currents caressed him with velveteen softness, batting him about. It swarmed him.

It *purred*.

And suddenly Quare knew, again without question, what had happened to the cats in Master Magnus's study. They were here. Just as the watch had absorbed his blood, so had it absorbed their furry essences, sucking the spirits from their bodies and leaving only empty husks behind. And that meant . . .

I am inside the watch, he realized.

He, too, had been absorbed. Was he dead then? His body lying slumped over the Old Wolf's desk? Was he – his spirit, rather – trapped here now, a prisoner of the watch? Had the hunter captured its prey?

Panic and terror rose up in him, but he had no way to express them. He had no body here: no limbs to lash out with, no mouth with which to scream. He floated in the dark . . . yet was himself a thing of darkness. Would he, in time, flow into the surrounding dark, disperse into it, forget himself entirely? Even if he could have cried out, called on Tiamat, he did not think the dragon could hear him – or, if it did hear, breach the walls of this prison. The geis laid upon him had no power here. There would be no rescue. No escape.

He found himself thinking of Master Magnus, who had set

all this in motion by sending him to steal the timepiece from Lord Wichcote . . . and then given the watch a taste of his blood. Had he known somehow that this would be the result? Had he intended for it to happen?

Quare understood with dawning dismay that his mission on that moonlit night had been very different from what he had been told. Why had he not seen it sooner? He had been too busy running for his life, from one dire mishap to another. But now that there was no place left to run, the logic of it unfolded to him. Lord Wichcote – that is to say, Longinus – must have been in on it as well. Perhaps part of whatever had really been going on had been, as Longinus claimed, a trap laid to catch the false Grimalkin, the young woman he had overpowered upon the rooftop. But there was more to it than that. There had to be. The trap, Quare felt, had been laid for him as well. But why? To what purpose?

He had mourned Master Magnus's death. Now he cursed his name. For lying to him. Using him. Leaving him with questions that had no answers, and an eternity in which to ask them. *Why, this is hell*, he thought with a flicker of hysteria like the first hint of a madness that would engulf him whether he resisted it or not. And why should he resist? Better to surrender. Perhaps that was the only escape possible.

A ragged giggle issued from out of the dark. Or, no, it was the darkness itself that laughed. A terrible sound, like sanity ripping. Then it spoke, which was far, far worse.

'*Well, well. Look what the cats dragged in.*'

The words came from everywhere at once – including, it seemed, from inside him . . . to the extent he still had an inside. Was this his own voice that addressed him, a voice spun out of the threads of his unravelled reason? Quare was losing his sense of separateness, of self.

'You wound me, Mr Quare. Do you not recognize my voice?'

And with that, he did. It was not precisely the voice he remembered but instead a close facsimile, as if whatever addressed him now lacked the equipment for human speech and had been forced to make do with materials unsuited to the task. Even so, there was no mistaking the voice of his late master, Theophilus Magnus.

18

What the Cats Dragged In

THE VOICE OF QUARE'S DEAD MASTER GIGGLED AGAIN. *'BEHOLD.'*

Tendrils of darkness coalesced into the shape of a man, a living shadow cast by no light that Quare could see. Here he saw by some other means, as if with his mind's eye. The figure thus revealed stood tall and unbowed, not the hunched, twisted shape of Master Theophilus Magnus but a paragon of male perfection, a David carved from ebony rather than marble, sleek-muscled as a god ... yet sexless, its groin smooth. Around this statuesque figure, familiar details swam into focus: a desk, chairs, bookcases and stacks of books, even burning candles ... all bereft of colour: only black and white and shades of grey. Yet it was unquestionably Master Magnus's study – or, rather, a close facsimile of it ... just as the voice was a close facsimile of the master's. Quare perceived that he, too, now possessed a shape, a kind of inverse silhouette, a white space that felt less like the outline of his own body than what was left after the dark had drained away.

'You may speak,' said the shadow of the man.

'Is it really you, Master?' Quare asked, and the voice that issued from out of the white space that defined him was both

familiar and strange, like his own voice echoing from a great distance.

'It is I,' came the reply. 'And yet not I. That is to say, the man I was is only part of what I am becoming.'

'And what is that?' Quare asked, not at all sure he wanted to know.

The darkness opposite him unravelled, then re-formed. In an instant, the shadow of the man was gone, along with the furnishings on that side of the room and, indeed, the room itself: all blown away like so much smoke in a gust of wind. In their place hovered a wingless dragon so black it glowed. Quare's first thought was that Tiamat had found him, that merely thinking of the dragon had been enough to summon it, though he had not called for it to come. But of course this was not Tiamat.

'Is it not wonderful?' demanded the dragon in the voice of Master Magnus. 'Do you not see? The hunter is not a device for telling time. Nor is it a weapon, precisely. It is, rather, a chamber of sorts, an alembic in which the essences of various creatures may be combined to a new and higher purpose. In short, it is an egg. A dragon's egg.'

Quare was speechless. Longinus had told him that dragons had been born from the stuff of the Otherwhere, and Tiamat had indirectly confirmed that. Neither of them had said anything about an egg, however.

In the next instant, the dragon was gone, its dark substance shredding then coalescing again into the shape of Master Magnus's study. Of the master himself, there was no sign. Yet his voice continued to issue from all around. 'The egg draws sustenance from the outer world. It feeds upon our blood, our very lives. My blood and yours, Mr Quare. My life, and the lives of my cats. All mingled to quicken what lay quiescent until wakened by our presence.'

'*So I am dead, then. The hunter has killed me.*' He felt numb.

The disquieting giggle came again. '*Rather, it has saved your life.*'

'*I don't understand . . .*'

'*How could you? Even I succumbed to madness when I awakened here, a lone mind adrift in a sea of eternal night, with only the squalling spirits of my cats for company. Many years passed before I regained my reason, like a crippled man relearning the use of his limbs. Little wonder that you would be confused.*'

'*Master, you have only been dead a matter of days.*'

'*Time runs differently here, Mr Quare, as you shall learn. Perhaps it does not run at all. That is a question beyond the grasp of human intellect, I fear. But soon I shall leave all that behind and be born anew, with knowledge and power beyond anything you can imagine.*'

'*Born how?*' Quare asked.

'*Why, by hatching out of this egg, of course.*'

'*And then what?*'

'*I shall spread my wings, sir,*' Magnus answered as if this were a foregone conclusion and Quare a dunce for having failed to see it. '*I shall bring order and reason to the world. Superstition and ignorance will be eradicated. There will be no more war, no more religion, only the fearless pursuit of scientific inquiry, under my direction.*'

'*But Master . . . do you imagine a dragon will be welcomed with open arms – a creature of legend suddenly made real? You will be seen as a demon, a monster to be slain. Indeed, I can well imagine that your presence might end the war between England and her enemies – but only so that they may unite against you.*'

'*Let them try. They shall learn to fear – and to obey. But I will not be restricted to the body of a dragon, Mr Quare. Dragons are protean creatures, or so I now perceive. I will walk the Earth as a man – as*' *the man I should have been, my outer form at last a match for my inner qualities. People will follow such a man willingly – perhaps not all of them, but enough.'* Again the darkness took the shape of a godlike man.

Quare felt a shudder pass through him. *'Listen to yourself, Master – you are talking like a tyrant, not the man I knew . . . the man whose death I mourned.'*

'In that, you were too hasty – though I appreciate the sentiment, of course. But as to the other: perhaps you did not know me as well as you thought. Perhaps I did not know myself. My perceptions were as stunted and twisted as the body that was my prison. But now I have escaped from both.'

'This is monstrous,' Quare said.

'Miraculous, rather. Yes, science has its miracles, too! For what else is this mechanism but a thing of science – an artificial egg, incubator of dragons, of gods?'

'Of madness.'

'You disappoint me, Mr Quare, indeed you do. You, too, have known what it is to be mocked and scorned, to have the particulars of your birth held against you. Why would you not rejoice at the prospect of a world in which an orphan or a bastard could rise as far as his talents might take him?'

'That world I would welcome. But you speak of fear and compelled obedience. I will not be part of such a world.'

'You are part of it already. When the hunter – the egg – drank our blood, it tasted us. It sifted our qualities and judged us. It chose how to use us in its great work of growing a dragon.'

'You speak as if it were intelligent.'

'Is a clock intelligent? A loom? This is a device, Mr Quare. A machine. It does what it was built to do – no more, no less.'

'Built by whom?'

'That I do not know . . . yet.'

'But you knew the hunter was no ordinary timepiece. You've known that for years. You and Longinus – Lord Wichcote, that is – worked together once to discover its secrets. He has confessed as much to me. Surely he must have told you of his experiences in Märchen. Of the Otherwhere. Of Wachter, Doppler, and the rest.'

'Of course he did – though now I perceive, for everything you know is known to me in this place, that his lordship omitted some choice information. That extraordinary foot of his, for instance. And to think that Grimalkin was under my nose all that time!' His laughter rumbled. 'But Lord Wichcote is a man who likes his secrets. No matter. For many years, we did work together, as you say. If one of us had spilled even a drop of blood during those investigations, things might have gone very differently! But we had no inkling that blood was the key. No clue whatsoever. And finally, out of frustration, or greed, or an excess of caution, perhaps, fearful of drawing the attention of Doppler or some greater power, Lord Wichcote stopped cooperating. He refused to grant me access to the hunter, or even to tell me where he had hidden it. We continued to work together on other matters – he remained a key asset of the Most Secret and Exalted Order. But a certain mutual trust was spoiled.'

'Is that why you sent me to his house that night? To steal the hunter, so you could resume your investigations?'

'I had no delusions on that score. Even at his age, Lord Wichcote is a deadly swordsman, a consummate fighter. I doubt there is a regulator alive who could best him. Certainly not you. No, you could never have stolen the hunter from him.'

'What then? Did you expect him to simply give it to me?'

'In point of fact, yes, I did.'

'And why should he have done that?'

'Have you not marked the resemblance between you? Lord Wichcote is your father, Mr Quare.'

Quare had not thought he could be any more discomposed than he was already. But in that, he had been wrong. 'Lord Wichcote . . . Longinus . . . my father?'

'You are his bastard by-blow. I tracked you down, brought you to London, trained you in the skills of a journeyman and regulator – all so that I might have a trump card with his lordship. It is always wise, I have found, when dealing with the gentry, to do so from a position of strength. They do not generally feel themselves bound by honour or any other constraint when dealing with those they perceive to be their inferiors.'

'But you are wrong. I asked Lord Wichcote himself if he were not my father. I put the question to him directly, face to face. He denied it.'

'Of course he did. Such is the way of the world. But make no mistake: you are his son, his bastard, and he knows it well.'

'Has he always known?'

'No. He had not known of your existence until the very day I dispatched you to him. That same afternoon, I sent a confidential note to his lordship detailing the particulars of your parentage and informing him that you would be paying him a visit later that same night. Knowing that there are men in this world who do not welcome their by-blows with open arms, I warned him in no uncertain terms that if any harm befell you, I would release all the details to His Majesty . . . and to the vultures of Fleet Street. If he wished to avoid disgrace or worse, he need only hand over the hunter to you. I did not like to resort to blackmail, but there was no choice. Time was running out, you see. Others were on the trail of the hunter, among them, or so I thought, the notorious Grimalkin. I did not have faith in my old friend's ability to keep the hunter safe from this paragon of thievery. And was I not right to be concerned? So it was that I decided the time had come to play my trump card. And I feel certain that his lordship would have given you the hunter, Mr Quare . . . if

Grimalkin – a false Grimalkin, as it appears, and a woman no less! – had not got there first.'

'Why didn't you tell me any of this before?' Quare demanded. *'I trusted you . . . looked upon you as I might have a father.'*

'Yes, that made it all very easy, I must say. You would do well in the future, Mr Quare, to be a good deal less trusting. At least you need not search for a substitute father any longer. And after all, haven't things turned out for the best? You retrieved the watch from the female masquerading as Grimalkin and returned it to me. I pricked my finger in examining it, and discovered the secret key I had looked for in vain all those years. Thanks to you, I have shed my ruined body and will soon enjoy a better one, along with the power to reshape the world. I owe you much – and never let it be said that I do not repay my debts.'

'How – by killing me and bringing me here?'

'Did I not say that the hunter had saved your life? I sensed the moment Aylesford's dagger slid into your heart, Mr Quare. I watched your essence – your soul, for lack of a better word – crawl like a moth from its chrysalis. I called it to me, and it came, a poor blind thing drawn along a bloody umbilical. I grasped it in my hand. I hold it still.'

At this, he extended one hand. There, on a palm as black as midnight, sat a fragile moth the colour of blood – the only bit of colour Quare had glimpsed since he had awakened here. The sight of it sent a shock through him; though he had never before seen such a thing, still he recognized it, felt instinctively that it was a part of him. The moth seemed to recognize him as well. It fluttered its wings but could not rise from Master Magnus's palm, as if held down by an immense weight. Its blood-red colour flared as it struggled, like a cooling ember fanned by a breeze, but almost at once the colour ebbed, fading from scarlet through rouge to a pale rose, as the moth subsided in exhaustion. Magnus closed his fingers around it, caging it within.

'I know about the dragon Tiamat and the compulsion laid upon you. But I have broken its hold. That jealous creature has no dominion over you any more – not as long as I hold this part of you, and you hold the hunter. Thus joined, no man or dragon can stand against us. We are invincible, Mr Quare! I will protect you from your enemies. From death itself. In return, you will be my agent in the world. My protector. My voice. And more. For you see, I cannot hatch from this egg alone. I need your help. I must grow stronger, and for that I require sustenance.'

Quare felt a chill. *'You mean blood.'*

'Only then will I be strong enough to hatch. You will be midwife to that birth. That is your purpose, your glorious destiny!'

'Glorious? It is obscene. Is that how you would usher in your bright and shining age of reason? On a tide of blood?'

'There is no birth without blood. But I will kill no one.'

'No, I suppose that is to be my *task.'*

'You will carry me across the Channel, into the thick of the war. There I dare say we shall find a sufficiency of blood – blood that will be put to a better use than fertilizing some farmer's field.'

'I won't do it,' Quare said. *'The Master Magnus I knew would never have considered such a vile scheme. You are no longer the man you were – no longer even human – you have become what the others called you: Master Mephistopheles! If you are trapped here, so much the better. I will not help to loose you upon the world. Kill me if you like – I won't lift a finger to help you.'*

'We are both part of something greater than we were,' Magnus replied. *'Embrace that truth or fight against it – in the end it matters not. Our wants count for nothing against the needs of the dragon. That, too, I have learned. Now you will learn it.'*

With that, Quare found himself back in his body. How

much time had passed, he did not know, but he was still seated at the Old Wolf's desk, grasping the hunter in his maimed hand. But that hand was no longer bleeding, though the wound had not healed. He could see the raw, ravaged flesh, the white wink of bone . . .There was the stub of his finger on the desktop, just where it had been sliced away . . . but now shrivelled and dark as a raisin, as if every drop of vitality had been drained from it.

The hunter had lost its crimson glow and faded to a pale roseate hue, like the moth that Magnus had held in his hand. Quare could feel the flutter of its pulse, twinned to the rapid beating of his heart as if it were some kind of parasite sucking the life from him. The ornate hands of the watch were crawling in no ordered progression, moving neither clockwise nor anticlockwise but instead seeming to quest about the face of the timepiece like the roving antennae of a blind insect, pointing with unguessable intent towards those strange symbols he could not decipher . . . could barely even focus on, as if they, too, were in motion, squirming to escape his sight. Once he had gazed admiringly on those hands, carved with such exquisite craftsmanship into the shape of a dragon, but now he felt only revulsion. He tried to fling the hunter away, but his fingers would not open. They disobeyed his will; they had another master now, it seemed. Nor would his arm obey his command to smash the timepiece down upon the desk.

He pushed the chair back and stood . . . then froze.

Bodies lay strewn about the floor – including, beside him, that of the Old Wolf. The guards were down, lying motionless as dead men. Pickens, too. And Longinus.

Father . . .

Either Magnus had lied to him, or Longinus had. But which

one? What was the truth? If Longinus was dead, killed by the hunter, he might never know.

Quare moved to the older man and knelt beside him. He was breathing shallowly, his eyes open, the pupils dilated. Quare shook him by the shoulder with his free hand. 'Longinus – wake up. Longinus!'

A faint groan was his only answer.

And what of the others? Quare moved from one fallen form to another, finding that all of them were, like Longinus, unconscious. He took the opportunity to rearm himself, then hesitated, debating what to do next.

'Waste not, want not, Mr Quare.'

The voice was as intimate as his own thoughts, yet entirely unnatural. It was as if a worm had burrowed into his brain – or, no, a *tongue* . . . He could feel it rasping repulsively across the inside of his skull. He bent over, retching, his stomach emptying. But he could not purge himself of the invader. When he was done, the voice returned.

'These titbits will lend savour to the coming feast.'

Now, just as he had been unable to force his fingers to drop the hunter, so, too, was he helpless to resist as a will more powerful than his own exerted control over his body. He – or, rather, the puppet he had become – drew his dagger and proceeded methodically to cut the throats of the guards. Quare's right hand did not so much as quiver as it went about its grisly business, though he fought against it with every ounce of strength he possessed.

As before, the hunter drew the streams of blood into itself; he could not believe how much blood a human body held . . . nor how quickly it could be drained. Not a drop was wasted. And also as before, the timepiece began to glow as it drank, until it hurt to look upon. Yet Quare could not tear his eyes away. The fierce light shone right through the skin of his hand, so that he could see the bones, the veins, the blood within the veins. All the while, in his head, he heard the dragon singing. That was the only word for it. It was the same song that had called him here, only indescribably more beautiful . . . and terrible, as if he were watching a ravishing maiden bathing in a pool of blood. He felt himself stiffen within his breeches. Then, as had happened in the bath, when he had conversed with Tiamat, he was spilling his seed, convulsed with a pleasure that overwhelmed but did not eliminate the shame he felt. And the horror. For just as it drank the blood of his victims, so, too, did the hunter take into itself this other vital essence. Tears ran down his cheeks.

When he came to himself again, the blade was poised above the throat of the Old Wolf. His hand, which had been so firm, trembled now.

'Not him,' came Magnus's voice. '*We do not need his blood. We do not want it.*'

Quare realized with a jolt that Magnus was not addressing him. He was not commanding. He was entreating. It appeared that he, too, had a master. But if that master made reply, Quare could not hear it.

'*Please, anyone but him! I could not bear to know his blood had a part in making us . . .*'

For a long moment, Quare's shaking hand hovered over the exposed white flesh. Then, steady again, it lowered the blade, wiped it dry upon the Old Wolf's waistcoat, and sheathed it. As the dagger slid home, Quare felt the control of his body returned to him.

'*Best be off, Mr Quare,*' came Magnus's voice, restored to its customary authoritative tone. '*No time to dawdle.*'

'Who were you—' Quare began.

'*The dragon,*' Magnus interrupted, and now Quare detected, or thought he detected, a hint of fear in the voice.

'Why, you are as much in harness as I,' Quare said.

'*You understand nothing,*' Magnus replied. '*Is the hand a slave to the arm? The arm to the body? The body to the mind?*'

'Whom are you addressing, Mr Quare?'

He turned, startled, to find that Longinus had regained consciousness and climbed to his feet while Magnus had been busy pleading for the Old Wolf's life – less, it seemed, out of any impulse towards mercy than from the same deep-seated hatred and sense of rivalry that had always characterized relations between the two men. 'What?'

'Who is it that is as much in harness as you?'

Only then did Quare realize that his half of the conversation with Magnus had been spoken aloud. He had assumed that the two of them were conversing mind to mind – but that was evidently not the case. Longinus must think him mad. And telling the truth would confirm his opinion. 'Never mind that,' he said. 'I'll tell you later. We've got to get out of here before anyone else comes.' It wasn't his own safety that concerned him, but rather the bloodbath that would ensue if the hunter once more began to feed.

Longinus did not reply. Instead, he glanced about the room. 'You have been busy,' he said at last, inclining his head towards the nearest guard. 'You seem to have overcome your squeamishness about cold-blooded murder. The Old Wolf would be pleased. Or perhaps not, seeing as how you have cut the throats of his personal guards.'

'That wasn't me. It was . . .' He wasn't sure how to explain. 'The hunter?'

He was still holding the timepiece, his fingers locked around it. He raised it now, held it out before him as if in explanation. It was no longer glowing . . . and the hands had ceased their motion. It might have been no more than what it appeared to be. Except, of course, it wasn't.

'Your finger is no longer bleeding, I see,' Longinus went on. 'In fact, there is a conspicuous absence of blood all around, considering the abundance of slit throats. The hunter again?'

Quare gave a resigned nod.

'You had best give it to me, Mr Quare.'

'I beg your pardon?'

Suddenly, Quare was facing a drawn sword. He had not noticed that Longinus, too, had rearmed himself. 'The hunter, sir. Hand it over, if you please.'

Again Quare felt an invading presence slip into his skin like a hand inserted snugly into a glove. That hand drew his sword. 'I cannot.'

Longinus nodded, as if his suspicions had been confirmed. 'Because you are in harness, as you said. The hunter controls you. That much is plain to see. And I see as well that there is no hope of mastering it. I was a fool to think otherwise. What is it, Mr Quare? Can you tell me that, at least?'

'An abomination,' he said. 'It is no weapon. It is—'

'Oh, my aching head!'

Pickens climbed to his feet, rubbing his head with one hand and looking curiously from Quare to Longinus and back again. 'What the deuce is going on? For God's sake, this isn't the time to squabble amongst ourselves! You've got what you came for – can we please just get out of here?'

'He's right,' Quare said, eyes fixed on Longinus. 'Surely you can see that.'

''Course I'm right,' said Pickens, stooping to help himself to the sword of one of the dead guards. 'Afraid I didn't see how you turned the tables, Quare, old boy,' he added, seeming to take stock of the situation for the first time, 'but well done. Well done indeed! Only, you forgot the Old Wolf. I'll just carve him a second smile, shall I, and we can be on our merry way . . .'

'No,' Quare said, and this time, though it was his voice that spoke, the will behind it belonged to another. And that will was not Magnus's, either. Magnus was part of it, but looming behind Magnus like a mountainous shadow was something stronger, vaster, older . . . and yet, Quare sensed – because he, too, was part of it – something that was still taking shape, not fully formed, simultaneously ancient and new, like a possibility that had existed from the beginning of all things but was only now on the verge of being realized. Of being born. 'We don't want this one.'

Pickens drew back. 'Don't we? Got something else in mind for him, Quare?'

'Mr Quare is not himself,' Longinus said, advancing upon him, sword at the ready.

'Isn't he?' Pickens blinked owlishly. 'Who is he, then?'

'I should very much like to know that myself.'

It was the Old Wolf. He rolled to a sitting position, a pistol held in one meaty paw. This he kept pointed squarely at Quare's chest as he heaved himself to his feet, his sweaty face grimacing with the effort. 'Who are you, Mr Quare? Not the ordinary journeyman and regulator you have taken such pains to appear to be, I'll warrant. No matter – you have caused me more than enough trouble. I find my patience has reached its end.' And he pulled the trigger before Quare could say a word or so much as blink an eye.

The impact of the ball striking his chest knocked Quare off his feet. There was no pain, just an immense, stunning shock. The next thing he knew, he was flat on his back, gasping for breath and gazing up into Pickens's battered face, which wore an expression of horrified concern that was anything but comforting. The stink of spent gunpowder was heavy in the air; a grey haze of smoke drifted before his eyes.

'Quare! Good lord, man, are you all right?'

He managed to nod, sucking air into his burning lungs. Then erupted in a paroxysm of coughing.

'Lie back, man. Lie back.' Pickens was pulling one-handed at the shredded remnants of his shirt, frantically trying to get a clear view of the wound. 'I . . . I don't see any blood – yet how could he have missed at such close range?'

But he hadn't missed. Quare could feel the ball lodged inside him, a heavy, aching wrongness lying alongside his heart. He felt, too, an urgent throbbing in his hand . . . the hand that held the hunter. He forced his eyes down. His whole hand seemed to be on fire, so brightly was the timepiece glowing. He could see the bones of his fingers. The hands of the watch had resumed their insectile back-and-forthing, as if they were not so much registering the time or anything analogous to time as he understood it but rather feeling out a path, like a blind man with a cane tapping his way through a maze.

Now Pickens noticed it, too. 'What in the name of . . .?' He drew back. But not far or fast enough.

Quare felt it happening, but there was nothing he could do to stop it. No warning he could give. His hand came up of its own accord and pressed the glowing hunter to Pickens's chest. The man uttered a small sigh, shuddered once, then collapsed to the floor beside Quare. Where the hunter had touched, his shirt was shredded and blackened, as was the skin beneath. Quare gasped at the sudden absence of the ball from inside him, even as blood began to well up from a wound in Pickens's chest that hadn't been there an instant ago. And that blood streamed into the hunter like a river pouring into the sea.

Something snapped in Quare, then. He scrambled for the door on all fours, like a beaten cur fleeing more blows. He felt the hunter resist him, as if it were not finished drinking Pickens's blood. But Quare *was* finished. He pulled away, and the hunter did not haul him back but let the leash play out.

Reaching the door, he stood on shaky legs to open it.

'Quare!'

He glanced back at the forceful cry. On the far side of the room, Longinus and the Old Wolf were crossing swords – and the grandmaster seemed to be proving a formidable opponent despite his bulk; at least, neither man had yet drawn blood. Longinus seemed about to say something more, but now, seeing his adversary's attention fixed on Quare, the Old Wolf struck, sliding his blade into Longinus's torso. An expression of surprise and distaste came over the aristocratic features, as if to be skewered in this way were a faux pas of the very first order; then his eyes rolled up into his head. But his body had already responded like a mechanism designed for just such a purpose, and though the Old Wolf knocked the riposte aside, he was not able to avoid the thrust of the dagger held in Longinus's other hand, which plunged into his side and remained there as the body of the man who had wielded it winked out of sight.

The Old Wolf gave a startled shout at this uncanny disapparition, then toppled to the floor with a crash as the drug coating the dagger took effect.

Quare did not wait to see if Longinus would return from the Otherwhere. The wound he'd received had appeared to be a mortal one . . . but Quare had experienced too much of late to place any credence in mortality. Nor was he thinking clearly enough to consider what he should do now that the Old Wolf was once again helpless before him. Instead, the sight of the blood leaking from the Old Wolf's side inspired only a frantic need to get away before the hunter could begin to feed again. He turned back to the door, wrenched it open, and staggered through.

A pair of guardsmen lay unconscious or dead just outside; he didn't stop to check their condition but stumbled past them down the corridor, until he reached the closet by which he, Longinus and Pickens had entered this floor of the guild hall in quest of the object he now possessed – or, rather, that possessed him. He ducked inside.

The candle Longinus had lit was still burning, and by its light Quare opened the hinged false front of the stacked barrels that concealed the mechanism responsible for bringing them all here. He stepped in without hesitation, and the platform, registering his weight, began to descend into darkness.

When it stopped, he fumbled about his person until he produced the vial Longinus had given him – he shook it, and in the bloom of greenish light beheld the storeroom and the still-unconscious bodies of Master Malrubius and the guardsman. He feared the hunter would add these men to its ever-growing list of victims, but it seemed sated for now – though it also seemed to Quare that he could sense the watchful presence of Magnus and whatever entity lurked behind him – not the dragon, for that was as yet unborn, but some primal consciousness, dimly awakened, out of which the dragon would emerge, shaped by the blood and will of the humans it had consumed . . . and not only the humans, for he sensed Magnus's cats as well, arrogant and disdainful and savagely competent killers. Magnus would never control such a creature, Quare knew: he might at best hope to influence it.

But it seemed clear that the stronger influence went in the other direction, and Magnus had already been warped far out of true.

At any rate, Magnus kept his silence for now, no doubt because Quare was doing what he would have wished him to do in any case. He was bringing the hunter out of the guild hall. He was taking the first steps that would lead him across the Channel, to fresh horrors. Quare thought with dread of those who waited there, English and French alike, soldiers and civilians, none of them suspecting the doom he was about to bring upon them. Yet what choice did he have? He could not protect them; he could not even protect himself.

There was no courage left inside him. All was madness and despair. As if to underscore his helplessness, Quare felt a pulse from the hunter prodding him on. He was not just holding the thing any more – or so, at least, it seemed to him. The hunter, the egg, was part of him now, as if his fingers had sunk into its substance and fused with it as intimately as the flesh and bone of Longinus's leg had meshed with his artificial foot. He would have cut the hand from his arm if he could, but he knew that he would never be permitted to free himself in such a manner. Nor could he call to Tiamat; he could not even shape the dragon's name in the privacy of his thoughts. His thoughts were no longer private.

A second, more forceful pulse sent him scrambling from the platform and out of the storeroom. He did not pause to determine if the passage outside was clear; he did not bother to try to keep quiet; he fled headlong, as if pursuing Furies were at his back. But nothing pursued him. Whatever Furies there were, he carried with him.

Thus did Quare retrace the route by which Longinus had spirited them into the guild hall. He did not encounter another person and soon found himself at the stone wall separating the lowest level of the hall from the London underground. He did not pause there, either, but scraped through, hurrying into the rough-hewn passage that led downwards, into the domain of the Morecockneyans.

19

Magic of a Most Ordinary Kind

IT WAS NOT UNTIL HE'D LEFT THE PASSAGE BEHIND AND BURST into the cavern beyond that Quare remembered Cornelius and Starkey. He'd left the two men bound and gagged near the entrance to the passage, but they were bound and gagged no longer. Now they faced him, swords drawn.

And they were not alone. A dozen men or more stood with them, some holding torches, others swords or crossbows.

Quare skidded to a halt.

'Well, if it ain't Mr Quare,' said Starkey with a grin that promised all sorts of unpleasantness. 'What's yer 'urry, eh?'

'Where's Grimalkin?' Cornelius demanded, gesturing with his sword. 'I'll whittle 'im down to a splinter, see if I don't!'

'Oi, look, 'e's 'oldin a watch!' Starkey said before Quare could reply, turning to address someone behind him. 'I told yer they was goin' ter fetch it right to yer, didn't I?'

'So you did, Mr Starkey.' The man pushed forward into view.

It was Aylesford.

'Surprised to see me, Quare?' Aylesford asked as he drew his blade with a flourish.

Quare felt the hunter pulse in his hand. He groaned in despair. 'Run,' he gasped out. 'All of you – before it's too late!'

This provoked a chorus of mocking laughter and catcalls.

'I've got a better idea,' said Aylesford when the general mirth had subsided. 'Hand over the watch, and I'll spare your life.'

''Course, me and Corny might not be so mercerful,' added Starkey.

'I don't feel much inclined in that direction, to be sure,' Cornelius admitted.

Quare drew his sword. 'You should have left London, Aylesford. You should have gone back to France and kept on going.'

'Oh, I mean to return – just as soon as I have the hunter.'

'It is the hunter that will have you,' Quare said grimly. 'All of you.'

'He's barmy,' someone said.

'Just shoot 'im,' another voice suggested. 'Make 'im inter a pincushion!'

Aylesford raised a forestalling hand. 'You may do what you like with him once I am through, gentlemen. But I have the prior claim. Quare and I have unfinished business.'

'Go on, then,' Cornelius said. ''Is Majesty said you was ter 'ave carte blanche, Mr Aylesford, and carte blanche you shall 'ave.'

'His Majesty is most gracious. I won't forget it . . . and nor will my prince.'

'This man is a cowardly murderer and an agent of the French,' Quare said, glancing over the knot of men arrayed against him. 'By helping him, you are aiding the enemies of your king and country. Is there no loyal Englishman among you?'

'We're Morecockneyans,' Cornelius answered. '*This* is our

country. Not up there – down 'ere. And we've got our own king, fank yer very much.'

'Enough words,' Aylesford said, advancing on Quare with his sword at the ready, the tip inscribing tight circles in the air. 'I prefer to let my blade do the talking.'

Quare readied himself. He knew from his previous encounter with Aylesford that the Scotsman was the better swordsman, but that would not matter now. Aylesford was in for a nasty surprise. They all were. The throbbing of the hunter had grown stronger, more insistent.

'Gorblimey, 'is 'and!' exclaimed Starkey, pointing. 'Look at 'is bleedin' 'and!'

Quare's hand rose of its own accord, elevating the hunter like a beacon. It cast a blood-red light upon Aylesford, who came on with a resolute expression despite the fear Quare saw in his eyes. He was right to be afraid. He just wasn't afraid enough. Quare almost pitied him.

Aylesford was gripping the hilt of his sword with both hands now. He shouted something in his own language that was incomprehensible to Quare as he stepped up and swung with all his might.

Quare watched as if from a safe remove as the blade passed through his wrist. His severed hand spun through the air in a spray of blood. Absurdly, he tried to reach for it, to catch it, with the stump. Yet he felt as if he were the one being cast away, as if his own hand had rejected him.

Then the pain took him. He dropped to his knees with a strangled, disbelieving cry, cradling the stump to his chest as if to smother the flow of blood. Aylesford meanwhile darted to where the hand had fallen. It lay on the ground like something hewn from a statue, the fingers still locked tight about the hunter.

'Stand back!' Aylesford cried out in warning to the Morecockneyans, who needed no encouragement on that score and were retreating en masse from the grisly trophy as if from a fizzing grenado. 'Mr Starkey, if you please.'

Starkey edged forward, holding out a sack of some kind at arm's length.

Aylesford reached for it . . .

And someone stepped to block Quare's view. He glanced up dully. Cornelius loomed over him. 'Nighty-night, Quaresie.' The pommel of his sword came down hard on Quare's skull, and he saw no more.

Quare awoke shivering in a heap of damp, filthy, foul-smelling straw. His head hurt abominably, and there was an excruciating ache in his left hand, as if his fingers were cramping. Yet when he raised his arm, he saw that it ended in a swathe of bloodstained bandages even filthier than the straw, if that were possible. He bolted upright as memories flooded back of the confrontation in the Old Wolf's den, his headlong flight, its gruesome conclusion. Even so, it took him a moment to absorb what he was seeing . . . or rather *not* seeing. Then shock at the absence of the hand whose cramping he still felt gave way to gut-wrenching sobs so primal in intensity that he seemed merely to be their conduit, rather than their source. At the same time, the visceral certainty that he was free of the hunter and its control filled him with giddy joy, so that laughter mingled with his tears. He rocked back and forth, weeping and giggling like a madman.

After a time, drained alike of energy and emotion, he subsided into the straw and took in his surroundings. He was in a cell carved out of solid rock, or perhaps it was a wide natural crevice adapted to the purpose of confinement. He could not see much more: the only light came from the glow of the luminous mushroom powder used by the Morecockneyans in lieu of torches. An iron cuff around his right ankle chained him to one stone wall, but he would have been too weak to attempt an escape in any case. It took all the effort of which he was capable to roll onto his side, fumble his breeches open with his remaining hand, and piss away from himself. The acrid smell of his urine did not improve the stench of the straw.

He wondered what had become of the hunter. Why had it failed to protect him as it had done in the Old Wolf's den? He didn't understand it. But it was not his problem any more. He no longer felt the slightest connection to it. He was free of that burden. Yet the knowledge that it was still out there weighed on him. Aylesford carried it now, or so he assumed. Perhaps he had already departed, heading back to his masters across the Channel. But Aylesford would soon discover, if he hadn't yet, that he had a new master now. Nor would that be the end of it. Only the beginning. The beginning of the end of everything. For as bad as things were now, Quare did not think they would improve once the dragon hatched out of the egg.

And Quare was the only one left who understood the threat. Pickens was dead, murdered by Quare's hand, his blood and his essence absorbed into the egg to nurture the monstrosity growing there. Longinus was gone, vanished into the Otherwhere with a wound that must surely prove mortal. Now Quare would never learn if Magnus had told him the truth about Lord Wichcote. Had the man really been his father, despite his denial when Quare had asked him point-blank? Not that it mattered. Not any more. Even if the Morecockneyans didn't kill him outright, his wound required better medical attention than he was likely to receive here.

Quare shouted, calling out for his captors, but there was no reply. It seemed he was on his own.

Or was he?

Magnus had removed Tiamat's geis, but that did not mean Quare could not call upon the dragon now, of his own free will. He did not know what that would accomplish, if Tiamat would even hear him – or, if it did, heed his call. He did not know what would happen if he brought a dragon into the world. But all things considered, it could hardly make things worse. Perhaps it would take a dragon to defeat a dragon.

'Tiamat,' he said, gazing into the greenish-yellow glow of the mushroom spores that had been dusted over the wall as if searching for a portal into the Otherwhere. 'Tiamat, if you can hear me, I need your help. Please.'

'Oi, 'oo yer talkin' to?' came a rough voice that startled Quare. The door banged open, and in barged his old friend Cornelius. 'Whatcher up to, eh?'

'Just praying,' Quare said. 'A man can pray, can't he?'

Cornelius shrugged. 'Pray all yer like.' He was carrying a wooden tray, and as he spoke he squatted, placed the tray on the ground, then stood again and nudged it towards Quare with the toe of one stained boot, as if afraid to draw too close to his prisoner . . . or to the no-doubt vermin-infested straw on which he lay. Upon the tray was a wooden bowl of grey and greasy porridge and a wooden mug filled with something that had the look of small beer. 'Go on,' he urged when Quare made no move to take the tray. 'It ain't gonter kill yer.'

Quare wasn't convinced of that. But he had other things on his mind than hunger and thirst. 'Where's Aylesford?'

'Gone, ain't he?' Cornelius replied. ''ippity-opped back ter Froggy land wif that ticker o' yers. Good riddance, says I. Give me the creeps, it did, glowin' like the devil's own pocket watch!'

'He must be stopped, Mr Cornelius! The hunter must be destroyed. Surely he can't have got far by now! We have to go after him before it's too late!'

Cornelius gave an ugly laugh. 'You been dead to the world for more than a day, Quaresie, old boy. Mr Aylesford is on 'is way across the Channel by now and no mistake.'

'Then I demand to speak with your king at once. There is no time to lose.'

'Perhaps you've not noticed that you are chained ter the wall in a prison cell. That is 'cause you are a prisoner. As such, Mr Quare, you are not in a position ter demand anyfing – certainly not an audience wif 'is Majesty.'

'Then you must take him a message. Tell him—'

Cornelius kicked suddenly and viciously at the tray he'd deposited on the floor, scattering everything on it. The bowl struck Quare in the shoulder, dumping its slimy contents along the side of his face and down his neck; the thick goop smelled of mushrooms. 'What, do you fink I'm to be ordered about like a bleedin' errand boy? You fink 'cause I'm a lowly Morecockneyan, that makes you my master? Is that it?'

'No . . .'

Cornelius ignored him. 'You surface dwellers are all the same. Fink you're better than us 'cause yer 'appen ter live under open sky. Well, that's about ter change, fanks to 'is Majesty.'

'I don't understand you,' Quare protested, angry himself now. 'Granted, you live below the surface of London . . . but this is still English soil, is it not? English blood runs in your veins. The bonds of history and family tie you to the surface and those who live upon it, burrow however deep you like. Yet you conspire with England's enemies; indeed, you have given them a weapon more potent and deadly than you – or they – know.'

''At's where you're wrong, Quaresie. 'Is Majesty knows more than you fink. More than Aylesford finks.'

'Who is your king?' Quare asked.

'Wouldn't yer like ter know,' Cornelius replied, laying a thick finger alongside his carbuncle of a nose. 'Suffice it ter say, 'is Majesty knows very well what is likely to transpire when Mr Aylesford reaches France. Indeed, I dare say 'e is countin' on it.'

'Does he imagine, then, that what is about to be loosed upon the world will stop at the surface, and that you people will be safe from it here? If so, I fear he is very much mistaken.'

'Might be 'e is. Might be 'e ain't. I reckon we'll just 'ave ter wait and see. But if I was you, I'd be finkin' less about Mr Aylesford and more about me own prospects.'

'I don't imagine they are any too bright.'

'They are not bright at all, Quaresie. In fact, you might say they are black as pitch.'

'So, you mean to kill me, then.'

'There'll be a trial first. We 'ave judges and juries 'ere, just like up above.'

'And what am I charged with?'

'A capital crime. Trespassin'.'

'What? Trespassing? You would kill a man for that?'

'Aye, we would. If Mr Pitt should 'ear of us, 'e'd 'unt us down like so many rats. Don't fink it ain't 'appened before.'

'Why not just kill me now and get it over with?' Quare said bitterly.

'That would be murder, not justice. 'Oo knows? Perhaps yer barrister will speak wif such eloquence as ter persuade the jury ter acquit – though I wouldn't count on it. I wouldn't count on it at all.'

'And why is that?'

'Because 'is Majesty 'as done me the great 'onour o' appointin' me ter act in that capacity,' Cornelius said. With a mocking bow, he turned to go.

'Wait,' called Quare.

Cornelius looked back from the doorway.

Quare raised his bandaged stump; he could not help but notice that the bloodstains had grown darker since he had awakened. His arm felt as if it were on fire. 'I find I am more in need of a physician than I am a barrister . . .'

'I regret we do not 'ave one available at present.'

'But . . . what then am I to do?'

'The trial is set for tomorrow,' Cornelius said. 'Until then – well, a man can pray, can't 'e?'

After that, Quare was left alone . . . in a manner of speaking. Fever took him, and he sank into a fitful half slumber in which figures from his distant and more recent past appeared in the cell to harangue him in so tedious a fashion as to constitute a form of torture. Though he was aware for the most part that these interminable one-sided conversations – for he could not get a word in edgewise, try as he might – were hallucinations, that knowledge proved insufficient to escape from them. Fellow orphans he'd known in the workhouse, whose very existence he had consigned to oblivion, returned to tax him with the crime of having forgotten them, of having left them behind to suffer while he went on to a life of luxury as the apprentice of Master Halsted. And here came old Halsted himself, walking him step by step through the most rudimentary clock repairs, as if he were once again the untutored apprentice he had been so long ago. Grandmaster Wolfe, meanwhile, berated him yet again for having bungled his rooftop opportunity with Grimalkin. Master Magnus chimed right in, as if the two men were allies now. Nor was Longinus absent – in all his various guises, each more critical than the last. Aylesford, too, was present, as were Pickens, Mansfield and Farthingale, along with Arabella and Clara. Even Mrs Puddinge put in an appearance, hectoring him about the fate of her late husband's second-best coat . . . and there as if on cue came the malodorous thing itself, flapping through the air like a disreputable ghost. Indeed, the cell was full to bursting with ghosts, not only people Quare recognized and remembered but others who seemed to be perfect strangers, as if another person's hallucinations had spilled over into his own. They seemed to be getting on very well together, having a grand old time. Most disconcerting of all was the return of his missing hand. Yes, there it was, back on the end of his wrist, as if it had never left. Except now it seemed to have only perched there, for to his amazement it rose like a bird and took flight, joining the coat in its airborne perambulations even as it dripped blood with the perfect regularity of a clepsydra on all those below.

So vivid were these apparitions that it was some time before Quare became convinced a particular voice among the throng was real. Or at any rate so insistent that it compelled his attention away from all the others. Especially since it was accompanied by a stinging slap across his cheek. And then another.

'Mr Quare! Can you hear me? Wake up!'

Quare attempted to focus his bleary gaze. Gradually the ghosts faded from view, until he found himself looking into fierce, dark eyes in a grey-masked and hooded face. His mouth worked to shape a name.

'Drink this.' A grey-gloved hand tipped a wooden mug to his lips. He drank the cool water, spluttering in his haste.

'Easy.' A strong hand slipped behind his head.

He swallowed until the mug was empty. Then spoke, his voice so faint as to be barely audible. 'How . . .?'

'Come on.' The mug clattered to the floor. 'We're getting out of here.'

'Can't.'

'I think you can.'

Quare found himself hauled to his feet. 'No.' He shook his head, trying to clear it. 'Chained.'

'Not any more.'

Sure enough, the cuff was gone from his ankle. Quare took a faltering step, then another, leaning heavily against his rescuer. He felt himself slipping back into his fever dreams and fought to remain anchored in the here and now. His tongue was swollen, his thoughts muddled, and his words slurred, but still he forced them out. 'Aylesford. He's got the hunter.'

'Shh. Save your strength.'

'We've got to stop him, Longinus. There's no one else but us.'

'Sorry to disappoint you, but I'm not Longinus.' The rescuer reached up and pulled hood and mask aside. Blonde hair tumbled free.

'You!'

It was the young woman from the rooftop. The false Grimalkin. Her expression was almost mischievous as she regarded him. The corners of her lips ticked upward in the hint of a smile. Then, compounding his shock, she leaned forward and pressed her mouth to his.

The result of this kiss was even more astonishing than the fact of it. Blessed coolness radiated out from the touch of her lips, and Quare felt his fever retreat before it, all the way to the end of his arm, where it pulsed distantly.

The woman pulled away. 'Better?'

He was – so much so, in fact, that whereas mere seconds ago it was the struggle of marshalling his sluggish thoughts into speech that had impeded him, now it was the rapidity of thought that made articulation difficult. 'I . . . How . . .'

She laughed. 'You may ask as many questions as you like – only not here. Not now. My kiss is no cure – you require more help than I can give. We must away, before your captors return.'

'But . . . who are you? How did you know to find me here?'

'You called, and so I came, as was promised.'

But he hadn't called her. The only one he'd called was . . .

'My God. Tiamat?'

'You may call me that if you like,' she said with a smile and a sly sideways glance, as if enjoying his befuddlement.

Quare's questions – of which he had many – were brushed aside by this self-assured if not imperious young woman who went by the name of a dragon. She led him out of the cell and into a narrow corridor extending in one direction only. They followed it, coming to a room whose sole occupant – the turnkey, Quare assumed – lay dead or unconscious upon the floor.

'How did you get in here?' he asked.

'The same way we are getting out.'

'But why did you not come sooner? I could have used your help that night at the Pig and Rooster, and many times since then.'

'I am sorry,' she said, wincing as if at a painful memory. 'I was unavoidably . . . detained. But no more questions, Mr Quare – in fact, it would be best if you not talk at all. The Morecockneyans have sharp ears, among other things.' She accompanied her words with a gesture, as if flicking away an insect, and Quare felt – as he had before – the sovereign weight of an implacable will descend upon him, sealing his lips. 'Stay close,' she whispered, pulling her hood and mask back into place so that she was once again, to all outward appearances, Grimalkin. 'Stay quiet.'

She had given him no choice but to obey, yet he did so gladly, eager to be gone. He could tell that time was short, not only because it seemed certain that his escape would be noticed, or, even if it were not, that they would encounter one or more Morecockneyans along the way to wherever it was they were going, and so raise a general alarum, but also because he could feel the hot tingle of his banished fever creeping back up his arm. It would break upon him again, and sooner rather than later. He did not want to be here when that happened.

Leaving the room behind, Tiamat led him with utter assurance through a maze of passages that would have left Quare baffled had he been forced to navigate them on his own. The most he could say was that they seemed to be descending rather than climbing towards the surface. But it was plain that Tiamat knew where she was going. He stuck to her like a shadow.

From time to time as they descended, Tiamat would halt, or backtrack, or pull him into a side passage – all in response to some warning signal he had not heard or seen. Twice groups of Morecockneyans walked by their hiding place, talking and laughing among themselves as if they were strolling down any busy London thoroughfare, and once a silent, armed patrol stalked past, glowing like grim spectres. More than once Quare reproached himself for not having thought to take a weapon from the turnkey, though in his present condition, weak as he was, and with the fever flowing back inch by inch, already beginning to cloud his thoughts again, he doubted that he would be much good in a fight.

At last, after what might have been hours, the sound of a great hunting horn reverberated from behind them, its urgent echoes multiplying even as the blast was repeated again and yet again. Quare knew then what the fox must feel.

'Pity,' Tiamat remarked. 'I had hoped we might have a bit more time. I'm afraid it's going to be a race now, Mr Quare.'

Yes, but a race to where?

He could not ask, could only follow as she picked up the pace, pulling him along. The horn continued to blow, further harrying them. Perhaps it was the exertion, or just the fading effects of Tiamat's kiss, but Quare's head was soon buzzing, and his stump was throbbing so painfully with each step that he could barely think at all . . . though he did wonder why it was that a dragon would be running from anything, and why Tiamat, who plainly possessed more than ordinary abilities, did not simply whisk them away through the Otherwhere as Longinus would surely have done.

After a while, Quare noticed a yellowish glow in front of them; it was hard to say just how far away it was, but it seemed to be growing brighter. Tiamat slowed, then halted. 'Just a little farther, Mr Quare. Can you manage it?'

He nodded, though in fact he was anything but certain of how much longer he could stay on his feet.

'You have suffered much,' she said now, and he could feel her gaze upon him though shadows hid her features. 'Much has been asked of you. Little has been offered in return. That is about to change.'

He heard her take a breath as if about to say more, but instead he felt the soft pressure of her lips on his own again.

This time there was no cooling effect, no ebbing of his fever, but there was, or anyway seemed to be, magic of another sort, for his heart swelled with courage, and he felt himself ready to do anything she asked of him, and more. Though perhaps that was not magic at all. Or if it was, only magic of a most ordinary kind.

She pulled away. 'They are behind us. We must hurry.'

Quare glanced back and, indeed, could see faint glimmers dancing in the dark.

'Ahead lies an ancient structure,' she informed him matter-of-factly. 'As soon as you can, run to the centre of it.'

'And what of you?' he asked – for he found that her kiss had unlocked his tongue.

'I will join you when I can.'

'If there is fighting to be done—'

'I will do it. You are not fit. Nor do you have a weapon. Trust me, Mr Quare.'

'I do,' he said and meant it.

She did not reply but was already pulling him onwards. Soon enough he could see that the light was coming from around a corner. Tiamat did not pause but broke into a loping run, leaving Quare to follow as best he could.

When he came around the corner, he stopped in astonishment. He stood at the entrance to a huge cavern – the largest by far that he had seen in his time underground. The floor and walls – and, as far as he could make out, the ceiling, too – were blanketed in mushrooms that emitted the yellowish glow he had noted earlier. A constant bright haze of incandescent spores drizzled down from the ceiling. It took him a moment to grow accustomed to it, as if he had emerged blinking into the light of day. But once his vision had adjusted, his gaze was drawn to the centre of the cavern, where stood a circle of dark stones such as were popularly believed to have been deposited upon the plains of England and Scotland by giants or fairies or druids in bygone days. One such site – the Nine Stones – was located on the outskirts of Dorchester, and as an apprentice Quare had sometimes ventured there to study his books and dream of clockworks and more than clockworks: of ages past, when magic had suffused the land, and of ages yet to come, when a science more wondrous would hold sway. But those had been small and stunted stones, lichen-covered, precariously tilted, two or three even toppled into the grass, so that the effect had been rather like a cemetery gone to seed. Not so here.

These stones, half again as tall as a man, stood straight and true, as if they had been erected yesterday. There were twelve of them, irregular in shape but evenly spaced, forming a circle that must have been at least fifteen yards in diameter. They had been polished to an extraordinary shine, like obsidian; yet they did not seem to reflect the light of the mushrooms so much as swallow it, giving them the look of empty, gaping holes, doorways cut into the air. There was something familiar about the shapes of the stones, but he could not quite bring it to mind.

What held Quare frozen in place despite Tiamat's clear instructions to make for the centre of this strange and imposing edifice was less the shock of coming upon such a thing deep below the metropolis of London than the sight of her at work amidst the mushrooms, single-handedly fighting what appeared to be at least a dozen robed figures. They looked like monks in heavy brown cassocks but moved more like soldiers ... or, rather, like seasoned regulators: men trained to fight and to kill with brutal economy and grace. Yet they might have been blind bumblers compared with the grey-clad demon who moved among them like a tiger – or, he thought, like a dragon.

He had never seen such fighting skill. He had never imagined it. Even Longinus would have stood no chance against her – and he was by far the best swordsman Quare had ever faced. She fought with a peculiar short sword in one hand and a long dagger in the other. The two weapons wove about her in a blur that no assailing blade or whip – for the men fought with both swords and braided ropes worn about their waists like cinctures – could penetrate. Yet notwithstanding the completeness of her defence, she somehow found or made opportunities to go on the attack. And in this she was more impressive still, as the blood of her enemies attested. She was in constant motion, her entire body a weapon: darting, tumbling, leaping, at times seeming almost to fly. Her speed was uncanny; there were moments it seemed that her opponents were standing still. This was death-dealing brought to the highest level of art . . . or even beyond art, to a kind of mechanized perfection. It was beautiful and terrible to watch. Her brown-robed adversaries were brave: they did not cry out, did not make any sound at all, as if they had taken vows of silence. They continued to fight even after it must have been plain to them that they stood no chance. Quare could not help but pity them. Yet he did not tear his eyes away as they fell like stalks of wheat before a merciless scythe.

So engrossed was he in this consummate display of killing craft that he forgot about the pursuing Morecockneyans until a crossbow bolt clattered off the wall beside him. Looking back, he saw a group of palely glowing men charging up the passage – which, luckily for him, was so narrow as to compel them to come in single file. That was why he had faced only a single bolt rather than half a dozen. But his pursuers would soon have ample room to spread out and fire upon him without fear of shooting each other. Cursing under his breath, he turned and ran into the cavern, making for the circle of stones.

It was not easy to run through the mushrooms; his boots crushed them into a slick paste that made every step perilous. His progress consisted more of slipping and sliding than it did of running. But he managed – just – to keep his feet. The constant rain of glowing spores from above, added to those stirred up by his passage, had soon turned his grey clothing into a suit of light. He could not help breathing the spores in; their brightness seemed to concentrate inside him, coming together into a single point of light behind his breast, hot and focused as a small sun, and it occurred to him that he might be turning into a spore himself and would soon float up from the ground. But then he thought that must be the influence of his fever rather than any transformation effected by the spores.

As he ran, too intent on keeping his balance to spare a backward glance for his pursuers, one of the remaining brown-robed men noticed him and broke away from Tiamat, angling towards him through the field of mushrooms. He was not glowing as Quare and Tiamat were; the brown robes, it seemed, were proof against the shining of the spores, which winked out like sparks settling on water upon alighting there. Quare did not think he would reach the stone circle before the man was upon him, and in any case he had no reason to believe the monument would afford him any protection from attack. Tiamat had told him that she had come this way to find him; he wondered how – assuming that were true – she had managed to avoid these silent, stalwart defenders. It was beginning to look as though he would not have the opportunity to ask her, however, for the man was close enough now that Quare could make out his features: a bulbous nose, dark eyes that regarded him with fierce, unreasoning hatred, lips bared in a soundless howl, displaying teeth filed to sharp points and an empty space where a tongue should have been. The man had lost his sword in the fight with Tiamat but was whipping his cincture in a wicked circle over his head as he came on; the thick hempen rope, Quare saw now, had an iron clasp at the end. It filled the air with a low, ominous thrumming that he felt in the very marrow of his bones.

As he tried to swerve aside, Quare's feet shot out from under him and he went down, hearing, even as he fell, something whistle past his head. He hit hard and slid on one hip through the mushrooms, still moving in the direction of his attacker – who, he was certain, would have gathered the cincture back by now and made ready to cast it anew. But when he had slowed sufficiently to look up again, holding his bloody, rag-wrapped stump out before him as if to deflect the blow by a mute appeal to the loss he had already suffered, he saw, instead of the iron clasp descending towards his skull, his attacker falling backwards, clawing at a crossbow bolt buried in his throat. Had Quare not slipped when he had, the bolt would have struck him between the shoulder blades.

The stone circle was close now: no more than fifteen or twenty yards away. Suddenly he remembered where he had seen those shapes before. They were the same as the symbols on the hunter. And, like those symbols, the more he tried to focus upon them, the shakier they became, like living things intent on eluding his grasp, even if it were only visual. The stones, he realized, were moving, vibrating, spinning so fast that they appeared to be standing still.

He tried to pick himself up and go on, but he had landed badly, twisting his ankle, and it would not support him. Nor, he found, did he have the strength to crawl. He felt weak as a newborn babe. He lay on his back, gazing up at the ceiling of the cavern, which was lost in the sunny glow of the mushrooms growing there and in the steady downward drift of spores. There was something restful about it, like lying at the bottom of a huge hourglass as warm golden sand trickled down to cover him.

Then he was being lifted in strong arms. It was Tiamat. She did not speak, but swept him up and ran for the stone circle, shielding him with her body. Quare felt the jolt of crossbow bolts hitting home – once, twice, three times – and each time she was struck, Tiamat grunted in pain . . . but it was a sound that did not have much that was human about it, not at first and even less each subsequent time he heard it, as if she were casting her humanity aside like a hindering cloak, shrugging out of it as she ran. And indeed the arms that held him seemed to be changing, becoming larger, fingers lengthening into claws, the grey costume of Grimalkin toughening into leathery skin.

But was Tiamat shedding some fleshly disguise, or, instead, was the stone circle stripping it from her, skinning her alive? For the closer they drew to it, the more the air resisted them, as if the spinning stones had conjured a wind, a gale that pushed back unrelentingly. Tiamat snarled and pressed on. It seemed to Quare that she was trying to force herself through a space too small to admit her, a narrow opening or channel in the world . . . or rather out of it, the sides of which were scraping her raw. And yet the shape that was emerging seemed larger by far than what had contained it. It made no sense. Quare could not tell any longer what was real and what the product of his fever. The spores that had been falling like a gentle dusting of sand now pelted them like hailstones, forcing him to bury his head in the crook of his bandaged arm. Then he heard Tiamat snarl again as her body shuddered with the impact of more bolts than he could count. She gathered herself and, with a deafening roar, gave a mighty leap.

She did not come down.

Quare was in the grasp of claws larger than his body. They held him in a gentle but unbreakable grip, like the bars of an iron cage. On the other end of those claws was the dragon he had first seen in the vision he'd experienced at Lord Wichcote's house. Tiamat, as she truly was: sleek, sinuous, serpentine, with scales as blue as the sky ... so blue they seemed translucent. She was huge; he did not see how she could have squeezed herself into the body of the woman who had kissed him.

As before, the effect of her presence was immediate and intense. He had no sense that resistance was possible; it was not a matter of will or even desire but instead the plain working of some natural – or supernatural – law to which he was subject by virtue of being human. It had been no different inside the egg; there, too, he had yielded up his seed in reflexive paroxysms that were anything but pleasant. For a time, he was lost in it, swallowed up.

But at last there was nothing left. He was limp, wrung out, fever-stricken. Only then did Quare begin to take in his surroundings, though in a dreamy kind of way. Tiamat was flying with a peculiar wingless grace, seeming to swim through the air like a snake squirming through water; she did not glance down at him or seem to be aware of him at all other than by the fact that she did not drop him. There must have been a dozen or more crossbow bolts embedded in her body, but she seemed unaware of them as well. They were like thorns in the hide of an elephant.

Quare knew at once that he was back in the Otherwhere. Not so much by anything he saw – the desert landscape of reddish sand and rolling dunes far beneath them, over which Tiamat's stark shadow glided, clinging to every indentation and swell, might have been the sands of some African or Asian desert undulating below the baleful, white-hot sun – as by the overwhelming impression he had that everything could change in an instant, that the underlying reality of the scene was very different from what his senses were equipped to perceive. He had felt the same way when Longinus had first taken him into the Otherwhere, and it had been much the same within the egg.

The egg that Aylesford was carrying to France.

At that, recalled to the urgency of things, Quare called to Tiamat, but his voice was too weak, his words borne away by the blast of the wind that was the sole indication of the dragon's prodigious speed. Where was she taking him? And what would become of him when they got there? *Much has been asked of you*, she had told him. *Little has been offered in return. That is about to change.* But Quare had had enough change to last a lifetime. He didn't want any more.

The desert stretched ahead without end. The sun might have been nailed to the sky.

Tiamat flew on. She did not slow, did not seem to tire. She did not once address a word to him, or glance in his direction. He wondered if she had forgotten about him. Racked by fever, he shivered and baked by turns.

It was in this state that he noticed a second shadow on the sand below. It was small, and at first he thought it was not a shadow at all but something physically present on the ground, a herd of horses, perhaps, or a caravan. But it grew, spreading like a black stain . . . or an angry cloud rising up to confront them. Or no, he realized dimly, with a certain distant interest, not rising but rather *falling* . . .

Tiamat swerved as something big came roaring past. At once, all was confusion. Buffeted within the cage of the dragon's claws, Quare saw flashes of ground and sky and what might have been a living shadow, night poured into flesh. The air rang with shrieks and bellows until he thought his eardrums must burst.

Then Tiamat stopped dead in the air and hung there, her body eeling slowly, the movement somehow keeping her aloft. Streaks of a silvery liquid trickled down her blue scales. An angry hiss escaped her massive jaws.

Hovering a hundred feet away or less was a black dragon even bigger than she was. It exuded age and power. Silver ichor dripped from its claws. Its head was like a sun-blasted mountainside scored with fissures and ravines. One eye was a pearlescent orb whose surface rippled like the placid mirror of a lake disturbed by the movement of some hidden swimmer. Where the pair of that eye should have been was a dark, gaping pit into which Quare thought he might fall for ever without touching bottom. To gaze into its abyssal depths was to already be falling into them, or so it seemed. He felt himself stiffening despite his terror; then he was coming again, burning with humiliation at his helplessness, hating his human frailty, this flesh that responded without his leave, slave to masters he did not know.

Neither dragon paid him the slightest heed.

'Where is it?' the black thundered. 'What have you done with my eye?'

Or was it 'egg'? Quare, half deafened, was not sure what he had heard.

'I do not have it,' Tiamat replied. 'Sister, move aside.'

'You lie,' the black raged. 'You reek of time and generation! Give back what is mine – or I will take it!'

Before Tiamat could answer, the black struck. The two dragons twined together in a murderous flux, slashing, biting. They rose entangled, knotting and unknotting. The noise of their roaring was a physical thing.

The claws caging Quare came open; he fell.

He watched the dragons, still locked together, dwindle above him to a single speck. Then he began to tumble. The air swaddled him in a rough silence all its own. A flash of blue sky and sun gave way to the tawny pelt of a brown landscape leaping to meet him. Then he saw blue sky again, only a different sky, in which two suns blazed; but in the blink of an eye, this impossible vision was replaced by a slate-grey ocean stretching endlessly, wave upon wave. Another blink, and he was gazing at a night sky spangled with strange stars. Blink: a city greater than London lay buried beneath a blanket of unspoiled snow. Blink: a fleet of great ships depending from greater balloons, like Magnus's Personal Flotation Device on an immense scale, glided through the air.

With each revolution of Quare's tumbling body, the scene changed, as if he were flipping between worlds. But then it came to him that he wasn't falling at all, that he was hovering in place as the dragons had done, and the sights he was seeing were glimpses of what lay beyond the spinning windows of the standing stones between which Tiamat had carried him. For all the time he had been here, for all the distance Tiamat had carried him, still he was somehow at the very centre of those stones. And if that were so, why couldn't he just, as he had done the last time he'd been in the Otherwhere, choose a path out of it? The windows . . . or doors, rather, were here before him, offering themselves in swift succession. Were their shapes in some way symbolic of what they led to, like the alchemical symbols of planets and stars? If so, it was a code he could not decipher. He would have to trust to luck.

Now, without understanding what he was doing or how, as if in the grip of an instinct he hadn't known he possessed until the moment came for its exercise, Quare groped towards a doorway, not caring where it might lead. He only knew, with a blind, animal certainty he did not question, that he could not remain here. He must escape or die. He reached out with his mind, or some aspect of his mind, like a drunken man fumbling to fit a key into a door. He thrust, thrust again. Felt himself slip in. He turned, or the world did.

All was darkness. And cold. And then it was as if he had been falling the whole time, after all. For he struck ground, or something as solid as ground, with a force that snuffed the candle of his consciousness.

Epilogue

WAR HAD COME TO THE VILLAGE, STAYED A WHILE, AND THEN moved on. What structures remained were little more than skeletons, blackened shards of timber and stone standing desolate beneath a grey sky from which flakes of snow drifted down like ash to settle upon wreckage half locked in ice, as though these ruins were of no recent vintage but had passed long centuries at the heart of a glacier only now, begrudgingly, yielding them back to the world. Nothing stirred in the frozen, stark tableau. Not the faintest whisper of wind could be heard. If whatever battle had been fought here had left survivors, it seemed they had long since fled, taking the bodies of their dead with them. Even the birds had departed.

Into the silence came a keening, a rising wail that split the air like the cry of an angel cast out of heaven. A shining arc traced a steep descent, ending in an explosion of snow and ice and billowing clouds of steam.

The ground shuddered.

A bell began to toll.

The steam thinned, returning to the ground as a new and whiter dusting of snow that clung to a grey-garbed man sprawled on his back in a soup of half-melted ice and snow at the base of a clock tower that hadn't been there before, as if it had crashed to earth along with the splayed and unmoving figure beside it.

The tower, like the surrounding buildings, was heavily damaged. Gaping holes punctured its sides where cannonballs had bitten deep, leaving splintered fragments of carved figures whose postures and expressions seemed to reflect the horror of the instant in which their artistry had been obliterated, while the proscenium, where once automatons would have paraded, was a jumble of stone and exposed machinery in which could be glimpsed portions of those same automatons, an arm here, a leg there, heads and torsos mixed willy-nilly, like a graveyard after an earthquake. The clock itself, which had been set above the proscenium, had also been struck. Its face was as pocked and cratered as the moon. Most of its numbers were missing, and its metal hands were bent and twisted, pointing outwards, away from what was left of the clock, as though registering a time that could not be represented there. Yet despite the carnage, the campanile was intact, and it was from there that the single bell rang out its insistent summons, as if to wake the man lying at the foot of the tower, half sunk in a bloody slush already re-hardening to ice around him.

But the man did not wake. Instead, a door opened at the base of the tower, and from its interior emerged an elderly man in a powdered wig and gold-framed spectacles, dressed all in black. He hurried to the prone figure as if he'd been expecting just such a visitation. He was so thin, his movements so jerky, that he might almost have been an automaton. All the while, the bell in the campanile kept up its ringing.

This man was more supple than his angular appearance or evident age indicated; stronger, too, for he stooped and lifted the fallen man with ease. Cradling his burden, he retraced his steps to the tower and slipped back inside, turning as he entered to ensure that no portion of the limp and lanky body in his arms would brush against the doorway.

The door closed behind him.

The echoes of the bell faded. The devastated village stood silent and still under a feathering of falling snow.

Meanwhile, in a moonlit attic filled with a variety of clocks, no two of which told a common time, so that the air was thronged with a quarrelsome murmur of ticking and tocking, a peal of bells began to ring. Every clock able to announce the hour in some fashion or other did so now, as if, despite the discordant times displayed upon their faces, they had come to an inner agreement . . . or were reacting to a common stimulus, like a London crowd that in one instant fuses its separate members into a single organism able to cry out with one voice at the passage of a king or the hanging of a highwayman.

As abruptly as they had rung out, the clocks quieted. Silence reigned in the attic. Even the sounds of ticking had ceased. The hands on every dial had stopped dead, pointing straight up at XII.

A whisper of air, like a sigh, as the casing of a tall clock swung open.

A groan, as a grey-clad figure slumped from within to the sawdust-covered attic floor. And began to crawl, ever so slowly, across it.

Leaving a bloody trail.

A second whisper, exactly like the first, as another casing opened in a clock that stood alongside the other.

A second grey-clad figure slumped groaning to the floor and began to crawl after the first.

'Lord Wichcote,' called this second figure. 'Wait.'

At which the first figure halted and, with visible effort, using a nearby table for leverage, pulled itself erect and turned to face the other, a dagger in hand.

Which, too, had pulled itself erect by similar means. And held a rapier en garde.

The two stood in mutual trembling regard in a dim fall of moonlight that concealed more than it illuminated. Each might have been the reflection of the other. At their feet inky shadows spread.

'What do you here?' asked Lord Wichcote. 'Have you not stolen enough from me already?'

'We need not be enemies, you and I,' the other said, and just then the room brightened, as if a mask of cloud had been pulled away from the face of the moon, revealing a young blonde-haired woman with skin like porcelain, her expression one of suffering stoically endured. Upon her shoulder, tucked against her neck, sat a mouse.

Lord Wichcote staggered back against the table. 'Corinna?'

'Her daughter,' answered a dwindling voice, 'and yours.' The woman dwindled along with it, falling in a slow faint. The mouse had already vanished into the shadows by the time the rapier clattered to the floor. It rolled a half turn on the wheel of its guard, then lay as still as its owner.

The City

Stella Gemmell

Built up over millennia, layer upon layer, the City is ancient and vast. Over the centuries it has sprawled beyond its walls, the cause of constant war with neighbouring peoples and kingdoms, laying waste to what was once green and fertile.

And at the heart of the City resides the emperor. Few have ever seen him. Those who have remember a man in his prime and yet he should be very old. Some speculate that he is no longer human; others wonder if indeed he ever truly was. And a small number have come to a desperate conclusion: that the only way to stop the ceaseless slaughter is to end the emperor's unnaturally long life.

From the rotting, flood-ruined catacombs beneath the City, where the poor struggle to stay alive, to the blood-soaked fields of battle, where so few heroes survive, these rebels pin their hopes on one man. A man who was once the emperor's foremost general. A revered soldier, who could lead an uprising and unite the City. But a man who was betrayed, imprisoned and tortured, and is now believed to be dead . . .

Available in hardback, paperback & ebook.

Queen of Kings

Maria Dahvana Headley

'So magical, so dark' NEIL GAIMAN

Once there was a queen of Egypt . . . a queen who became through magic something else . . .

In 30BC, as Octavian Caesar and his legions marched into Alexandria, Cleopatra, Queen of Egypt, learned that her beloved Mark Antony had taken his own life. Desperate to save her kingdom, her husband and all she held dear, Cleopatra turned to the gods for help. She summoned Sekhmet, goddess of death and destruction, and struck a mortal bargain. And not even the wisest scholar could have fore told what would follow . . .

For saving Antony's soul Sekhmet demands something in return: Cleopatra herself. Transformed into a shape-shifting, not-quite-human manifestation of a deity who seeks to destroy the world, Cleopatra follows Octavian back to Rome. She desires revenge, she yearns for her children . . . and she craves human blood.

'Genre-bending, myth-breaking'
TEA OBREHT, AUTHOR OF THE TIGER'S WIFE

'A miracle, a marvel'
PETER STRAUB, AUTHOR OF GHOST STORY

'A page turner: an epic historical thriller'
DANIELLE TRUSSONI, AUTHOR OF ANGELOLOGY

Available in paperback & ebook

Unholy Night

Seth Grahame-Smith

'Akin to fusing *Game of Thrones* with the Gospel of Luke'
ENTERTAINMENT WEEKLY

It is one of history's most iconic moments: three men on camels arrive at a stable, bearing gifts of gold, frankincense and myrrh. An impossibly bright star is suspended in the vast desert sky above. It's a moment of serenity and of grace. A holy night.

The Bible tells us little about these wise men from the East. Not even their names are mentioned. The historical record is vague. How do we know they were kings? What if they were petty, murderous thieves led by one called Balthazar who, on the run and fleeing through Judaea under cover of night, stumbled upon the celebrated manger with its newborn child?

The last thing they'd have wanted would be to be slowed down by Joseph, Mary and their infant, but when King Herod's men began their slaughter of the firstborn, they'd have been left with no choice but to help the young family on their flight to Egypt . . .

Here, the maverick imagination behind *Pride and Prejudice* and Zombies has taken a little mystery and played with history to tell a fantastical tale . . .

'Grahame-Smith has forsaken neither graphic gore nor gleeful historical and religious revisionism . . . Great fun'
ELIZABETH HAND, *WASHINGTON POST*

Available in paperback & ebook

❖

Jasper Kent

The Danilov Quintet

The enthralling, chilling and highly acclaimed historical vampire
sequence continues . . .

'Brilliantly weaving together history and family drama with
supernatural horror, political intrigue, espionage and suspense'
FANTASYBOOKCRITIC

TWELVE

*Russia, 1812. What began as a last stand against Napoleon's invading
army would end as a fight against an enemy of mankind itself . . .*

'An accomplished, entertaining blend of historical
fiction and dark fantasy'
THE TIMES

THIRTEEN YEARS LATER

*Russia,1825. A country on the brink of revolution – a dynasty
enslaved by blood . . .*

'Brilliant . . . this is a masterpiece of alternative Russian history'
SFCROWSNEST

THE THIRD SECTION

*Russia, 1855. They lay entombed beneath the earth. But a thirst
for blood cannot be buried for ever . . .*

'Magnificent and inventive . . . one of the most compelling
portraits it would like to be a vampire yet'
BLACK STATIC

THE PEOPLE'S WILL

*Russia, 1881. The blood of two great families flows in the veins of one
man. And blood must be spilled if either is to survive . . .*

'Truly unique, compelling, and thoroughly enjoyable . . . deserves
the highest possible recommendation'
FANTASYHOTLIST

Each available in paperback & ebook